BINGO 63

LOVE

Jackpot Edition

Tee Franklin • Jenn St-Onge
Joy San • Cardinal Rae

with additional material in this edition by:
Katie Cook • Shawn Pryor • Marguerite Bennett
Alyssa Cole • Amanda Deibert • Gail Simone
Genevieve FT • Carla "Speed" McNeil • Rori!
Alex Robinson • Paulina Ganucheau • Shae Beagle
Megan Hutchinson • Bev Johnson • Cat Staggs
Ariela Kristantina • Angael Davis • Margaux Saltel
Christopher The Wolffe

Bingo Love Volume 1 edited by Erica Schultz
Bingo Love: Jackpot Edition edited by Laurenn McCubbin
Bingo Love: Jackpot Edition designed by Laurenn McCubbin
Bingo Love logo by Kevin Maher

IMAGE COMICS, INC.

Robert Kirkman: Chief Operating Officer
Erik Larsen: Chief Financial Officer
Todd McFarlane: President
Marc Silvestri: Chief Executive Officer
Jim Valentino: Vice President
Eric Stephenson: Publisher / Chief Creative Officer
Corey Hart: Director of Sales
Jeff Boison: Director of Publishing Planning & Book Trade Sa
Chris Ross: Director of Digital Sales
Jeff Stang: Director of Specialty Sales
Kat Salazar: Director of PR & Marketing
Drew Gill: Art Director
Heather Doornink: Production Director
Nicole Lapalme: Controller

IMAGECOMICS.COM

BINGO LOVE, VOL. 1: JACKPOT EDITION. First printing. Nove
2018. Published by Image Comics, Inc. Office of publication: 2701 NW Va
St., Suite 780, Portland, OR 97210. *Bingo Love* is © 2018 by Tee Franklir
rights reserved. "Bingo Love," its logos, and the likenesses of all chara
herein are trademarks of Tee Franklin, unless otherwise noted. "Image" an
Image Comics logos are registered trademarks of Image Comics, Inc. No pa
this publication may be reproduced or transmitted, in any form or by any m
(except for short excerpts for journalistic or review purposes), without the ex
written permission of Tee Franklin or Image Comics, Inc. All names, chara
events, and locales in this publication are entirely fictional. Any resemb
to actual persons (living or dead), events, or places, without satiric inte
coincidental. Printed in the USA. For information regarding the CPSIA or
printed material call: 203-595-3636 and provide reference #RICH–815
For international rights, contact: foreignlicensing@imagecomics.com.

Trade Paperback ISBN 978-1-5343-1024-7
Hardcover ISBN 978-1-5343-0983-8

BINGO LOVE
Jackpot Edition

63

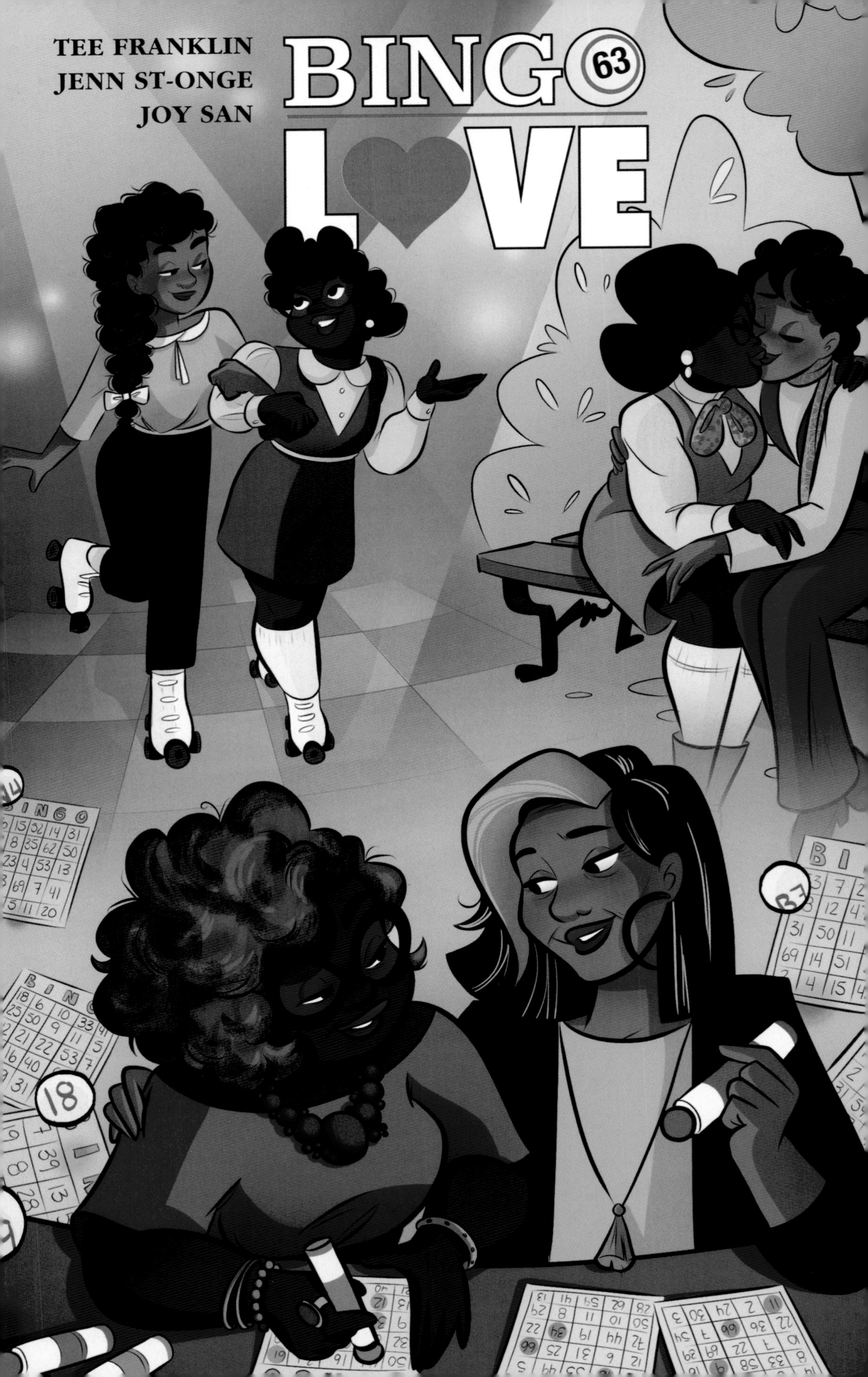
TEE FRANKLIN
JENN ST-ONGE
JOY SAN
BINGO
63
LOVE

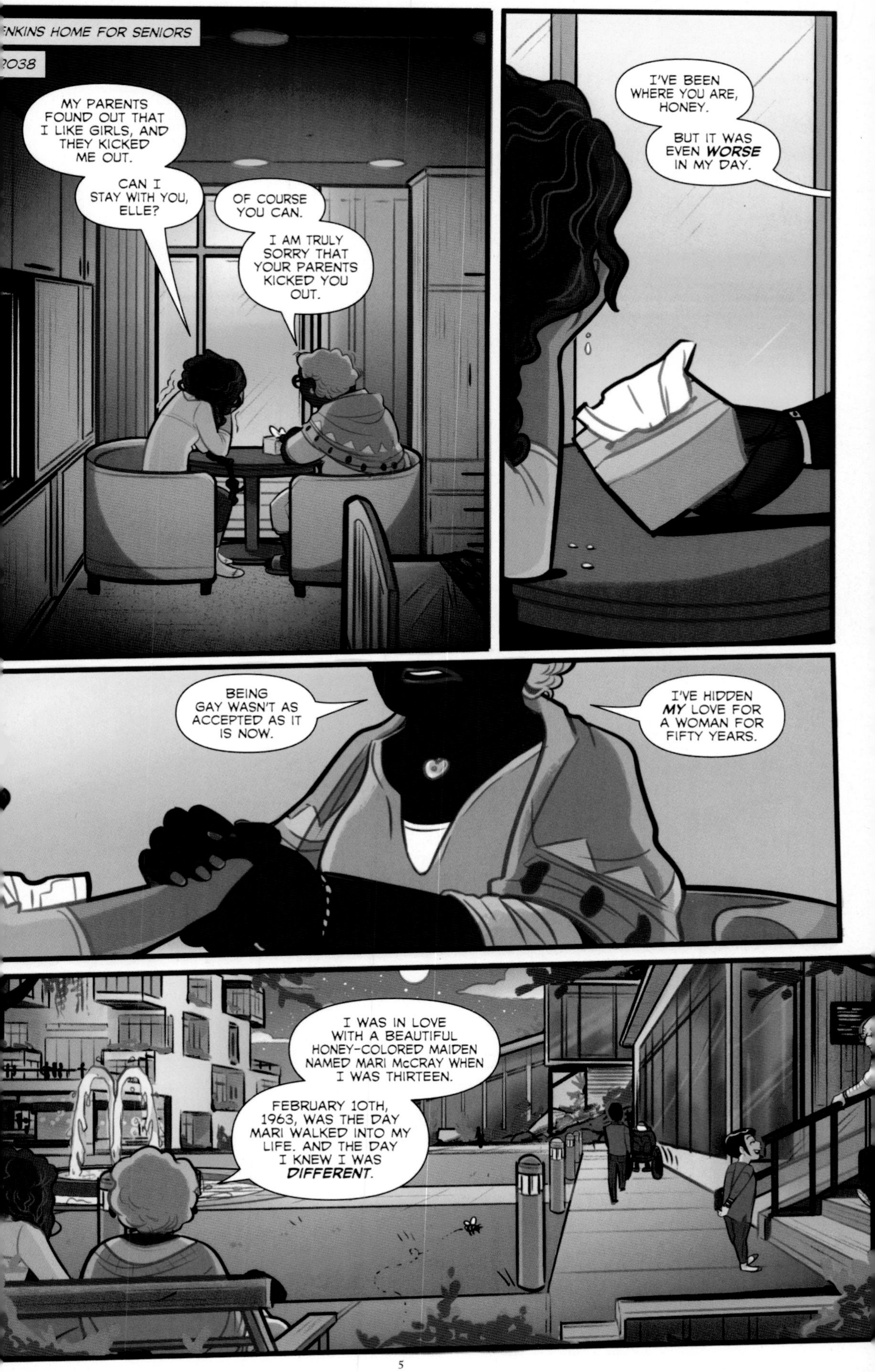

NKINS HOME FOR SENIORS
2038
MY PARENTS FOUND OUT THAT I LIKE GIRLS, AND THEY KICKED ME OUT.
CAN I STAY WITH YOU, ELLE?
OF COURSE YOU CAN.
I AM TRULY SORRY THAT YOUR PARENTS KICKED YOU OUT.
I'VE BEEN WHERE YOU ARE, HONEY.
BUT IT WAS EVEN WORSE IN MY DAY.
BEING GAY WASN'T AS ACCEPTED AS IT IS NOW.
I'VE HIDDEN MY LOVE FOR A WOMAN FOR FIFTY YEARS.
I WAS IN LOVE WITH A BEAUTIFUL HONEY-COLORED MAIDEN NAMED MARI McCRAY WHEN I WAS THIRTEEN.
FEBRUARY 10TH, 1963, WAS THE DAY MARI WALKED INTO MY LIFE. AND THE DAY I KNEW I WAS DIFFERENT.

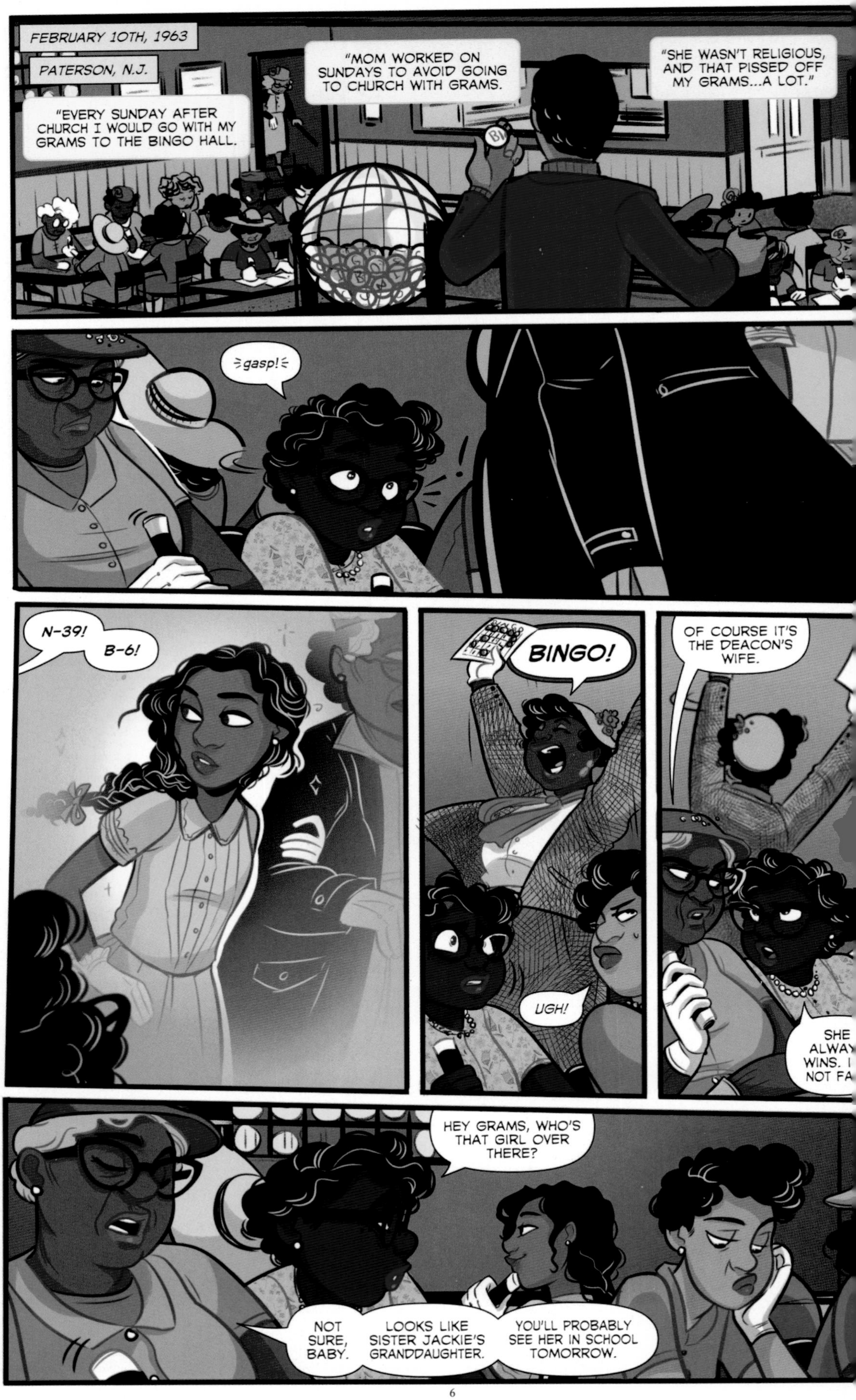
FEBRUARY 10TH, 1963
PATERSON, N.J.
"EVERY SUNDAY AFTER CHURCH I WOULD GO WITH MY GRAMS TO THE BINGO HALL.
"MOM WORKED ON SUNDAYS TO AVOID GOING TO CHURCH WITH GRAMS.
"SHE WASN'T RELIGIOUS, AND THAT PISSED OFF MY GRAMS...A LOT."
gasp!
N-39!
B-6!
BINGO!
UGH!
OF COURSE IT'S THE DEACON'S WIFE.
HEY GRAMS, WHO'S THAT GIRL OVER THERE?
NOT SURE, BABY.
LOOKS LIKE SISTER JACKIE'S GRANDDAUGHTER.
YOU'LL PROBABLY SEE HER IN SCHOOL TOMORROW.

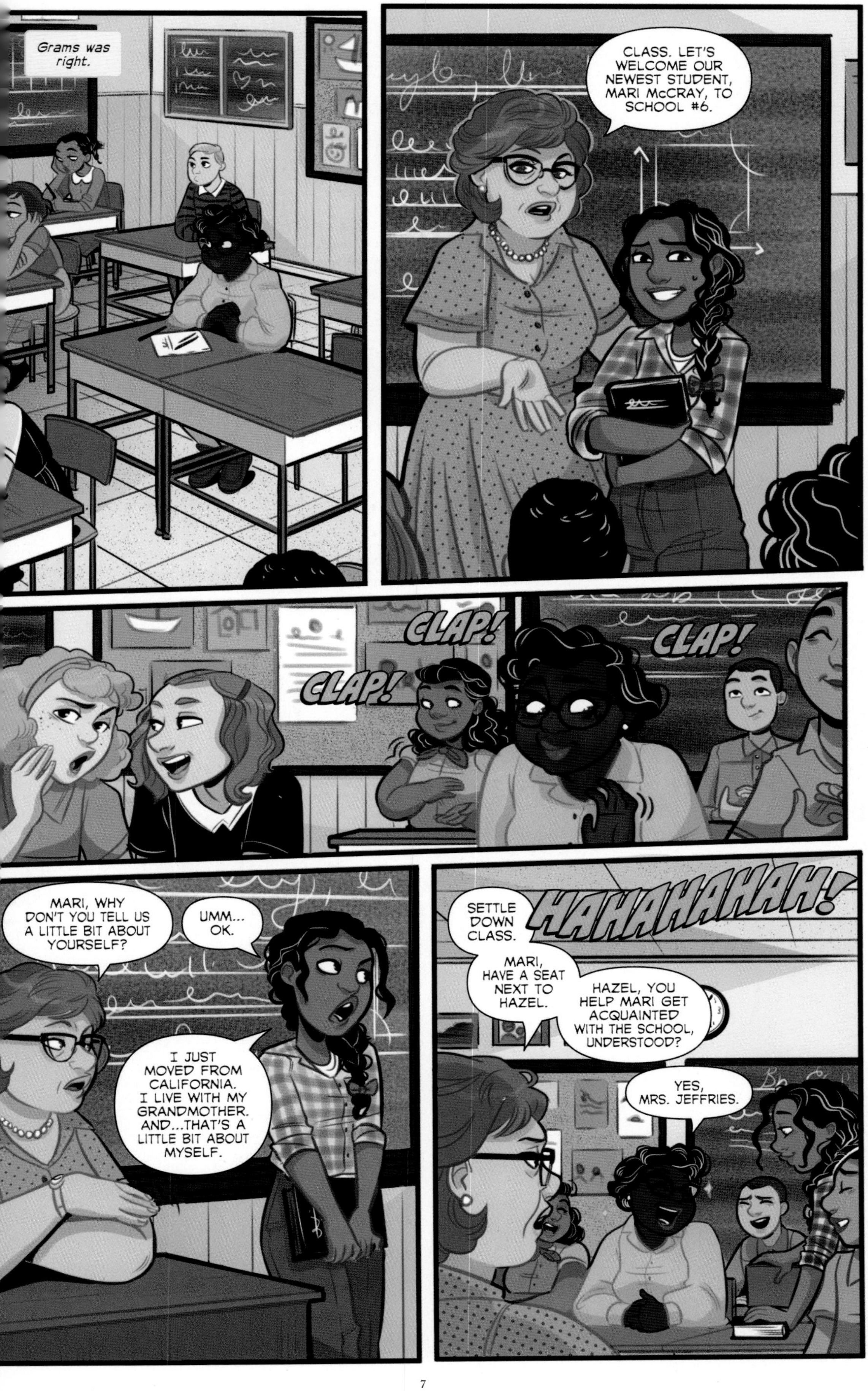
Grams was right.
CLASS. LET'S WELCOME OUR NEWEST STUDENT, MARI McCRAY, TO SCHOOL #6.
CLAP!
CLAP!
CLAP!
MARI, WHY DON'T YOU TELL US A LITTLE BIT ABOUT YOURSELF?
UMM... OK.
I JUST MOVED FROM CALIFORNIA. I LIVE WITH MY GRANDMOTHER. AND...THAT'S A LITTLE BIT ABOUT MYSELF.
HAHAHAHAHAH!
SETTLE DOWN CLASS.
MARI, HAVE A SEAT NEXT TO HAZEL.
HAZEL, YOU HELP MARI GET ACQUAINTED WITH THE SCHOOL, UNDERSTOOD?
YES, MRS. JEFFRIES.

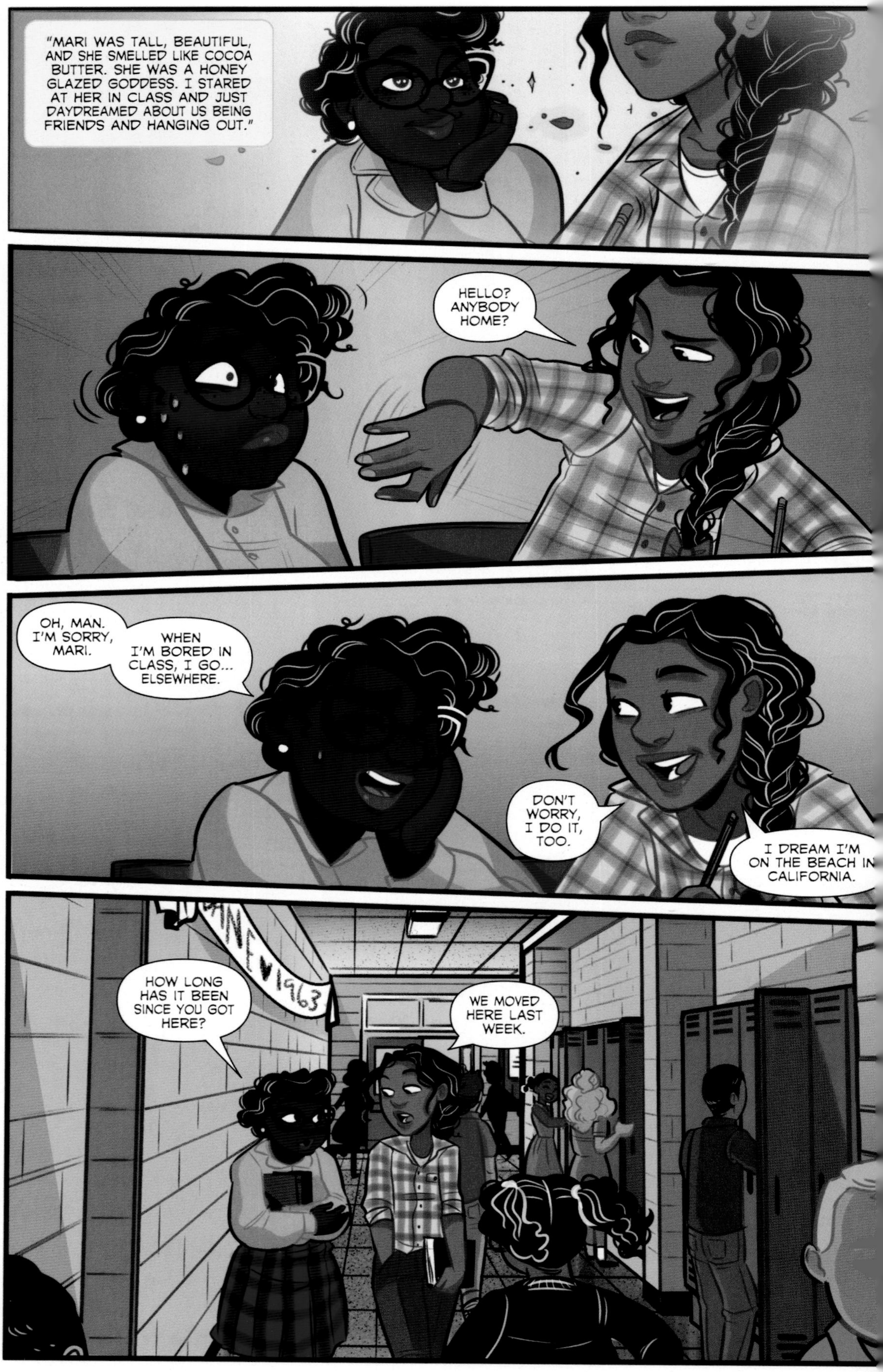
"MARI WAS TALL, BEAUTIFUL, AND SHE SMELLED LIKE COCOA BUTTER. SHE WAS A HONEY GLAZED GODDESS. I STARED AT HER IN CLASS AND JUST DAYDREAMED ABOUT US BEING FRIENDS AND HANGING OUT."
HELLO? ANYBODY HOME?
OH, MAN. I'M SORRY, MARI.
WHEN I'M BORED IN CLASS, I GO... ELSEWHERE.
DON'T WORRY, I DO IT, TOO.
I DREAM I'M ON THE BEACH IN CALIFORNIA.
HOW LONG HAS IT BEEN SINCE YOU GOT HERE?
WE MOVED HERE LAST WEEK.

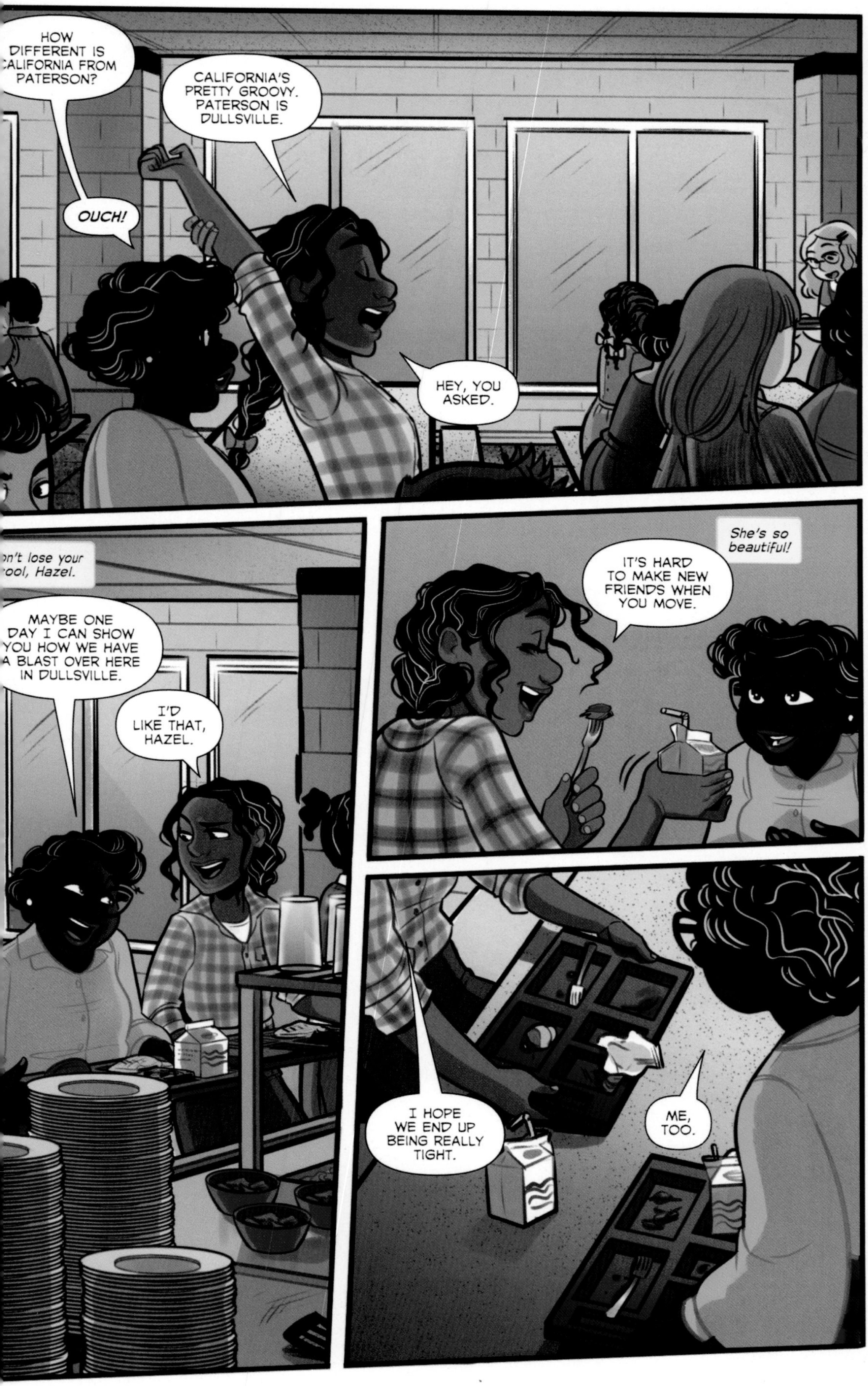
HOW DIFFERENT IS ALIFORNIA FROM PATERSON?
CALIFORNIA'S PRETTY GROOVY. PATERSON IS DULLSVILLE.
OUCH!
HEY, YOU ASKED.
n't lose your ool, Hazel.
MAYBE ONE DAY I CAN SHOW YOU HOW WE HAVE A BLAST OVER HERE IN DULLSVILLE.
I'D LIKE THAT, HAZEL.
She's so beautiful!
IT'S HARD TO MAKE NEW FRIENDS WHEN YOU MOVE.
I HOPE WE END UP BEING REALLY TIGHT.
ME, TOO.

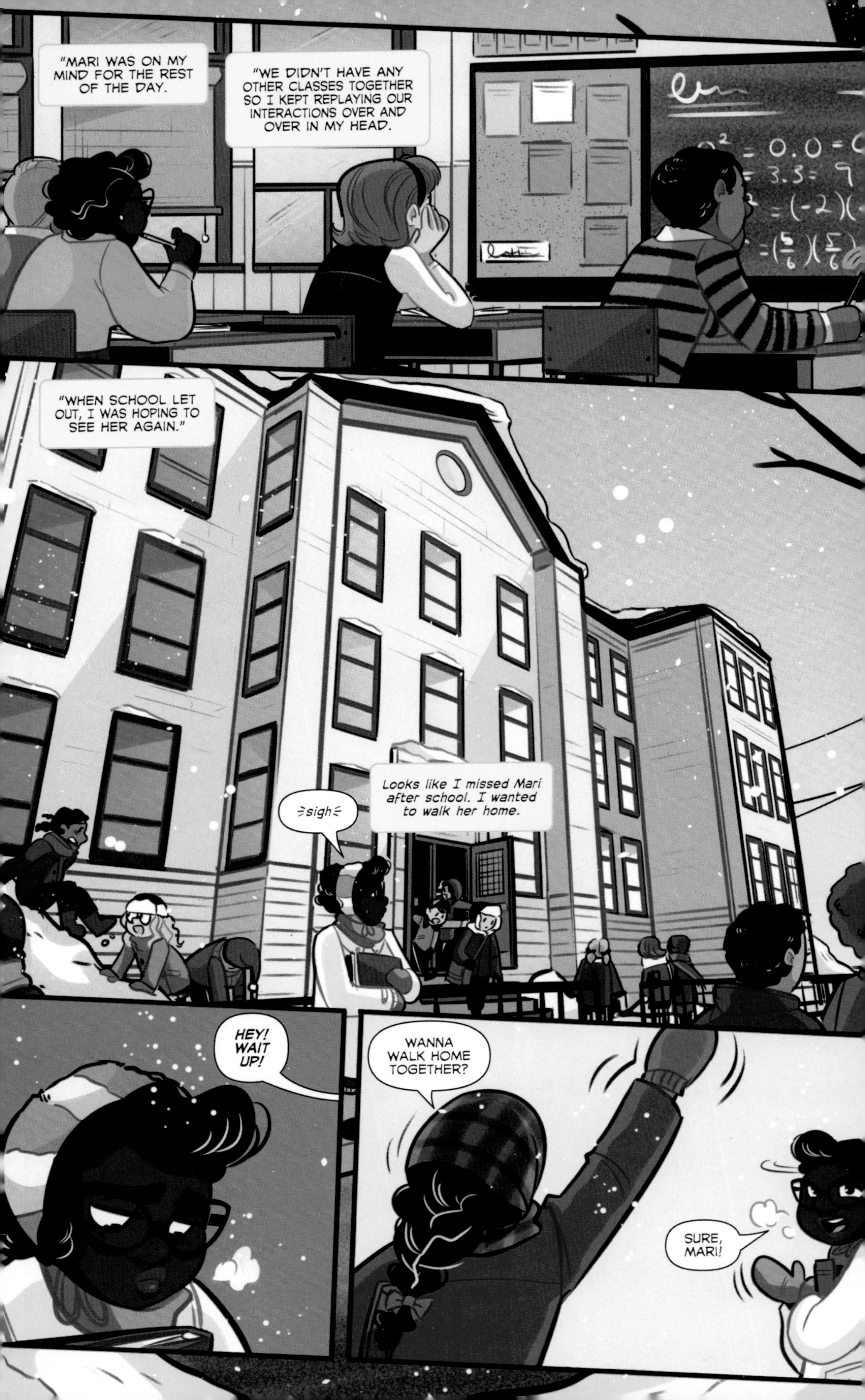
"MARI WAS ON MY MIND FOR THE REST OF THE DAY.
"WE DIDN'T HAVE ANY OTHER CLASSES TOGETHER SO I KEPT REPLAYING OUR INTERACTIONS OVER AND OVER IN MY HEAD.
"WHEN SCHOOL LET OUT, I WAS HOPING TO SEE HER AGAIN."
sigh
Looks like I missed Mari after school. I wanted to walk her home.
HEY! WAIT UP!
WANNA WALK HOME TOGETHER?
SURE, MARI!

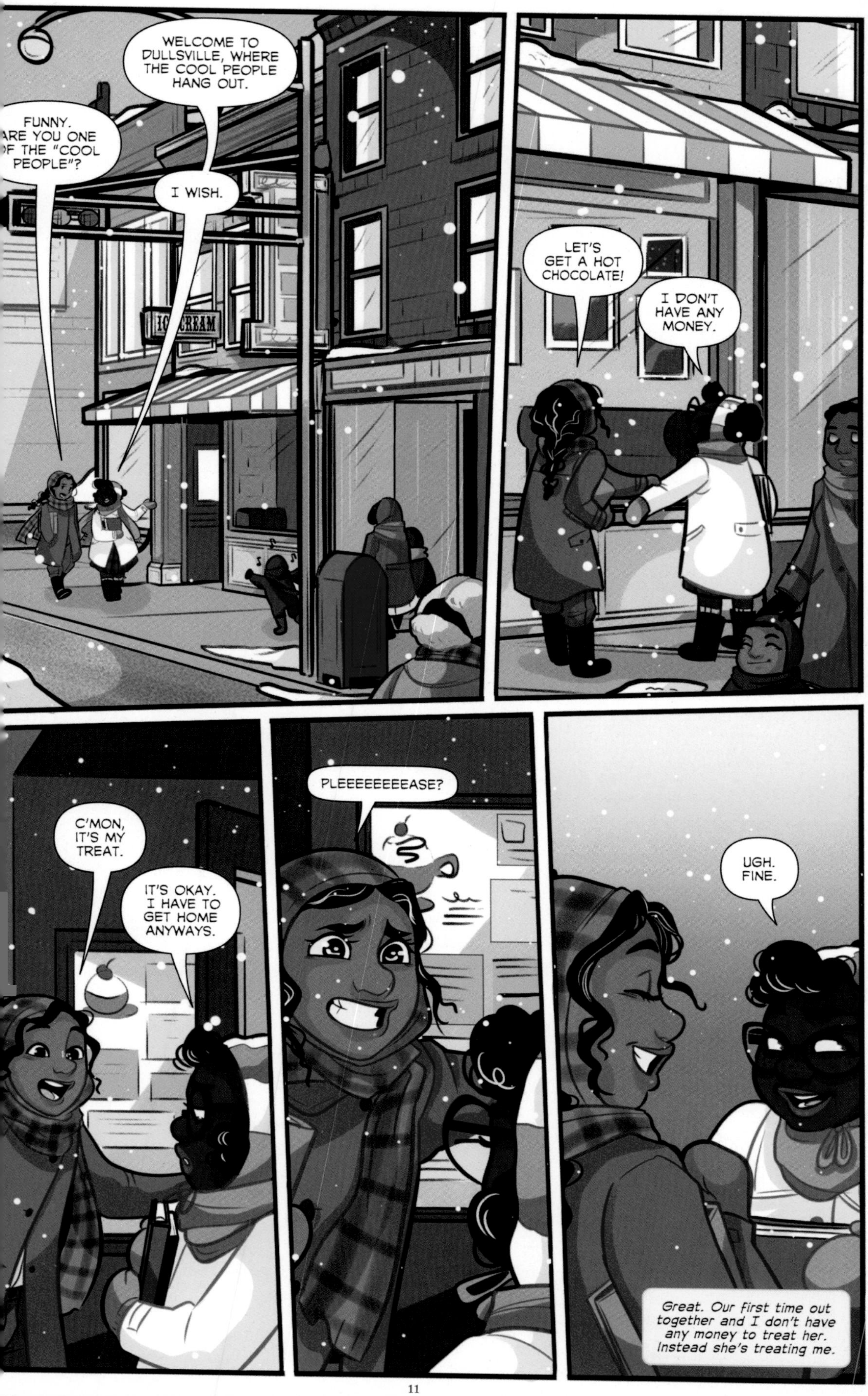
WELCOME TO DULLSVILLE, WHERE THE COOL PEOPLE HANG OUT.
FUNNY. ARE YOU ONE OF THE "COOL PEOPLE"?
I WISH.
ICE CREAM
LET'S GET A HOT CHOCOLATE!
I DON'T HAVE ANY MONEY.
C'MON, IT'S MY TREAT.
IT'S OKAY. I HAVE TO GET HOME ANYWAYS.
PLEEEEEEEEEASE?
UGH. FINE.
Great. Our first time out together and I don't have any money to treat her. Instead she's treating me.

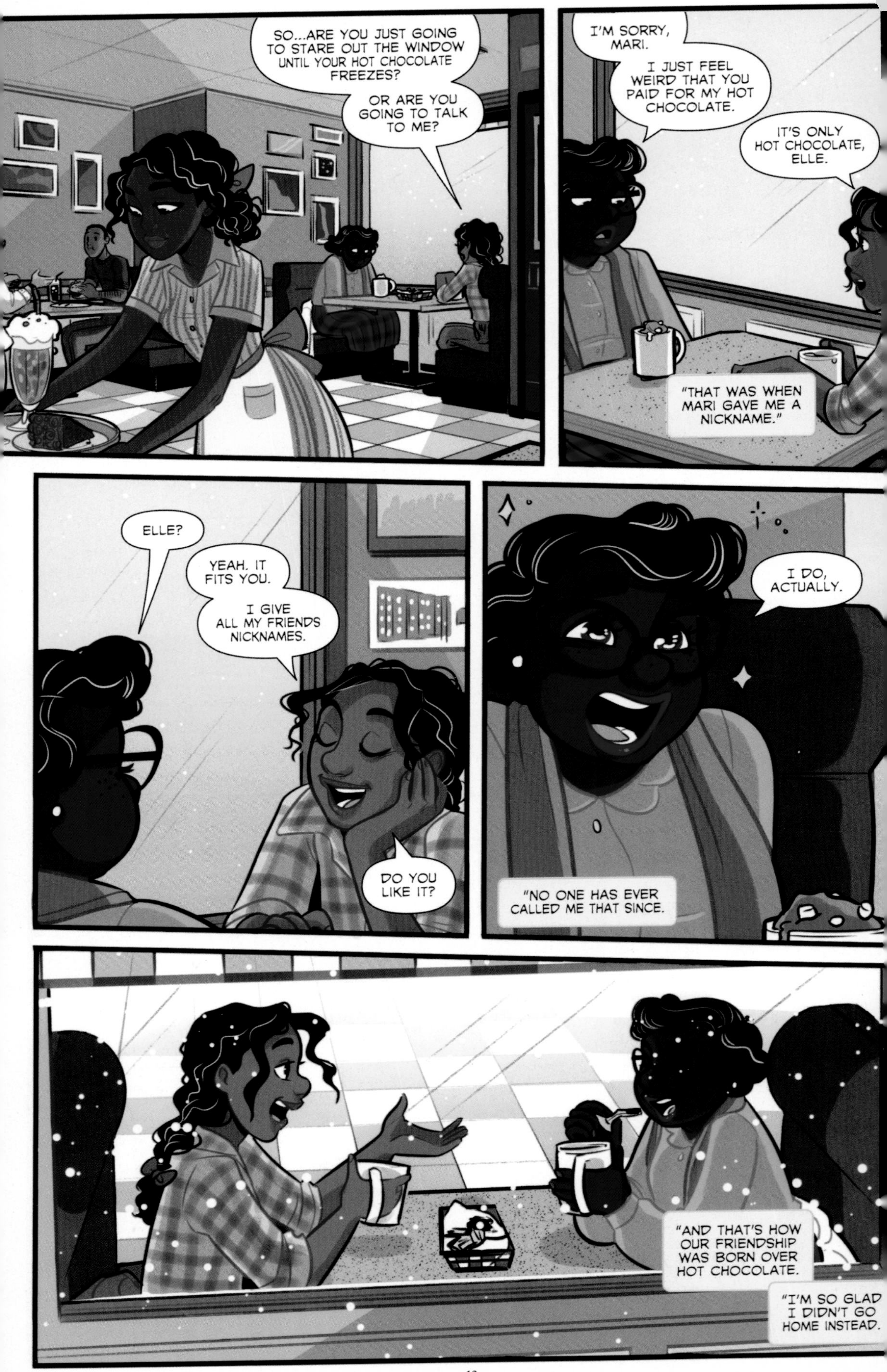
SO...ARE YOU JUST GOING TO STARE OUT THE WINDOW UNTIL YOUR HOT CHOCOLATE FREEZES?
OR ARE YOU GOING TO TALK TO ME?
I'M SORRY, MARI.
I JUST FEEL WEIRD THAT YOU PAID FOR MY HOT CHOCOLATE.
IT'S ONLY HOT CHOCOLATE, ELLE.
"THAT WAS WHEN MARI GAVE ME A NICKNAME."
ELLE?
YEAH. IT FITS YOU.
I GIVE ALL MY FRIENDS NICKNAMES.
DO YOU LIKE IT?
I DO, ACTUALLY.
"NO ONE HAS EVER CALLED ME THAT SINCE.
"AND THAT'S HOW OUR FRIENDSHIP WAS BORN OVER HOT CHOCOLATE.
"I'M SO GLAD I DIDN'T GO HOME INSTEAD.

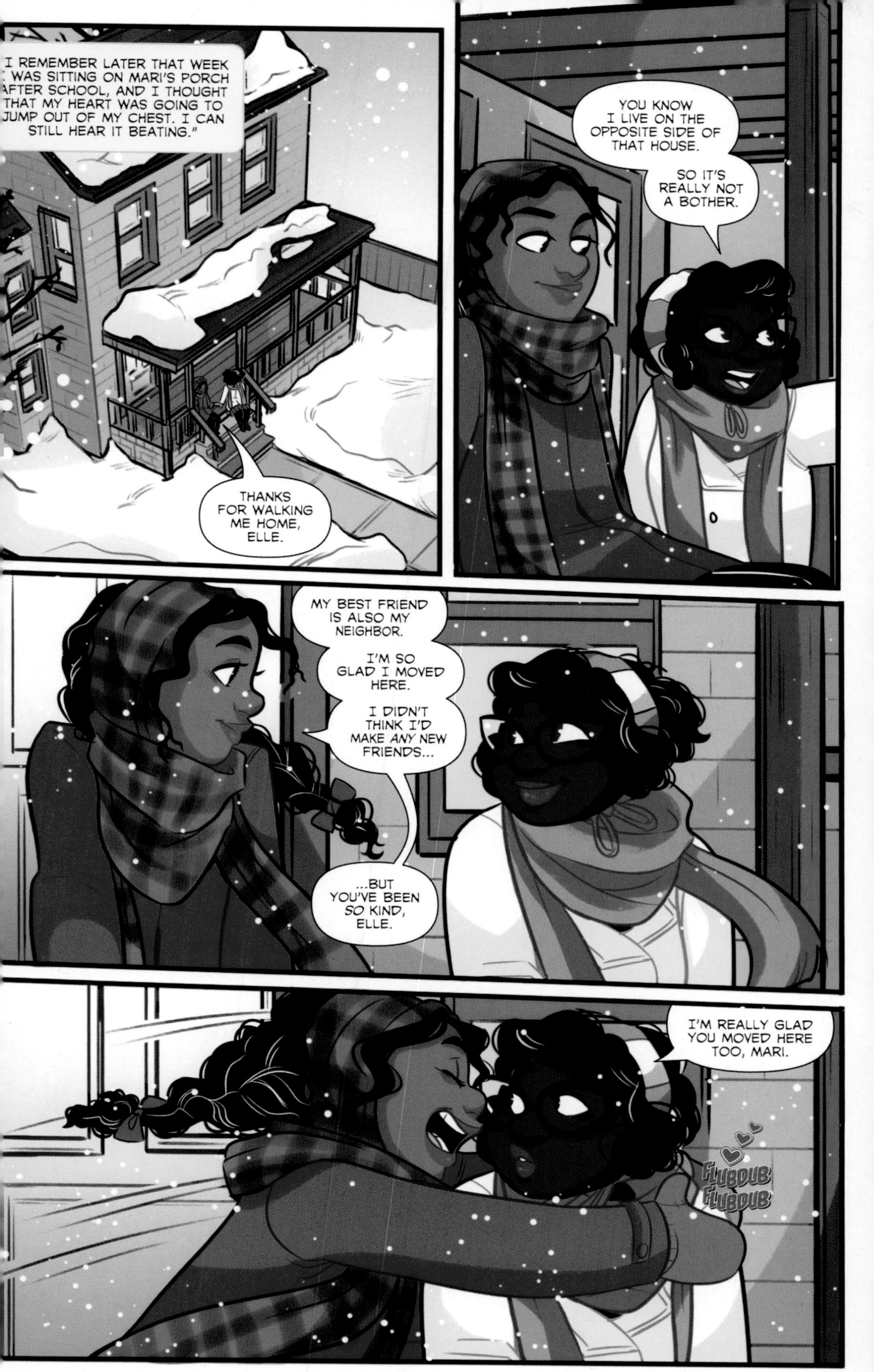

I REMEMBER LATER THAT WEEK I WAS SITTING ON MARI'S PORCH AFTER SCHOOL, AND I THOUGHT THAT MY HEART WAS GOING TO JUMP OUT OF MY CHEST. I CAN STILL HEAR IT BEATING."
THANKS FOR WALKING ME HOME, ELLE.
YOU KNOW I LIVE ON THE OPPOSITE SIDE OF THAT HOUSE.
SO IT'S REALLY NOT A BOTHER.
MY BEST FRIEND IS ALSO MY NEIGHBOR.
I'M SO GLAD I MOVED HERE.
I DIDN'T THINK I'D MAKE *ANY* NEW FRIENDS...
...BUT YOU'VE BEEN *SO* KIND, ELLE.
I'M REALLY GLAD YOU MOVED HERE TOO, MARI.
FLUBDUB FLUBDUB

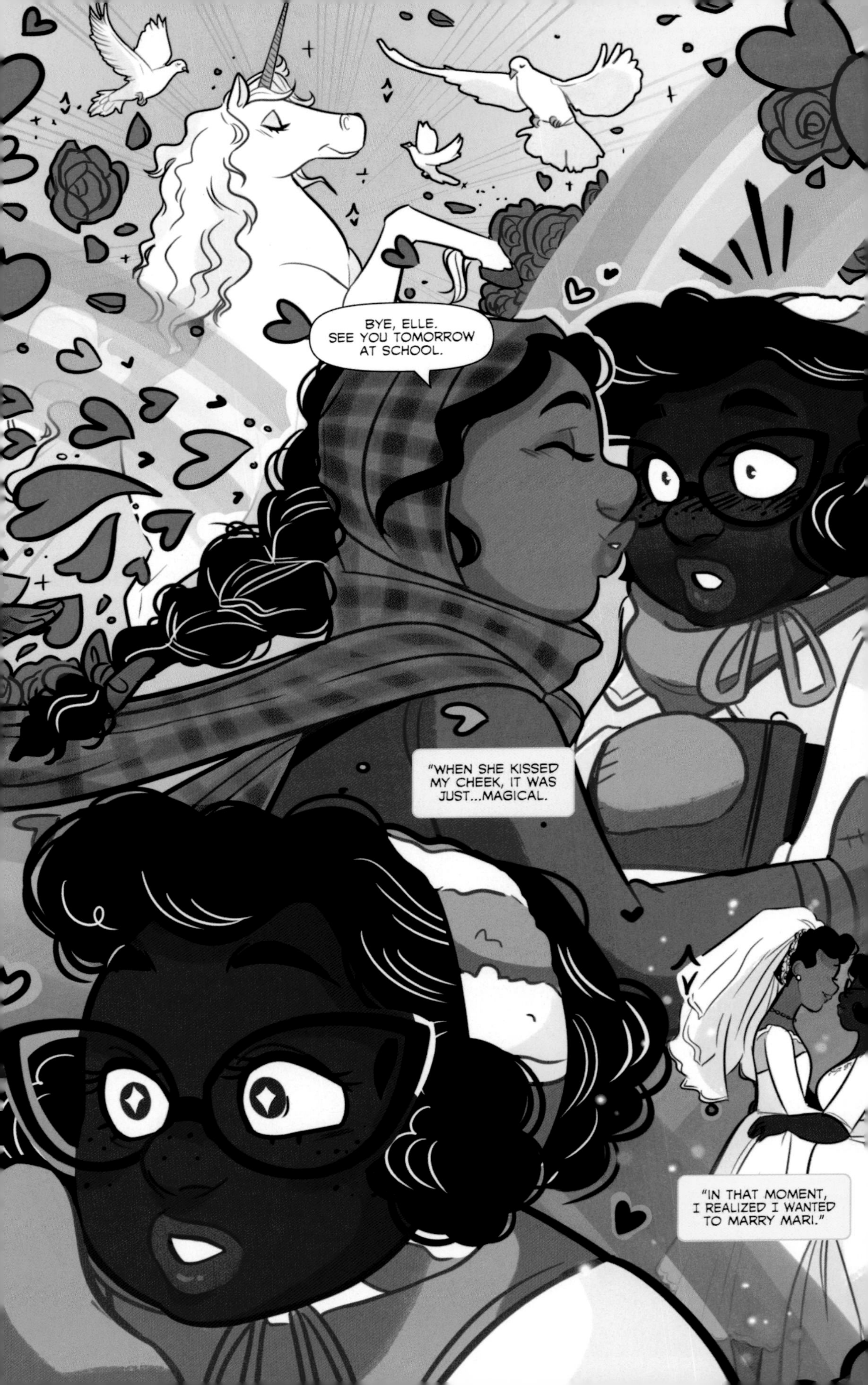
BYE, ELLE.
SEE YOU TOMORROW
AT SCHOOL.
"WHEN SHE KISSED
MY CHEEK, IT WAS
JUST...MAGICAL.
"IN THAT MOMENT,
I REALIZED I WANTED
TO MARRY MARI."

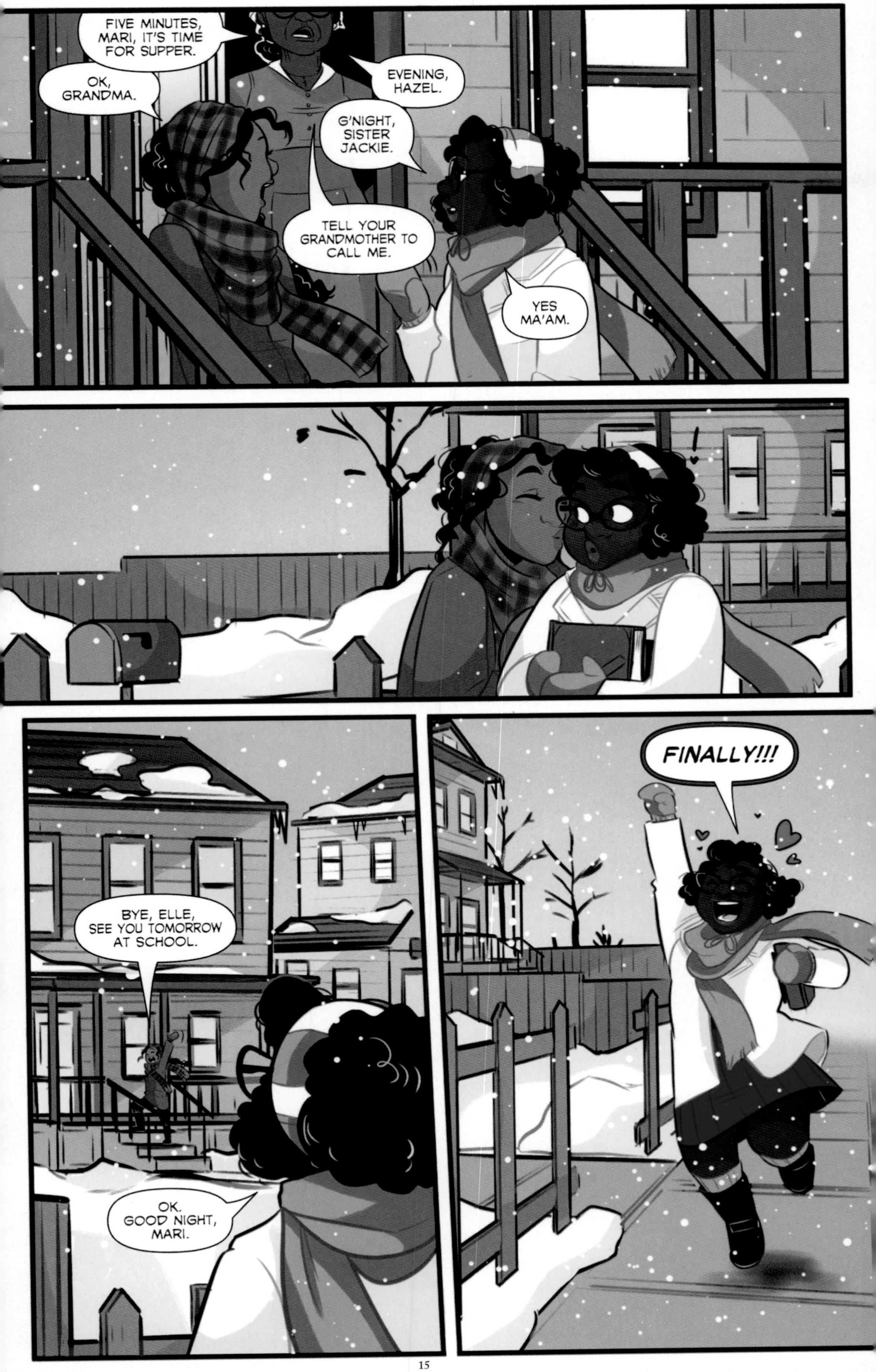
FIVE MINUTES, MARI, IT'S TIME FOR SUPPER.
OK, GRANDMA.
EVENING, HAZEL.
G'NIGHT, SISTER JACKIE.
TELL YOUR GRANDMOTHER TO CALL ME.
YES MA'AM.
BYE, ELLE, SEE YOU TOMORROW AT SCHOOL.
OK. GOOD NIGHT, MARI.
FINALLY!!!

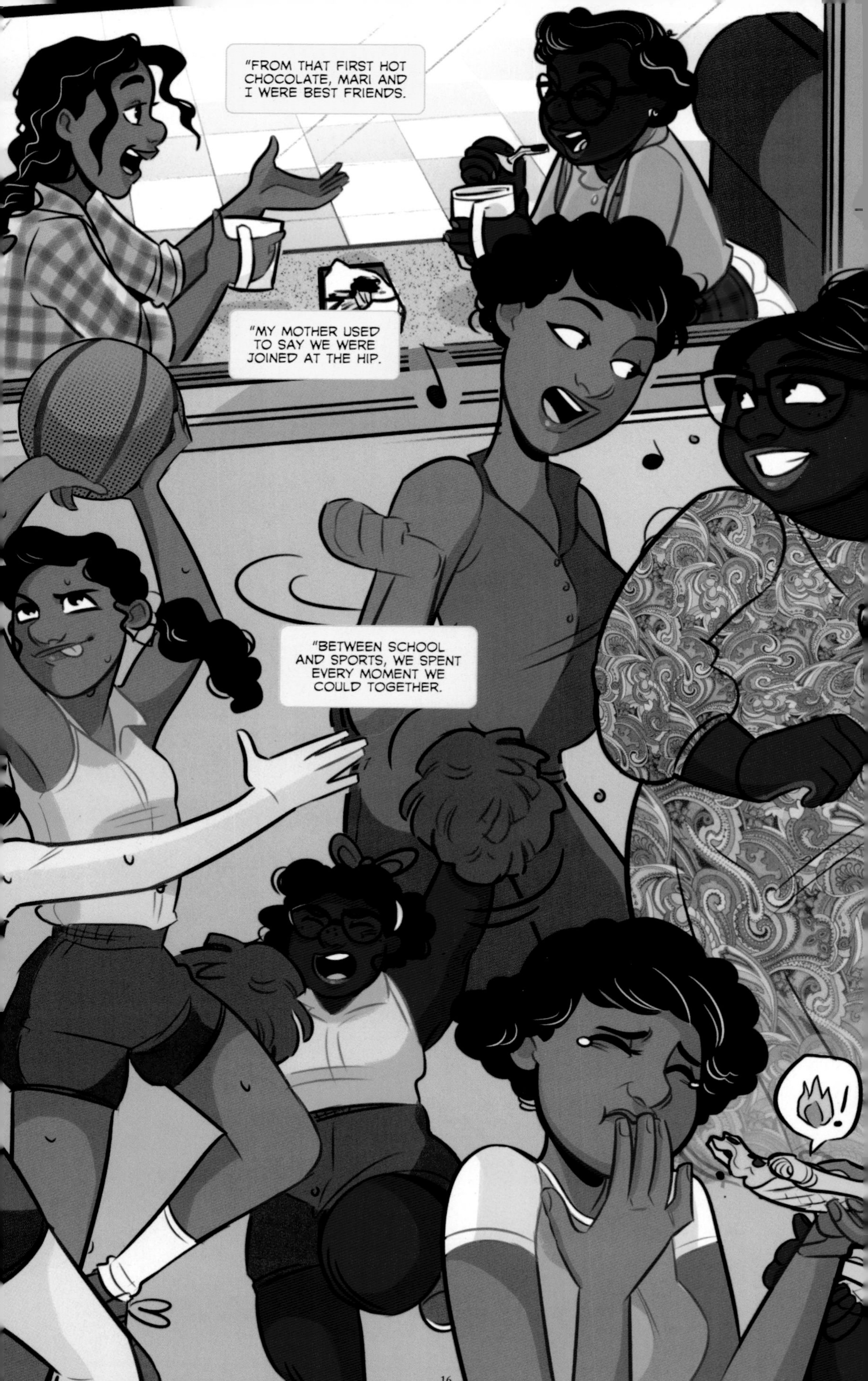
"FROM THAT FIRST HOT CHOCOLATE, MARI AND I WERE BEST FRIENDS.
"MY MOTHER USED TO SAY WE WERE JOINED AT THE HIP.
"BETWEEN SCHOOL AND SPORTS, WE SPENT EVERY MOMENT WE COULD TOGETHER.
!

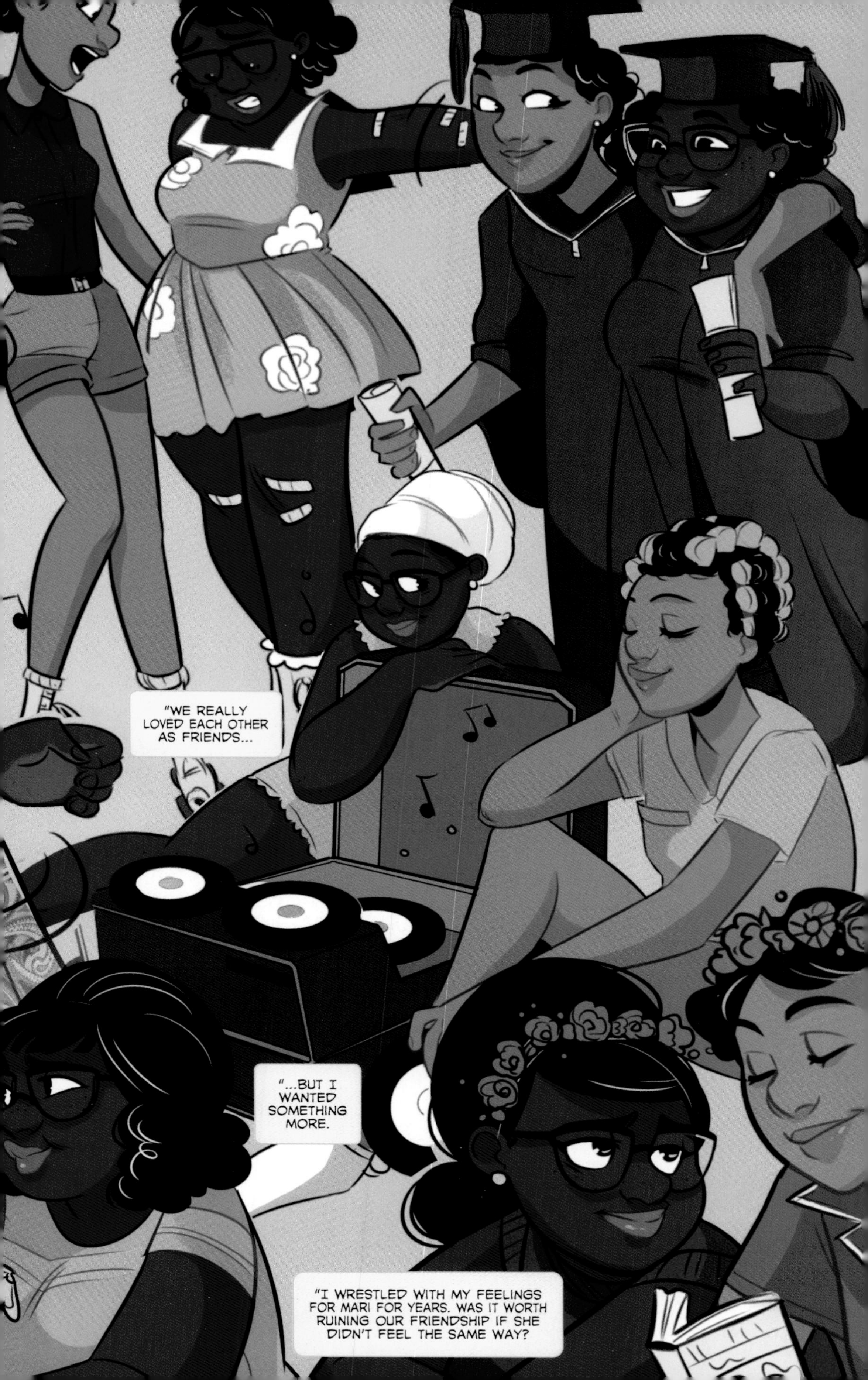
"WE REALLY LOVED EACH OTHER AS FRIENDS...
"...BUT I WANTED SOMETHING MORE.
"I WRESTLED WITH MY FEELINGS FOR MARI FOR YEARS. WAS IT WORTH RUINING OUR FRIENDSHIP IF SHE DIDN'T FEEL THE SAME WAY?

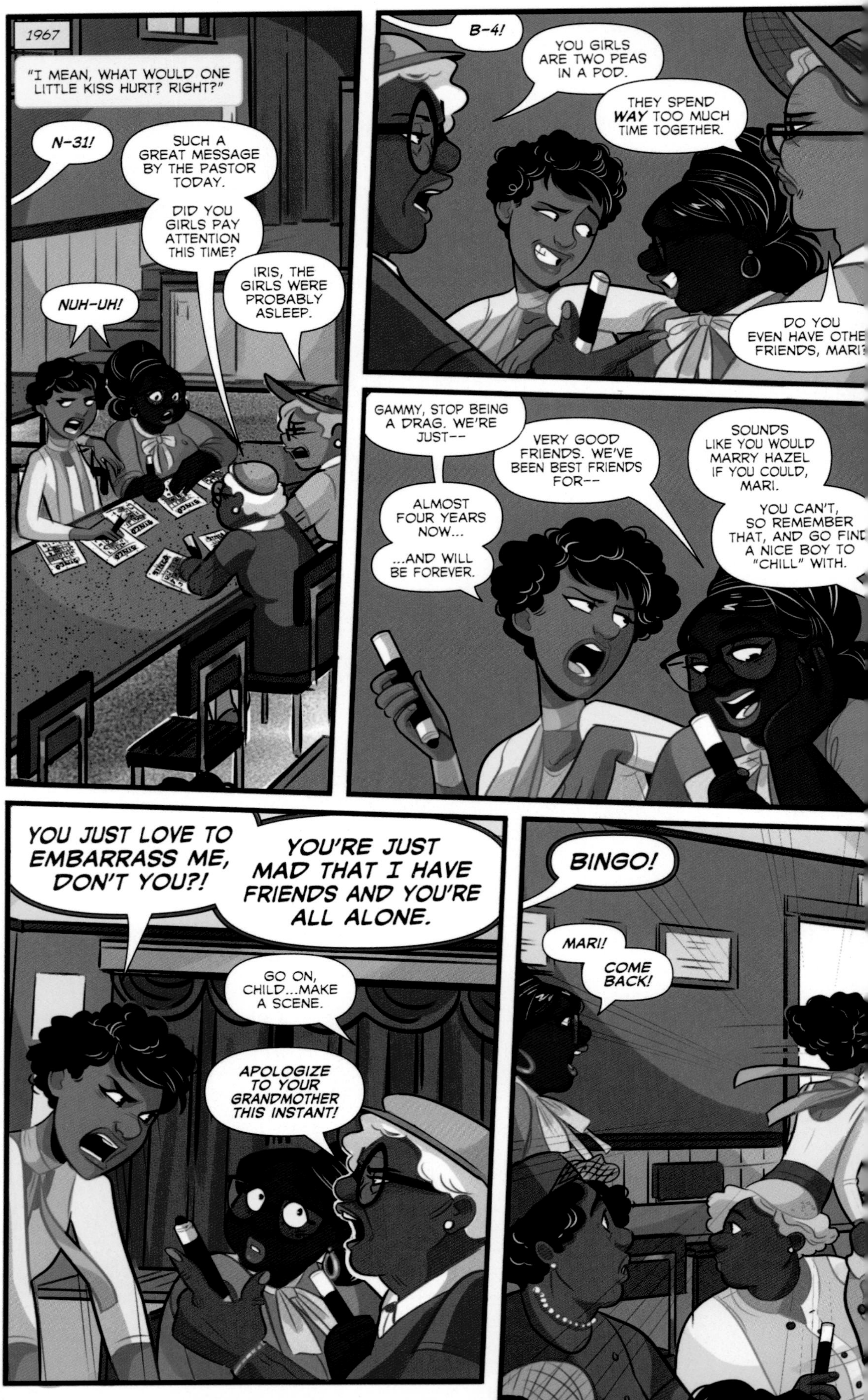
1967
"I MEAN, WHAT WOULD ONE LITTLE KISS HURT? RIGHT?"
N-31!
SUCH A GREAT MESSAGE BY THE PASTOR TODAY.
DID YOU GIRLS PAY ATTENTION THIS TIME?
NUH-UH!
IRIS, THE GIRLS WERE PROBABLY ASLEEP.
B-4!
YOU GIRLS ARE TWO PEAS IN A POD.
THEY SPEND WAY TOO MUCH TIME TOGETHER.
DO YOU EVEN HAVE OTHE FRIENDS, MARI?
GAMMY, STOP BEING A DRAG. WE'RE JUST--
VERY GOOD FRIENDS. WE'VE BEEN BEST FRIENDS FOR--
ALMOST FOUR YEARS NOW...
...AND WILL BE FOREVER.
SOUNDS LIKE YOU WOULD MARRY HAZEL IF YOU COULD, MARI.
YOU CAN'T, SO REMEMBER THAT, AND GO FIND A NICE BOY TO "CHILL" WITH.
YOU JUST LOVE TO EMBARRASS ME, DON'T YOU?!
YOU'RE JUST MAD THAT I HAVE FRIENDS AND YOU'RE ALL ALONE.
GO ON, CHILD...MAKE A SCENE.
APOLOGIZE TO YOUR GRANDMOTHER THIS INSTANT!
BINGO!
MARI!
COME BACK!

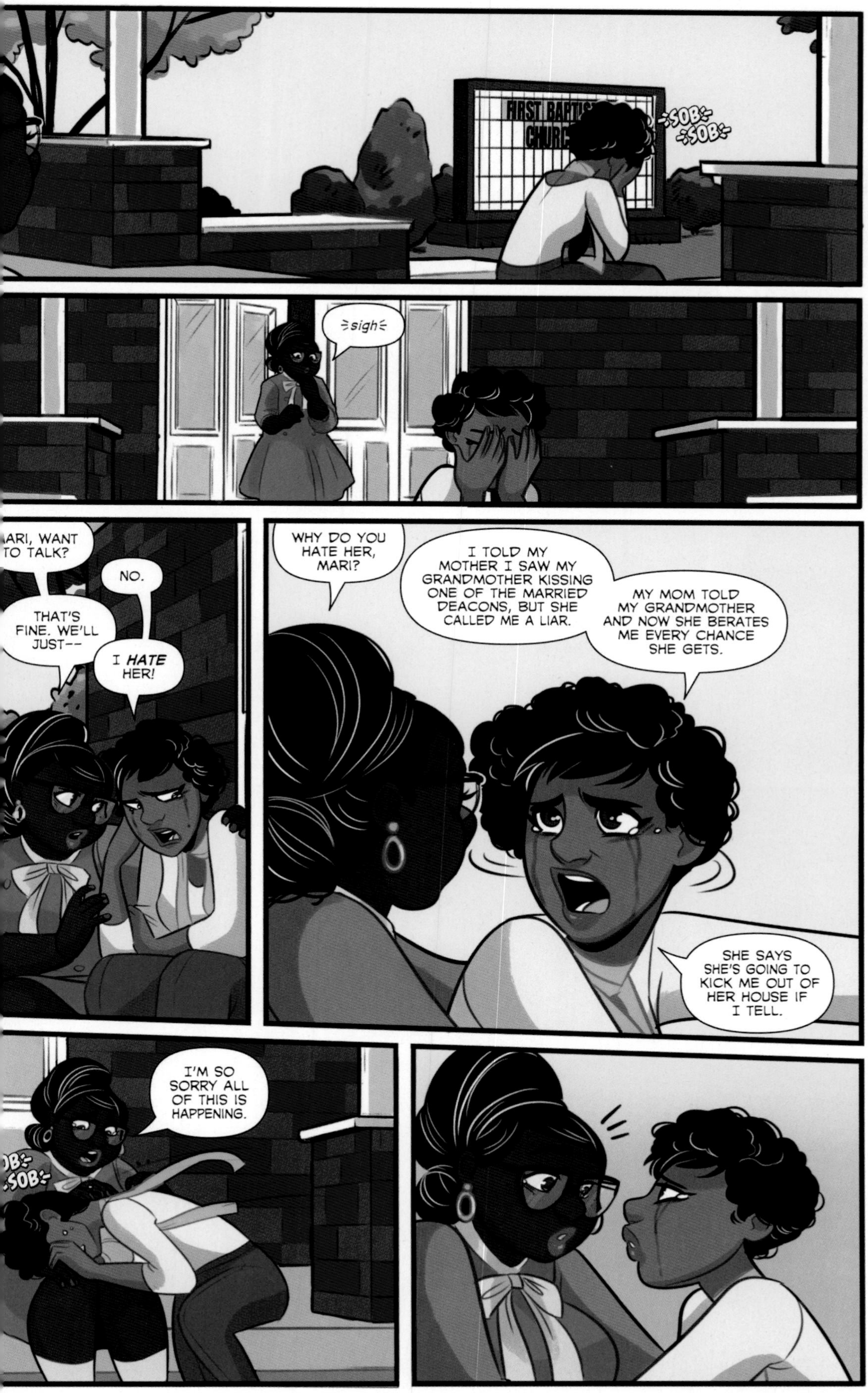
SOB
SOB
sigh
ARI, WANT TO TALK?
NO.
THAT'S FINE. WE'LL JUST--
I **HATE** HER!
WHY DO YOU HATE HER, MARI?
I TOLD MY MOTHER I SAW MY GRANDMOTHER KISSING ONE OF THE MARRIED DEACONS, BUT SHE CALLED ME A LIAR.
MY MOM TOLD MY GRANDMOTHER AND NOW SHE BERATES ME EVERY CHANCE SHE GETS.
SHE SAYS SHE'S GOING TO KICK ME OUT OF HER HOUSE IF I TELL.
I'M SO SORRY ALL OF THIS IS HAPPENING.
SOB

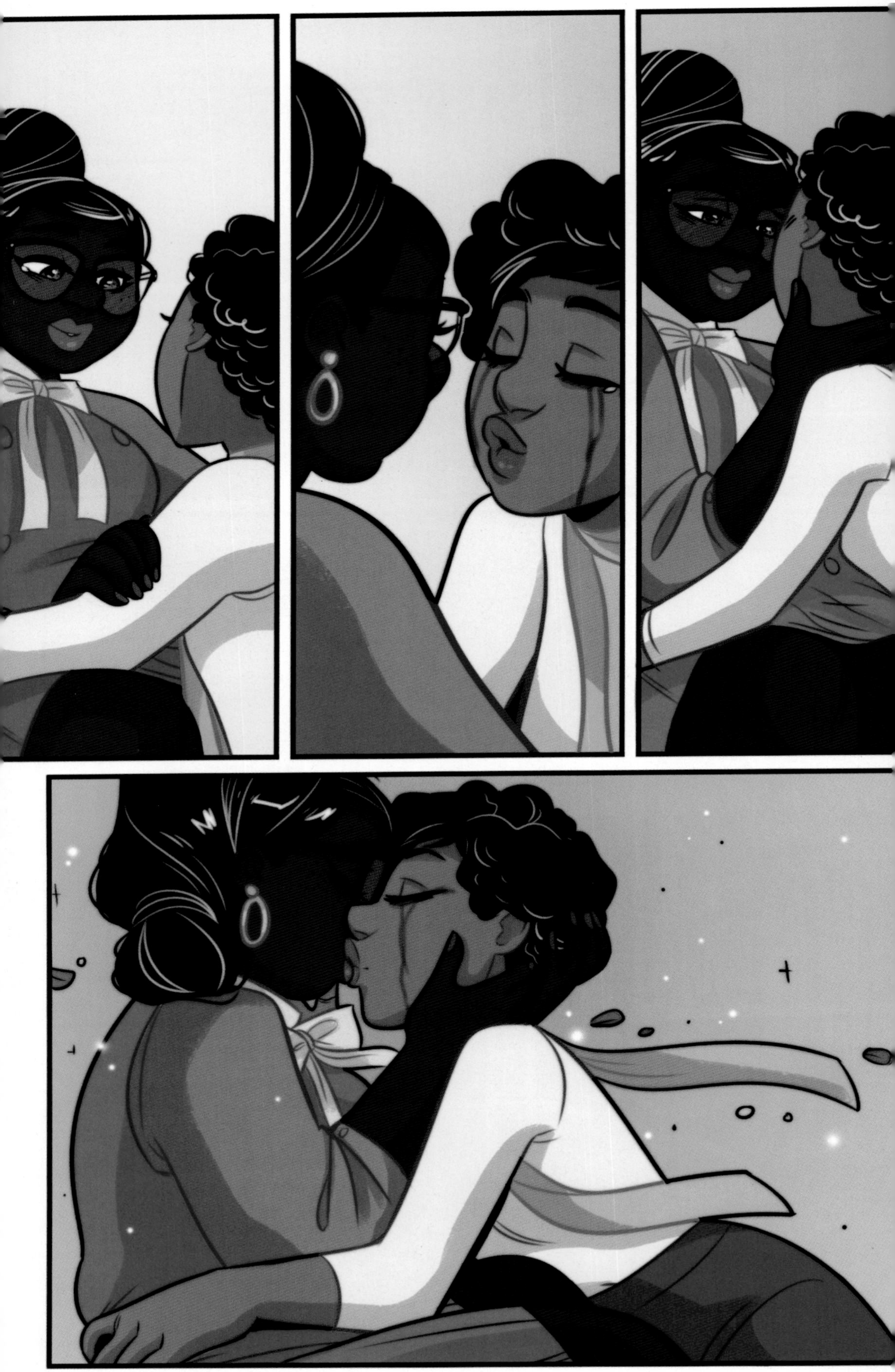

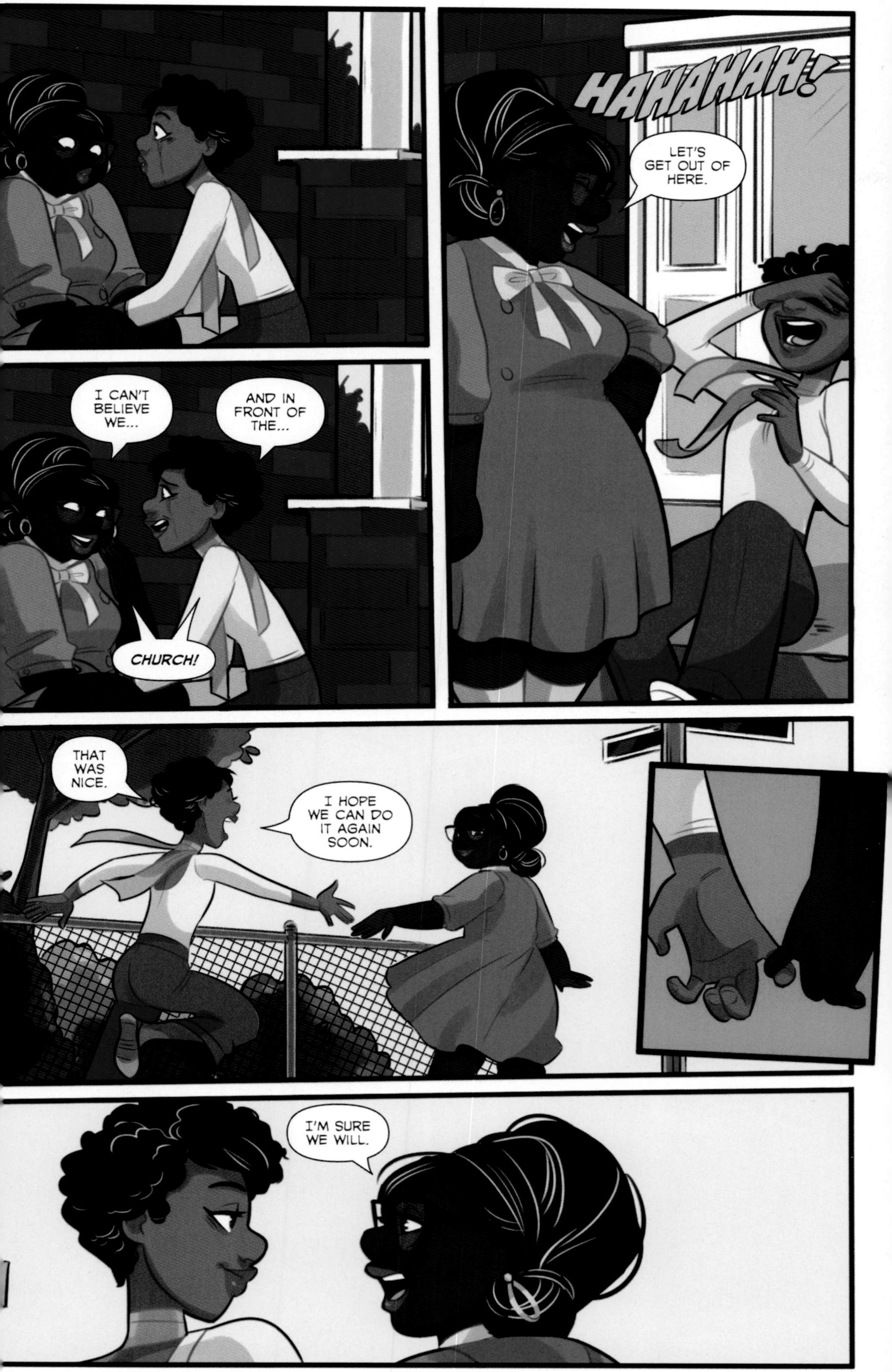
I CAN'T BELIEVE WE...
AND IN FRONT OF THE...
CHURCH!
HAHAHAH!
LET'S GET OUT OF HERE.
THAT WAS NICE.
I HOPE WE CAN DO IT AGAIN SOON.
I'M SURE WE WILL.

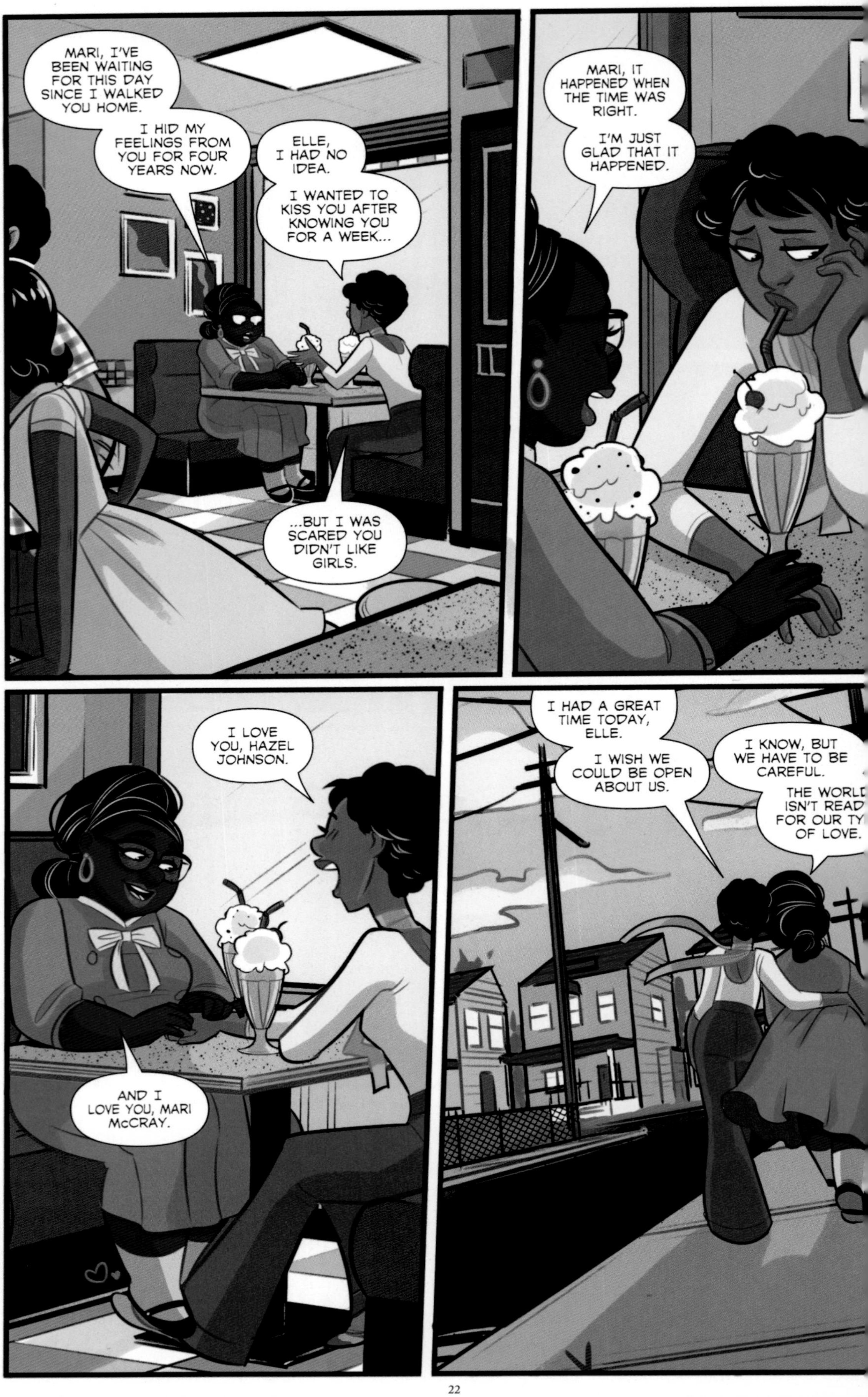
MARI, I'VE BEEN WAITING FOR THIS DAY SINCE I WALKED YOU HOME.
I HID MY FEELINGS FROM YOU FOR FOUR YEARS NOW.
ELLE, I HAD NO IDEA.
I WANTED TO KISS YOU AFTER KNOWING YOU FOR A WEEK...
...BUT I WAS SCARED YOU DIDN'T LIKE GIRLS.
MARI, IT HAPPENED WHEN THE TIME WAS RIGHT.
I'M JUST GLAD THAT IT HAPPENED.
I LOVE YOU, HAZEL JOHNSON.
AND I LOVE YOU, MARI McCRAY.
I HAD A GREAT TIME TODAY, ELLE.
I WISH WE COULD BE OPEN ABOUT US.
I KNOW, BUT WE HAVE TO BE CAREFUL.
THE WORLD ISN'T READ FOR OUR TY OF LOVE.

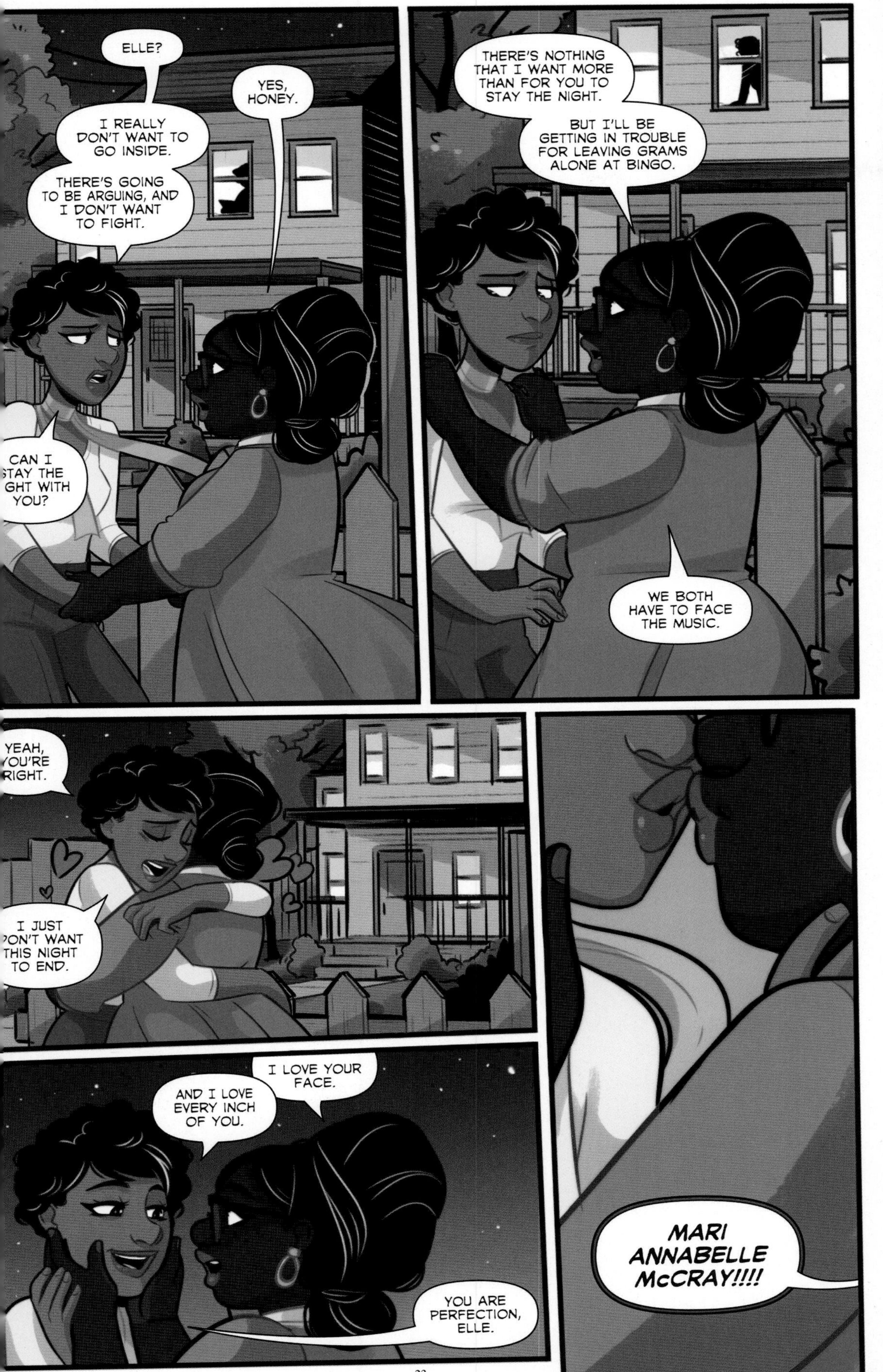
ELLE?
I REALLY DON'T WANT TO GO INSIDE.
THERE'S GOING TO BE ARGUING, AND I DON'T WANT TO FIGHT.
YES, HONEY.
CAN I STAY THE NIGHT WITH YOU?
THERE'S NOTHING THAT I WANT MORE THAN FOR YOU TO STAY THE NIGHT.
BUT I'LL BE GETTING IN TROUBLE FOR LEAVING GRAMS ALONE AT BINGO.
WE BOTH HAVE TO FACE THE MUSIC.
YEAH, YOU'RE RIGHT.
I JUST DON'T WANT THIS NIGHT TO END.
I LOVE YOUR FACE.
AND I LOVE EVERY INCH OF YOU.
YOU ARE PERFECTION, ELLE.
MARI ANNABELLE McCRAY!!!!

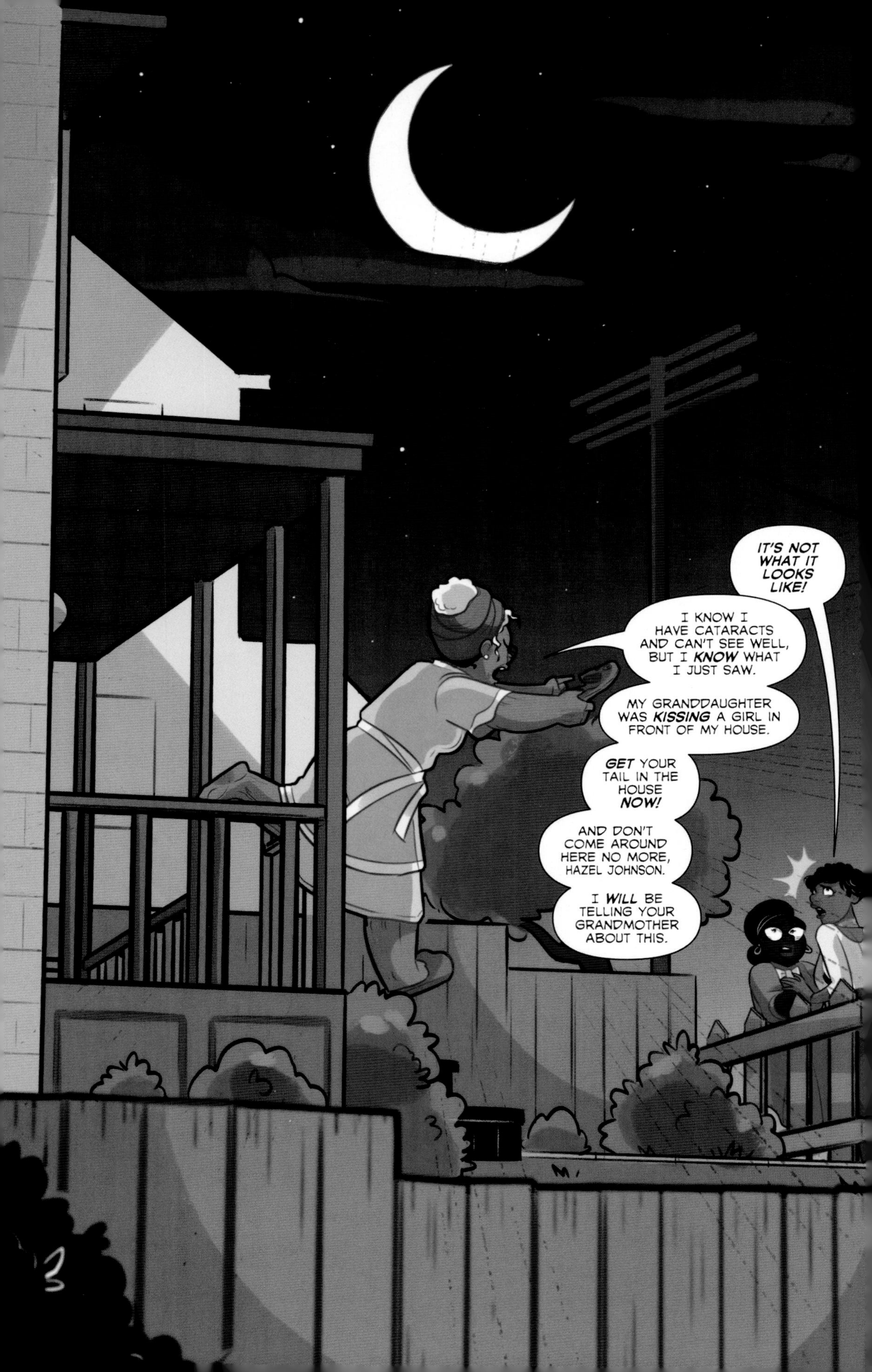
IT'S NOT WHAT IT LOOKS LIKE!
I KNOW I HAVE CATARACTS AND CAN'T SEE WELL, BUT I **KNOW** WHAT I JUST SAW.
MY GRANDDAUGHTER WAS **KISSING** A GIRL IN FRONT OF MY HOUSE.
GET YOUR TAIL IN THE HOUSE **NOW!**
AND DON'T COME AROUND HERE NO MORE, HAZEL JOHNSON.
I **WILL** BE TELLING YOUR GRANDMOTHER ABOUT THIS.

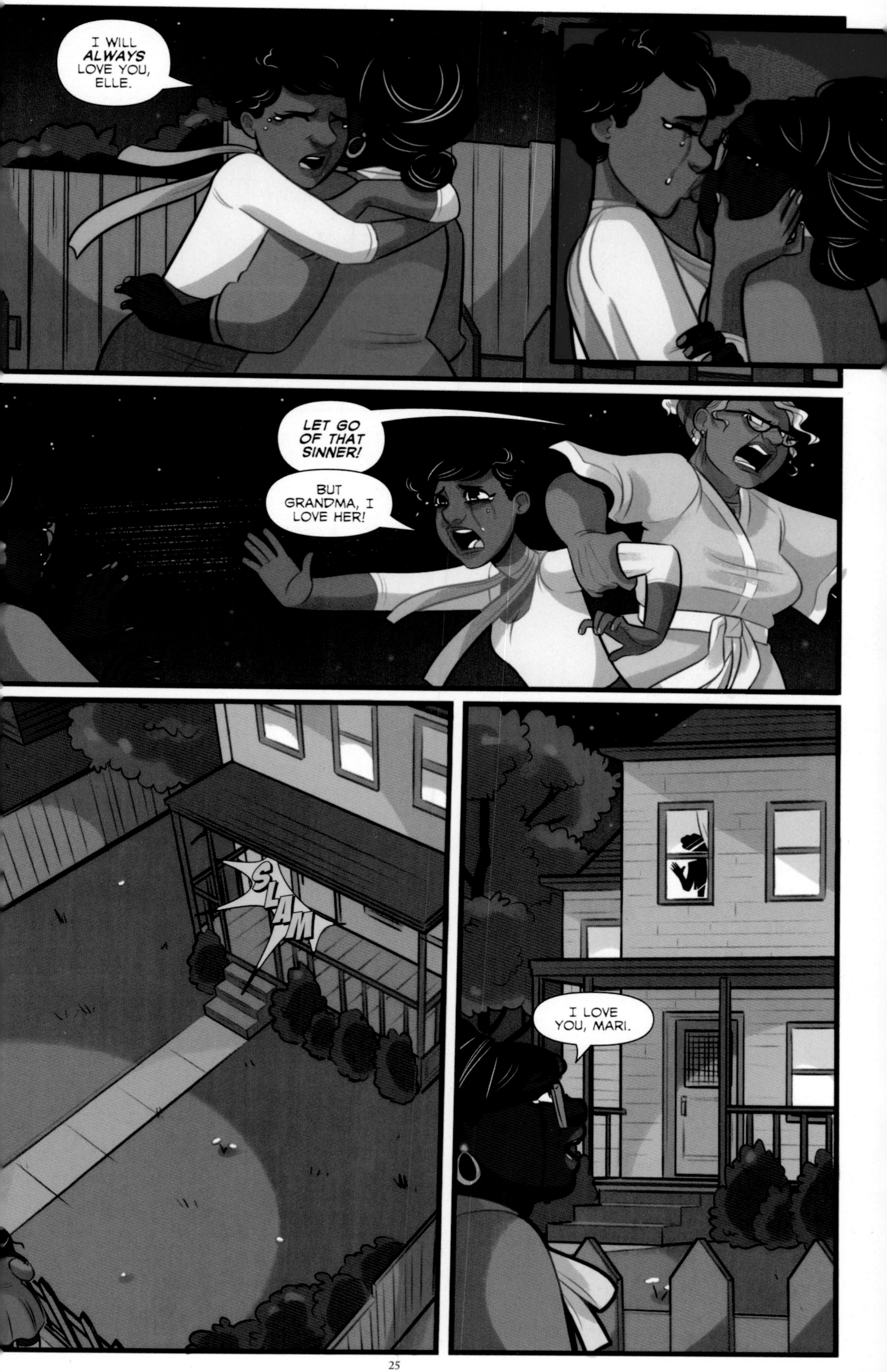
I WILL ALWAYS LOVE YOU, ELLE.
LET GO OF THAT SINNER!
BUT GRANDMA, I LOVE HER!
SLAM
I LOVE YOU, MARI.

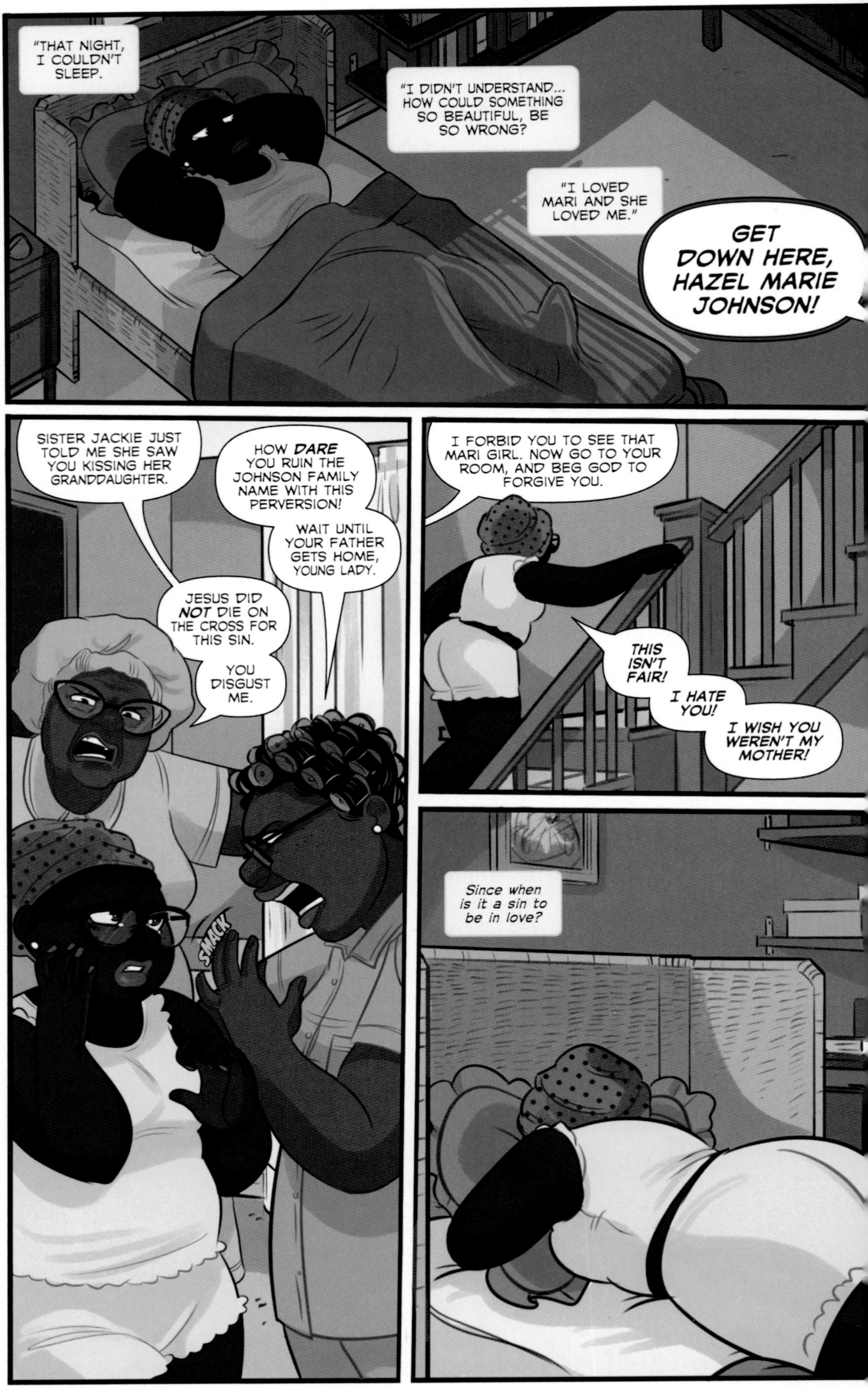
"THAT NIGHT, I COULDN'T SLEEP.
"I DIDN'T UNDERSTAND... HOW COULD SOMETHING SO BEAUTIFUL, BE SO WRONG?
"I LOVED MARI AND SHE LOVED ME."
GET DOWN HERE, HAZEL MARIE JOHNSON!
SISTER JACKIE JUST TOLD ME SHE SAW YOU KISSING HER GRANDDAUGHTER.
HOW DARE YOU RUIN THE JOHNSON FAMILY NAME WITH THIS PERVERSION!
WAIT UNTIL YOUR FATHER GETS HOME, YOUNG LADY.
JESUS DID NOT DIE ON THE CROSS FOR THIS SIN.
YOU DISGUST ME.
SMACK
I FORBID YOU TO SEE THAT MARI GIRL. NOW GO TO YOUR ROOM, AND BEG GOD TO FORGIVE YOU.
THIS ISN'T FAIR!
I HATE YOU!
I WISH YOU WEREN'T MY MOTHER!
Since when is it a sin to be in love?

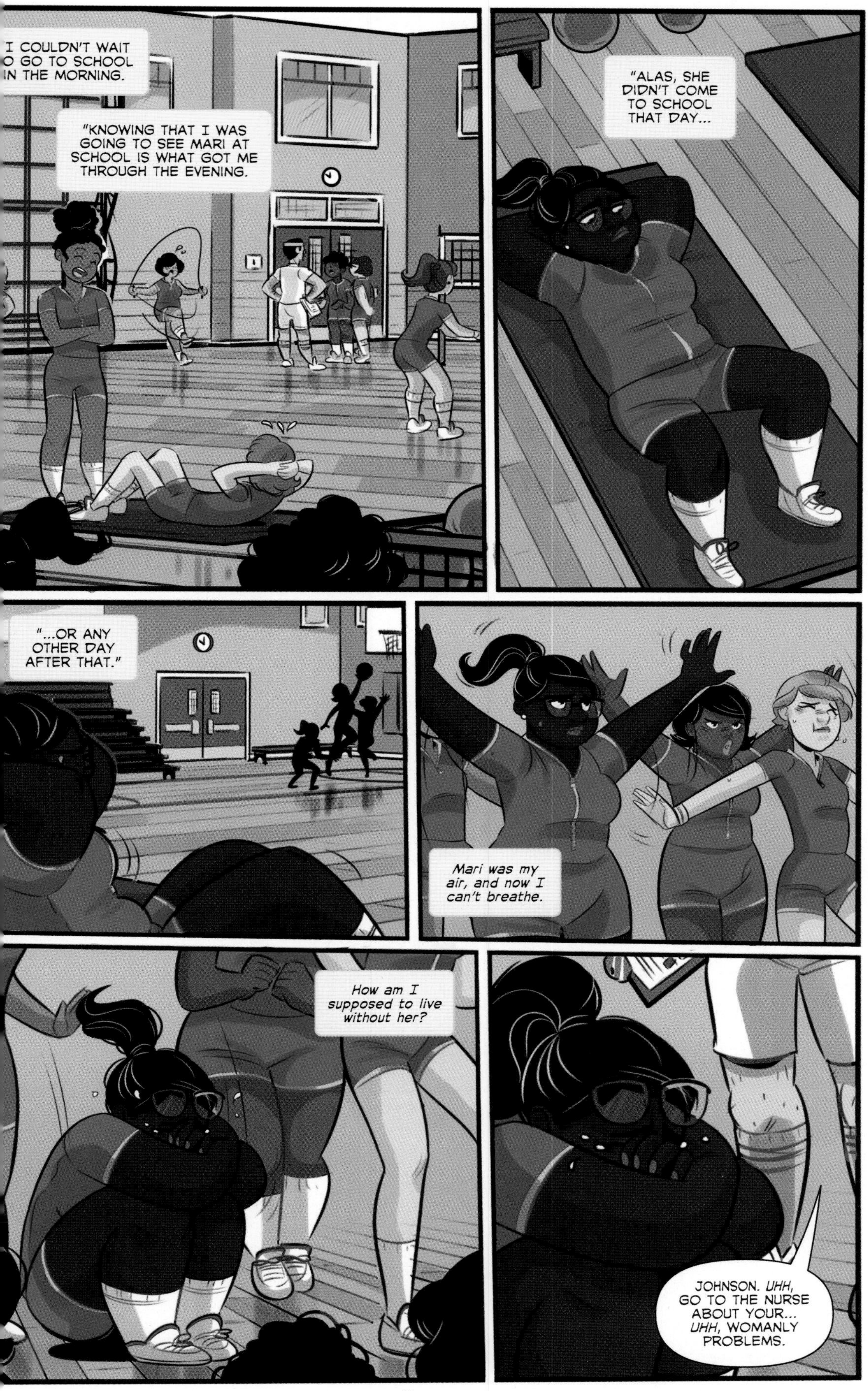
I COULDN'T WAIT
O GO TO SCHOOL
IN THE MORNING.
"KNOWING THAT I WAS GOING TO SEE MARI AT SCHOOL IS WHAT GOT ME THROUGH THE EVENING.
"ALAS, SHE DIDN'T COME TO SCHOOL THAT DAY...
"...OR ANY OTHER DAY AFTER THAT."
Mari was my air, and now I can't breathe.
How am I supposed to live without her?
JOHNSON. *UHH*, GO TO THE NURSE ABOUT YOUR... *UHH*, WOMANLY PROBLEMS.

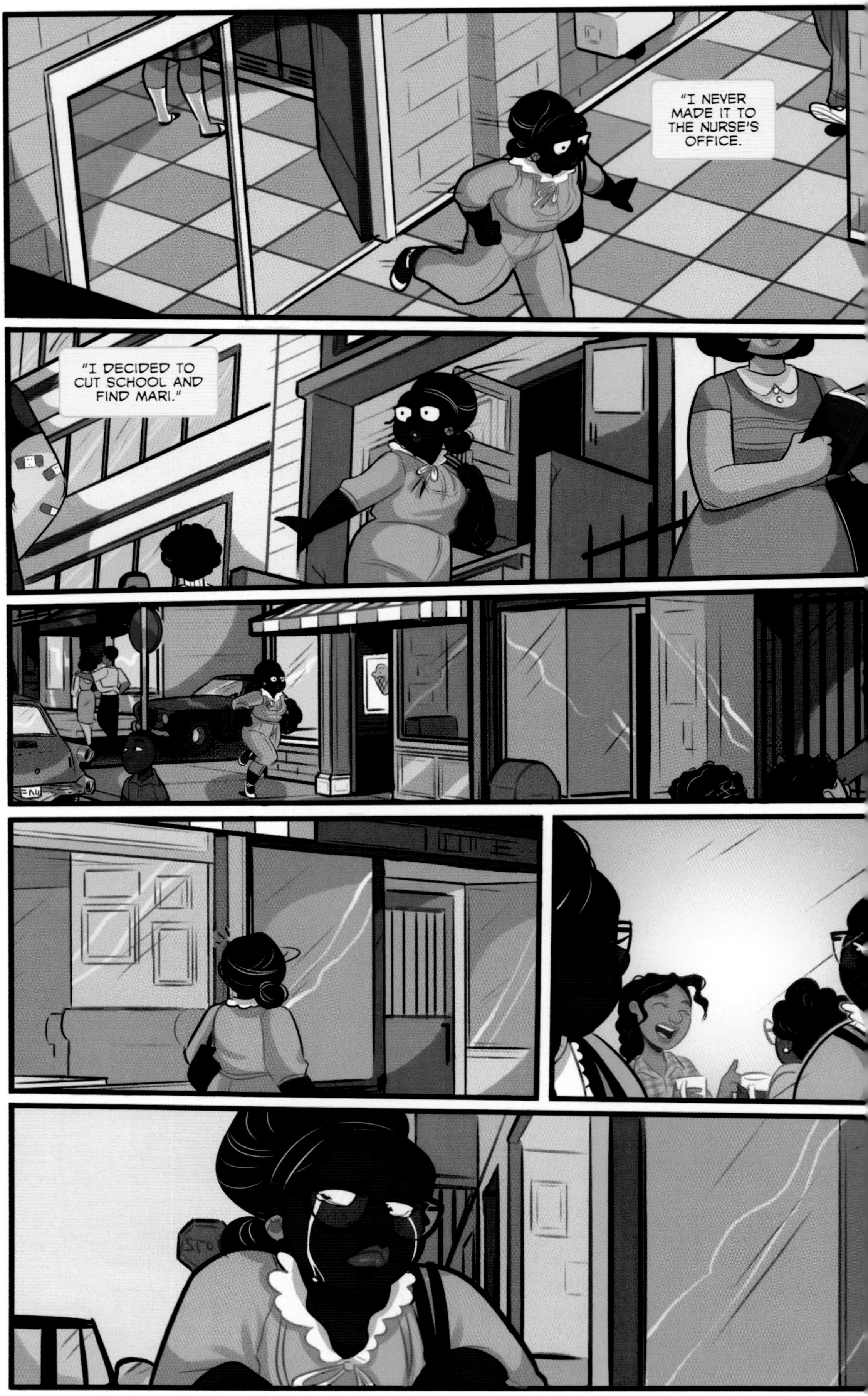
"I NEVER MADE IT TO THE NURSE'S OFFICE.
"I DECIDED TO CUT SCHOOL AND FIND MARI."

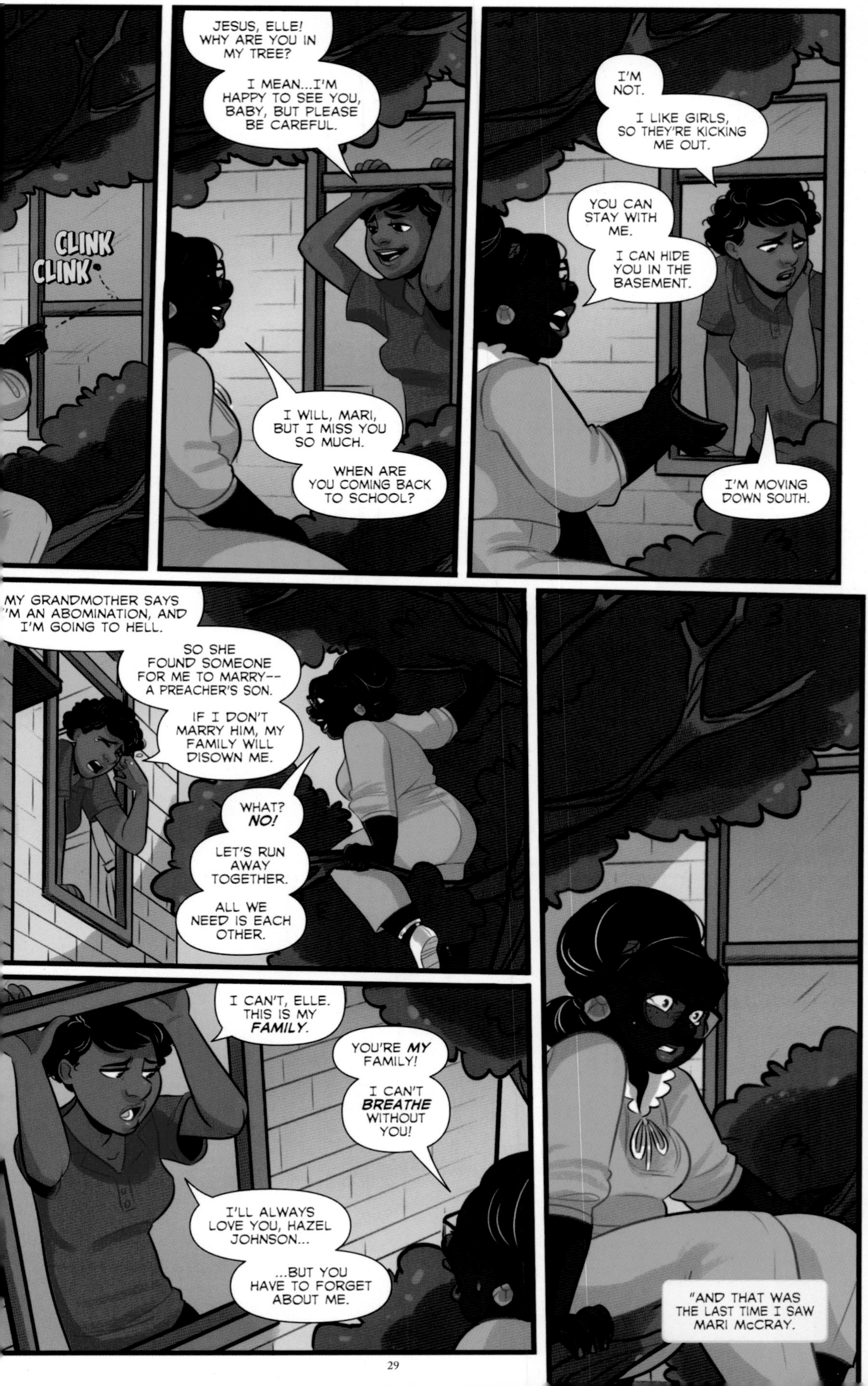
CLINK CLINK
JESUS, ELLE! WHY ARE YOU IN MY TREE?
I MEAN...I'M HAPPY TO SEE YOU, BABY, BUT PLEASE BE CAREFUL.
I WILL, MARI, BUT I MISS YOU SO MUCH.
WHEN ARE YOU COMING BACK TO SCHOOL?
I'M NOT.
I LIKE GIRLS, SO THEY'RE KICKING ME OUT.
YOU CAN STAY WITH ME.
I CAN HIDE YOU IN THE BASEMENT.
I'M MOVING DOWN SOUTH.
MY GRANDMOTHER SAYS I'M AN ABOMINATION, AND I'M GOING TO HELL.
SO SHE FOUND SOMEONE FOR ME TO MARRY-- A PREACHER'S SON.
IF I DON'T MARRY HIM, MY FAMILY WILL DISOWN ME.
WHAT? NO!
LET'S RUN AWAY TOGETHER.
ALL WE NEED IS EACH OTHER.
I CAN'T, ELLE. THIS IS MY FAMILY.
YOU'RE MY FAMILY!
I CAN'T BREATHE WITHOUT YOU!
I'LL ALWAYS LOVE YOU, HAZEL JOHNSON...
...BUT YOU HAVE TO FORGET ABOUT ME.
"AND THAT WAS THE LAST TIME I SAW MARI McCRAY.

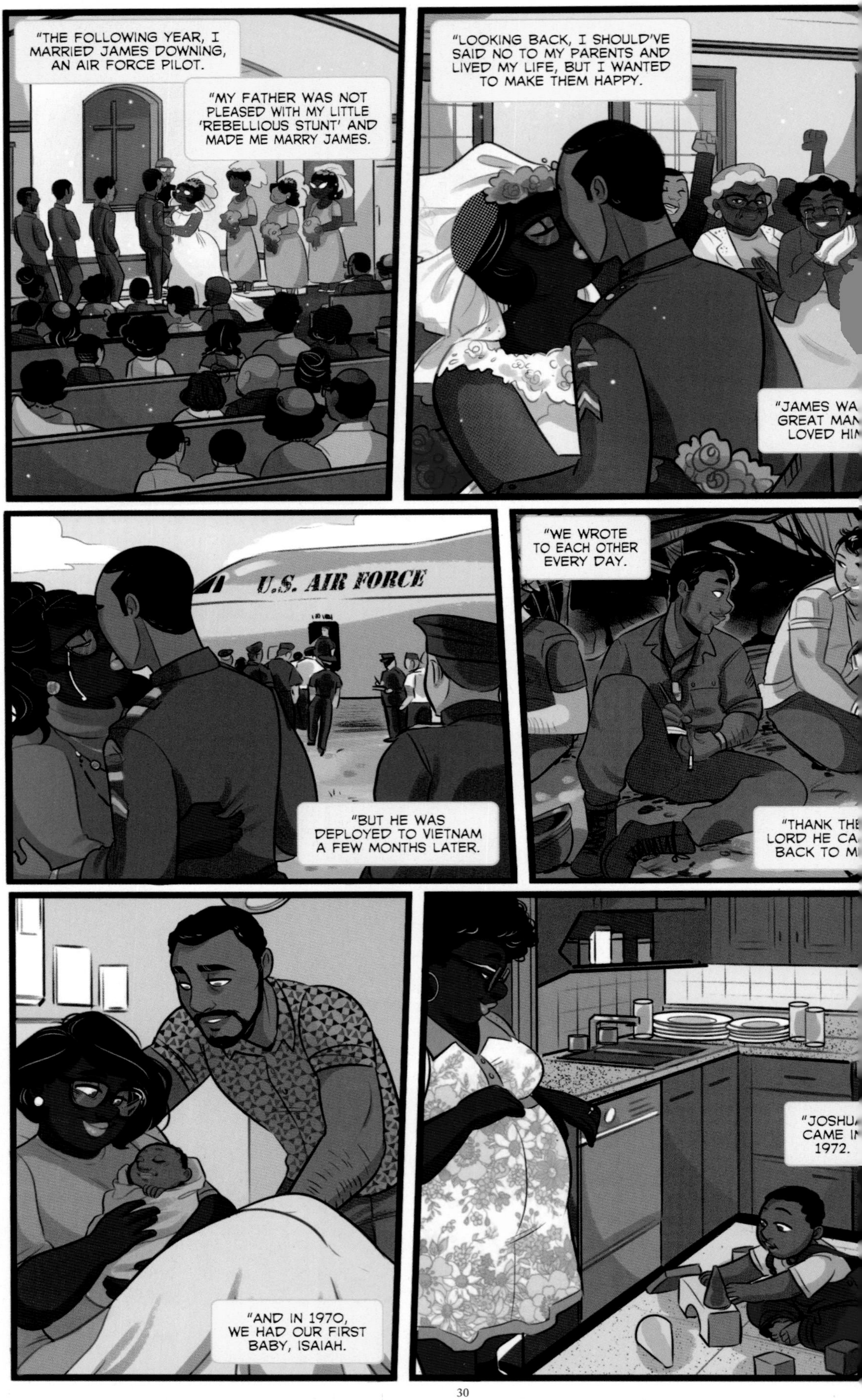
"THE FOLLOWING YEAR, I MARRIED JAMES DOWNING, AN AIR FORCE PILOT.
"MY FATHER WAS NOT PLEASED WITH MY LITTLE 'REBELLIOUS STUNT' AND MADE ME MARRY JAMES.
"LOOKING BACK, I SHOULD'VE SAID NO TO MY PARENTS AND LIVED MY LIFE, BUT I WANTED TO MAKE THEM HAPPY.
"JAMES WA GREAT MAN LOVED HIM
U.S. AIR FORCE
"BUT HE WAS DEPLOYED TO VIETNAM A FEW MONTHS LATER.
"WE WROTE TO EACH OTHER EVERY DAY.
"THANK THE LORD HE CA BACK TO M
"AND IN 1970, WE HAD OUR FIRST BABY, ISAIAH.
"JOSHU CAME I 1972.

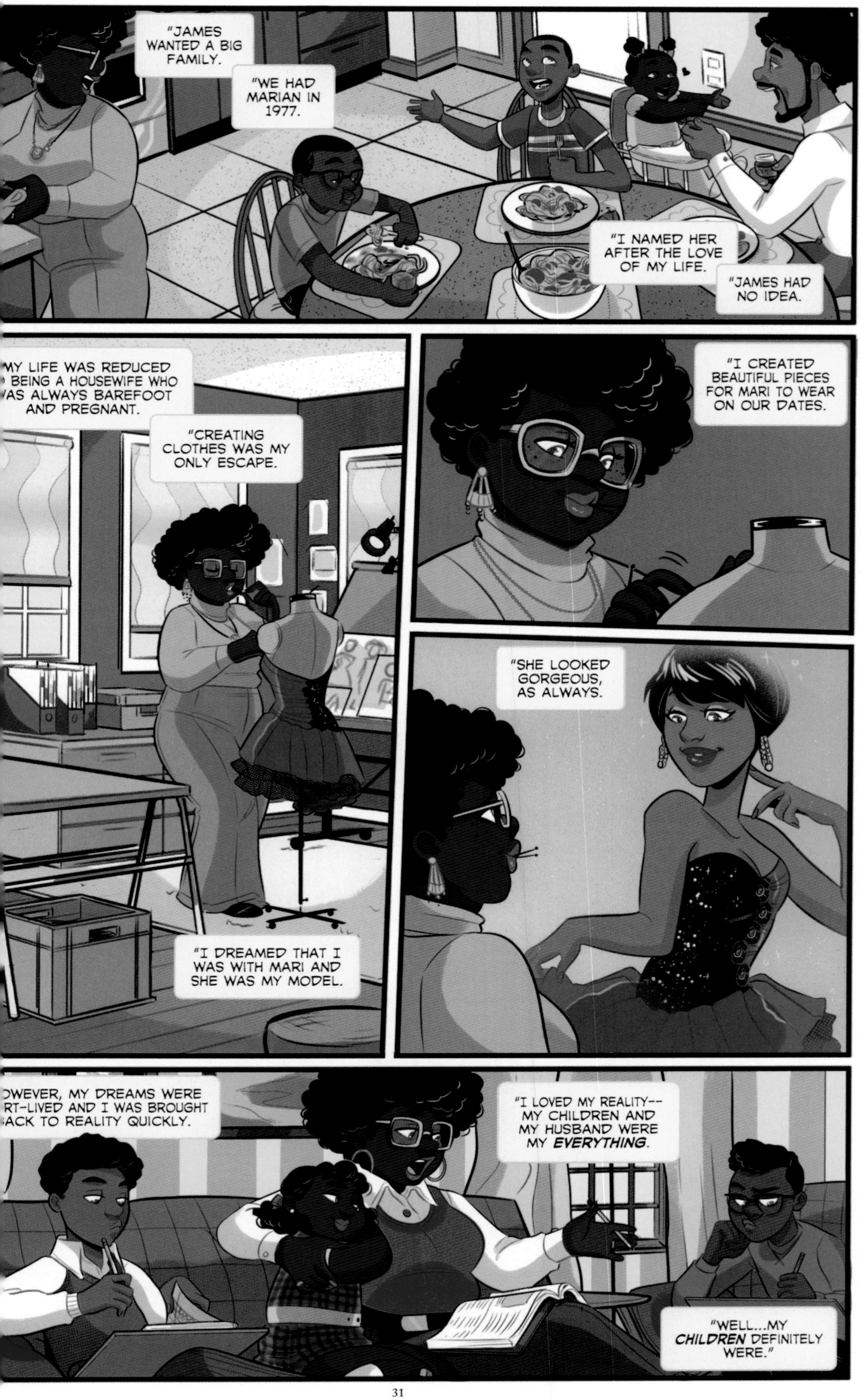
"JAMES WANTED A BIG FAMILY.
"WE HAD MARIAN IN 1977.
"I NAMED HER AFTER THE LOVE OF MY LIFE.
"JAMES HAD NO IDEA.
MY LIFE WAS REDUCED BEING A HOUSEWIFE WHO AS ALWAYS BAREFOOT AND PREGNANT.
"CREATING CLOTHES WAS MY ONLY ESCAPE.
"I DREAMED THAT I WAS WITH MARI AND SHE WAS MY MODEL.
"I CREATED BEAUTIFUL PIECES FOR MARI TO WEAR ON OUR DATES.
"SHE LOOKED GORGEOUS, AS ALWAYS.
OWEVER, MY DREAMS WERE RT-LIVED AND I WAS BROUGHT ACK TO REALITY QUICKLY.
"I LOVED MY REALITY-- MY CHILDREN AND MY HUSBAND WERE MY *EVERYTHING*.
"WELL...MY *CHILDREN* DEFINITELY WERE."

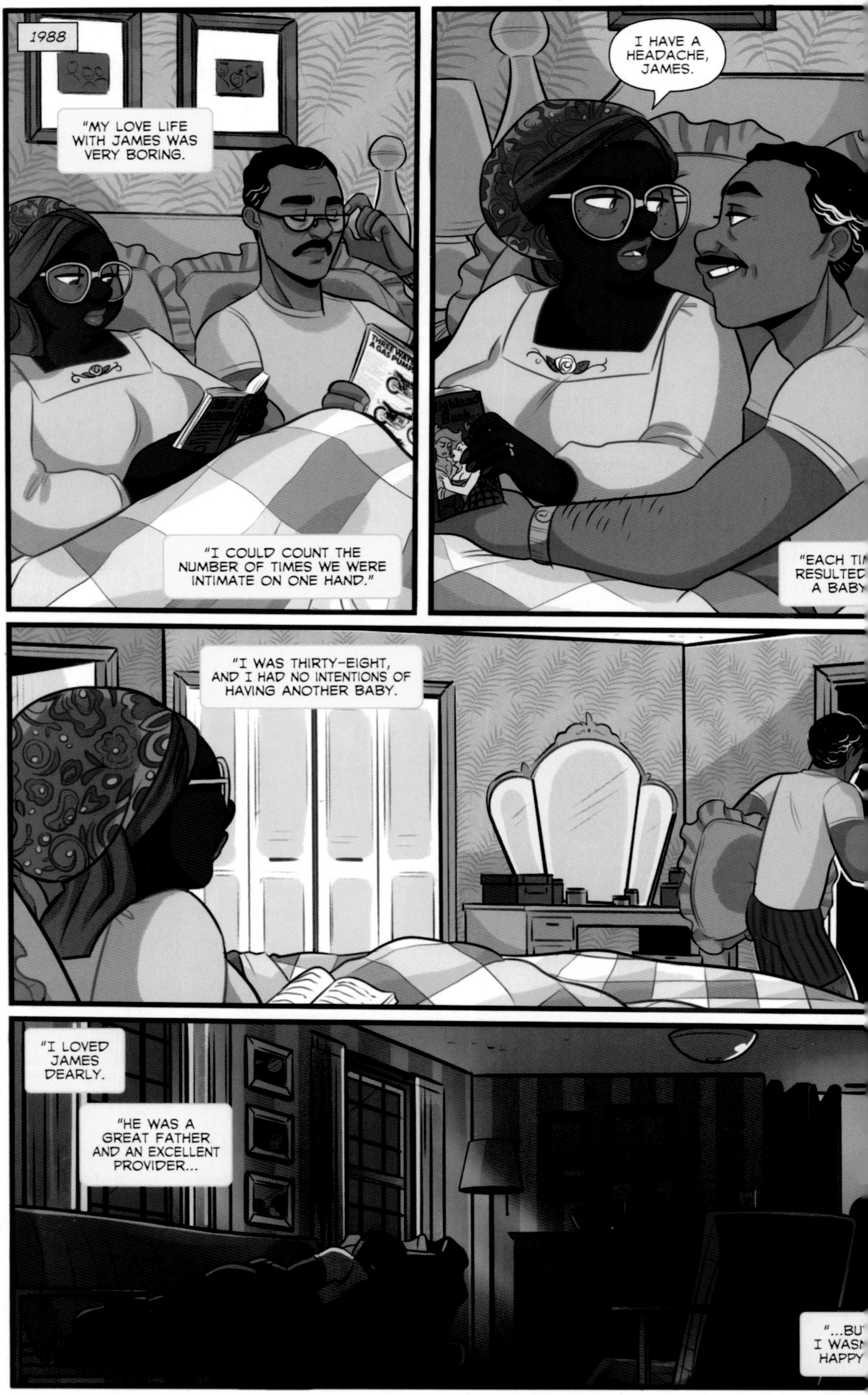
1988
"MY LOVE LIFE WITH JAMES WAS VERY BORING.
"I COULD COUNT THE NUMBER OF TIMES WE WERE INTIMATE ON ONE HAND."
I HAVE A HEADACHE, JAMES.
"EACH TI
RESULTED
A BABY
"I WAS THIRTY-EIGHT, AND I HAD NO INTENTIONS OF HAVING ANOTHER BABY.
"I LOVED JAMES DEARLY.
"HE WAS A GREAT FATHER AND AN EXCELLENT PROVIDER...
"...BU
I WASN
HAPPY

MOTHER'S DAY, 2015
ENGLEWOOD, N.J.

"THIS WENT ON FOR DECADES.

I COULD HAVE LEFT, BUT I STAYED BECAUSE OF THE KIDS...

"...AND THEN THE GRANDKIDS.

GRAND
THE MA
THE MYT
THE LEGEN

33

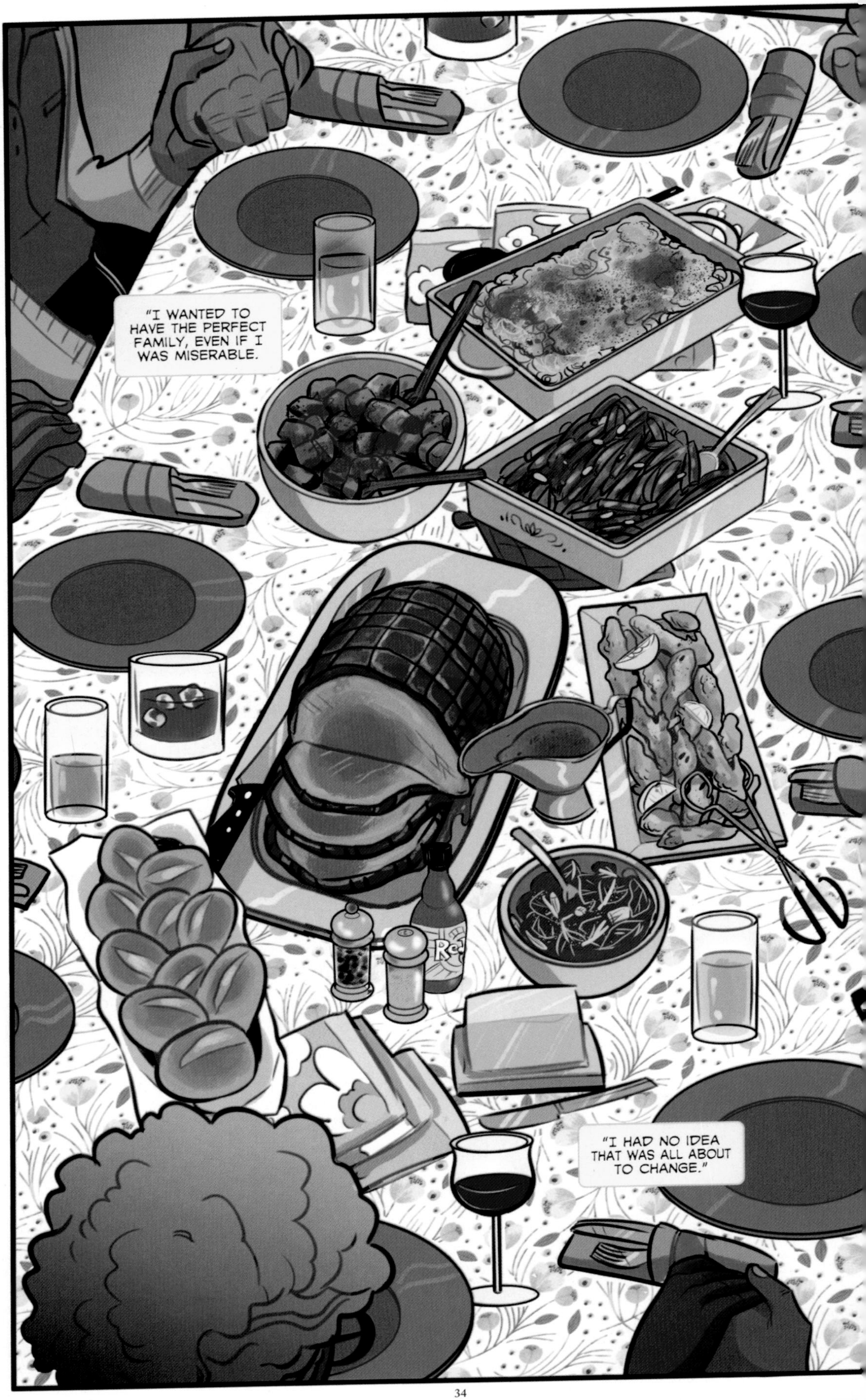
"I WANTED TO HAVE THE PERFECT FAMILY, EVEN IF I WAS MISERABLE.
"I HAD NO IDEA THAT WAS ALL ABOUT TO CHANGE."

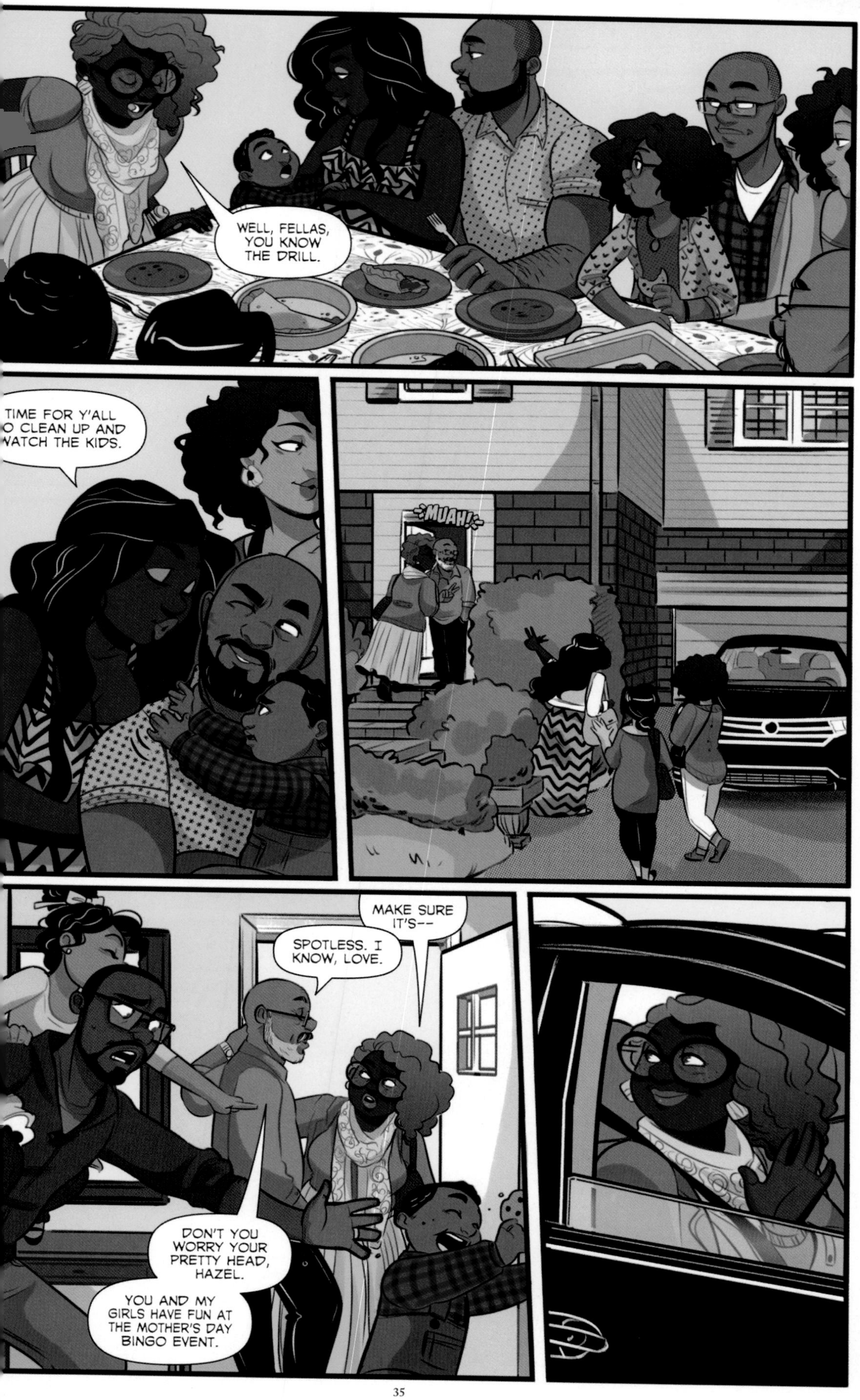
WELL, FELLAS, YOU KNOW THE DRILL.
TIME FOR Y'ALL O CLEAN UP AND WATCH THE KIDS.
MUAH!
MAKE SURE IT'S--
SPOTLESS. I KNOW, LOVE.
DON'T YOU WORRY YOUR PRETTY HEAD, HAZEL.
YOU AND MY GIRLS HAVE FUN AT THE MOTHER'S DAY BINGO EVENT.

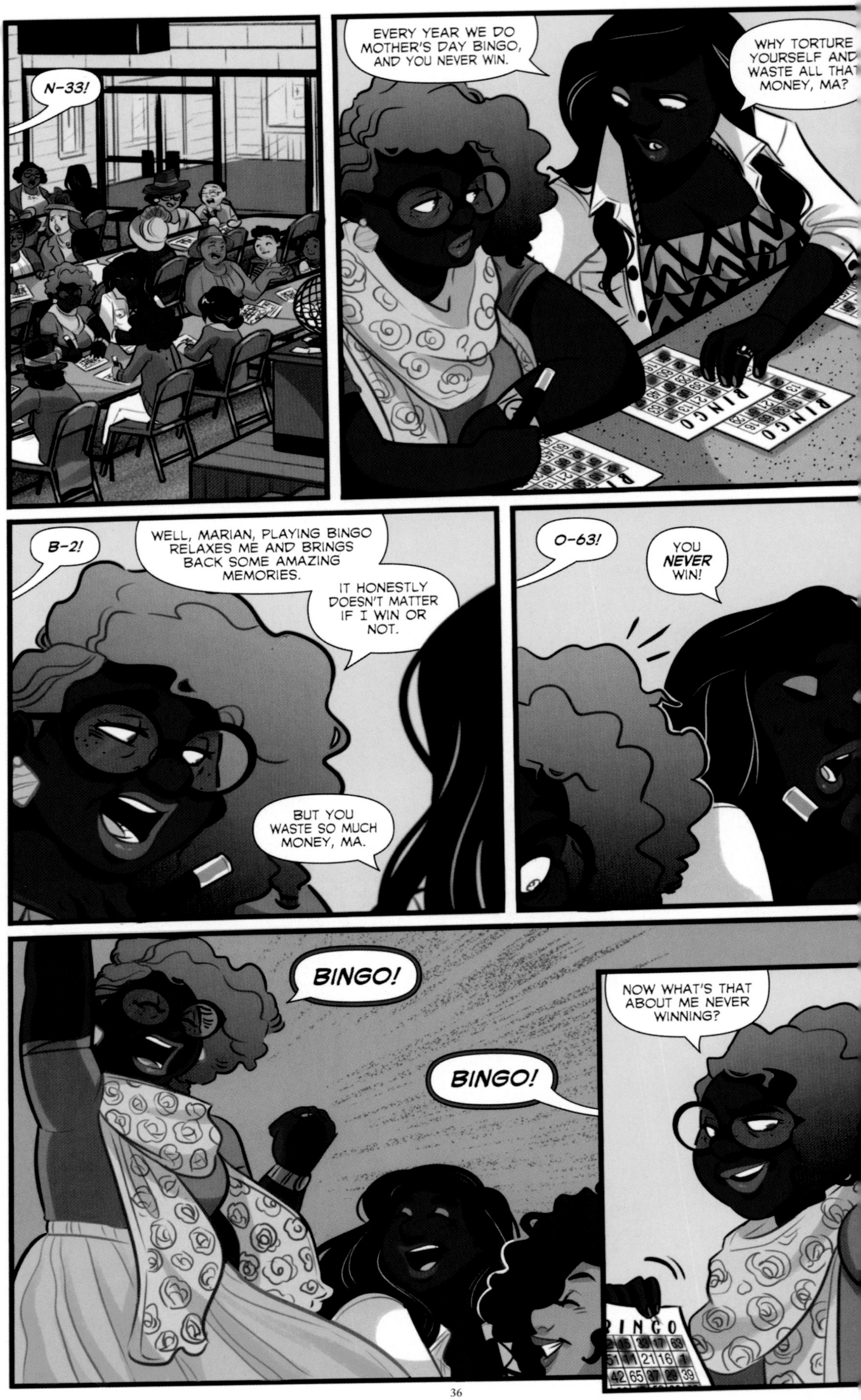
N-33!
EVERY YEAR WE DO MOTHER'S DAY BINGO, AND YOU NEVER WIN.
WHY TORTURE YOURSELF AND WASTE ALL THAT MONEY, MA?
B-2!
WELL, MARIAN, PLAYING BINGO RELAXES ME AND BRINGS BACK SOME AMAZING MEMORIES.
IT HONESTLY DOESN'T MATTER IF I WIN OR NOT.
BUT YOU WASTE SO MUCH MONEY, MA.
O-63!
YOU *NEVER* WIN!
BINGO!
BINGO!
NOW WHAT'S THAT ABOUT ME NEVER WINNING?

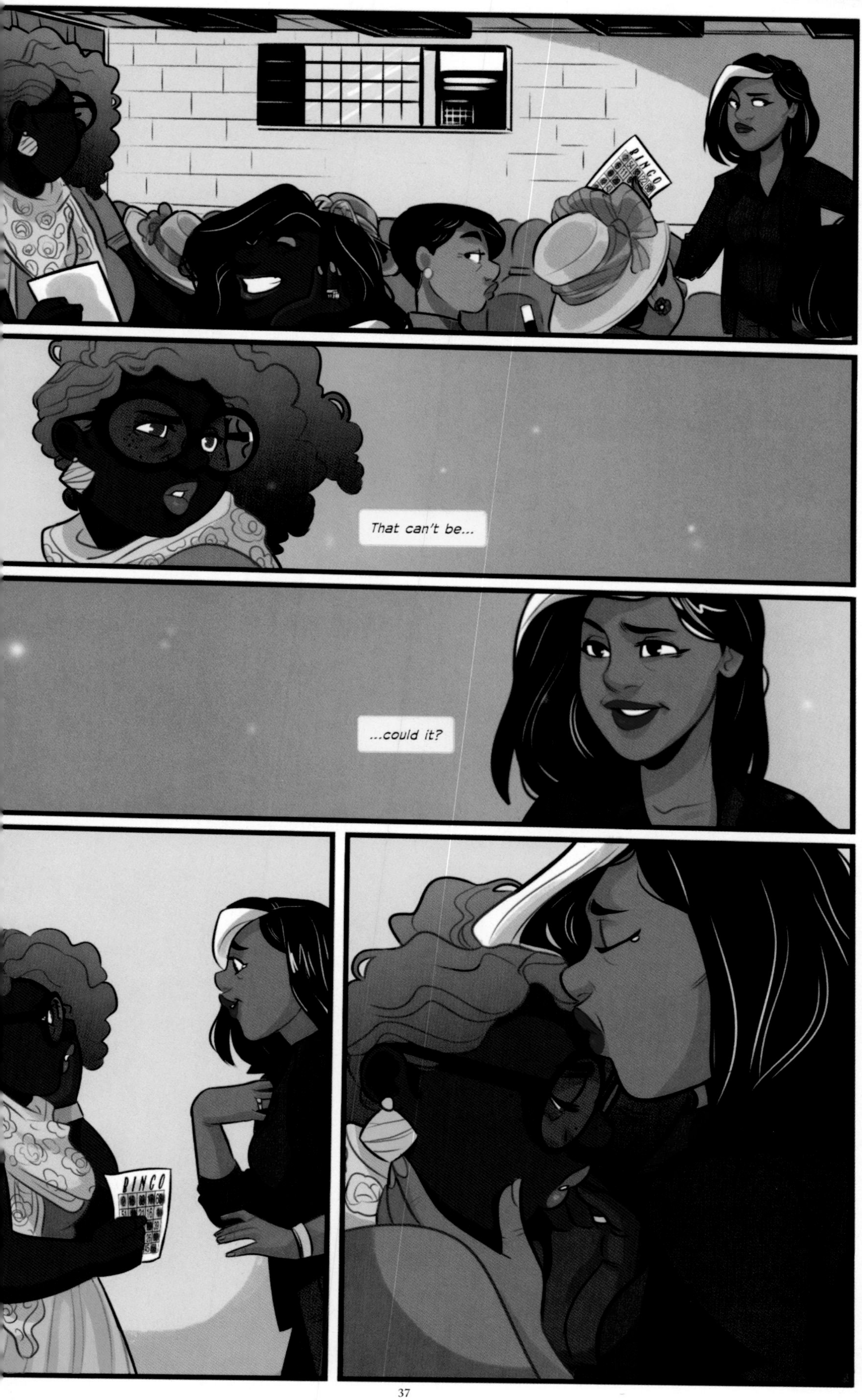
BINGO
That can't be...
...could it?
BINGO

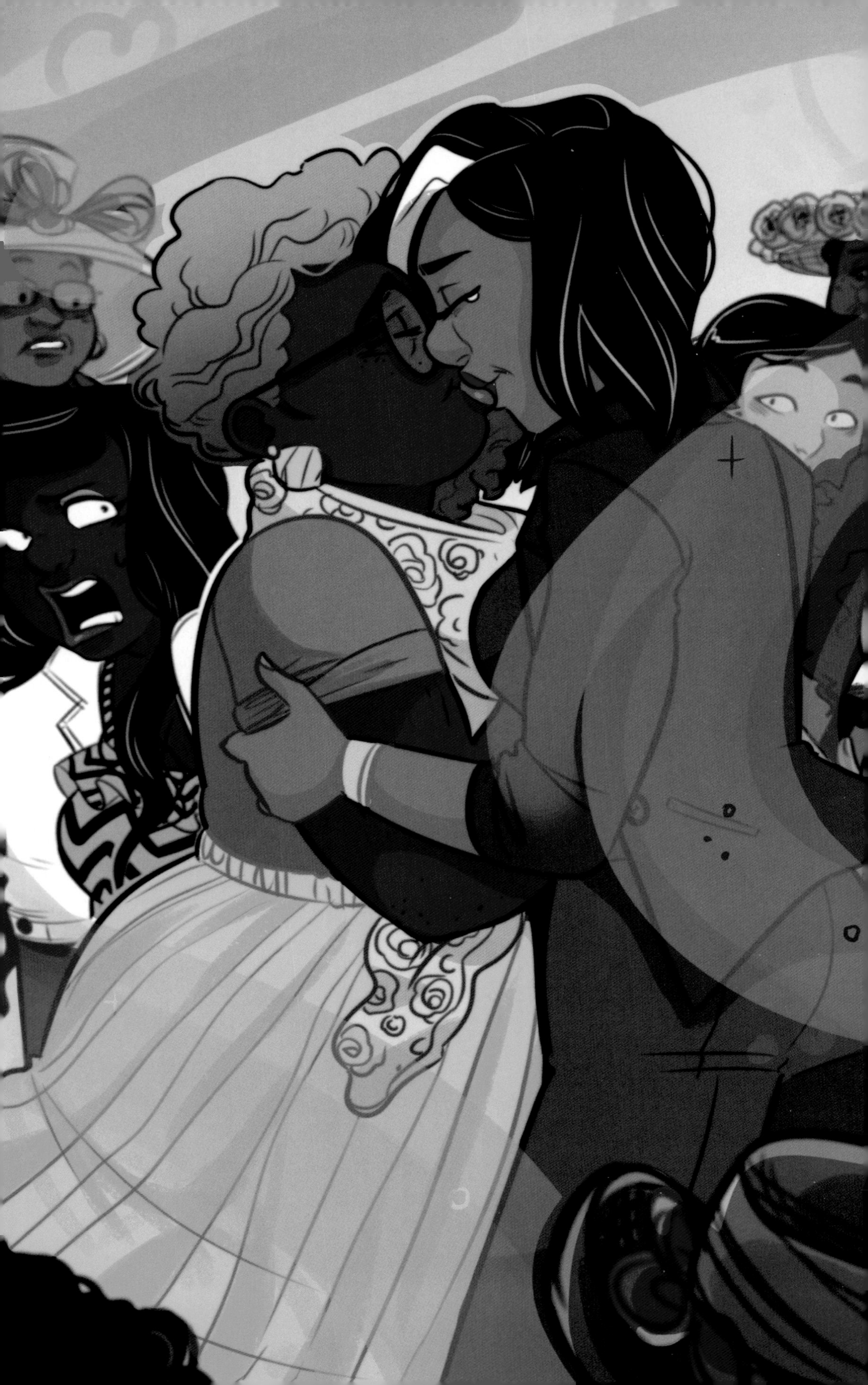

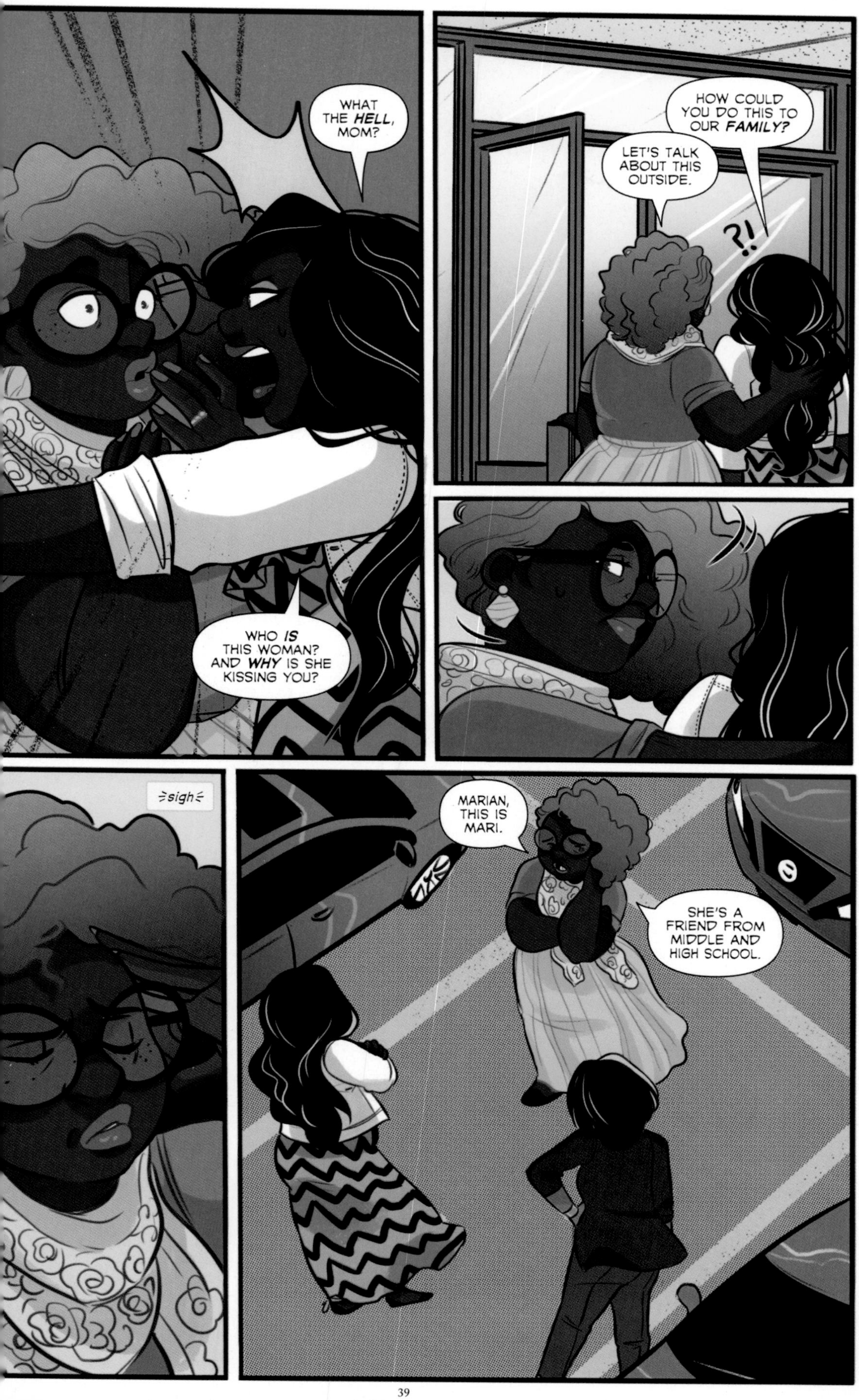
WHAT THE HELL, MOM?
WHO IS THIS WOMAN? AND WHY IS SHE KISSING YOU?
HOW COULD YOU DO THIS TO OUR FAMILY?
LET'S TALK ABOUT THIS OUTSIDE.
?!
sigh
MARIAN, THIS IS MARI.
SHE'S A FRIEND FROM MIDDLE AND HIGH SCHOOL.

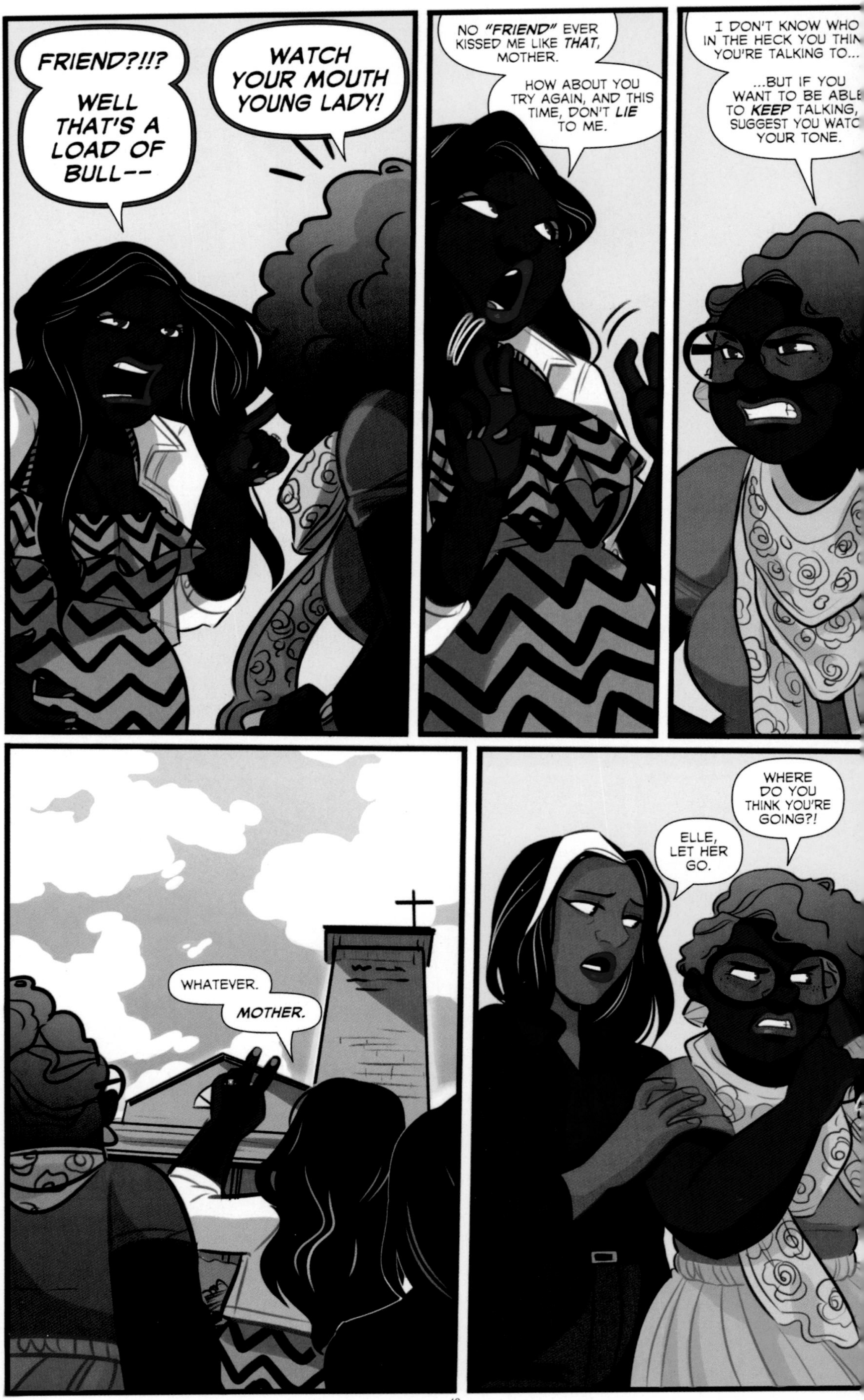
FRIEND?!!? WELL THAT'S A LOAD OF BULL--
WATCH YOUR MOUTH YOUNG LADY!
NO "FRIEND" EVER KISSED ME LIKE THAT, MOTHER.
HOW ABOUT YOU TRY AGAIN, AND THIS TIME, DON'T LIE TO ME.
I DON'T KNOW WHO IN THE HECK YOU THIN YOU'RE TALKING TO...
...BUT IF YOU WANT TO BE ABLE TO KEEP TALKING, SUGGEST YOU WATC YOUR TONE.
WHATEVER.
MOTHER.
WHERE DO YOU THINK YOU'RE GOING?!
ELLE, LET HER GO.

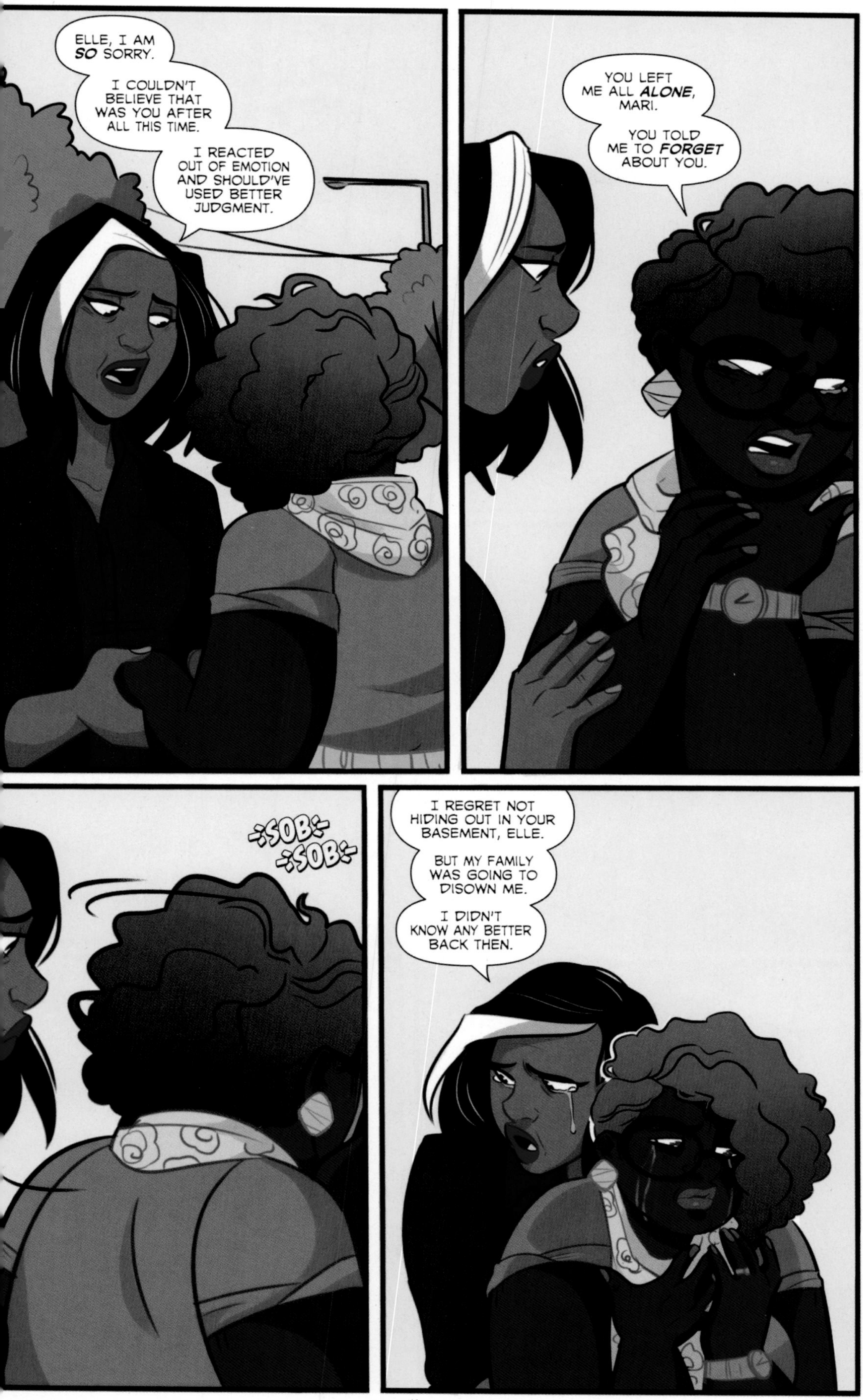

ELLE, I AM SO SORRY.
I COULDN'T BELIEVE THAT WAS YOU AFTER ALL THIS TIME.
I REACTED OUT OF EMOTION AND SHOULD'VE USED BETTER JUDGMENT.
YOU LEFT ME ALL ALONE, MARI.
YOU TOLD ME TO FORGET ABOUT YOU.
SOB SOB
I REGRET NOT HIDING OUT IN YOUR BASEMENT, ELLE.
BUT MY FAMILY WAS GOING TO DISOWN ME.
I DIDN'T KNOW ANY BETTER BACK THEN.

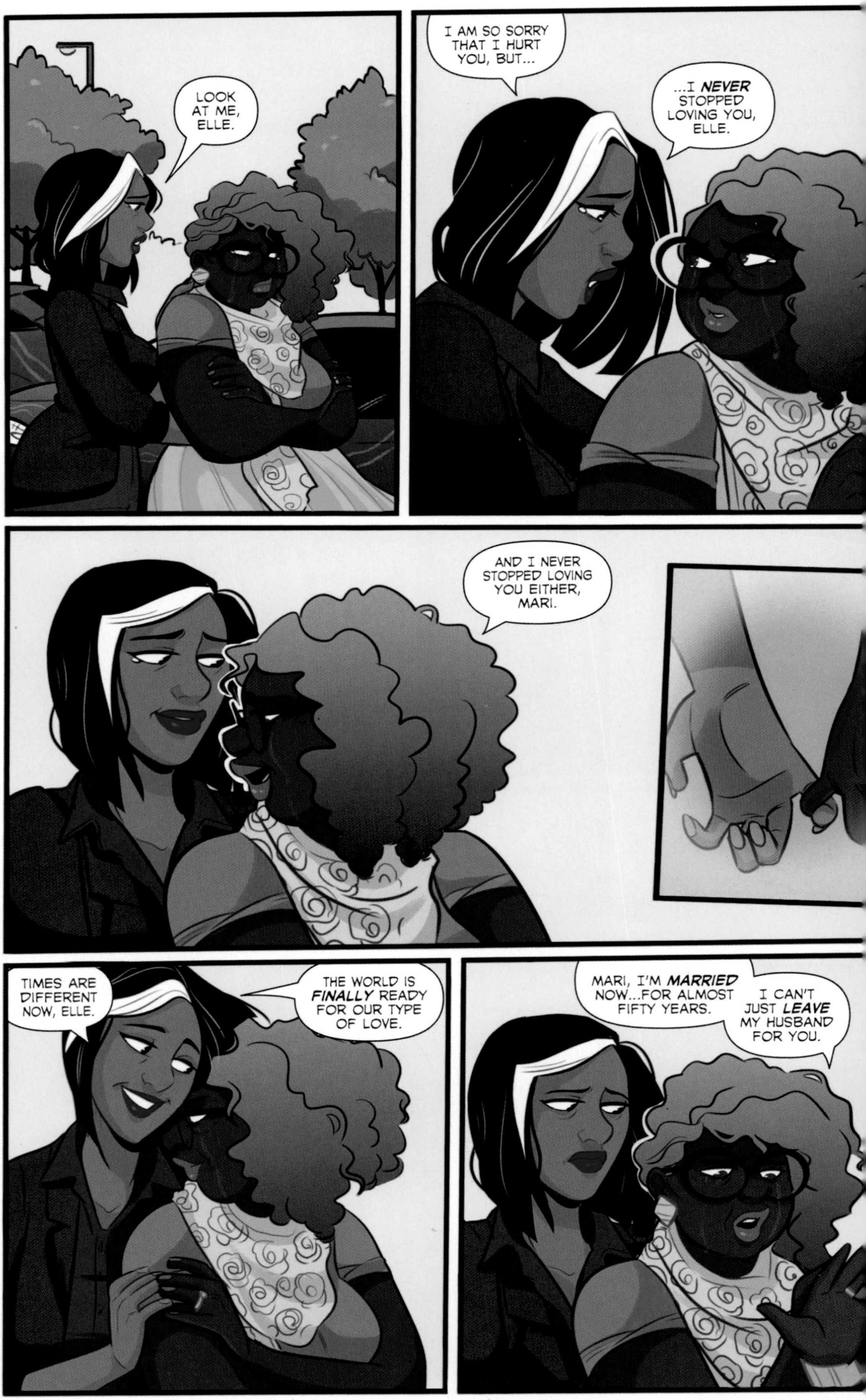

LOOK AT ME, ELLE.
I AM SO SORRY THAT I HURT YOU, BUT...
...I NEVER STOPPED LOVING YOU, ELLE.
AND I NEVER STOPPED LOVING YOU EITHER, MARI.
TIMES ARE DIFFERENT NOW, ELLE.
THE WORLD IS FINALLY READY FOR OUR TYPE OF LOVE.
MARI, I'M MARRIED NOW...FOR ALMOST FIFTY YEARS.
I CAN'T JUST LEAVE MY HUSBAND FOR YOU.

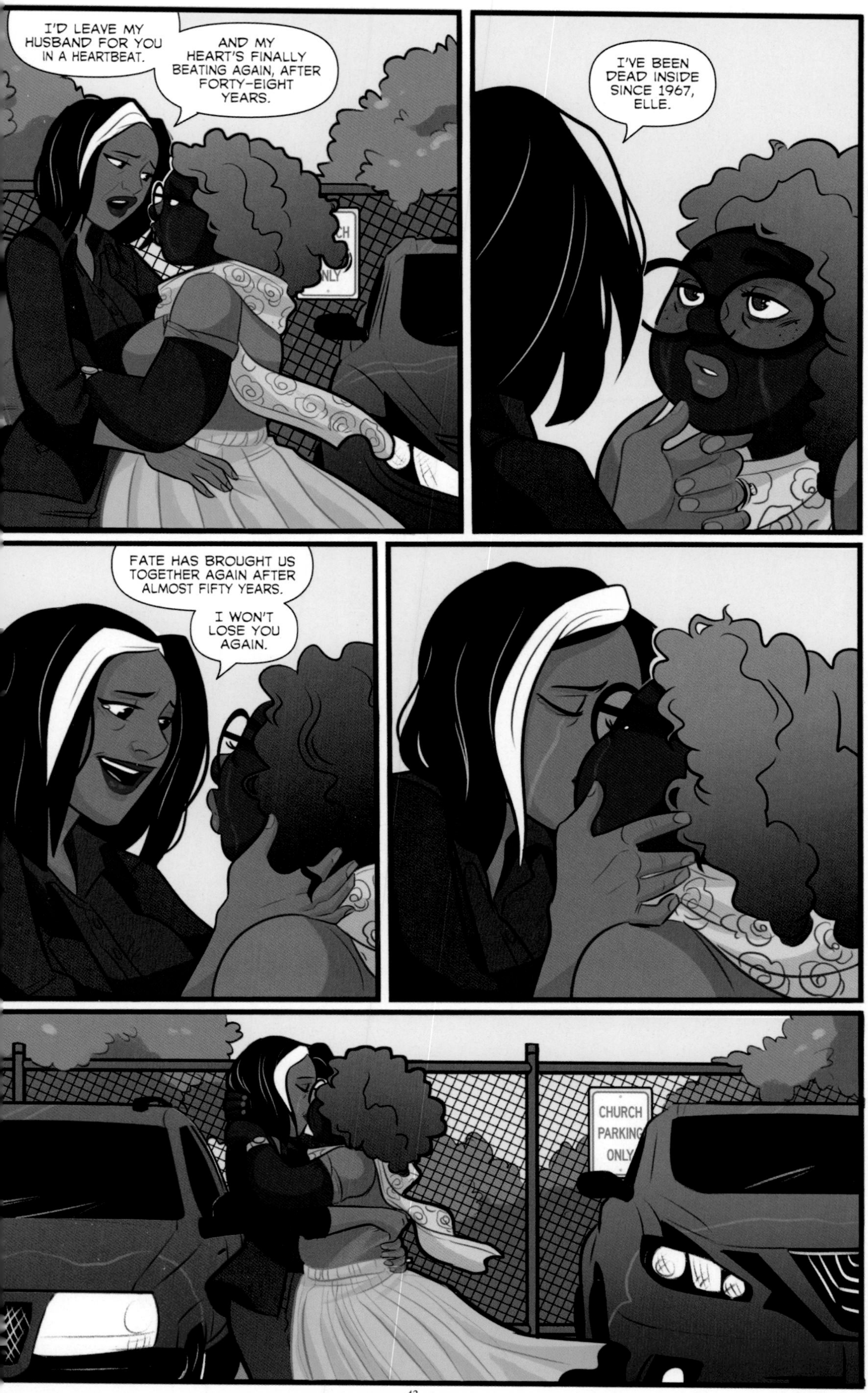
I'D LEAVE MY HUSBAND FOR YOU IN A HEARTBEAT.
AND MY HEART'S FINALLY BEATING AGAIN, AFTER FORTY-EIGHT YEARS.
I'VE BEEN DEAD INSIDE SINCE 1967, ELLE.
FATE HAS BROUGHT US TOGETHER AGAIN AFTER ALMOST FIFTY YEARS.
I WON'T LOSE YOU AGAIN.
CHURCH PARKING ONLY

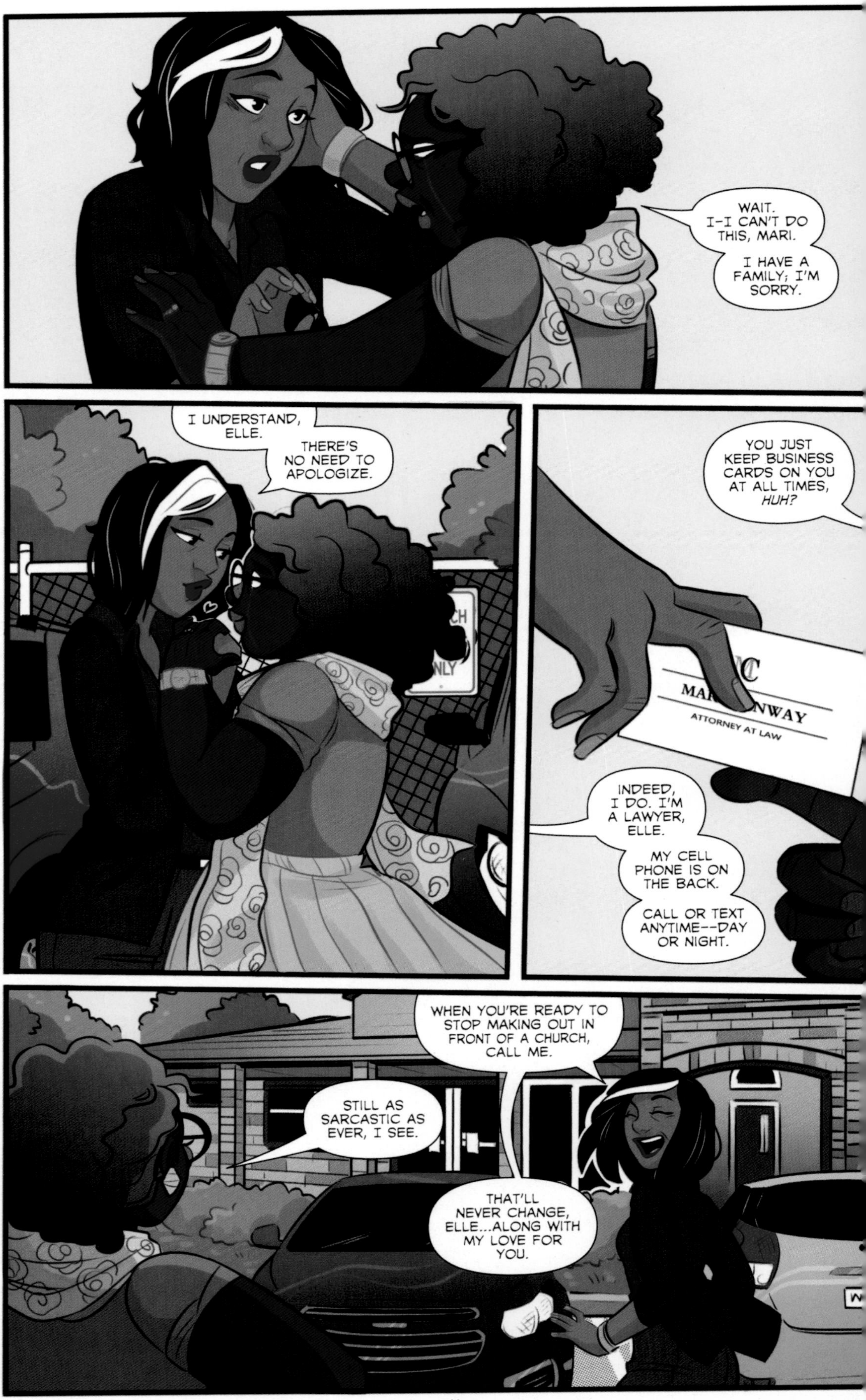
WAIT. I-I CAN'T DO THIS, MARI.
I HAVE A FAMILY; I'M SORRY.
I UNDERSTAND, ELLE.
THERE'S NO NEED TO APOLOGIZE.
YOU JUST KEEP BUSINESS CARDS ON YOU AT ALL TIMES, *HUH?*
ATTORNEY AT LAW
INDEED, I DO. I'M A LAWYER, ELLE.
MY CELL PHONE IS ON THE BACK.
CALL OR TEXT ANYTIME--DAY OR NIGHT.
WHEN YOU'RE READY TO STOP MAKING OUT IN FRONT OF A CHURCH, CALL ME.
STILL AS SARCASTIC AS EVER, I SEE.
THAT'LL NEVER CHANGE, ELLE...ALONG WITH MY LOVE FOR YOU.

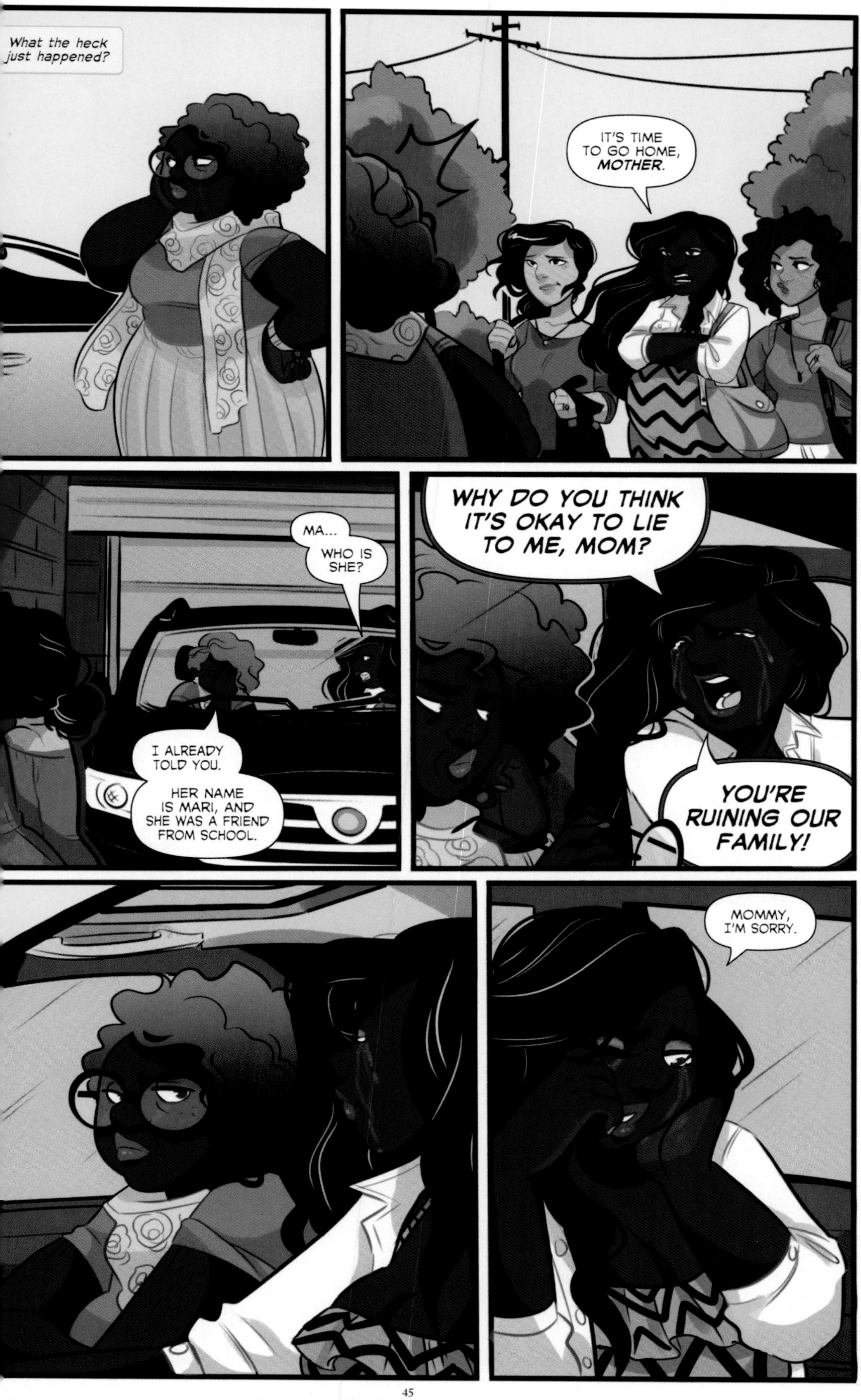
What the heck just happened?
IT'S TIME TO GO HOME, MOTHER.
MA...
WHO IS SHE?
I ALREADY TOLD YOU.
HER NAME IS MARI, AND SHE WAS A FRIEND FROM SCHOOL.
WHY DO YOU THINK IT'S OKAY TO LIE TO ME, MOM?
YOU'RE RUINING OUR FAMILY!
MOMMY, I'M SORRY.

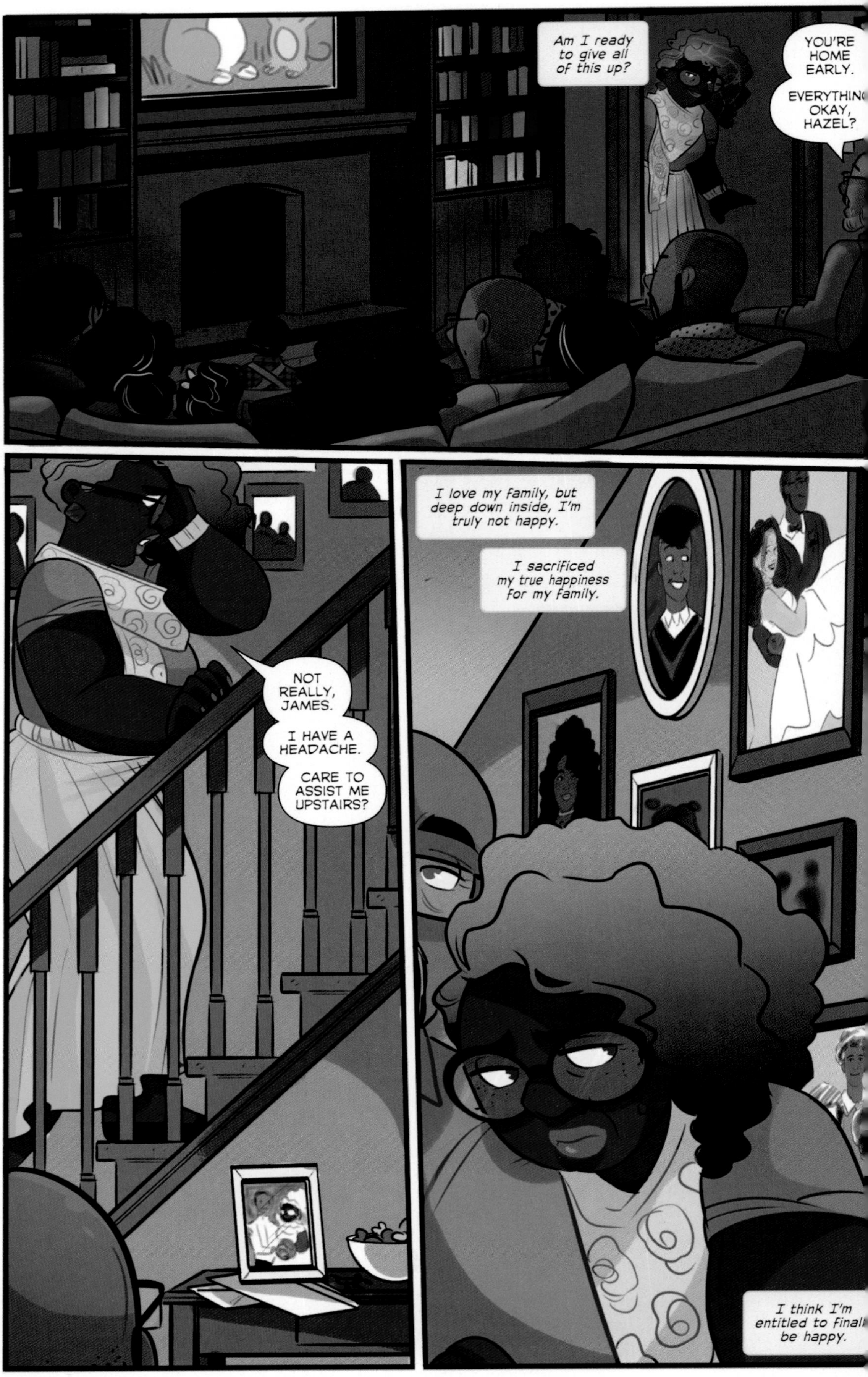

Am I ready to give all of this up?
YOU'RE HOME EARLY.
EVERYTHIN OKAY, HAZEL?
NOT REALLY, JAMES.
I HAVE A HEADACHE.
CARE TO ASSIST ME UPSTAIRS?
I love my family, but deep down inside, I'm truly not happy.
I sacrificed my true happiness for my family.
I think I'm entitled to final be happy.

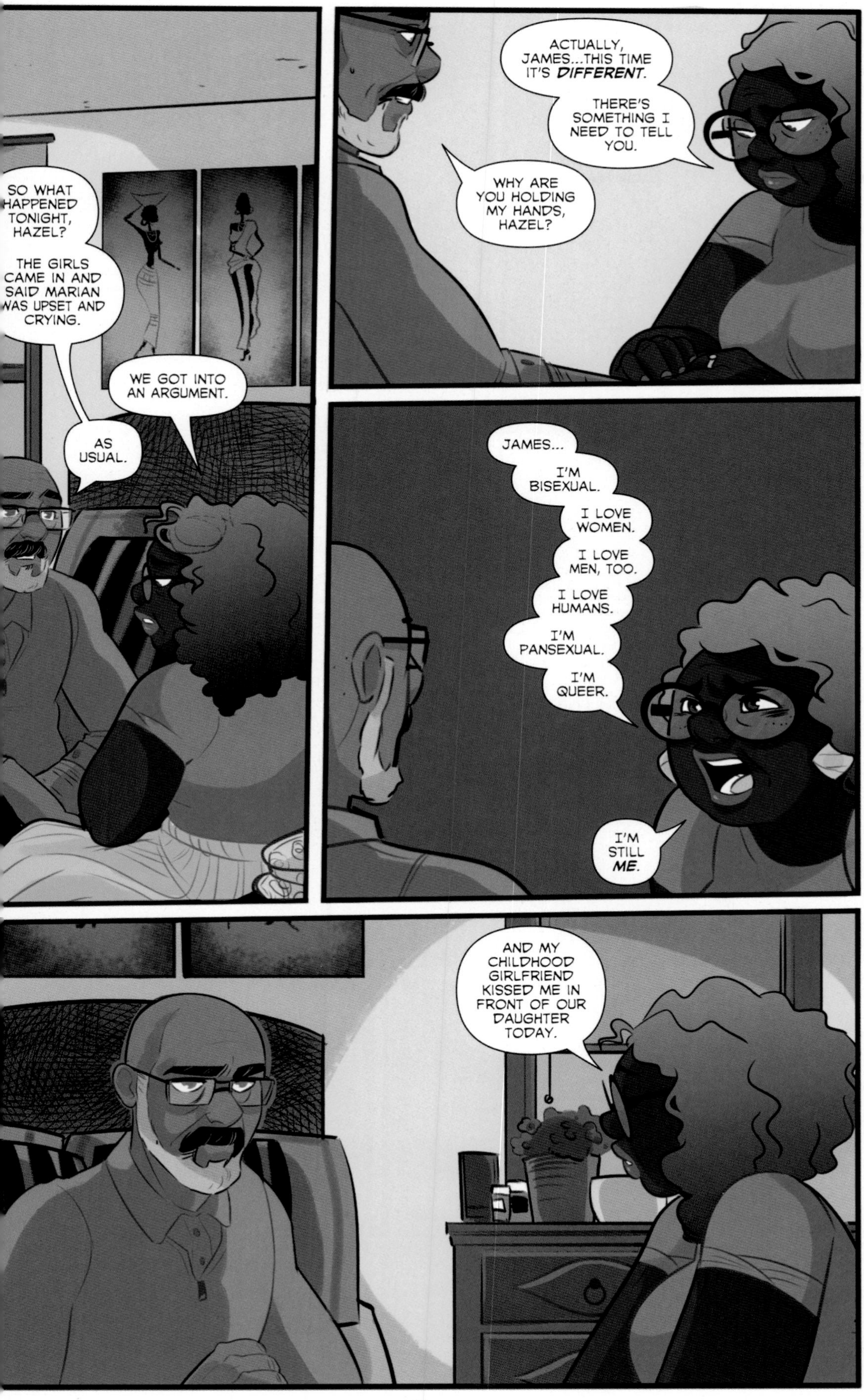
SO WHAT HAPPENED TONIGHT, HAZEL?
THE GIRLS CAME IN AND SAID MARIAN WAS UPSET AND CRYING.
WE GOT INTO AN ARGUMENT.
AS USUAL.
ACTUALLY, JAMES...THIS TIME IT'S DIFFERENT.
THERE'S SOMETHING I NEED TO TELL YOU.
WHY ARE YOU HOLDING MY HANDS, HAZEL?
JAMES...
I'M BISEXUAL.
I LOVE WOMEN.
I LOVE MEN, TOO.
I LOVE HUMANS.
I'M PANSEXUAL.
I'M QUEER.
I'M STILL ME.
AND MY CHILDHOOD GIRLFRIEND KISSED ME IN FRONT OF OUR DAUGHTER TODAY.

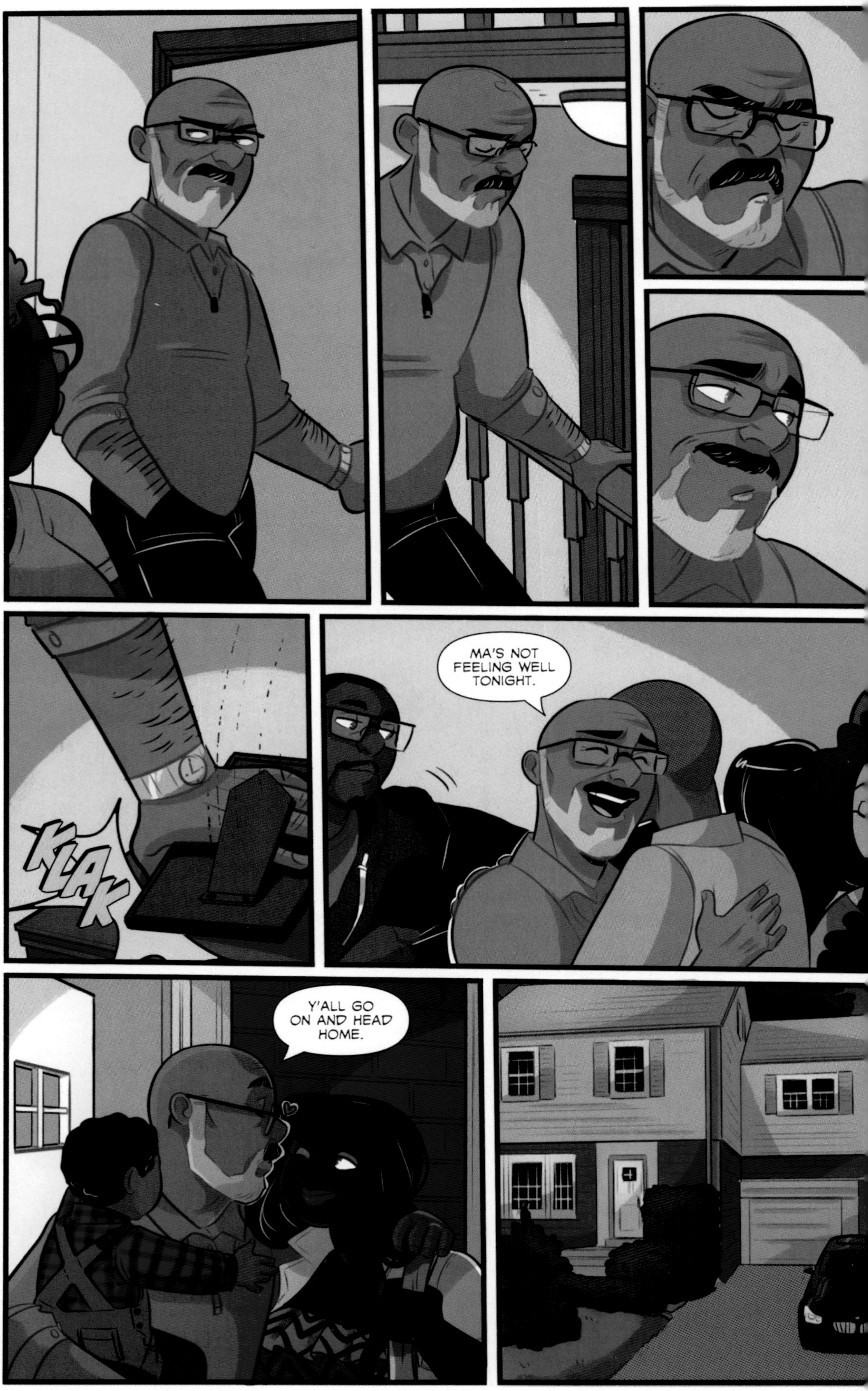
KLAK
MA'S NOT FEELING WELL TONIGHT.
Y'ALL GO ON AND HEAD HOME.

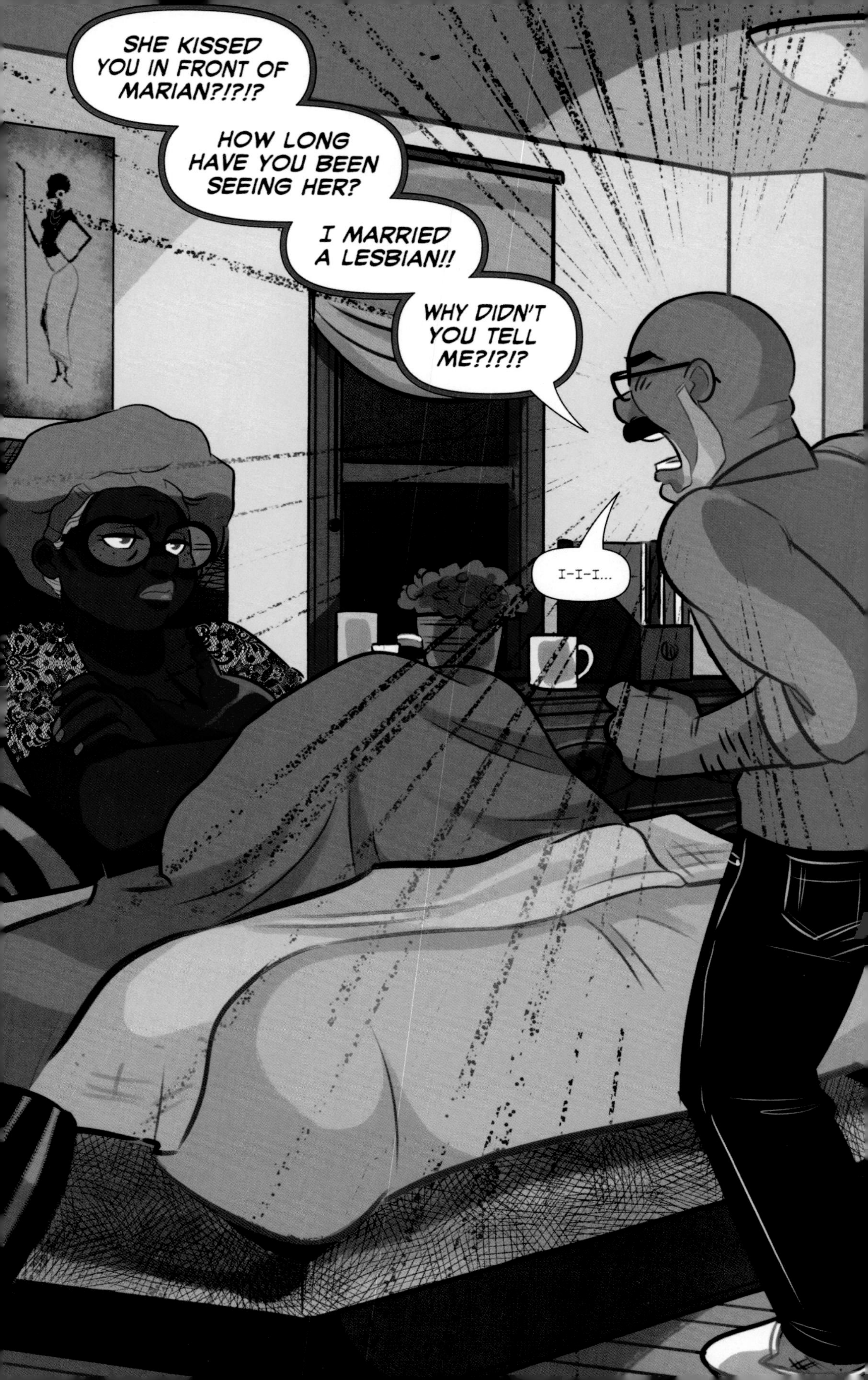
SHE KISSED YOU IN FRONT OF MARIAN?!?!?
HOW LONG HAVE YOU BEEN SEEING HER?
I MARRIED A LESBIAN!!
WHY DIDN'T YOU TELL ME?!?!?
I-I-I...

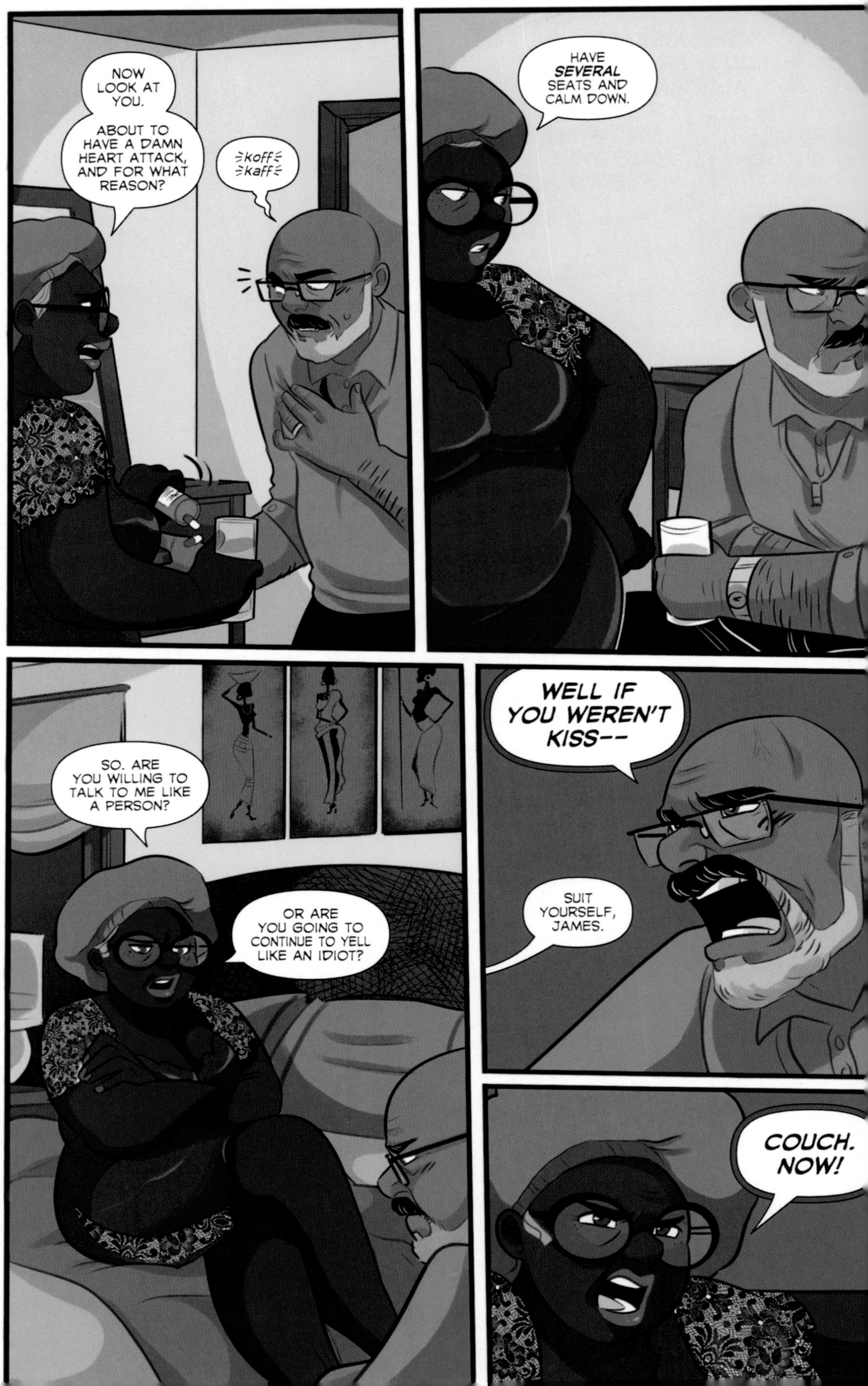
NOW LOOK AT YOU.
ABOUT TO HAVE A DAMN HEART ATTACK, AND FOR WHAT REASON?
koff kaff
HAVE SEVERAL SEATS AND CALM DOWN.
SO. ARE YOU WILLING TO TALK TO ME LIKE A PERSON?
OR ARE YOU GOING TO CONTINUE TO YELL LIKE AN IDIOT?
WELL IF YOU WEREN'T KISS--
SUIT YOURSELF, JAMES.
COUCH. NOW!

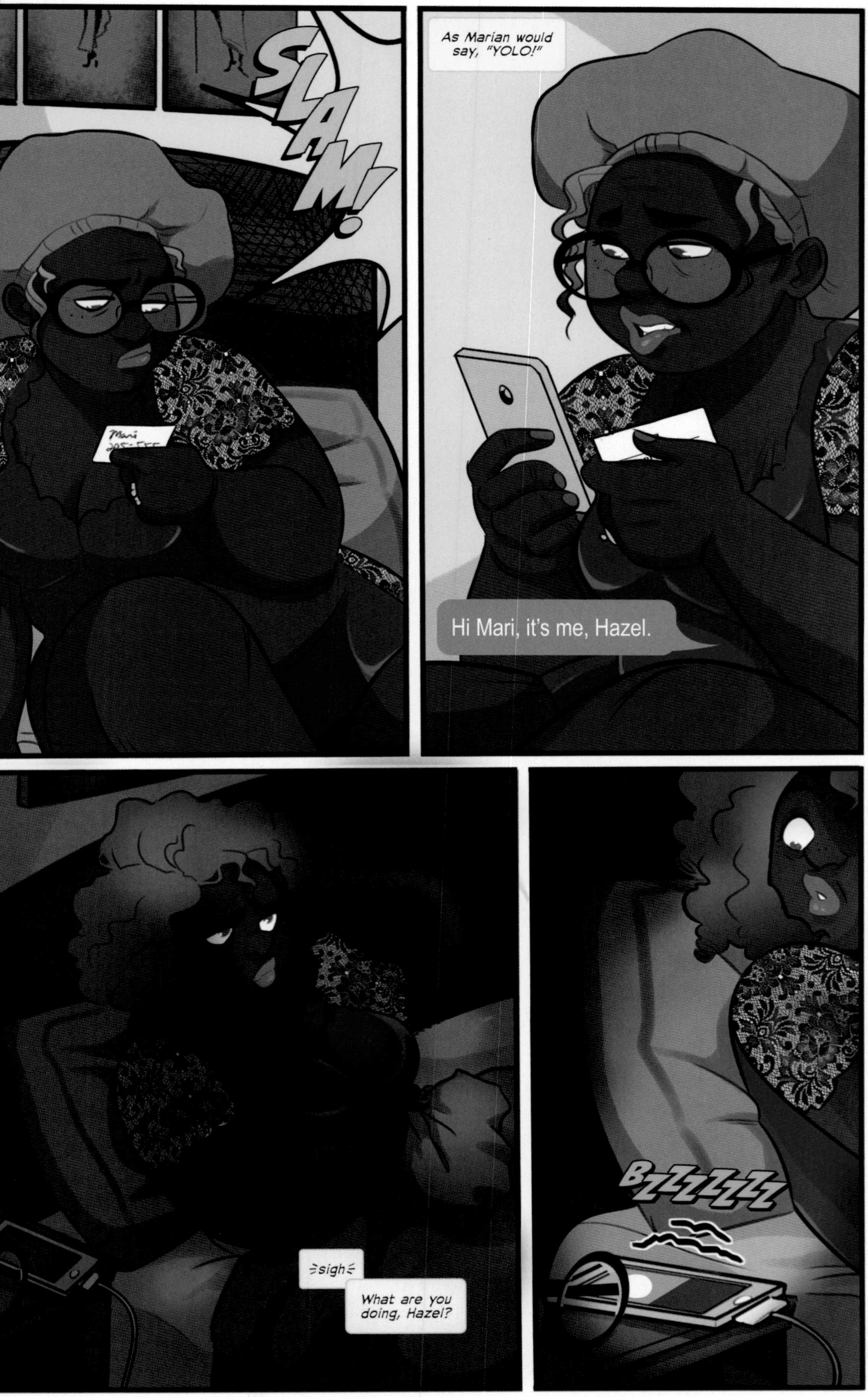
SLAM!
Mari
As Marian would say, "YOLO!"
Hi Mari, it's me, Hazel.
sigh
What are you doing, Hazel?
BZZZZZZ

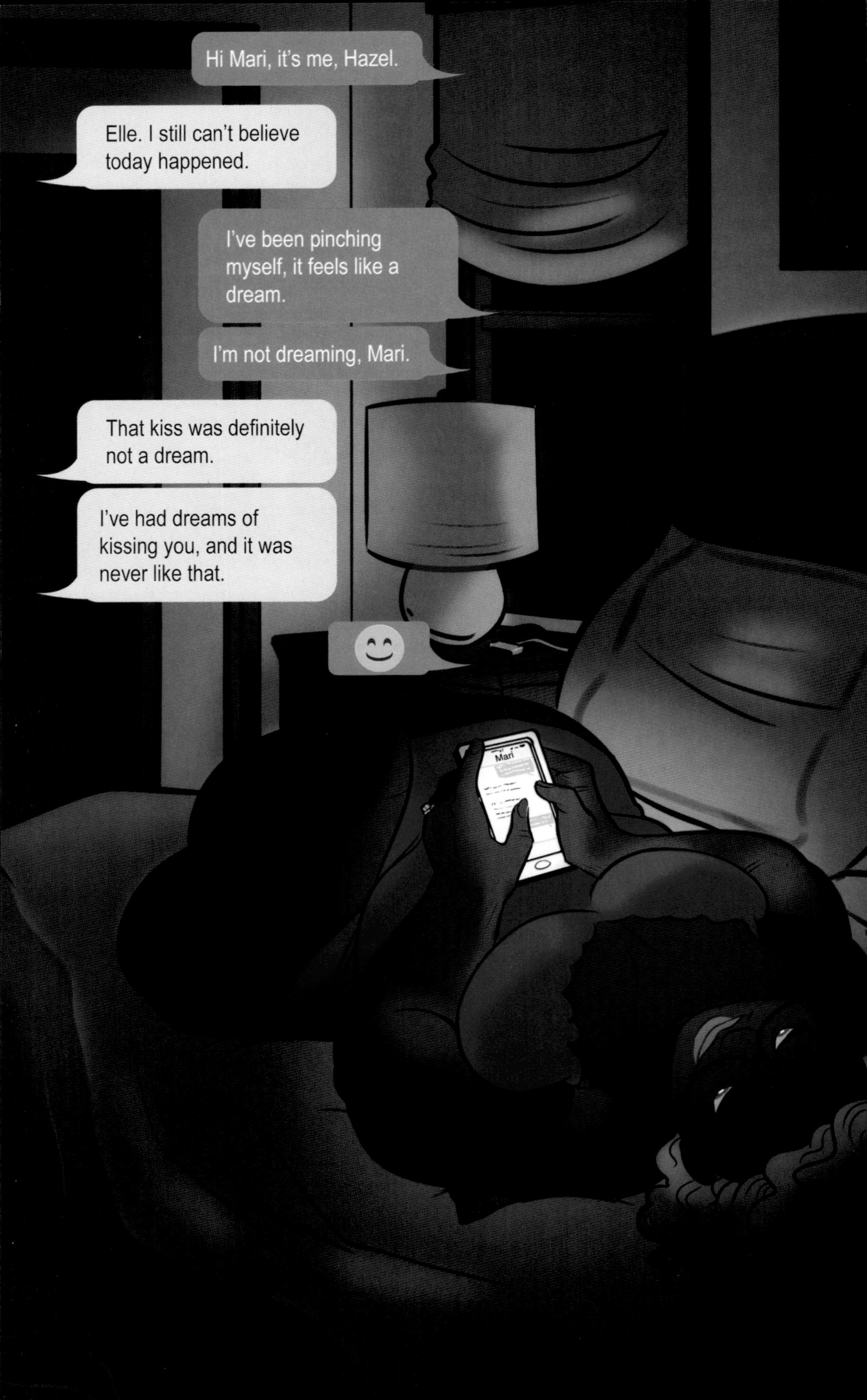
Hi Mari, it's me, Hazel.
Elle. I still can't believe today happened.
I've been pinching myself, it feels like a dream.
I'm not dreaming, Mari.
That kiss was definitely not a dream.
I've had dreams of kissing you, and it was never like that.
Mari

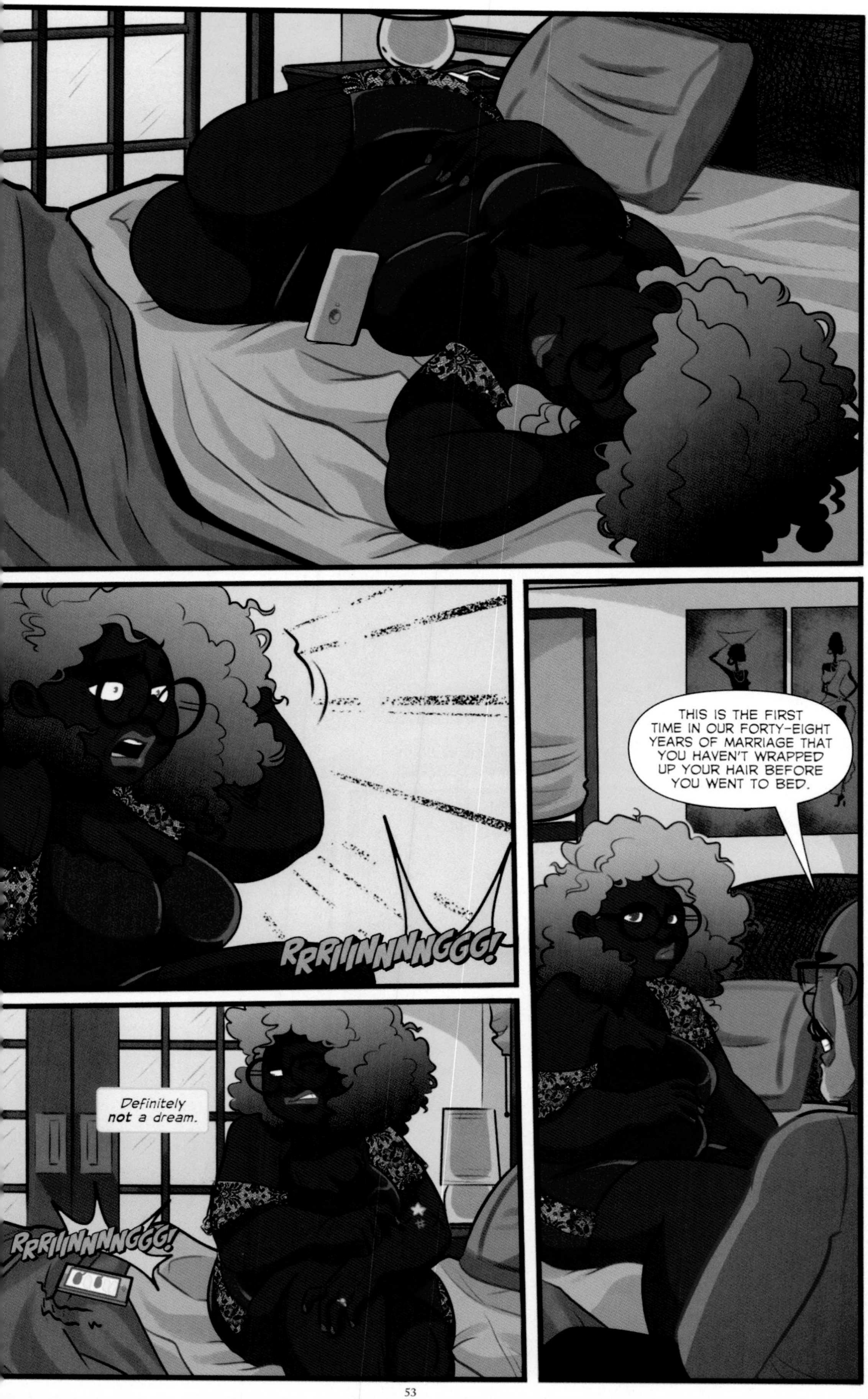
RRRIIINNNNGGG!
Definitely not a dream.
RRRIIINNNNGGG!
THIS IS THE FIRST TIME IN OUR FORTY-EIGHT YEARS OF MARRIAGE THAT YOU HAVEN'T WRAPPED UP YOUR HAIR BEFORE YOU WENT TO BED.

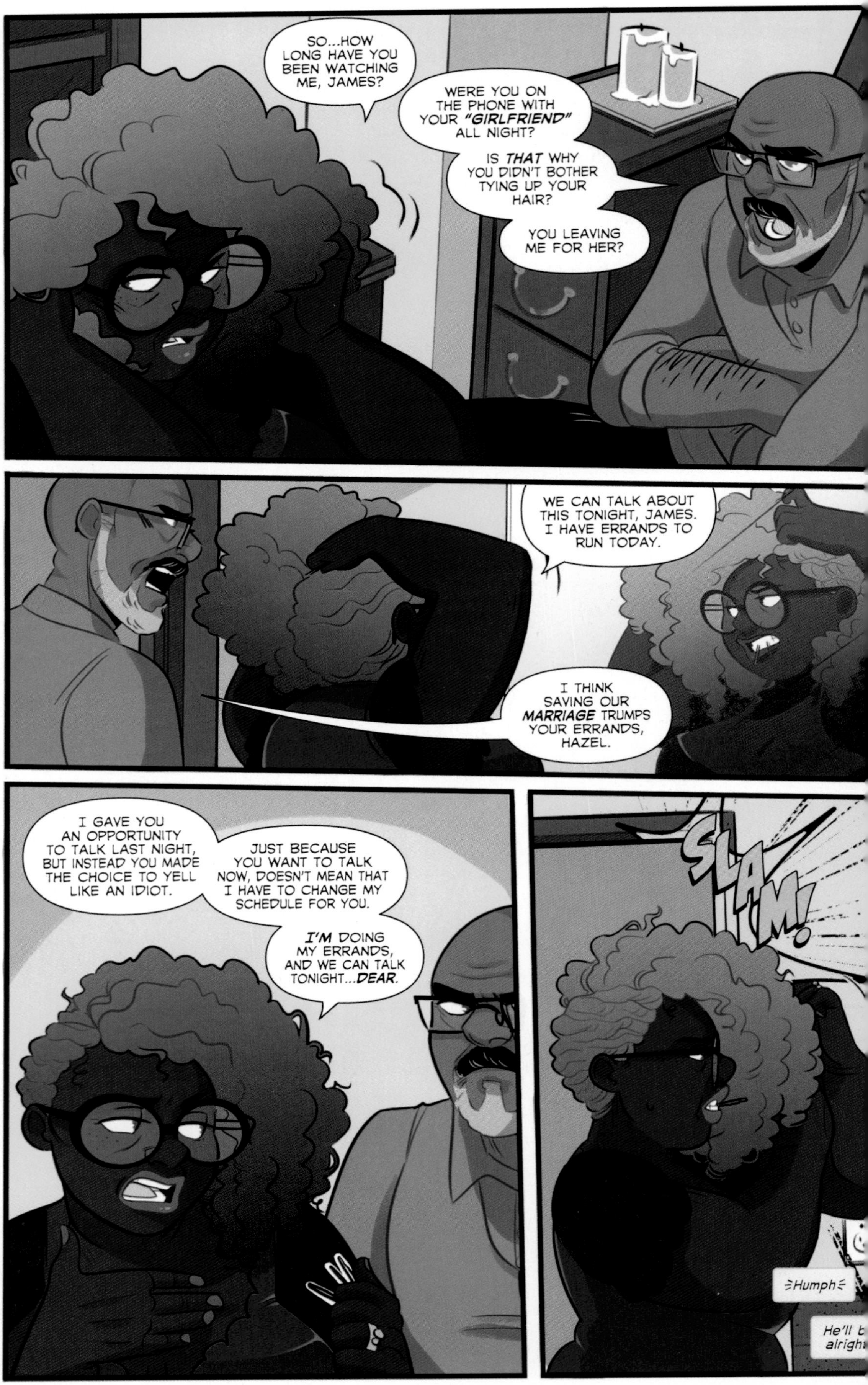
SO...HOW LONG HAVE YOU BEEN WATCHING ME, JAMES?
WERE YOU ON THE PHONE WITH YOUR "GIRLFRIEND" ALL NIGHT?
IS THAT WHY YOU DIDN'T BOTHER TYING UP YOUR HAIR?
YOU LEAVING ME FOR HER?
WE CAN TALK ABOUT THIS TONIGHT, JAMES. I HAVE ERRANDS TO RUN TODAY.
I THINK SAVING OUR MARRIAGE TRUMPS YOUR ERRANDS, HAZEL.
I GAVE YOU AN OPPORTUNITY TO TALK LAST NIGHT, BUT INSTEAD YOU MADE THE CHOICE TO YELL LIKE AN IDIOT.
JUST BECAUSE YOU WANT TO TALK NOW, DOESN'T MEAN THAT I HAVE TO CHANGE MY SCHEDULE FOR YOU.
I'M DOING MY ERRANDS, AND WE CAN TALK TONIGHT...DEAR.
SLAM!
Humph

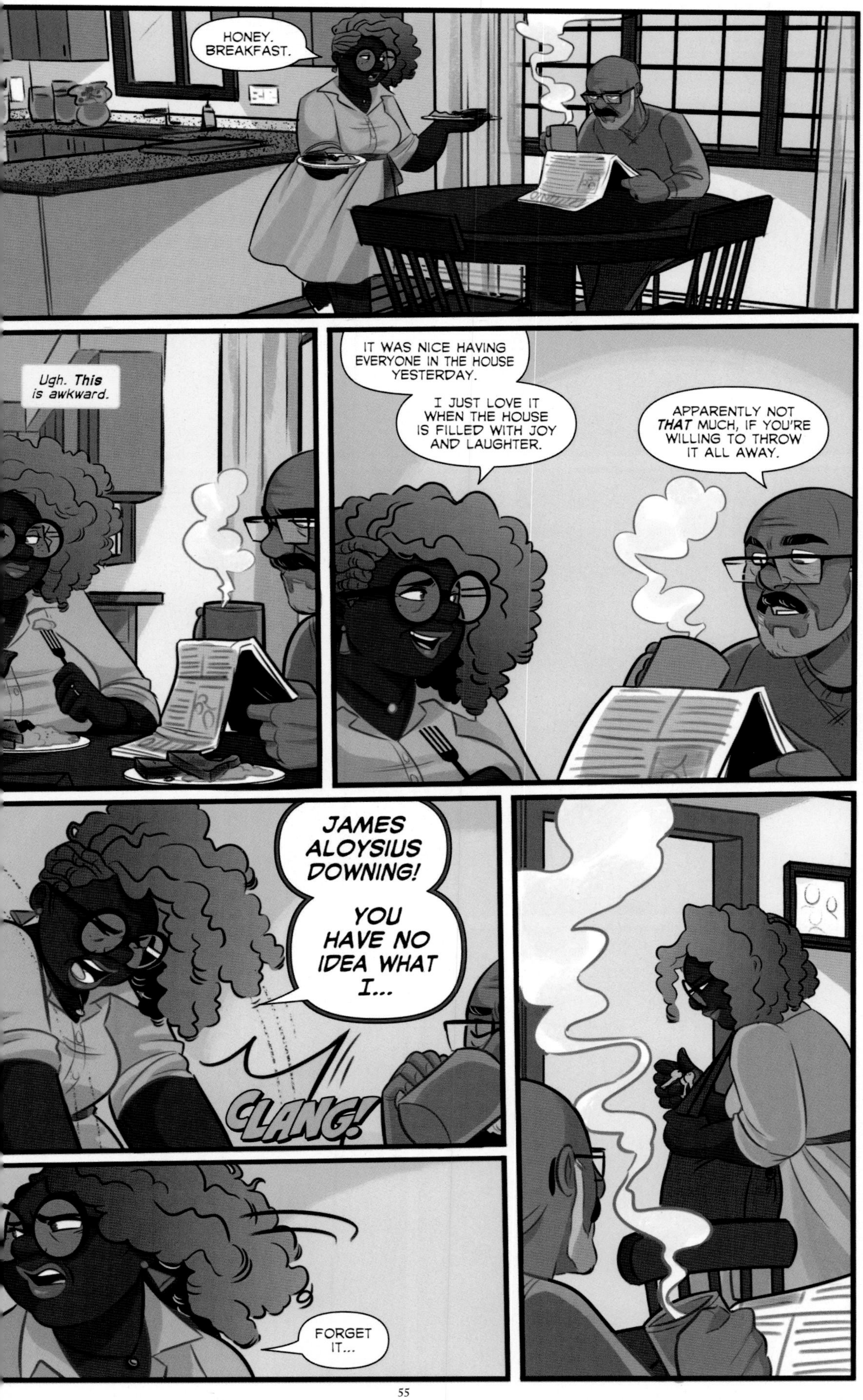
HONEY. BREAKFAST.
Ugh. This is awkward.
IT WAS NICE HAVING EVERYONE IN THE HOUSE YESTERDAY.
I JUST LOVE IT WHEN THE HOUSE IS FILLED WITH JOY AND LAUGHTER.
APPARENTLY NOT THAT MUCH, IF YOU'RE WILLING TO THROW IT ALL AWAY.
JAMES ALOYSIUS DOWNING!
YOU HAVE NO IDEA WHAT I...
CLANG!
FORGET IT...

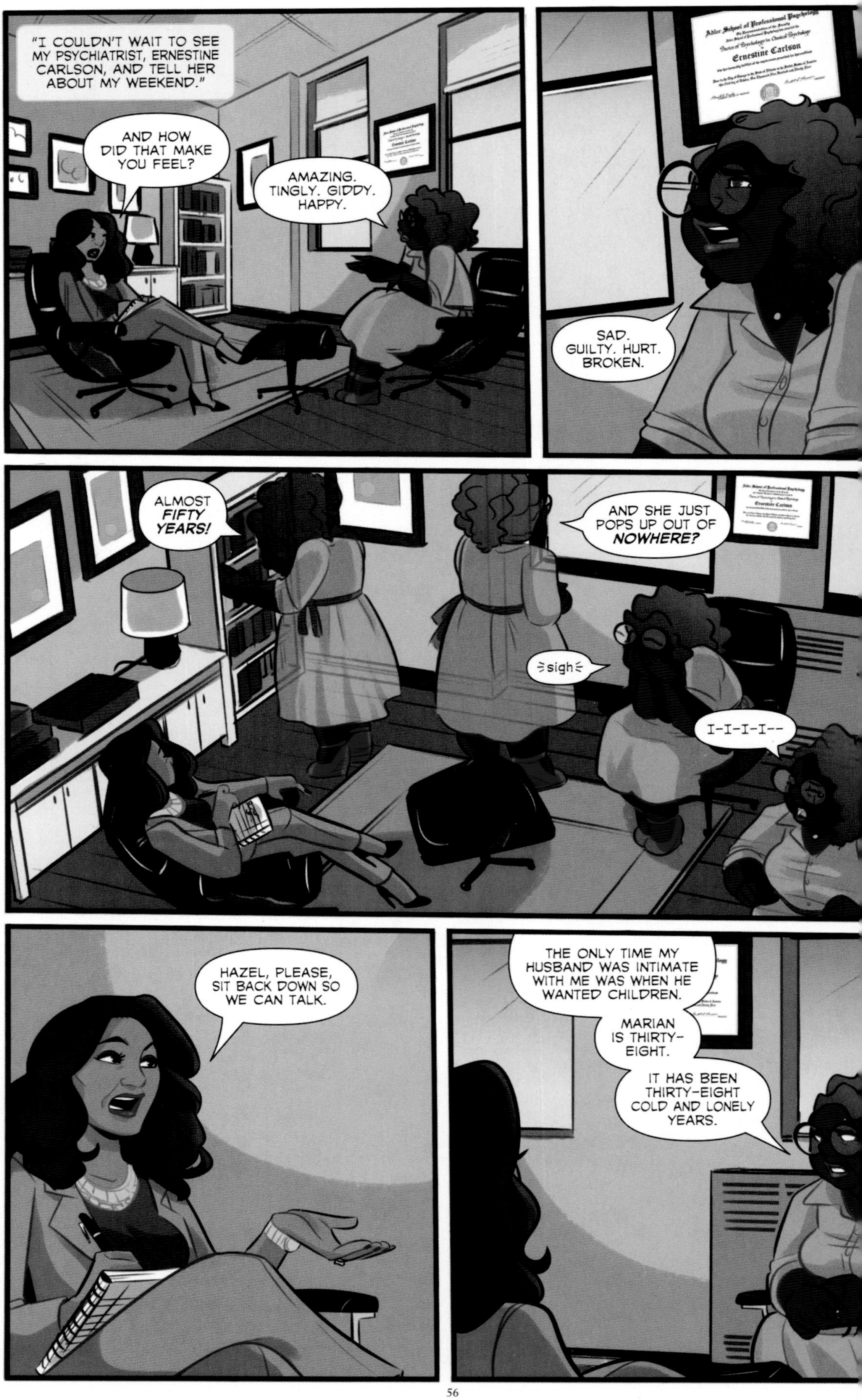
"I COULDN'T WAIT TO SEE MY PSYCHIATRIST, ERNESTINE CARLSON, AND TELL HER ABOUT MY WEEKEND."
AND HOW DID THAT MAKE YOU FEEL?
AMAZING. TINGLY. GIDDY. HAPPY.
Adler School of Professional Psychology
Doctor of Psychology in Clinical Psychology
Ernestine Carlson
SAD. GUILTY. HURT. BROKEN.
ALMOST *FIFTY YEARS!*
AND SHE JUST POPS UP OUT OF *NOWHERE?*
sigh
I-I-I-I--
HAZEL, PLEASE, SIT BACK DOWN SO WE CAN TALK.
THE ONLY TIME MY HUSBAND WAS INTIMATE WITH ME WAS WHEN HE WANTED CHILDREN.
MARIAN IS THIRTY-EIGHT.
IT HAS BEEN THIRTY-EIGHT COLD AND LONELY YEARS.

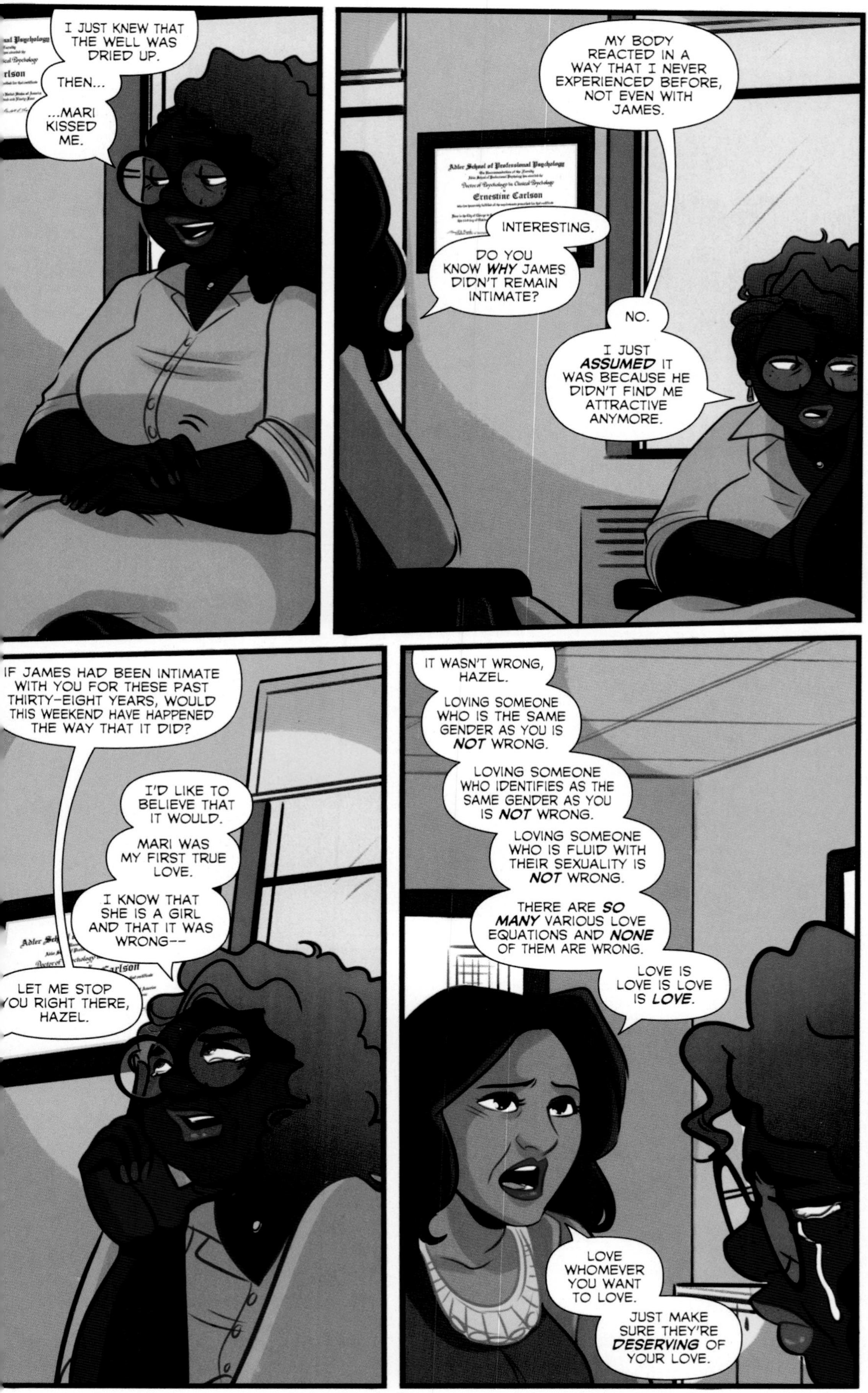
I JUST KNEW THAT THE WELL WAS DRIED UP.
THEN...
...MARI KISSED ME.
MY BODY REACTED IN A WAY THAT I NEVER EXPERIENCED BEFORE, NOT EVEN WITH JAMES.
INTERESTING.
DO YOU KNOW WHY JAMES DIDN'T REMAIN INTIMATE?
NO.
I JUST ASSUMED IT WAS BECAUSE HE DIDN'T FIND ME ATTRACTIVE ANYMORE.
IF JAMES HAD BEEN INTIMATE WITH YOU FOR THESE PAST THIRTY-EIGHT YEARS, WOULD THIS WEEKEND HAVE HAPPENED THE WAY THAT IT DID?
I'D LIKE TO BELIEVE THAT IT WOULD.
MARI WAS MY FIRST TRUE LOVE.
I KNOW THAT SHE IS A GIRL AND THAT IT WAS WRONG--
LET ME STOP YOU RIGHT THERE, HAZEL.
IT WASN'T WRONG, HAZEL.
LOVING SOMEONE WHO IS THE SAME GENDER AS YOU IS NOT WRONG.
LOVING SOMEONE WHO IDENTIFIES AS THE SAME GENDER AS YOU IS NOT WRONG.
LOVING SOMEONE WHO IS FLUID WITH THEIR SEXUALITY IS NOT WRONG.
THERE ARE SO MANY VARIOUS LOVE EQUATIONS AND NONE OF THEM ARE WRONG.
LOVE IS LOVE IS LOVE IS LOVE.
LOVE WHOMEVER YOU WANT TO LOVE.
JUST MAKE SURE THEY'RE DESERVING OF YOUR LOVE.

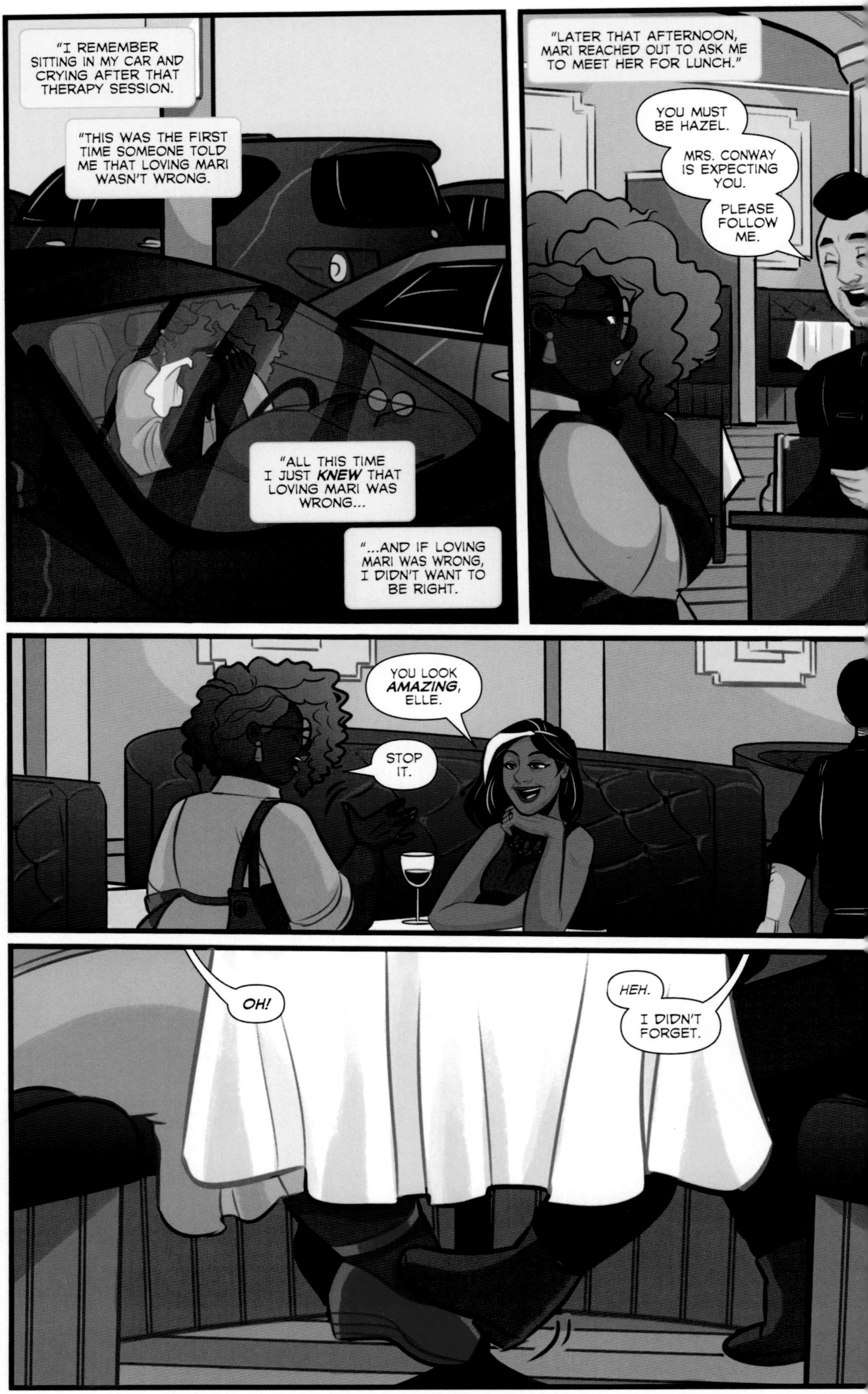
"I REMEMBER SITTING IN MY CAR AND CRYING AFTER THAT THERAPY SESSION.
"THIS WAS THE FIRST TIME SOMEONE TOLD ME THAT LOVING MARI WASN'T WRONG.
"ALL THIS TIME I JUST KNEW THAT LOVING MARI WAS WRONG...
"...AND IF LOVING MARI WAS WRONG, I DIDN'T WANT TO BE RIGHT.
"LATER THAT AFTERNOON, MARI REACHED OUT TO ASK ME TO MEET HER FOR LUNCH."
YOU MUST BE HAZEL.
MRS. CONWAY IS EXPECTING YOU.
PLEASE FOLLOW ME.
YOU LOOK AMAZING, ELLE.
STOP IT.
OH!
HEH.
I DIDN'T FORGET.

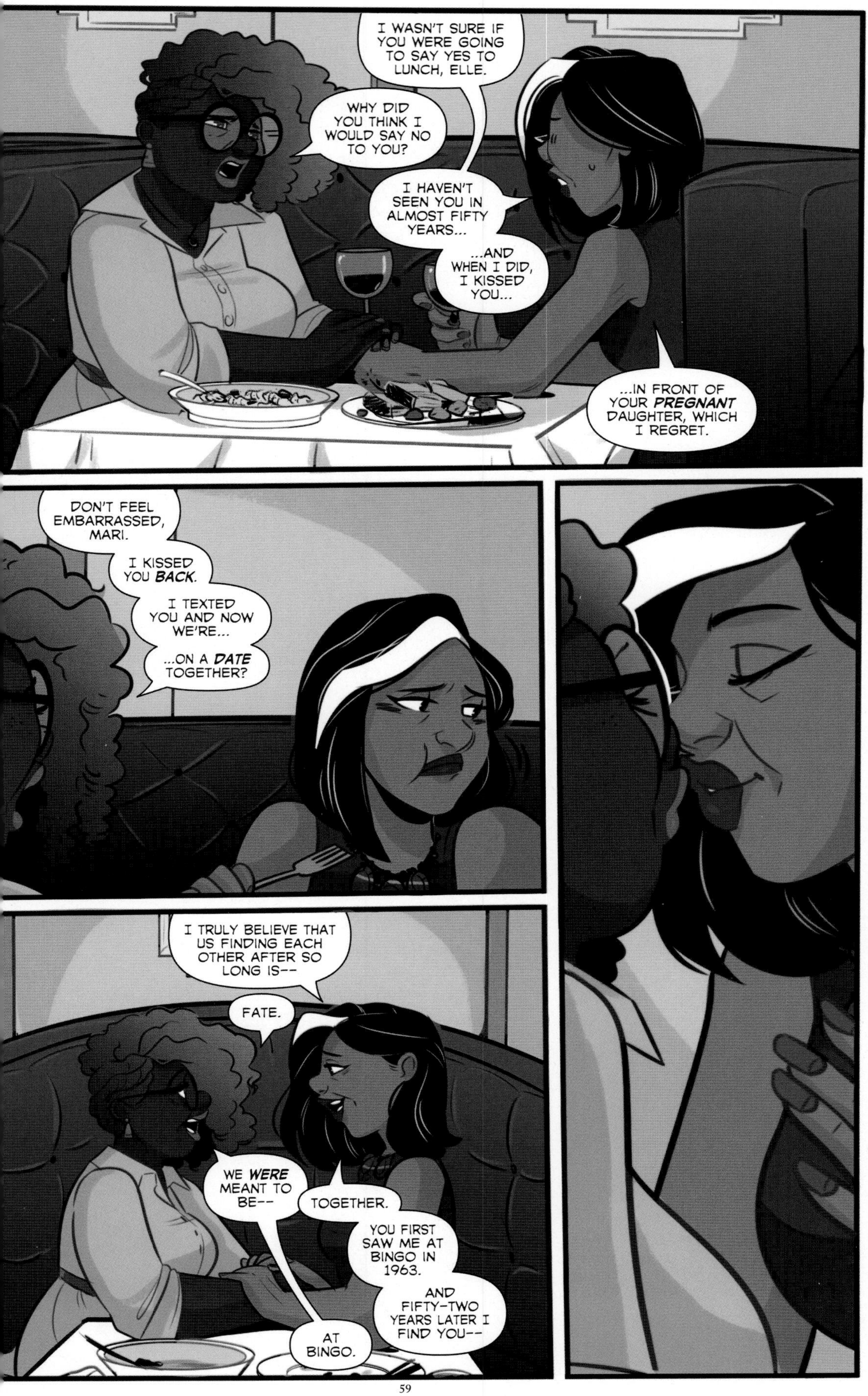

I WASN'T SURE IF YOU WERE GOING TO SAY YES TO LUNCH, ELLE.
WHY DID YOU THINK I WOULD SAY NO TO YOU?
I HAVEN'T SEEN YOU IN ALMOST FIFTY YEARS...
...AND WHEN I DID, I KISSED YOU...
...IN FRONT OF YOUR PREGNANT DAUGHTER, WHICH I REGRET.
DON'T FEEL EMBARRASSED, MARI.
I KISSED YOU BACK.
I TEXTED YOU AND NOW WE'RE...
...ON A DATE TOGETHER?
I TRULY BELIEVE THAT US FINDING EACH OTHER AFTER SO LONG IS--
FATE.
WE WERE MEANT TO BE--
TOGETHER.
YOU FIRST SAW ME AT BINGO IN 1963.
AND FIFTY-TWO YEARS LATER I FIND YOU--
AT BINGO.

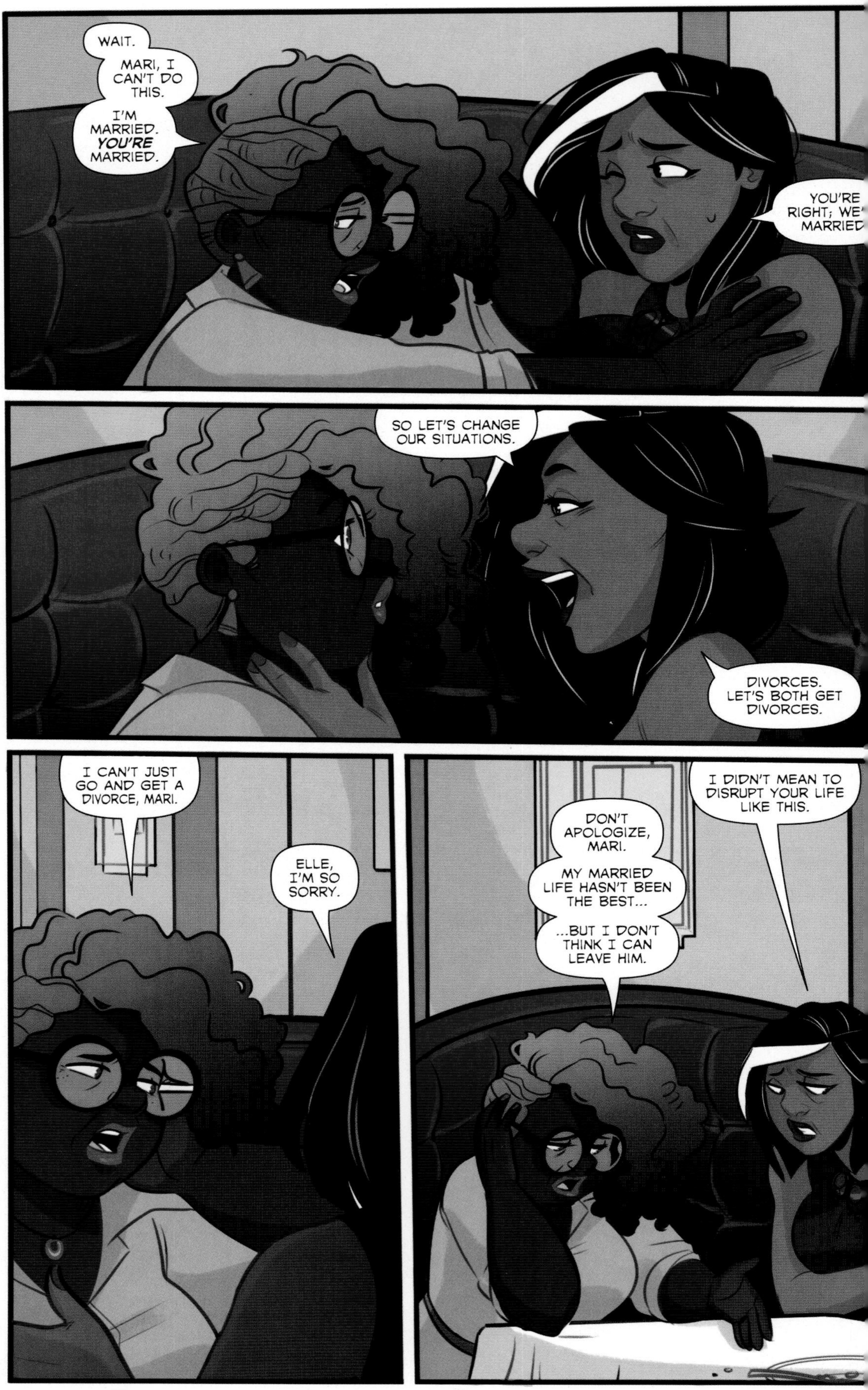
WAIT.
MARI, I CAN'T DO THIS.
I'M MARRIED. ***YOU'RE*** MARRIED.
YOU'RE RIGHT; WE MARRIED
SO LET'S CHANGE OUR SITUATIONS.
DIVORCES. LET'S BOTH GET DIVORCES.
I CAN'T JUST GO AND GET A DIVORCE, MARI.
ELLE, I'M SO SORRY.
I DIDN'T MEAN TO DISRUPT YOUR LIFE LIKE THIS.
DON'T APOLOGIZE, MARI.
MY MARRIED LIFE HASN'T BEEN THE BEST...
...BUT I DON'T THINK I CAN LEAVE HIM.

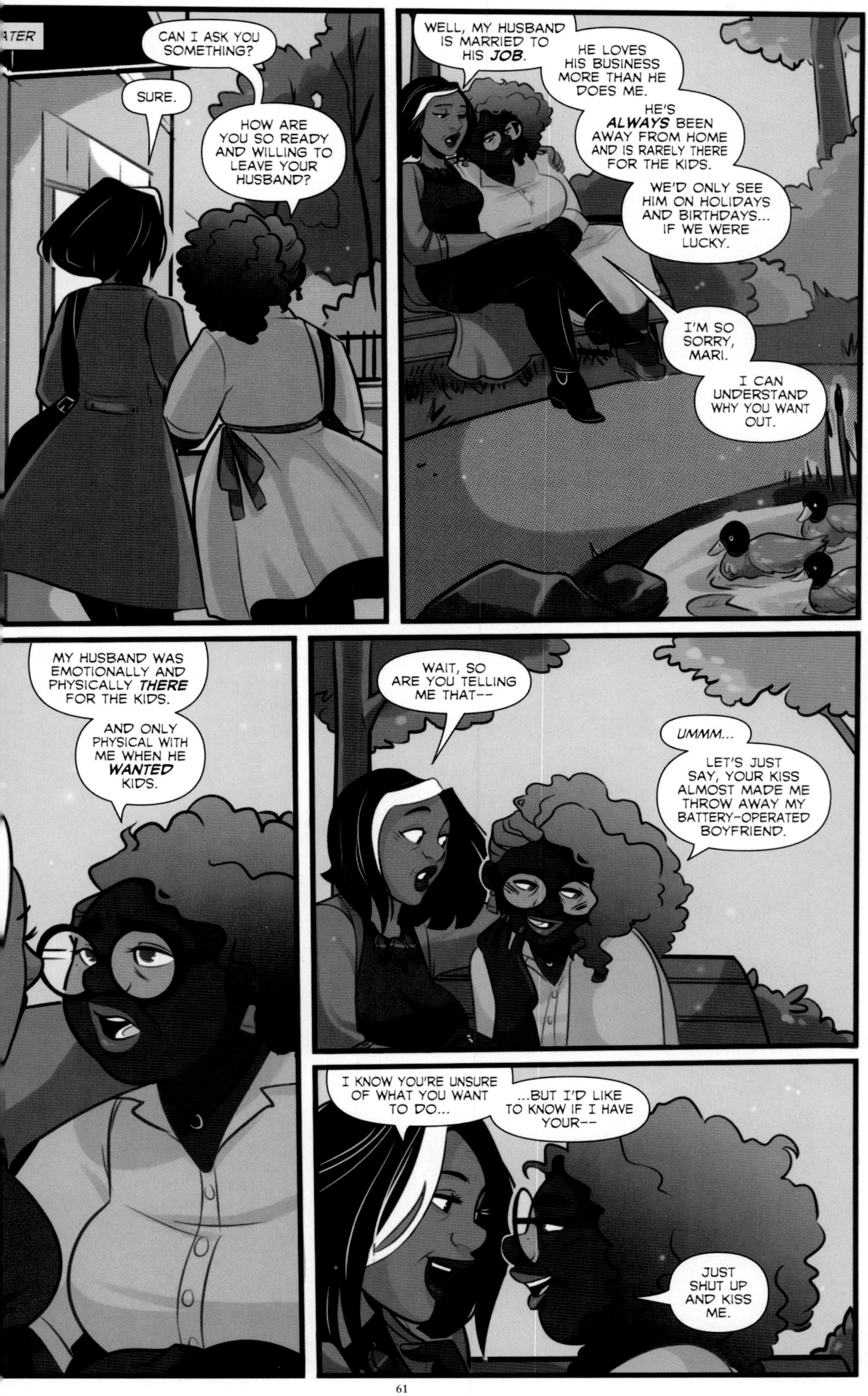
ATER
CAN I ASK YOU SOMETHING?
SURE.
HOW ARE YOU SO READY AND WILLING TO LEAVE YOUR HUSBAND?
WELL, MY HUSBAND IS MARRIED TO HIS *JOB*.
HE LOVES HIS BUSINESS MORE THAN HE DOES ME.
HE'S *ALWAYS* BEEN AWAY FROM HOME AND IS RARELY THERE FOR THE KIDS.
WE'D ONLY SEE HIM ON HOLIDAYS AND BIRTHDAYS... IF WE WERE LUCKY.
I'M SO SORRY, MARI.
I CAN UNDERSTAND WHY YOU WANT OUT.
MY HUSBAND WAS EMOTIONALLY AND PHYSICALLY *THERE* FOR THE KIDS.
AND ONLY PHYSICAL WITH ME WHEN HE *WANTED* KIDS.
WAIT, SO ARE YOU TELLING ME THAT--
UMMM...
LET'S JUST SAY, YOUR KISS ALMOST MADE ME THROW AWAY MY BATTERY-OPERATED BOYFRIEND.
I KNOW YOU'RE UNSURE OF WHAT YOU WANT TO DO...
...BUT I'D LIKE TO KNOW IF I HAVE YOUR--
JUST SHUT UP AND KISS ME.

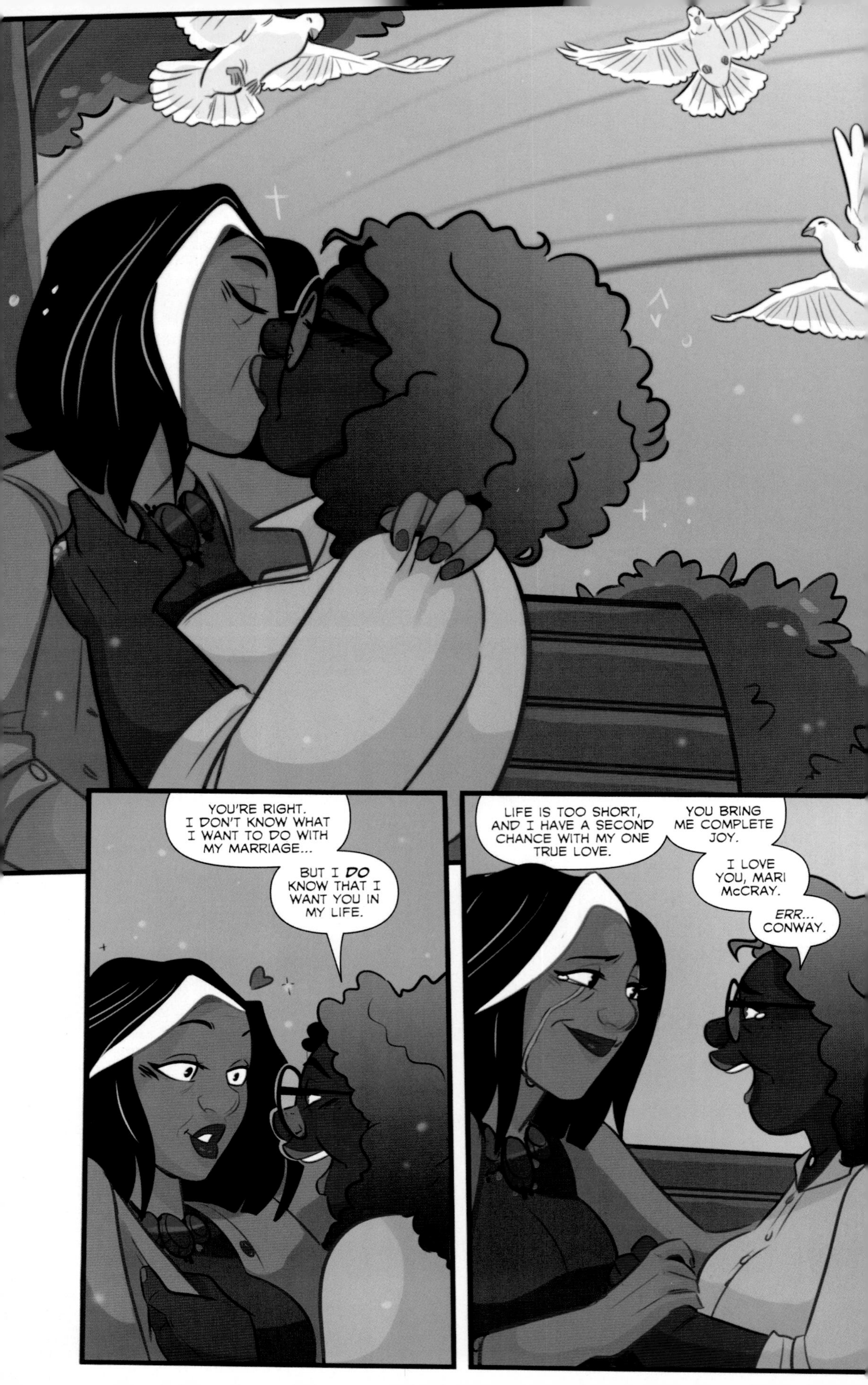

YOU'RE RIGHT. I DON'T KNOW WHAT I WANT TO DO WITH MY MARRIAGE...
BUT I *DO* KNOW THAT I WANT YOU IN MY LIFE.
LIFE IS TOO SHORT, AND I HAVE A SECOND CHANCE WITH MY ONE TRUE LOVE.
YOU BRING ME COMPLETE JOY.
I LOVE YOU, MARI McCRAY.
ERR... CONWAY.

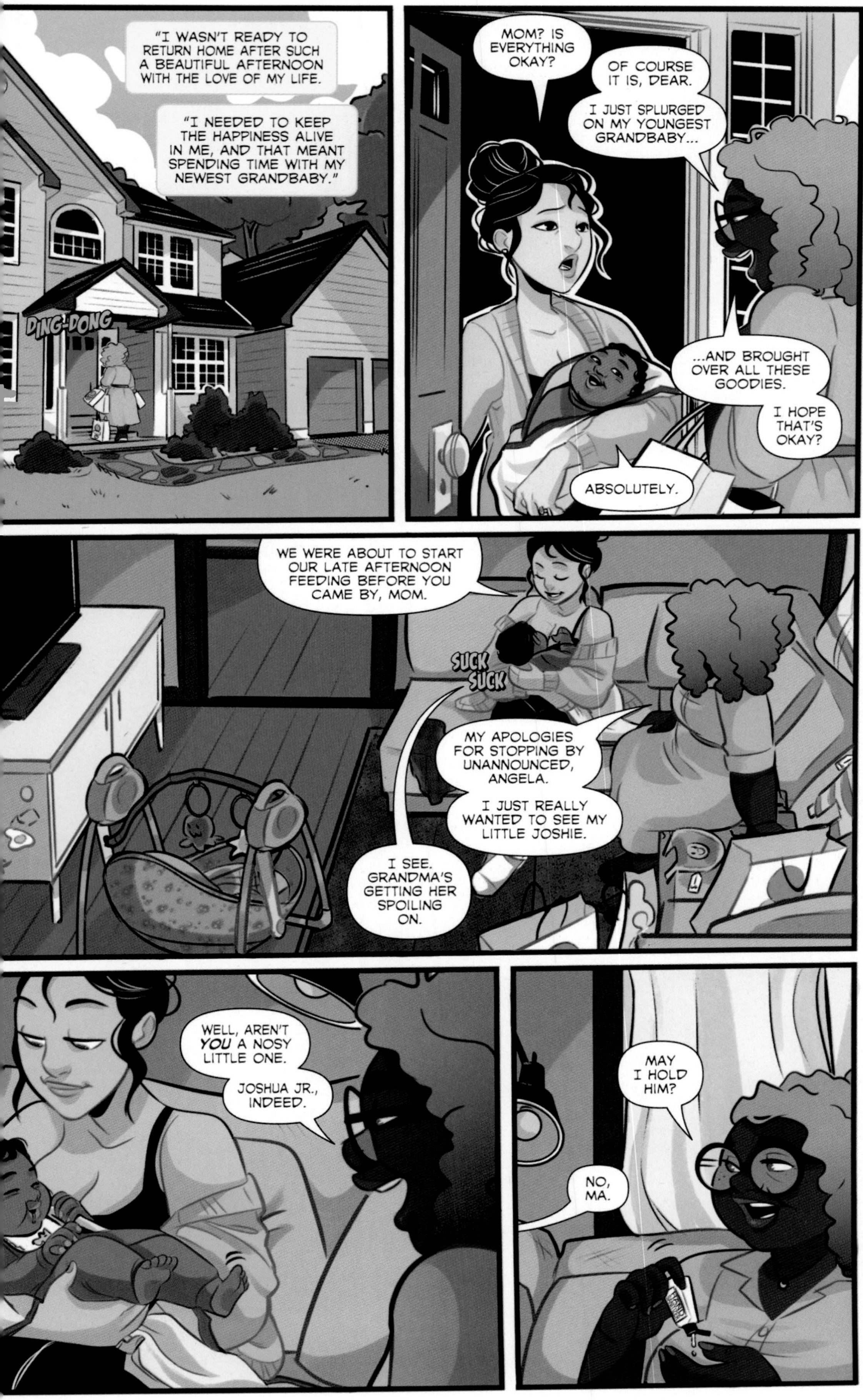
"I WASN'T READY TO RETURN HOME AFTER SUCH A BEAUTIFUL AFTERNOON WITH THE LOVE OF MY LIFE.
"I NEEDED TO KEEP THE HAPPINESS ALIVE IN ME, AND THAT MEANT SPENDING TIME WITH MY NEWEST GRANDBABY."
DING-DONG
MOM? IS EVERYTHING OKAY?
OF COURSE IT IS, DEAR.
I JUST SPLURGED ON MY YOUNGEST GRANDBABY...
...AND BROUGHT OVER ALL THESE GOODIES.
I HOPE THAT'S OKAY?
ABSOLUTELY.
WE WERE ABOUT TO START OUR LATE AFTERNOON FEEDING BEFORE YOU CAME BY, MOM.
SUCK SUCK
MY APOLOGIES FOR STOPPING BY UNANNOUNCED, ANGELA.
I JUST REALLY WANTED TO SEE MY LITTLE JOSHIE.
I SEE. GRANDMA'S GETTING HER SPOILING ON.
WELL, AREN'T *YOU* A NOSY LITTLE ONE.
JOSHUA JR., INDEED.
MAY I HOLD HIM?
NO, MA.

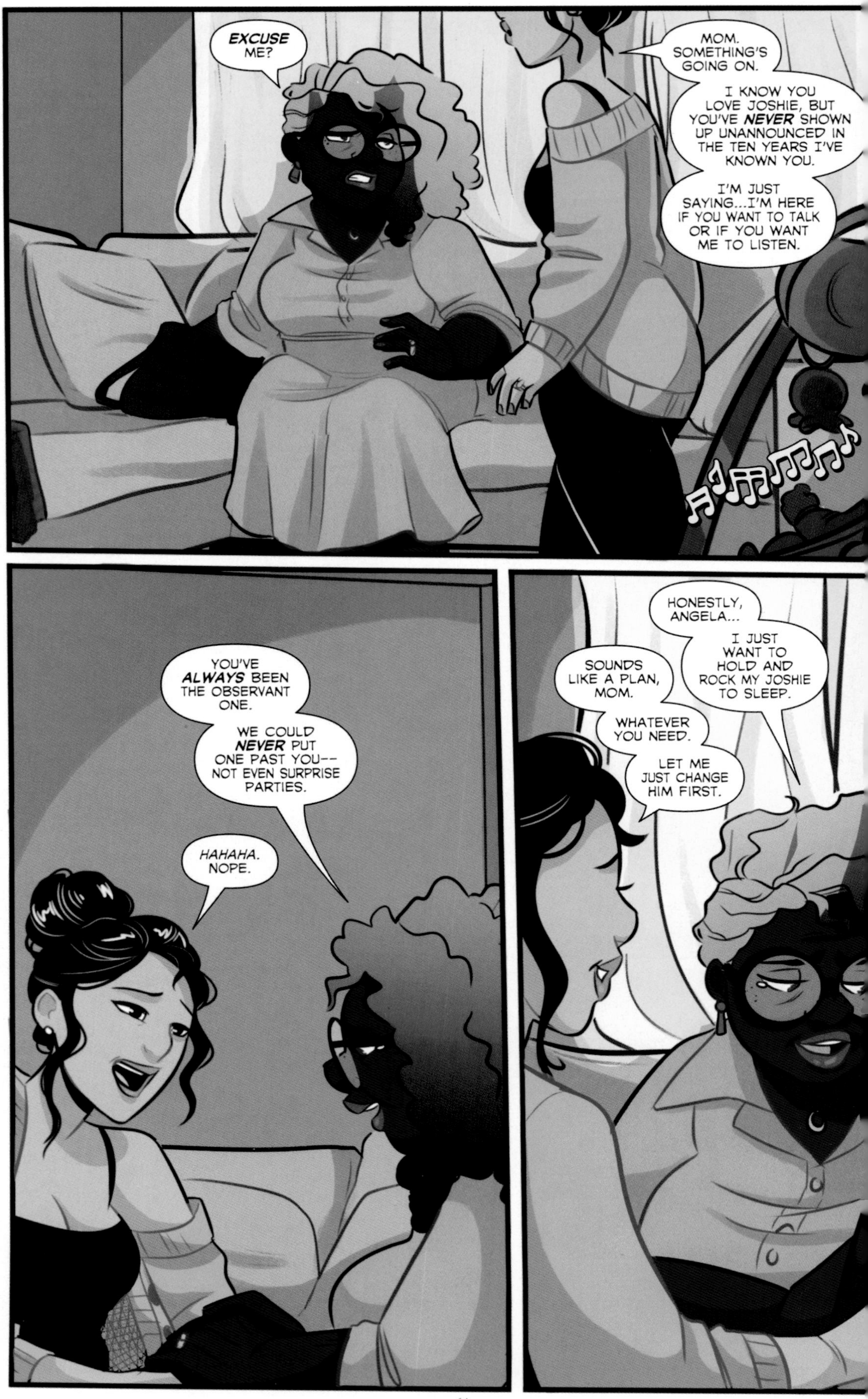
EXCUSE ME?
MOM. SOMETHING'S GOING ON.
I KNOW YOU LOVE JOSHIE, BUT YOU'VE NEVER SHOWN UP UNANNOUNCED IN THE TEN YEARS I'VE KNOWN YOU.
I'M JUST SAYING...I'M HERE IF YOU WANT TO TALK OR IF YOU WANT ME TO LISTEN.
YOU'VE ALWAYS BEEN THE OBSERVANT ONE.
WE COULD NEVER PUT ONE PAST YOU-- NOT EVEN SURPRISE PARTIES.
HAHAHA. NOPE.
HONESTLY, ANGELA...
I JUST WANT TO HOLD AND ROCK MY JOSHIE TO SLEEP.
SOUNDS LIKE A PLAN, MOM.
WHATEVER YOU NEED.
LET ME JUST CHANGE HIM FIRST.

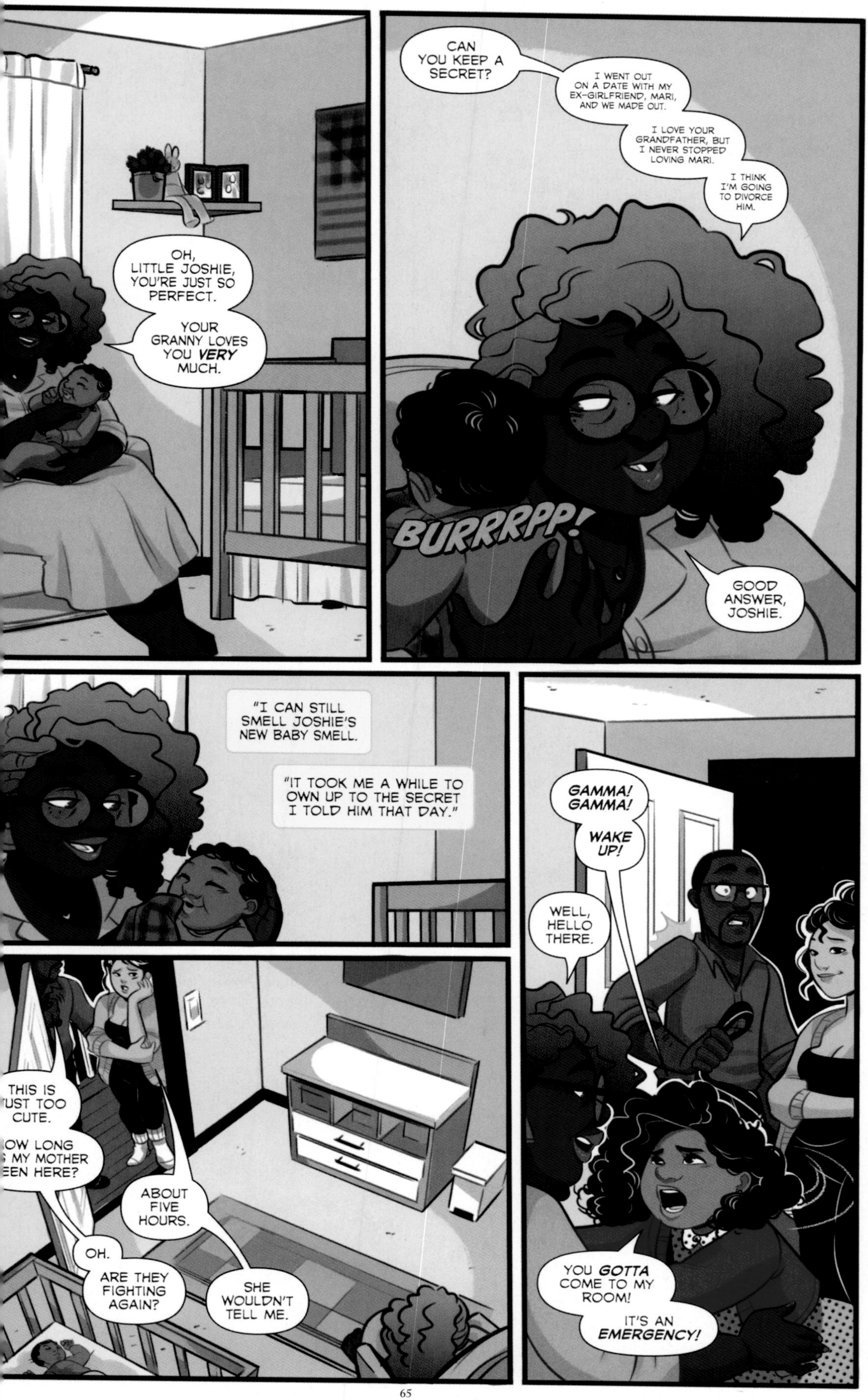
OH, LITTLE JOSHIE, YOU'RE JUST SO PERFECT.
YOUR GRANNY LOVES YOU VERY MUCH.
CAN YOU KEEP A SECRET?
I WENT OUT ON A DATE WITH MY EX-GIRLFRIEND, MARI, AND WE MADE OUT.
I LOVE YOUR GRANDFATHER, BUT I NEVER STOPPED LOVING MARI.
I THINK I'M GOING TO DIVORCE HIM.
BURRRPP!
GOOD ANSWER, JOSHIE.
"I CAN STILL SMELL JOSHIE'S NEW BABY SMELL.
"IT TOOK ME A WHILE TO OWN UP TO THE SECRET I TOLD HIM THAT DAY."
THIS IS
CUTE.
MY MOTHER
HERE?
ABOUT FIVE HOURS.
OH.
ARE THEY FIGHTING AGAIN?
SHE WOULDN'T TELL ME.
GAMMA! GAMMA!
WAKE UP!
WELL, HELLO THERE.
YOU GOTTA COME TO MY ROOM!
IT'S AN EMERGENCY!

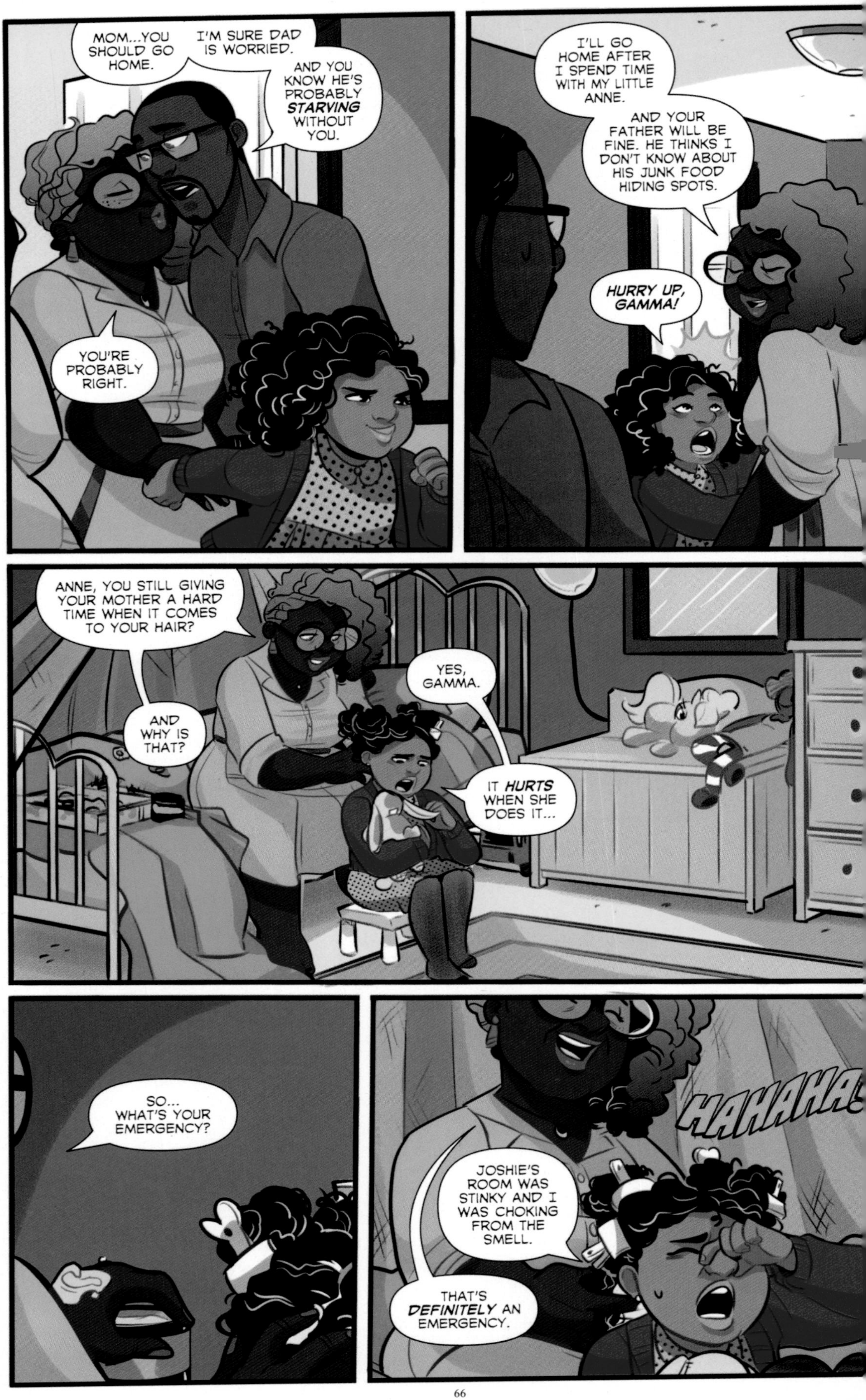
MOM...YOU SHOULD GO HOME.
I'M SURE DAD IS WORRIED.
AND YOU KNOW HE'S PROBABLY STARVING WITHOUT YOU.
YOU'RE PROBABLY RIGHT.
I'LL GO HOME AFTER I SPEND TIME WITH MY LITTLE ANNE.
AND YOUR FATHER WILL BE FINE. HE THINKS I DON'T KNOW ABOUT HIS JUNK FOOD HIDING SPOTS.
HURRY UP, GAMMA!
ANNE, YOU STILL GIVING YOUR MOTHER A HARD TIME WHEN IT COMES TO YOUR HAIR?
YES, GAMMA.
AND WHY IS THAT?
IT HURTS WHEN SHE DOES IT...
SO... WHAT'S YOUR EMERGENCY?
HAHAHA!
JOSHIE'S ROOM WAS STINKY AND I WAS CHOKING FROM THE SMELL.
THAT'S DEFINITELY AN EMERGENCY.

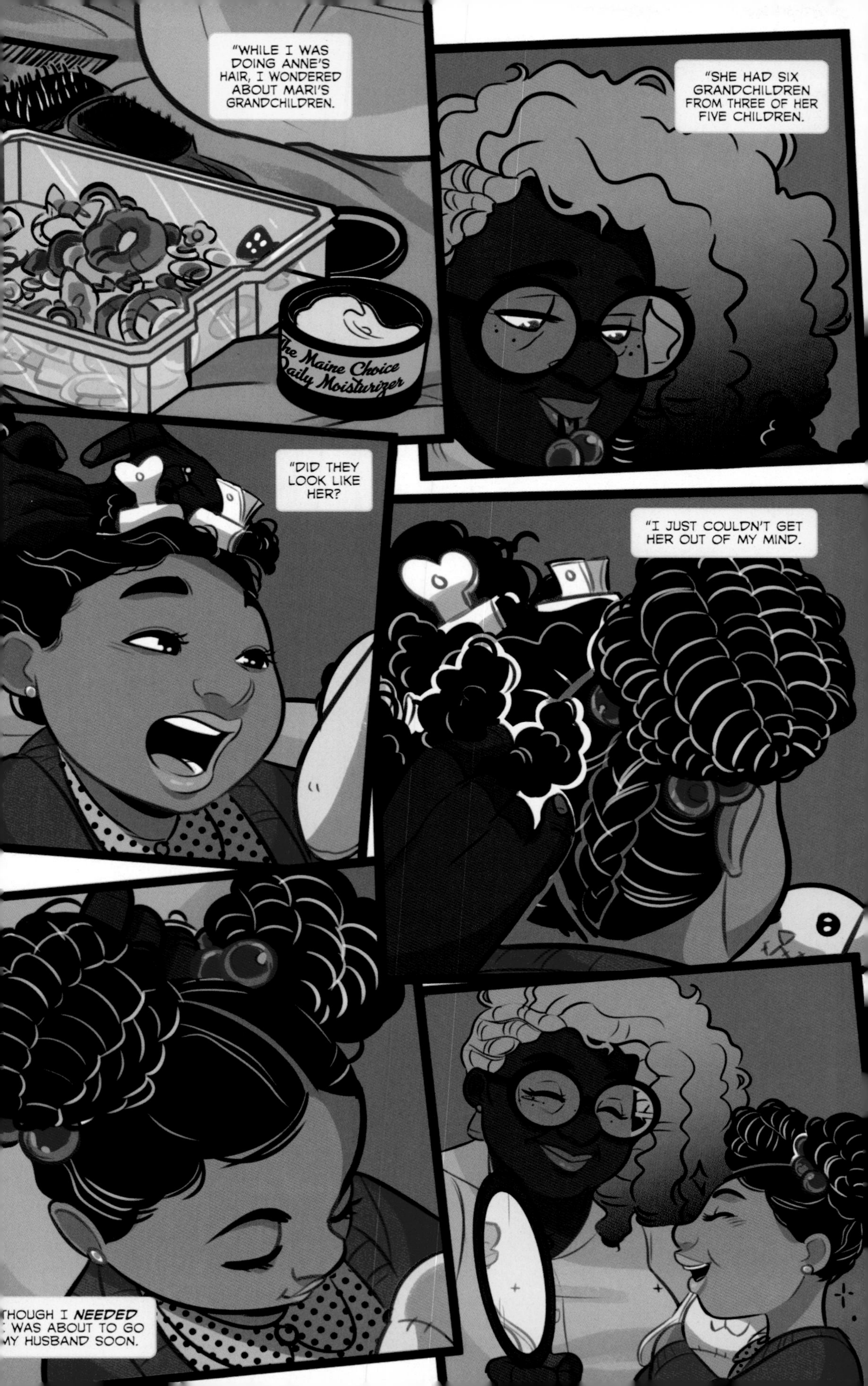
"WHILE I WAS DOING ANNE'S HAIR, I WONDERED ABOUT MARI'S GRANDCHILDREN.
"SHE HAD SIX GRANDCHILDREN FROM THREE OF HER FIVE CHILDREN.
The Maine Choice Daily Moisturizer
"DID THEY LOOK LIKE HER?
"I JUST COULDN'T GET HER OUT OF MY MIND.
THOUGH I *NEEDED*
WAS ABOUT TO GO
MY HUSBAND SOON.

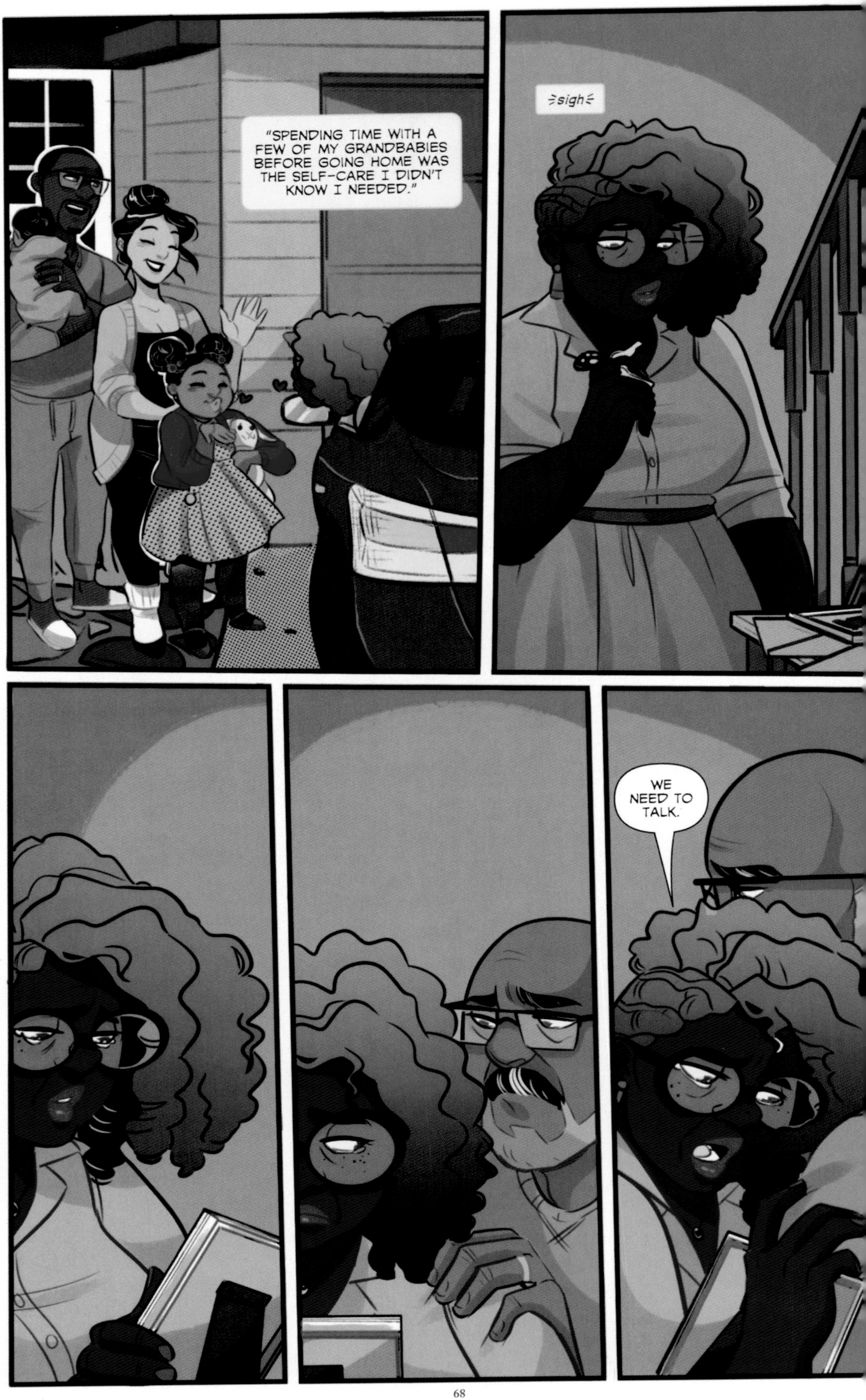
"SPENDING TIME WITH A FEW OF MY GRANDBABIES BEFORE GOING HOME WAS THE SELF-CARE I DIDN'T KNOW I NEEDED."
sigh
WE NEED TO TALK.

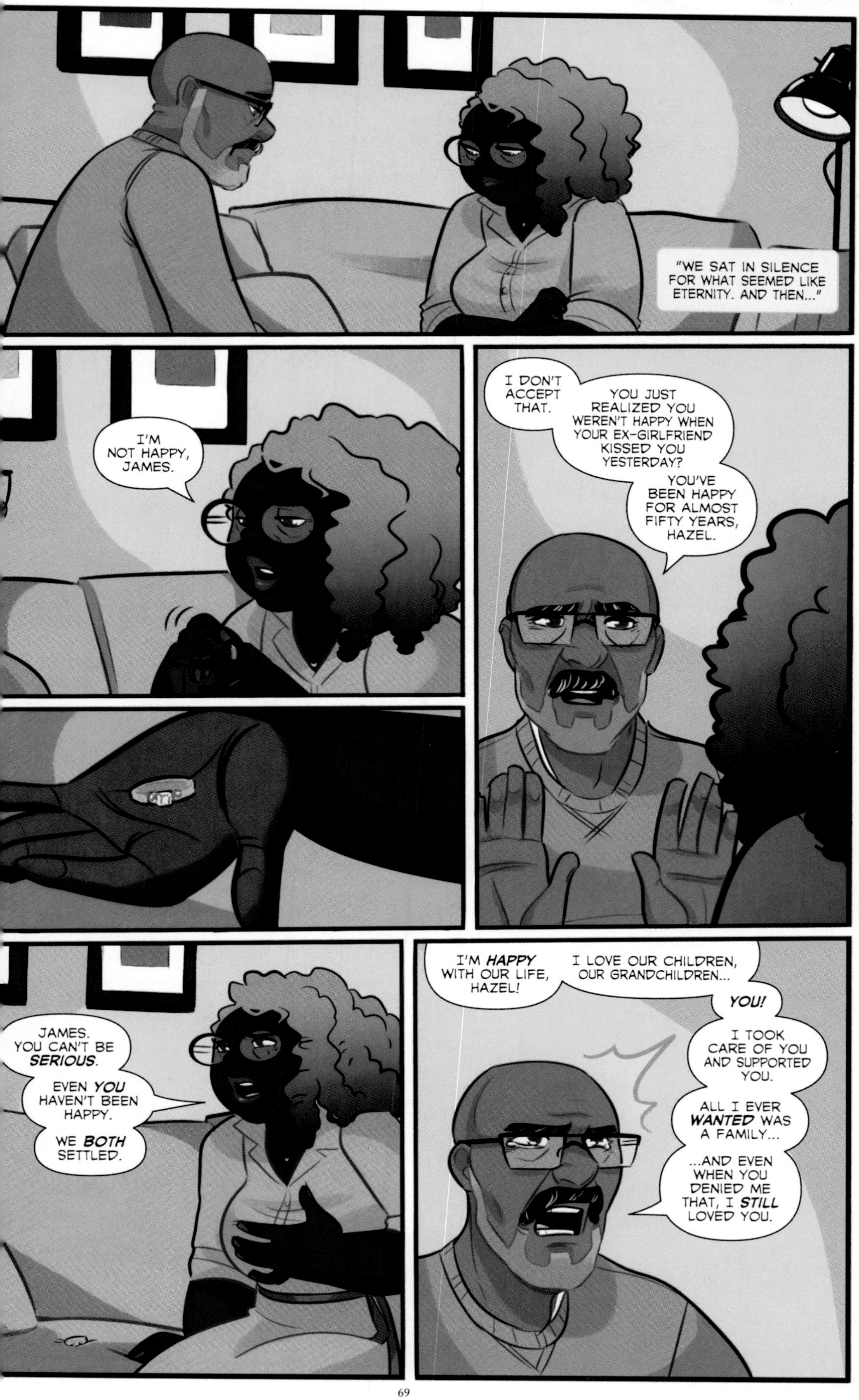
"WE SAT IN SILENCE FOR WHAT SEEMED LIKE ETERNITY. AND THEN..."
I'M NOT HAPPY, JAMES.
I DON'T ACCEPT THAT.
YOU JUST REALIZED YOU WEREN'T HAPPY WHEN YOUR EX-GIRLFRIEND KISSED YOU YESTERDAY?
YOU'VE BEEN HAPPY FOR ALMOST FIFTY YEARS, HAZEL.
JAMES. YOU CAN'T BE **SERIOUS**.
EVEN ***YOU*** HAVEN'T BEEN HAPPY.
WE ***BOTH*** SETTLED.
I'M ***HAPPY*** WITH OUR LIFE, HAZEL!
I LOVE OUR CHILDREN, OUR GRANDCHILDREN...
YOU!
I TOOK CARE OF YOU AND SUPPORTED YOU.
ALL I EVER ***WANTED*** WAS A FAMILY...
...AND EVEN WHEN YOU DENIED ME THAT, I ***STILL*** LOVED YOU.

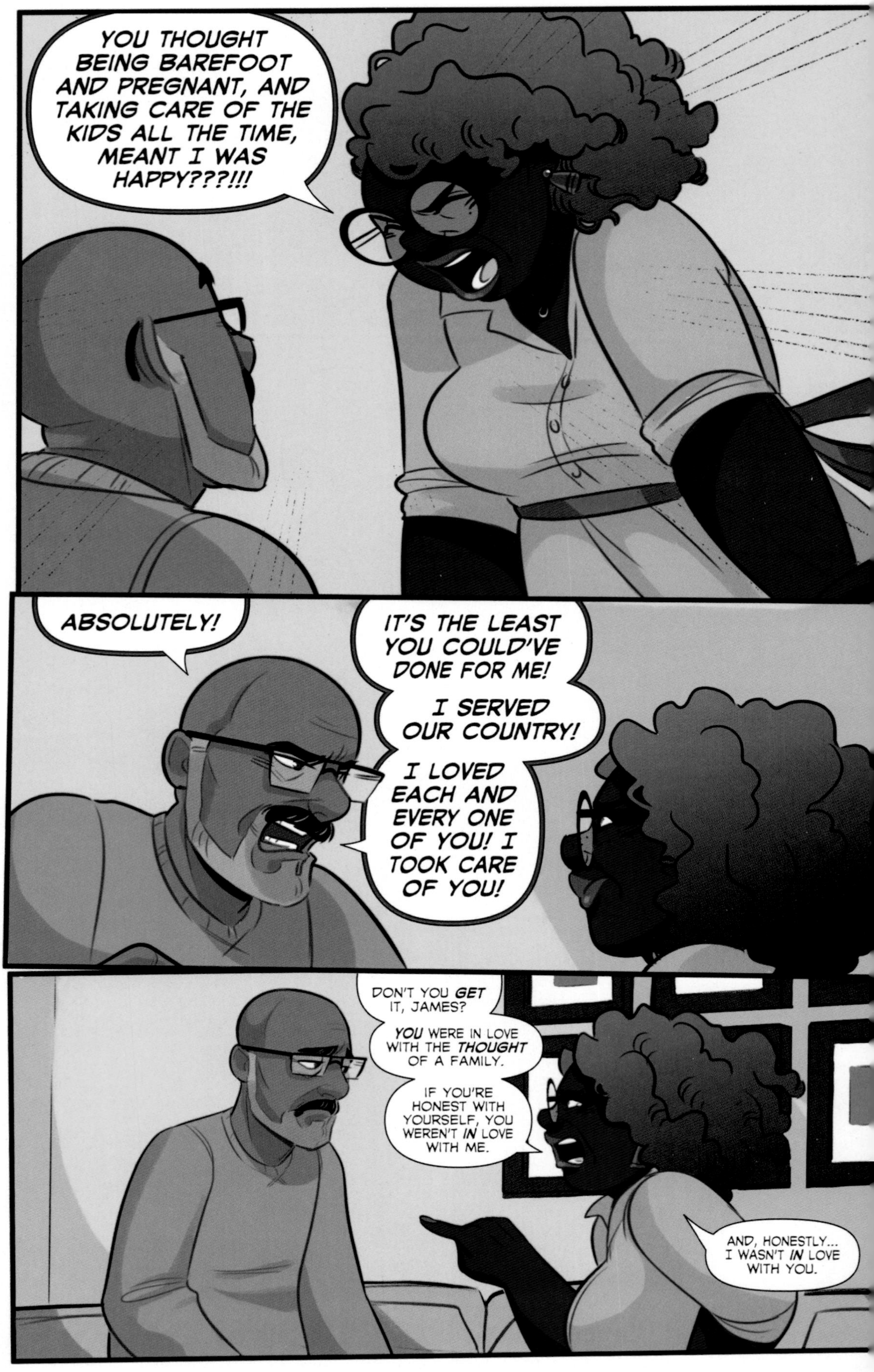
YOU THOUGHT BEING BAREFOOT AND PREGNANT, AND TAKING CARE OF THE KIDS ALL THE TIME, MEANT I WAS HAPPY???!!!
ABSOLUTELY!
IT'S THE LEAST YOU COULD'VE DONE FOR ME!
I SERVED OUR COUNTRY!
I LOVED EACH AND EVERY ONE OF YOU! I TOOK CARE OF YOU!
DON'T YOU GET IT, JAMES?
YOU WERE IN LOVE WITH THE THOUGHT OF A FAMILY.
IF YOU'RE HONEST WITH YOURSELF, YOU WEREN'T IN LOVE WITH ME.
AND, HONESTLY... I WASN'T IN LOVE WITH YOU.

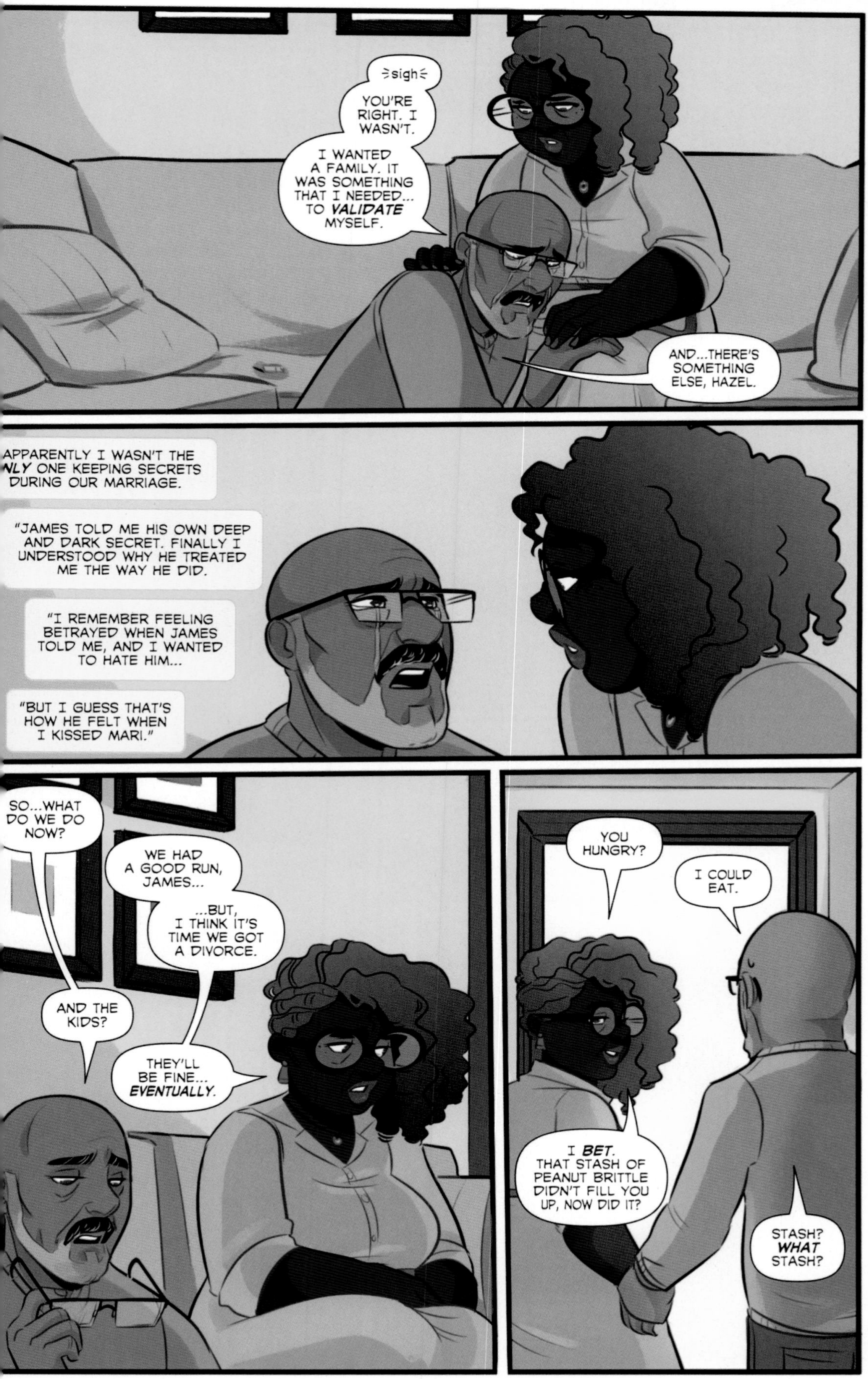

⋛sigh⋚
YOU'RE RIGHT. I WASN'T.
I WANTED A FAMILY. IT WAS SOMETHING THAT I NEEDED... TO *VALIDATE* MYSELF.
AND...THERE'S SOMETHING ELSE, HAZEL.
APPARENTLY I WASN'T THE *NLY* ONE KEEPING SECRETS DURING OUR MARRIAGE.
"JAMES TOLD ME HIS OWN DEEP AND DARK SECRET. FINALLY I UNDERSTOOD WHY HE TREATED ME THE WAY HE DID.
"I REMEMBER FEELING BETRAYED WHEN JAMES TOLD ME, AND I WANTED TO HATE HIM...
"BUT I GUESS THAT'S HOW HE FELT WHEN I KISSED MARI."
SO...WHAT DO WE DO NOW?
WE HAD A GOOD RUN, JAMES...
...BUT, I THINK IT'S TIME WE GOT A DIVORCE.
AND THE KIDS?
THEY'LL BE FINE... ***EVENTUALLY***.
YOU HUNGRY?
I COULD EAT.
I ***BET***. THAT STASH OF PEANUT BRITTLE DIDN'T FILL YOU UP, NOW DID IT?
STASH? ***WHAT*** STASH?

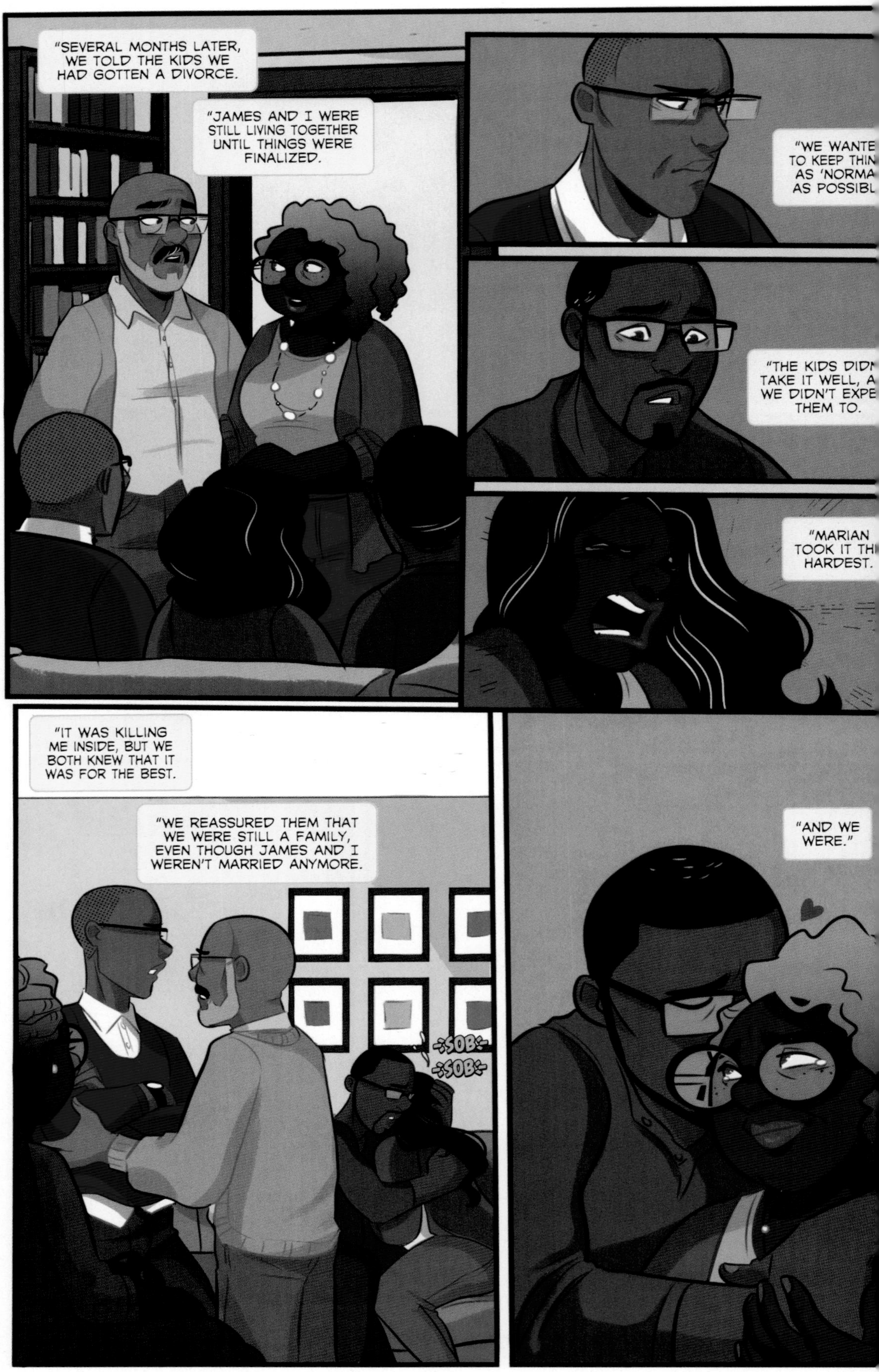
"SEVERAL MONTHS LATER, WE TOLD THE KIDS WE HAD GOTTEN A DIVORCE.
"JAMES AND I WERE STILL LIVING TOGETHER UNTIL THINGS WERE FINALIZED.
"WE WANTE TO KEEP THIN AS 'NORMA AS POSSIBL
"THE KIDS DIDN TAKE IT WELL, A WE DIDN'T EXPE THEM TO.
"MARIAN TOOK IT TH HARDEST.
"IT WAS KILLING ME INSIDE, BUT WE BOTH KNEW THAT IT WAS FOR THE BEST.
"WE REASSURED THEM THAT WE WERE STILL A FAMILY, EVEN THOUGH JAMES AND I WEREN'T MARRIED ANYMORE.
SOB
SOB
"AND WE WERE."

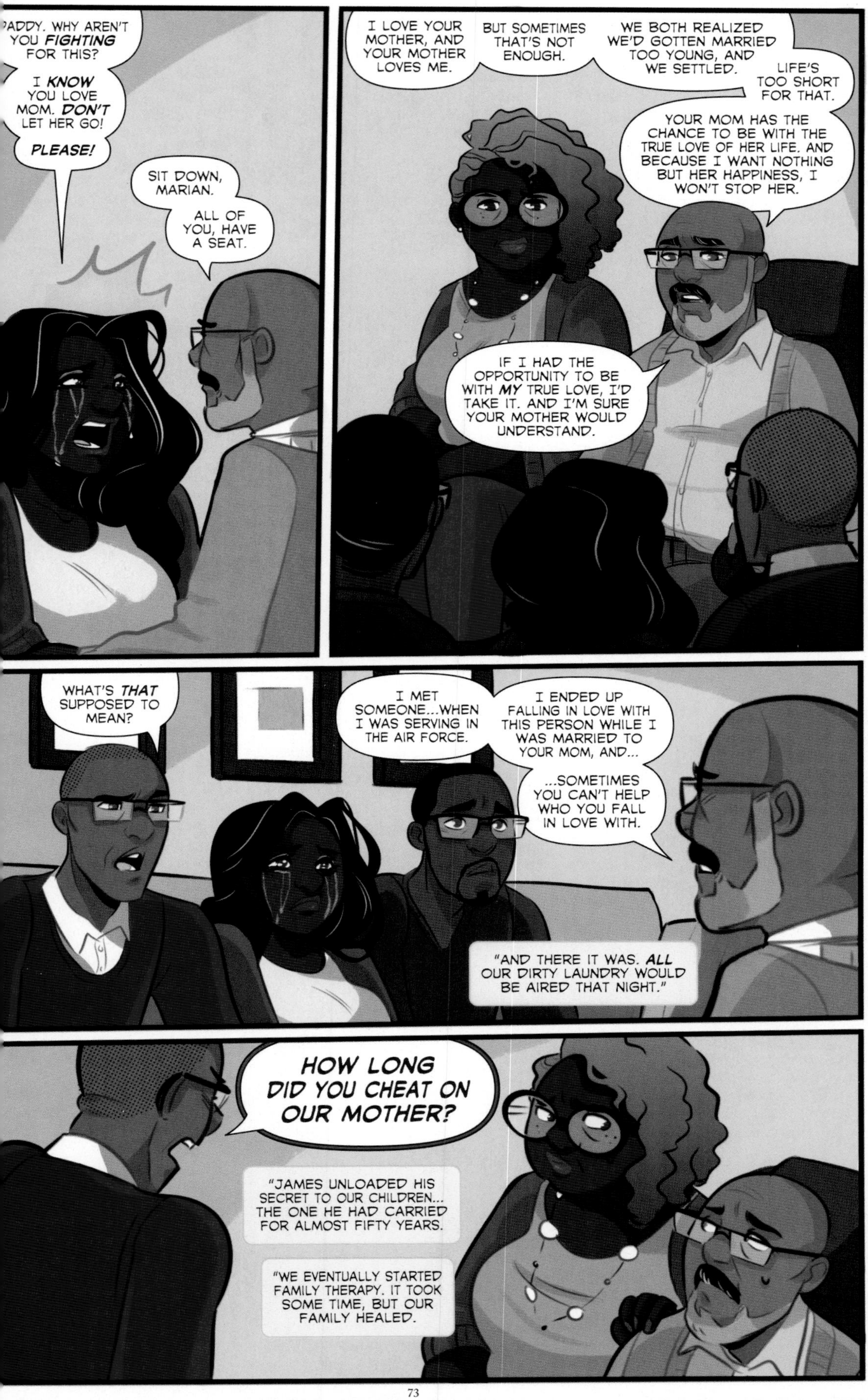
DADDY. WHY AREN'T YOU *FIGHTING* FOR THIS?
I *KNOW* YOU LOVE MOM. *DON'T* LET HER GO!
PLEASE!
SIT DOWN, MARIAN.
ALL OF YOU, HAVE A SEAT.
I LOVE YOUR MOTHER, AND YOUR MOTHER LOVES ME.
BUT SOMETIMES THAT'S NOT ENOUGH.
WE BOTH REALIZED WE'D GOTTEN MARRIED TOO YOUNG, AND WE SETTLED.
LIFE'S TOO SHORT FOR THAT.
YOUR MOM HAS THE CHANCE TO BE WITH THE TRUE LOVE OF HER LIFE. AND BECAUSE I WANT NOTHING BUT HER HAPPINESS, I WON'T STOP HER.
IF I HAD THE OPPORTUNITY TO BE WITH *MY* TRUE LOVE, I'D TAKE IT. AND I'M SURE YOUR MOTHER WOULD UNDERSTAND.
WHAT'S *THAT* SUPPOSED TO MEAN?
I MET SOMEONE...WHEN I WAS SERVING IN THE AIR FORCE.
I ENDED UP FALLING IN LOVE WITH THIS PERSON WHILE I WAS MARRIED TO YOUR MOM, AND...
...SOMETIMES YOU CAN'T HELP WHO YOU FALL IN LOVE WITH.
"AND THERE IT WAS. *ALL* OUR DIRTY LAUNDRY WOULD BE AIRED THAT NIGHT."
HOW LONG DID YOU CHEAT ON OUR MOTHER?
"JAMES UNLOADED HIS SECRET TO OUR CHILDREN... THE ONE HE HAD CARRIED FOR ALMOST FIFTY YEARS.
"WE EVENTUALLY STARTED FAMILY THERAPY. IT TOOK SOME TIME, BUT OUR FAMILY HEALED.

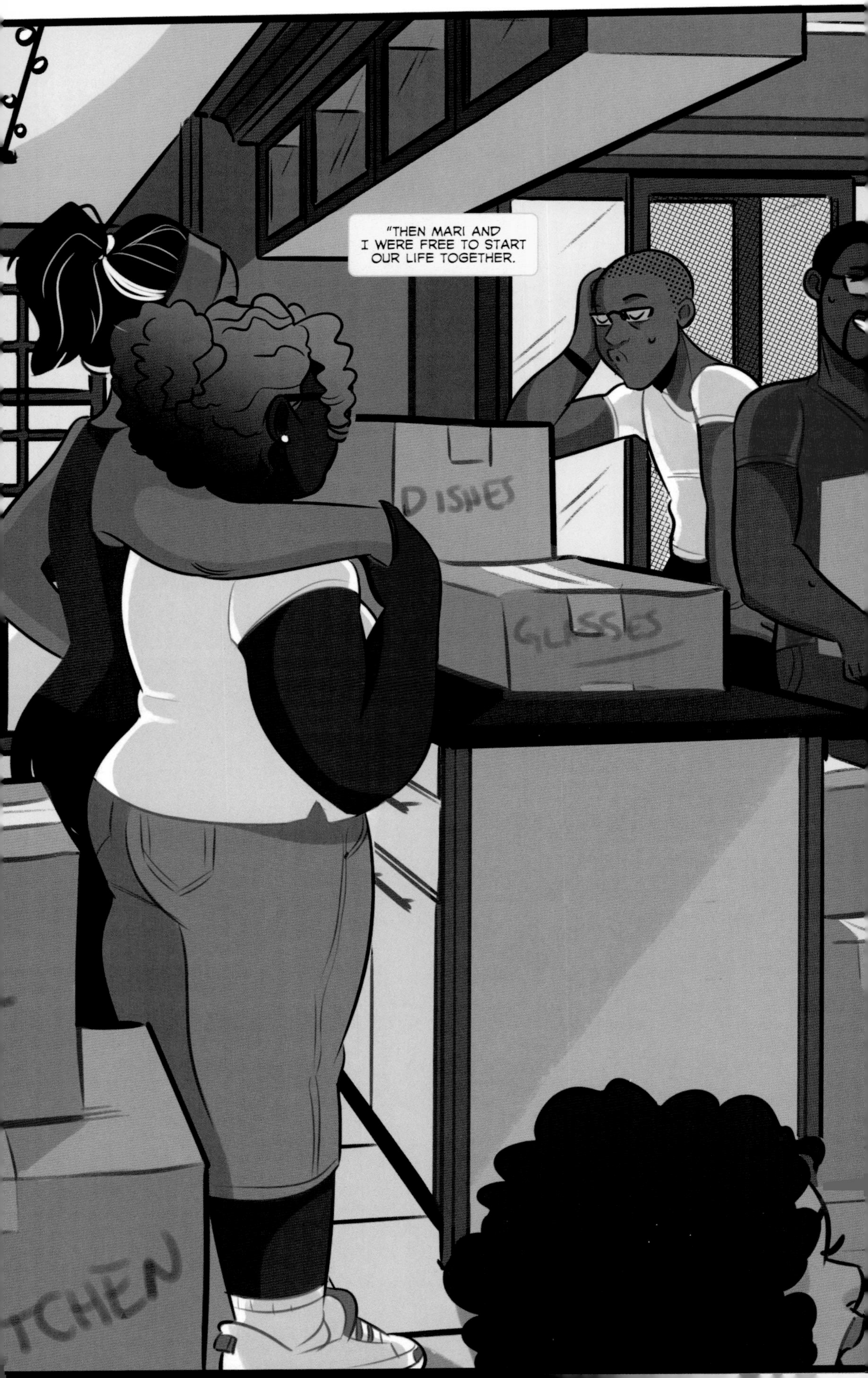
"THEN MARI AND I WERE FREE TO START OUR LIFE TOGETHER.
DISHES
GLASSES
TCHEN

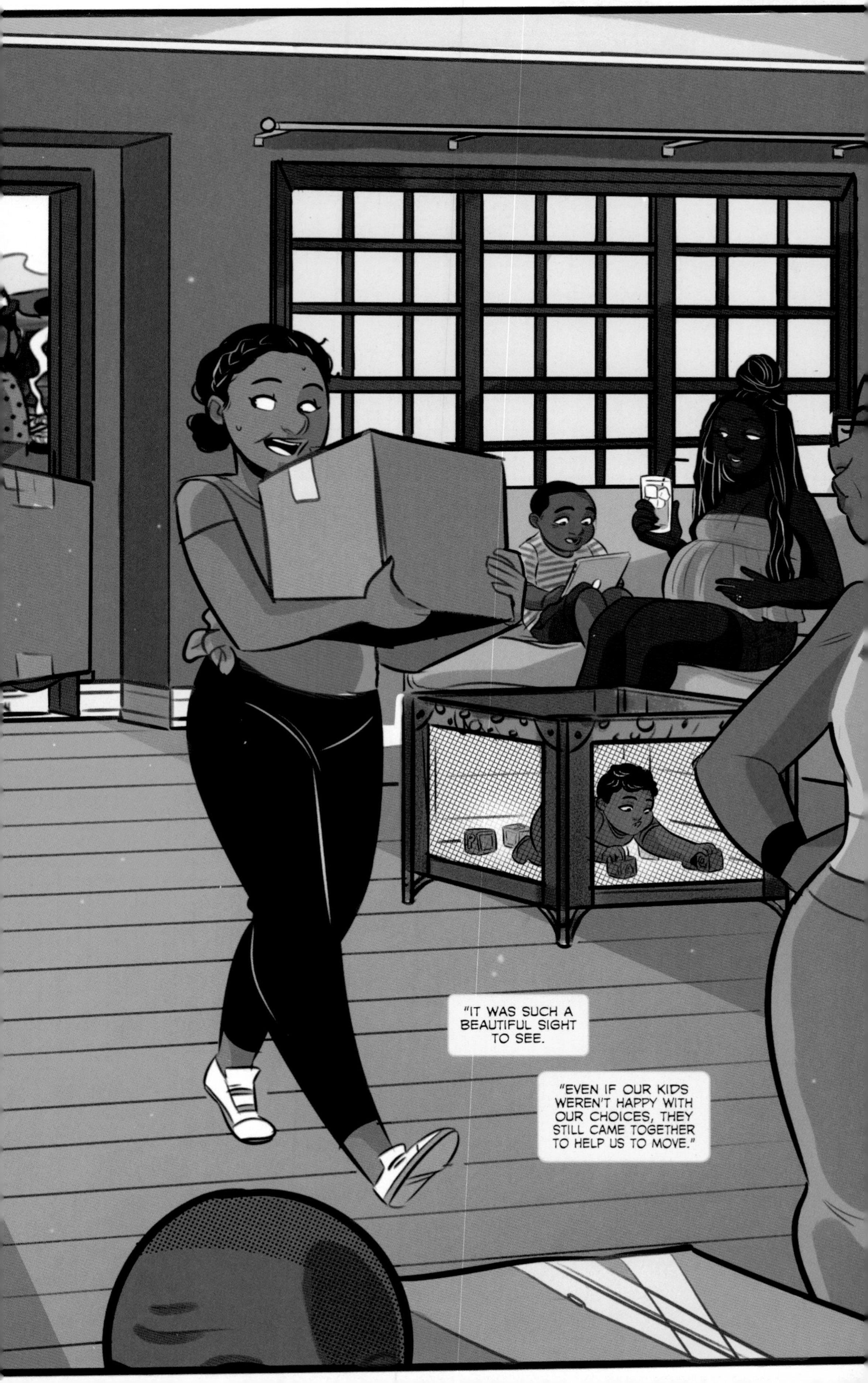
"IT WAS SUCH A BEAUTIFUL SIGHT TO SEE.
"EVEN IF OUR KIDS WEREN'T HAPPY WITH OUR CHOICES, THEY STILL CAME TOGETHER TO HELP US TO MOVE."

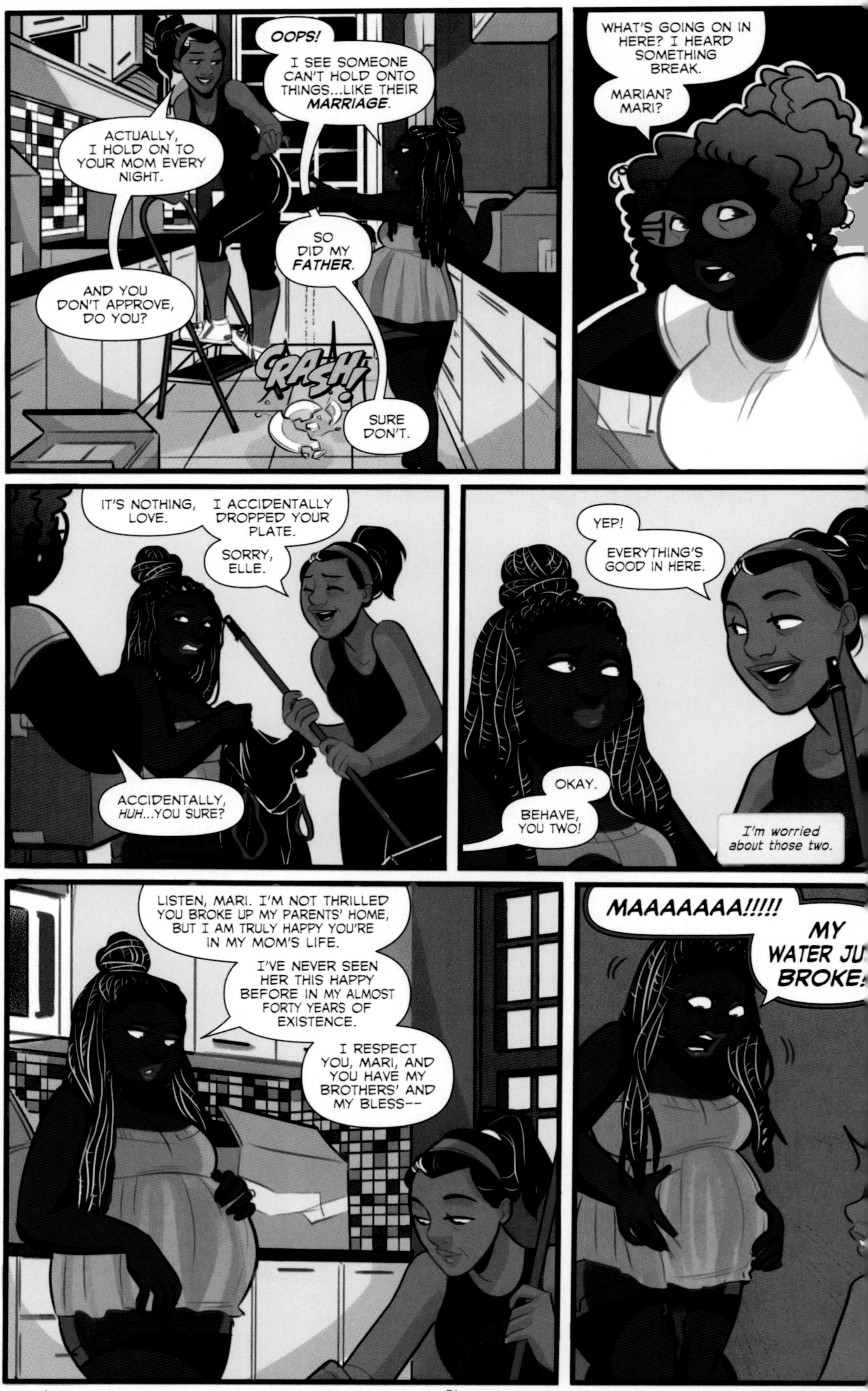

OOPS!
I SEE SOMEONE CAN'T HOLD ONTO THINGS...LIKE THEIR MARRIAGE.
ACTUALLY, I HOLD ON TO YOUR MOM EVERY NIGHT.
AND YOU DON'T APPROVE, DO YOU?
SO DID MY FATHER.
CRASH!
SURE DON'T.
WHAT'S GOING ON IN HERE? I HEARD SOMETHING BREAK.
MARIAN? MARI?
IT'S NOTHING, LOVE.
I ACCIDENTALLY DROPPED YOUR PLATE.
SORRY, ELLE.
ACCIDENTALLY, HUH...YOU SURE?
YEP!
EVERYTHING'S GOOD IN HERE.
OKAY.
BEHAVE, YOU TWO!
I'm worried about those two.
LISTEN, MARI. I'M NOT THRILLED YOU BROKE UP MY PARENTS' HOME, BUT I AM TRULY HAPPY YOU'RE IN MY MOM'S LIFE.
I'VE NEVER SEEN HER THIS HAPPY BEFORE IN MY ALMOST FORTY YEARS OF EXISTENCE.
I RESPECT YOU, MARI, AND YOU HAVE MY BROTHERS' AND MY BLESS--
MAAAAAAA!!!!!
MY WATER JU BROKE!

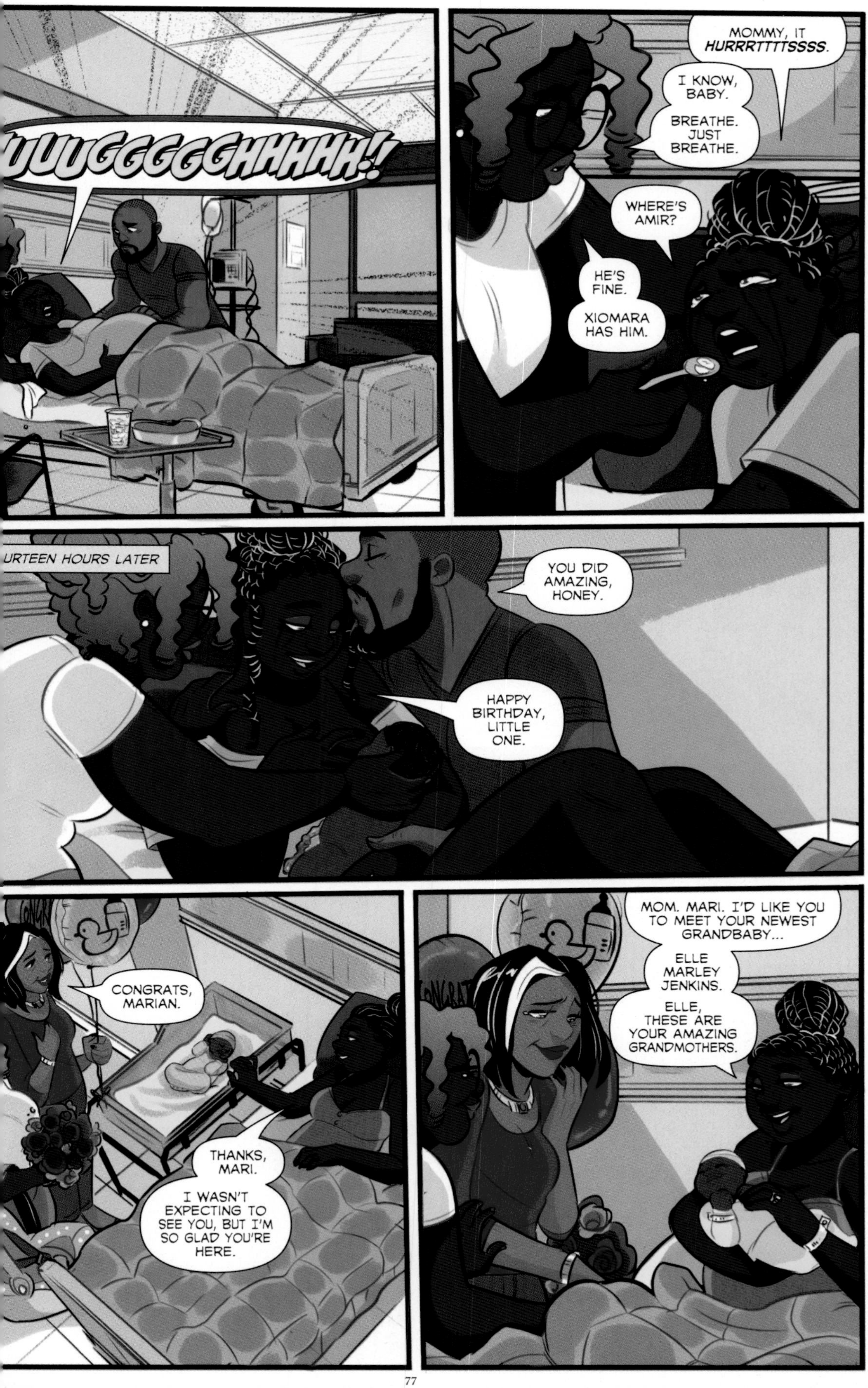
UUUUGGGGGGHHHHHH!
MOMMY, IT *HURRRTTTTSSSS*.
I KNOW, BABY.
BREATHE. JUST BREATHE.
WHERE'S AMIR?
HE'S FINE.
XIOMARA HAS HIM.
URTEEN HOURS LATER
YOU DID AMAZING, HONEY.
HAPPY BIRTHDAY, LITTLE ONE.
CONGRATS, MARIAN.
THANKS, MARI.
I WASN'T EXPECTING TO SEE YOU, BUT I'M SO GLAD YOU'RE HERE.
MOM. MARI. I'D LIKE YOU TO MEET YOUR NEWEST GRANDBABY...
ELLE MARLEY JENKINS.
ELLE, THESE ARE YOUR AMAZING GRANDMOTHERS.

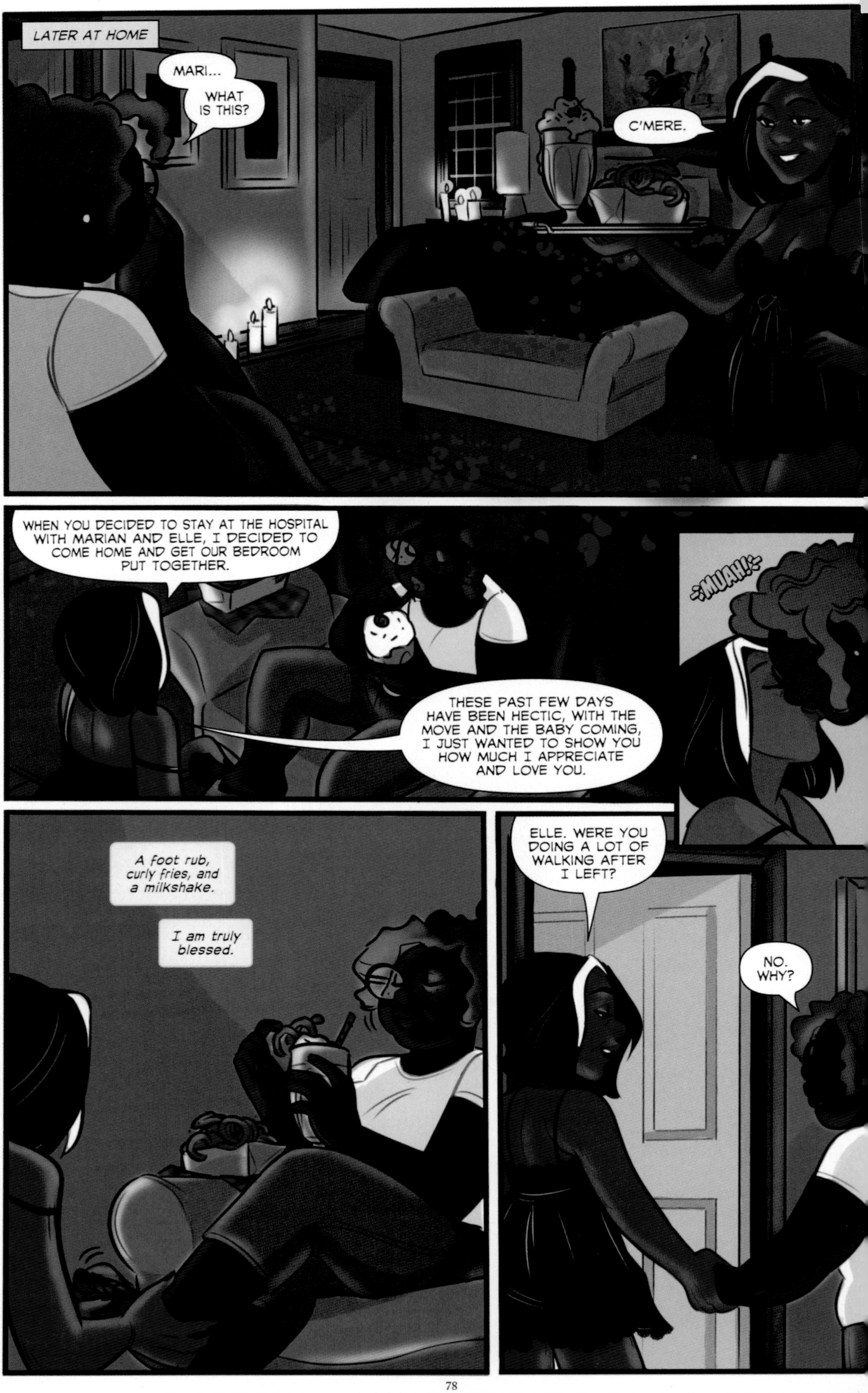
LATER AT HOME
MARI...
WHAT IS THIS?
C'MERE.
WHEN YOU DECIDED TO STAY AT THE HOSPITAL WITH MARIAN AND ELLE, I DECIDED TO COME HOME AND GET OUR BEDROOM PUT TOGETHER.
THESE PAST FEW DAYS HAVE BEEN HECTIC, WITH THE MOVE AND THE BABY COMING, I JUST WANTED TO SHOW YOU HOW MUCH I APPRECIATE AND LOVE YOU.
MUAH!
A foot rub, curly fries, and a milkshake.
I am truly blessed.
ELLE. WERE YOU DOING A LOT OF WALKING AFTER I LEFT?
NO. WHY?

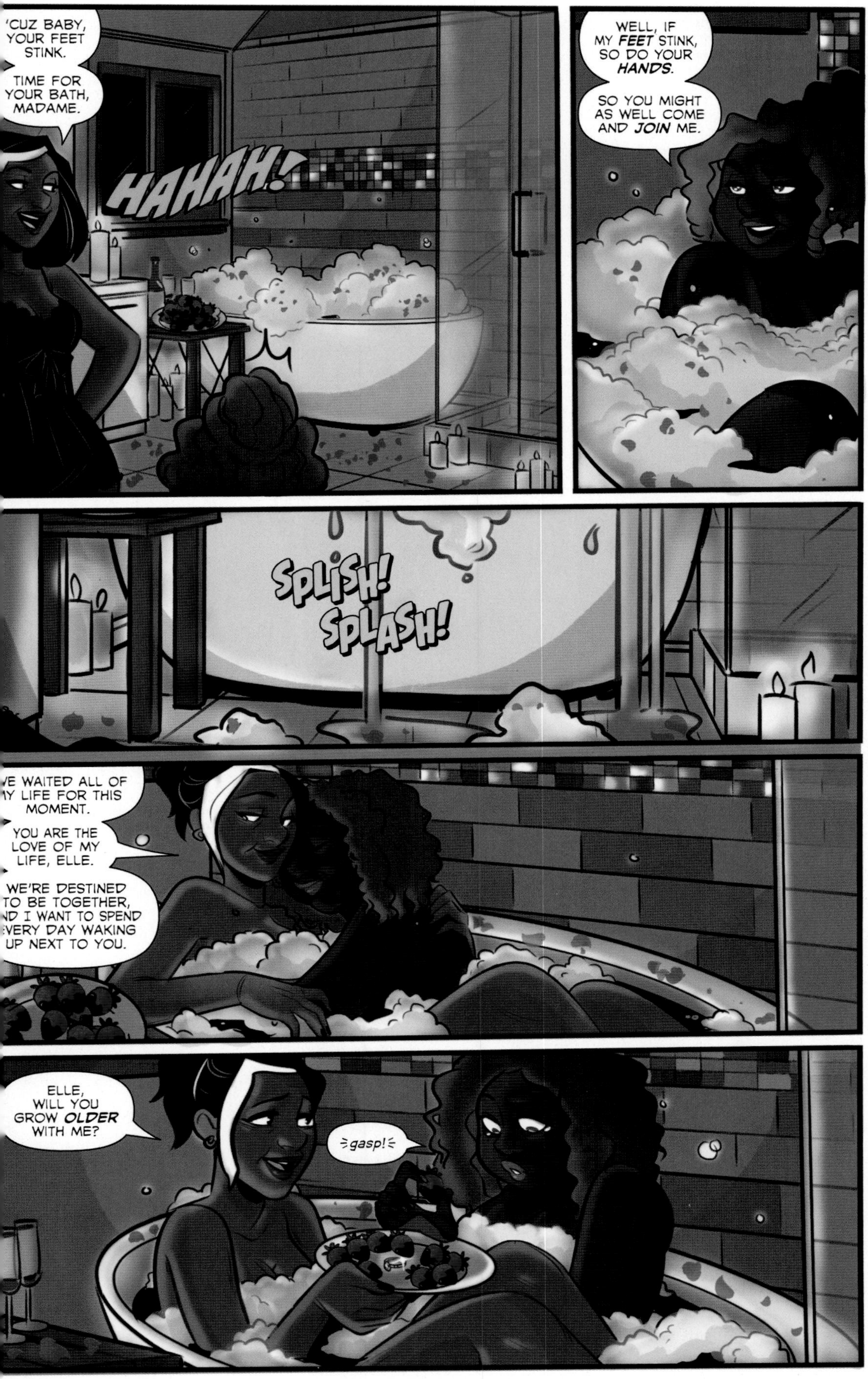

'CUZ BABY, YOUR FEET STINK.
TIME FOR YOUR BATH, MADAME.
HAHAH!
WELL, IF MY FEET STINK, SO DO YOUR HANDS.
SO YOU MIGHT AS WELL COME AND JOIN ME.
SPLISH! SPLASH!
VE WAITED ALL OF Y LIFE FOR THIS MOMENT.
YOU ARE THE LOVE OF MY LIFE, ELLE.
WE'RE DESTINED TO BE TOGETHER, ND I WANT TO SPEND VERY DAY WAKING UP NEXT TO YOU.
ELLE, WILL YOU GROW OLDER WITH ME?
gasp!

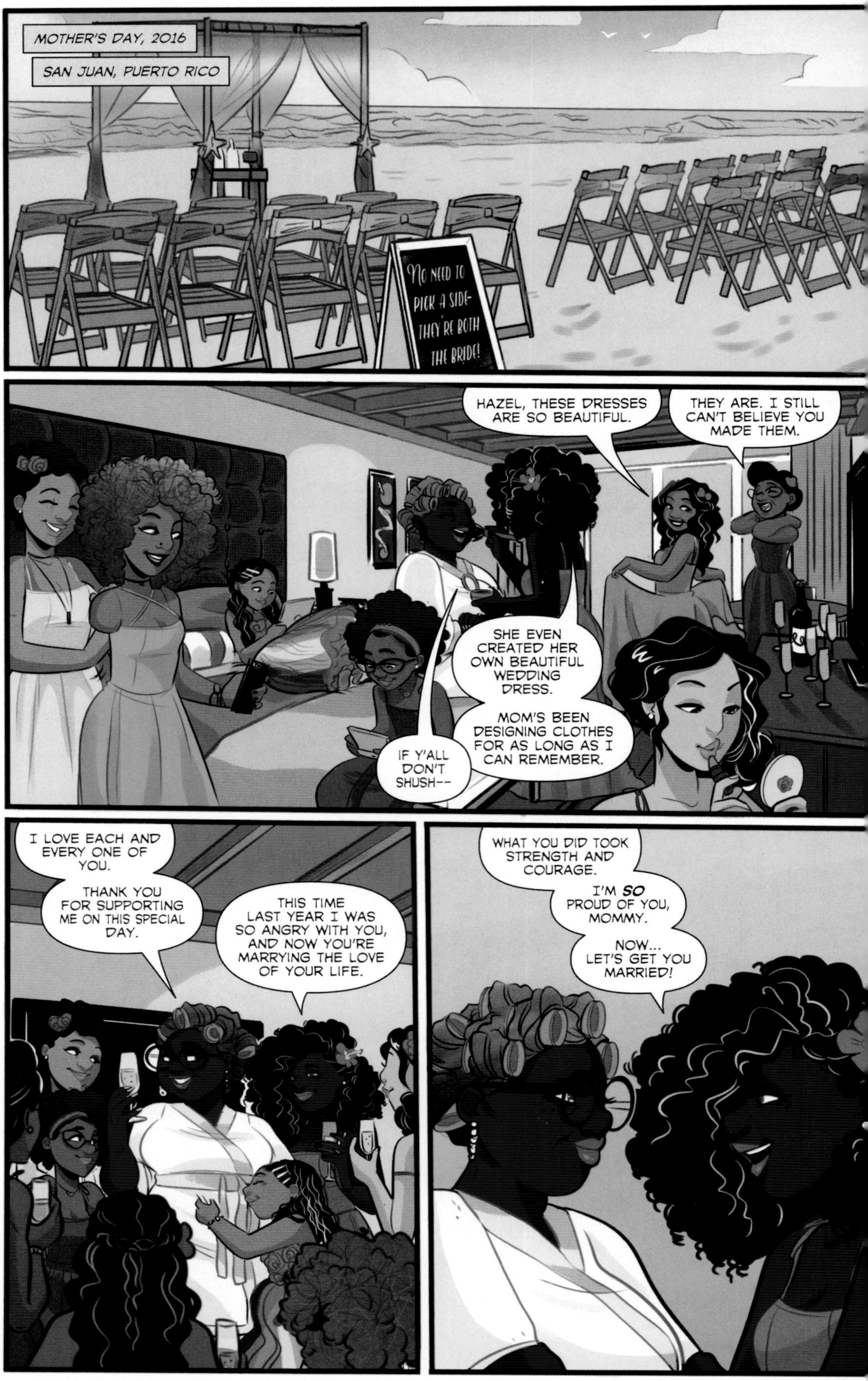
MOTHER'S DAY, 2016
SAN JUAN, PUERTO RICO
No need to pick a side-- they're both the bride!
HAZEL, THESE DRESSES ARE SO BEAUTIFUL.
THEY ARE. I STILL CAN'T BELIEVE YOU MADE THEM.
SHE EVEN CREATED HER OWN BEAUTIFUL WEDDING DRESS.
MOM'S BEEN DESIGNING CLOTHES FOR AS LONG AS I CAN REMEMBER.
IF Y'ALL DON'T SHUSH--
I LOVE EACH AND EVERY ONE OF YOU.
THANK YOU FOR SUPPORTING ME ON THIS SPECIAL DAY.
THIS TIME LAST YEAR I WAS SO ANGRY WITH YOU, AND NOW YOU'RE MARRYING THE LOVE OF YOUR LIFE.
WHAT YOU DID TOOK STRENGTH AND COURAGE.
I'M *SO* PROUD OF YOU, MOMMY.
NOW... LET'S GET YOU MARRIED!

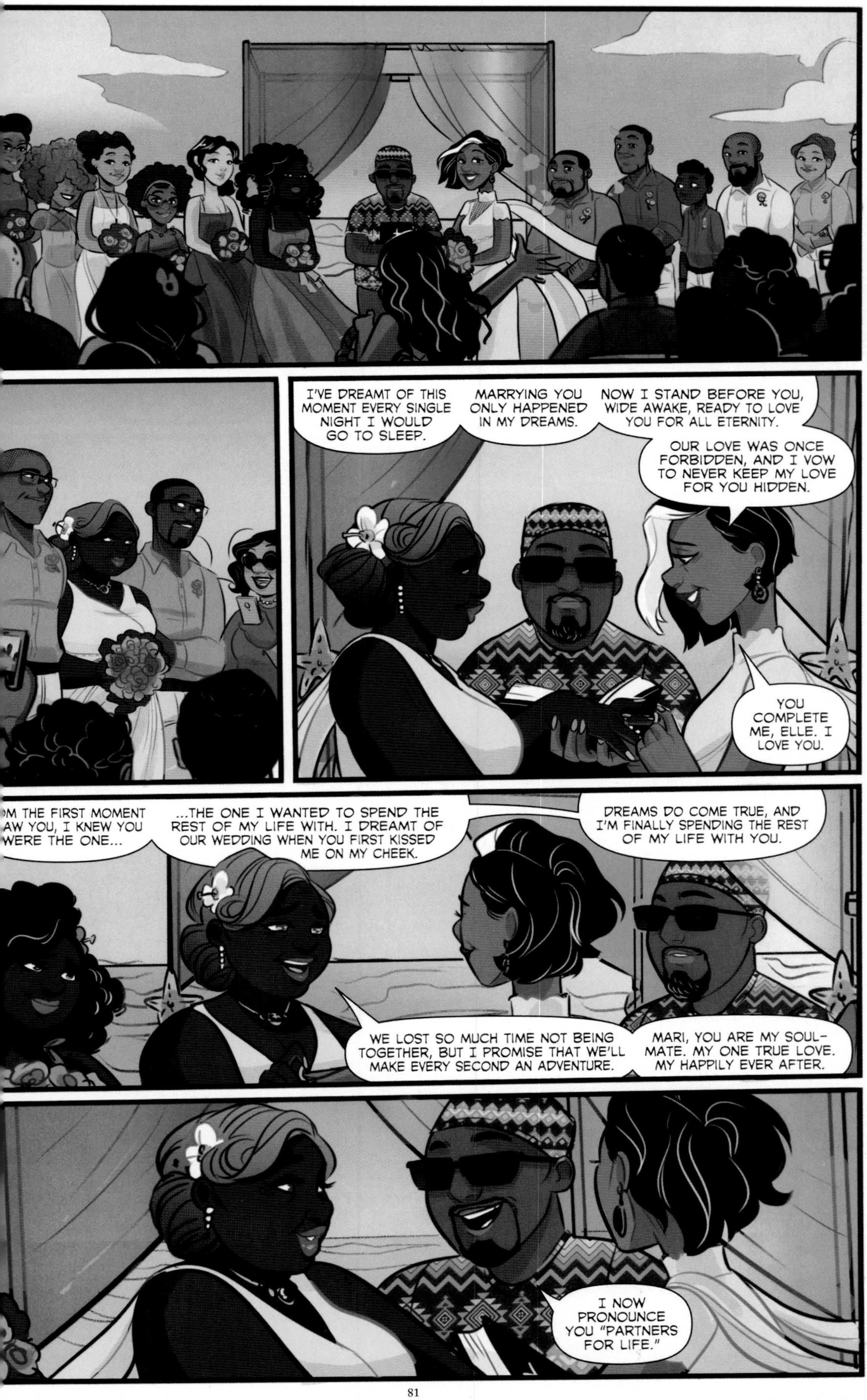
I'VE DREAMT OF THIS MOMENT EVERY SINGLE NIGHT I WOULD GO TO SLEEP.
MARRYING YOU ONLY HAPPENED IN MY DREAMS.
NOW I STAND BEFORE YOU, WIDE AWAKE, READY TO LOVE YOU FOR ALL ETERNITY.
OUR LOVE WAS ONCE FORBIDDEN, AND I VOW TO NEVER KEEP MY LOVE FOR YOU HIDDEN.
YOU COMPLETE ME, ELLE. I LOVE YOU.
M THE FIRST MOMENT AW YOU, I KNEW YOU WERE THE ONE...
...THE ONE I WANTED TO SPEND THE REST OF MY LIFE WITH. I DREAMT OF OUR WEDDING WHEN YOU FIRST KISSED ME ON MY CHEEK.
DREAMS DO COME TRUE, AND I'M FINALLY SPENDING THE REST OF MY LIFE WITH YOU.
WE LOST SO MUCH TIME NOT BEING TOGETHER, BUT I PROMISE THAT WE'LL MAKE EVERY SECOND AN ADVENTURE.
MARI, YOU ARE MY SOUL-MATE. MY ONE TRUE LOVE. MY HAPPILY EVER AFTER.
I NOW PRONOUNCE YOU "PARTNERS FOR LIFE."

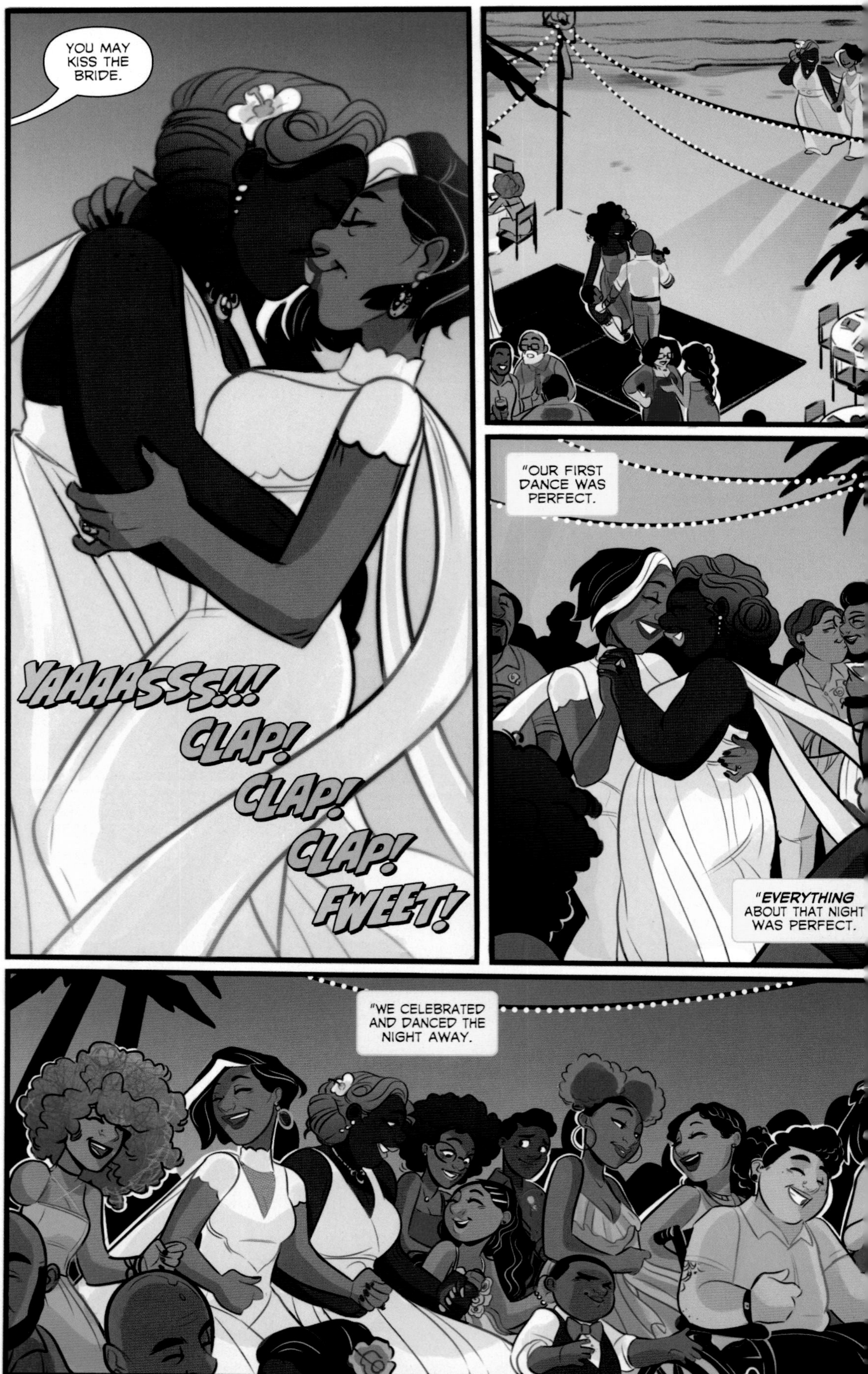
YOU MAY KISS THE BRIDE.
YAAAASSS!!!
CLAP!
CLAP!
CLAP!
FWEET!
"OUR FIRST DANCE WAS PERFECT.
"EVERYTHING ABOUT THAT NIGHT WAS PERFECT.
"WE CELEBRATED AND DANCED THE NIGHT AWAY.

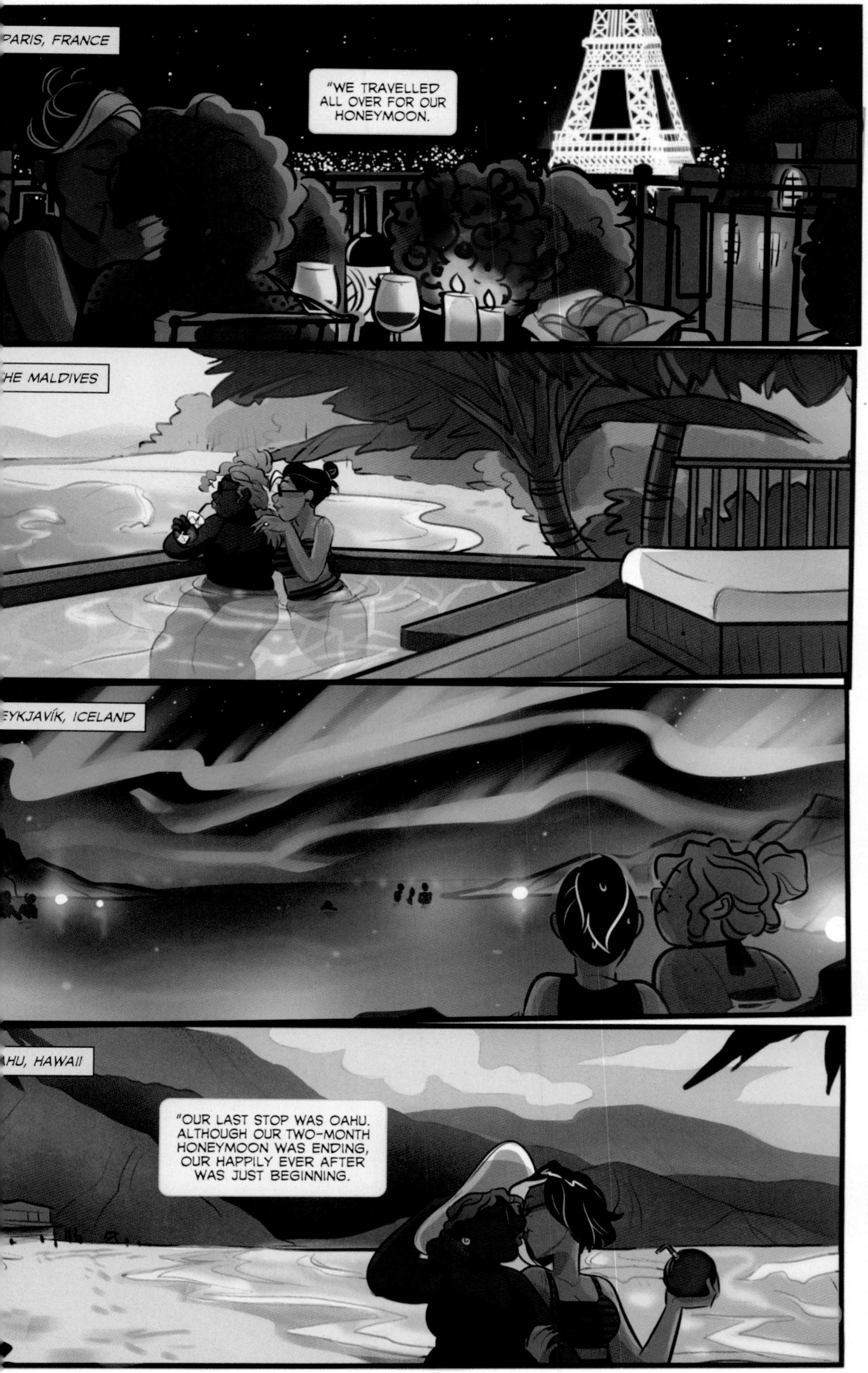
PARIS, FRANCE
"WE TRAVELLED ALL OVER FOR OUR HONEYMOON.
HE MALDIVES
EYKJAVÍK, ICELAND
HU, HAWAII
"OUR LAST STOP WAS OAHU. ALTHOUGH OUR TWO-MONTH HONEYMOON WAS ENDING, OUR HAPPILY EVER AFTER WAS JUST BEGINNING.

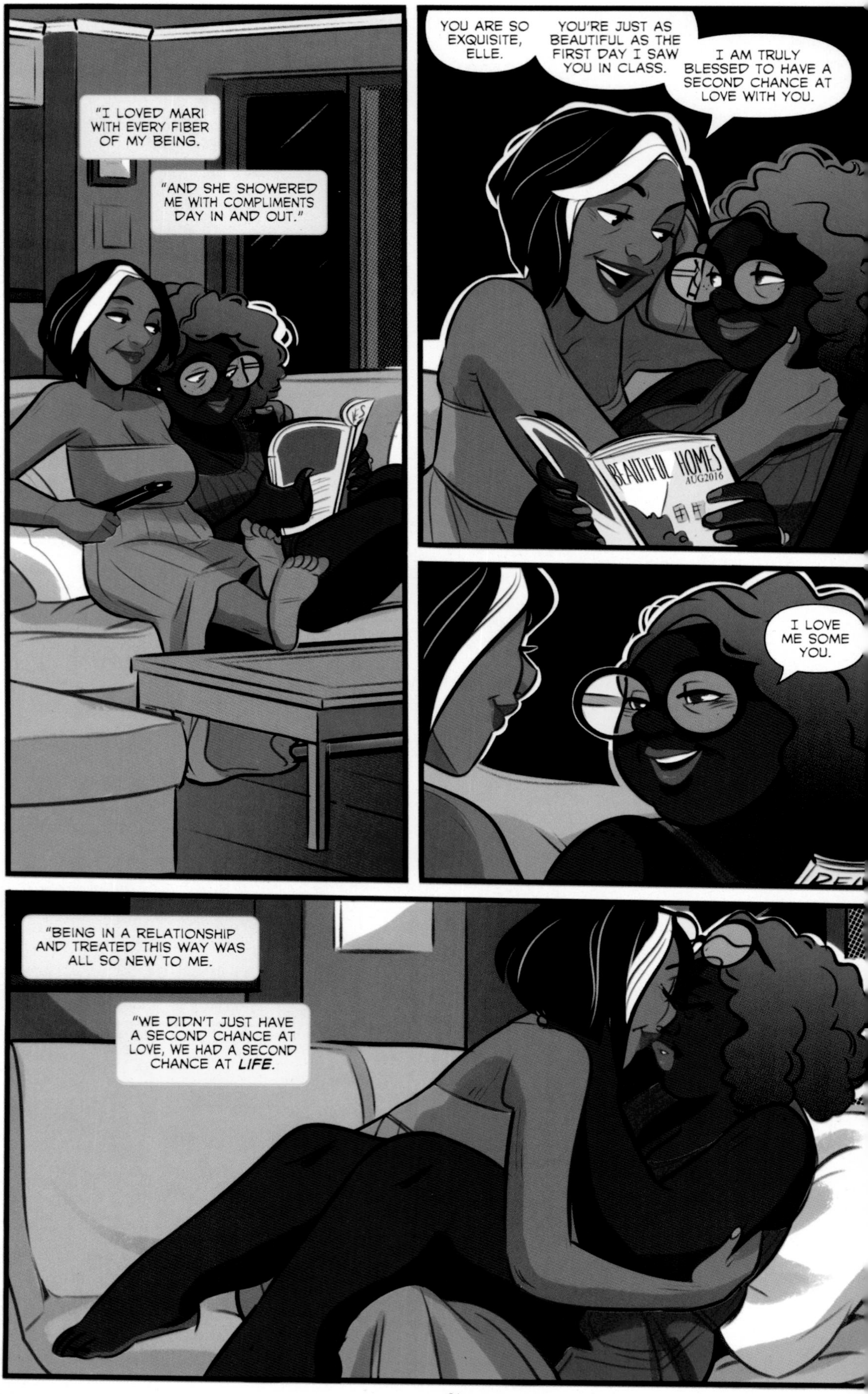
"I LOVED MARI WITH EVERY FIBER OF MY BEING.
"AND SHE SHOWERED ME WITH COMPLIMENTS DAY IN AND OUT."
YOU ARE SO EXQUISITE, ELLE.
YOU'RE JUST AS BEAUTIFUL AS THE FIRST DAY I SAW YOU IN CLASS.
I AM TRULY BLESSED TO HAVE A SECOND CHANCE AT LOVE WITH YOU.
BEAUTIFUL HOMES AUG2016
I LOVE ME SOME YOU.
"BEING IN A RELATIONSHIP AND TREATED THIS WAY WAS ALL SO NEW TO ME.
"WE DIDN'T JUST HAVE A SECOND CHANCE AT LOVE, WE HAD A SECOND CHANCE AT *LIFE*.

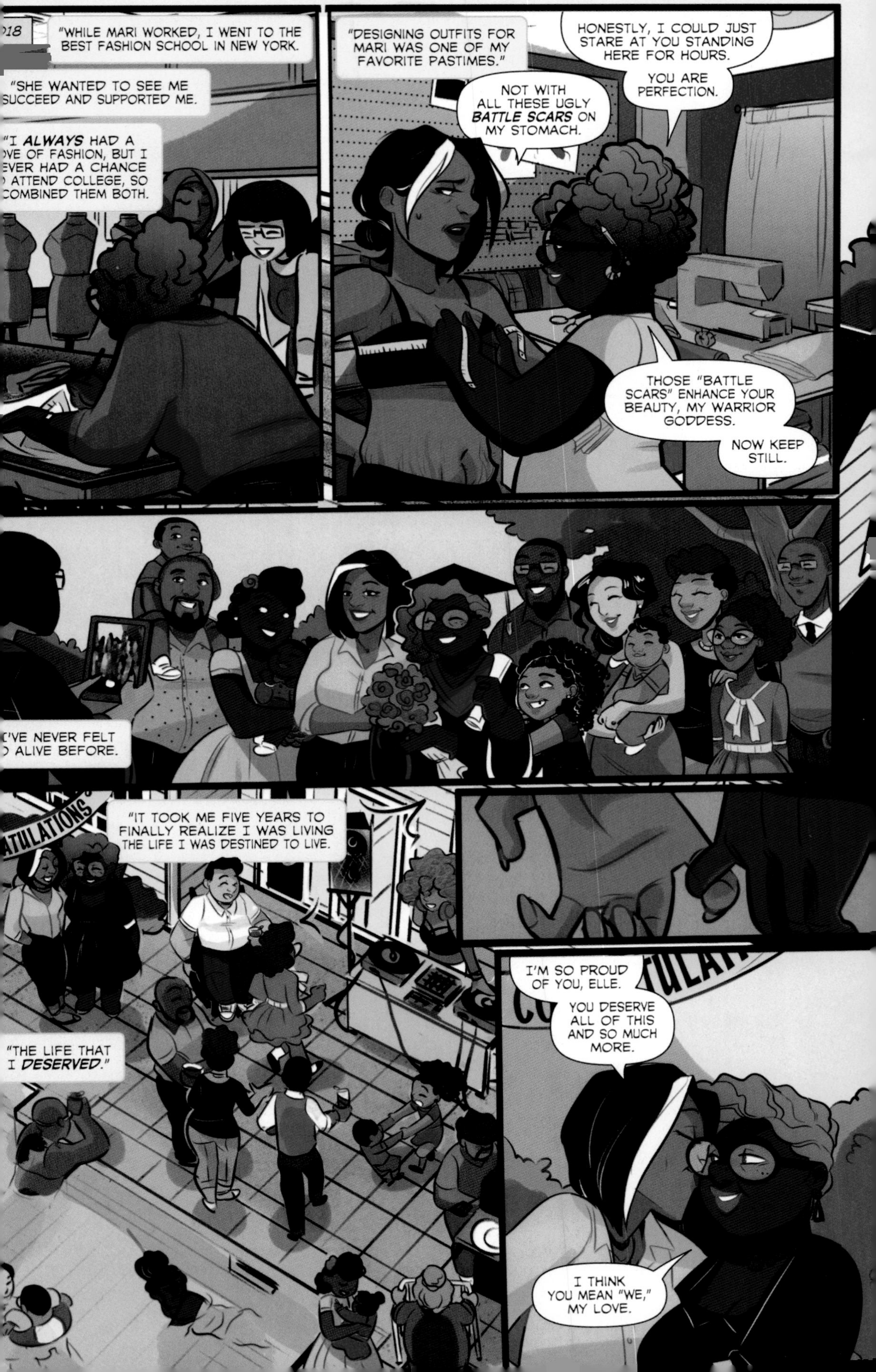

018
"WHILE MARI WORKED, I WENT TO THE BEST FASHION SCHOOL IN NEW YORK.
"SHE WANTED TO SEE ME SUCCEED AND SUPPORTED ME.
"I **ALWAYS** HAD A VE OF FASHION, BUT I EVER HAD A CHANCE ATTEND COLLEGE, SO COMBINED THEM BOTH.
"DESIGNING OUTFITS FOR MARI WAS ONE OF MY FAVORITE PASTIMES."
HONESTLY, I COULD JUST STARE AT YOU STANDING HERE FOR HOURS.
YOU ARE PERFECTION.
NOT WITH ALL THESE UGLY ***BATTLE SCARS*** ON MY STOMACH.
THOSE "BATTLE SCARS" ENHANCE YOUR BEAUTY, MY WARRIOR GODDESS.
NOW KEEP STILL.
'VE NEVER FELT ALIVE BEFORE.
ATULATIONS
"IT TOOK ME FIVE YEARS TO FINALLY REALIZE I WAS LIVING THE LIFE I WAS DESTINED TO LIVE.
"THE LIFE THAT I ***DESERVED***."
I'M SO PROUD OF YOU, ELLE.
YOU DESERVE ALL OF THIS AND SO MUCH MORE.
I THINK YOU MEAN "WE," MY LOVE.

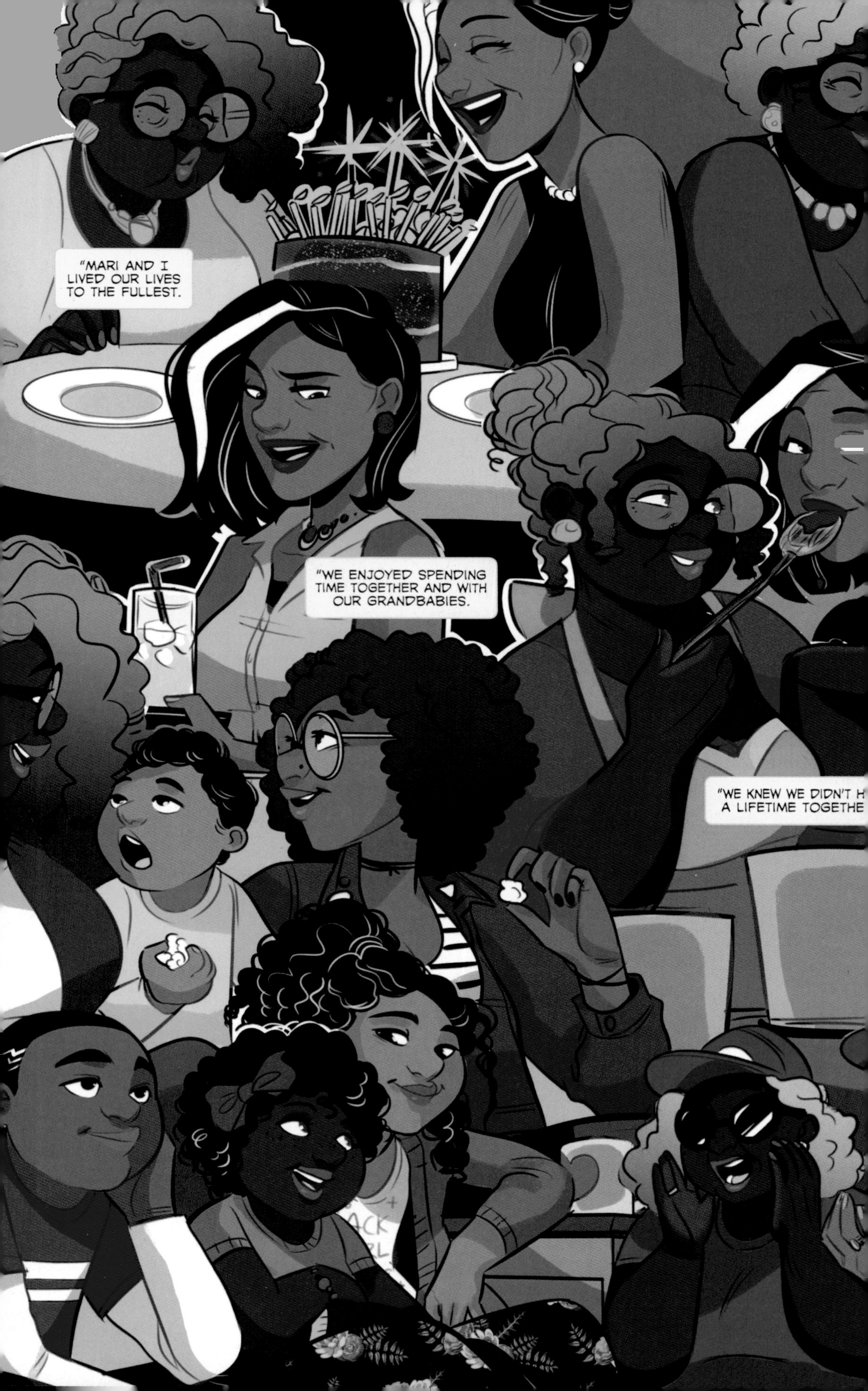
"MARI AND I LIVED OUR LIVES TO THE FULLEST.
"WE ENJOYED SPENDING TIME TOGETHER AND WITH OUR GRANDBABIES.
"WE KNEW WE DIDN'T H
A LIFETIME TOGETHE

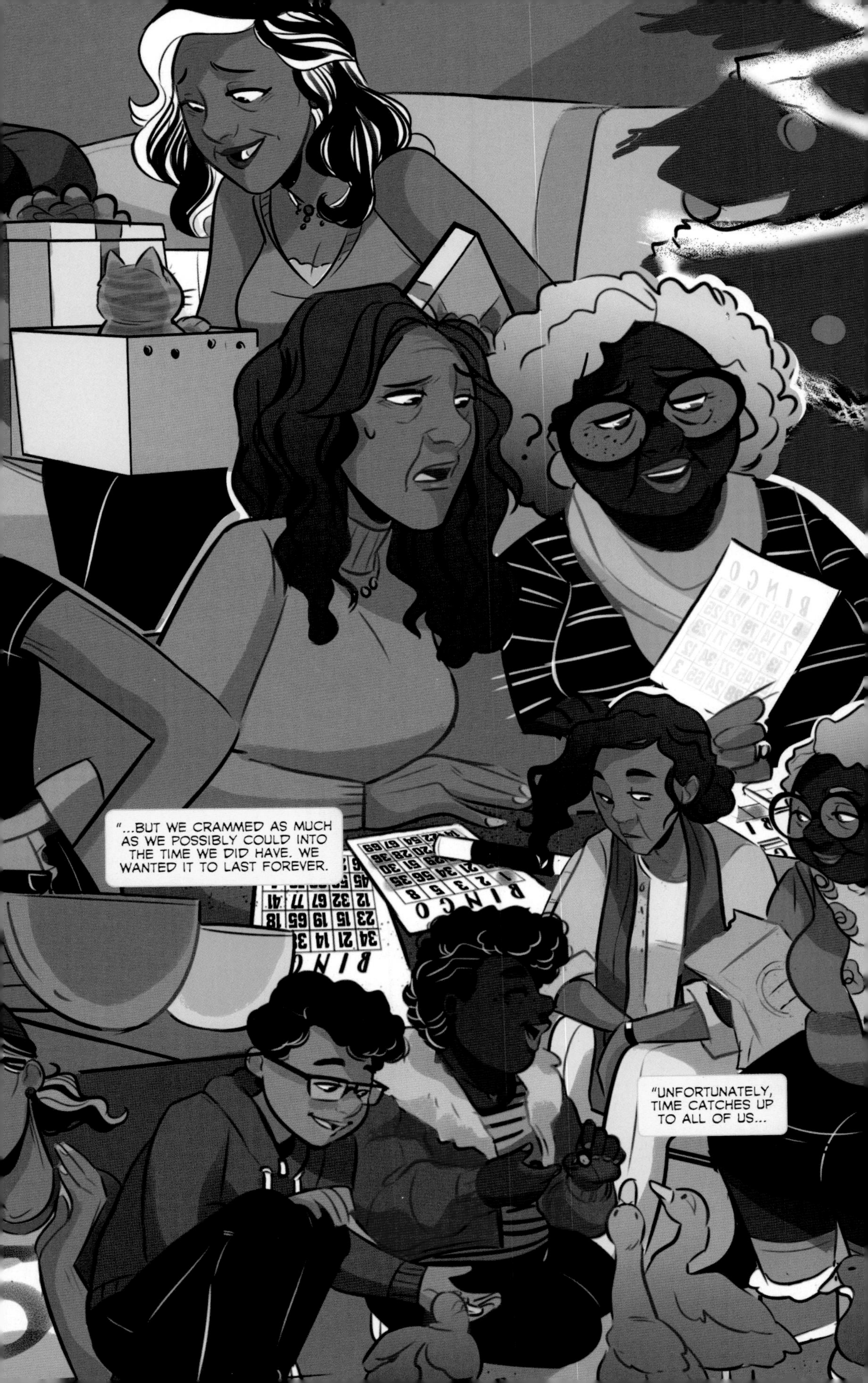
"...BUT WE CRAMMED AS MUCH AS WE POSSIBLY COULD INTO THE TIME WE DID HAVE. WE WANTED IT TO LAST FOREVER.
"UNFORTUNATELY, TIME CATCHES UP TO ALL OF US...

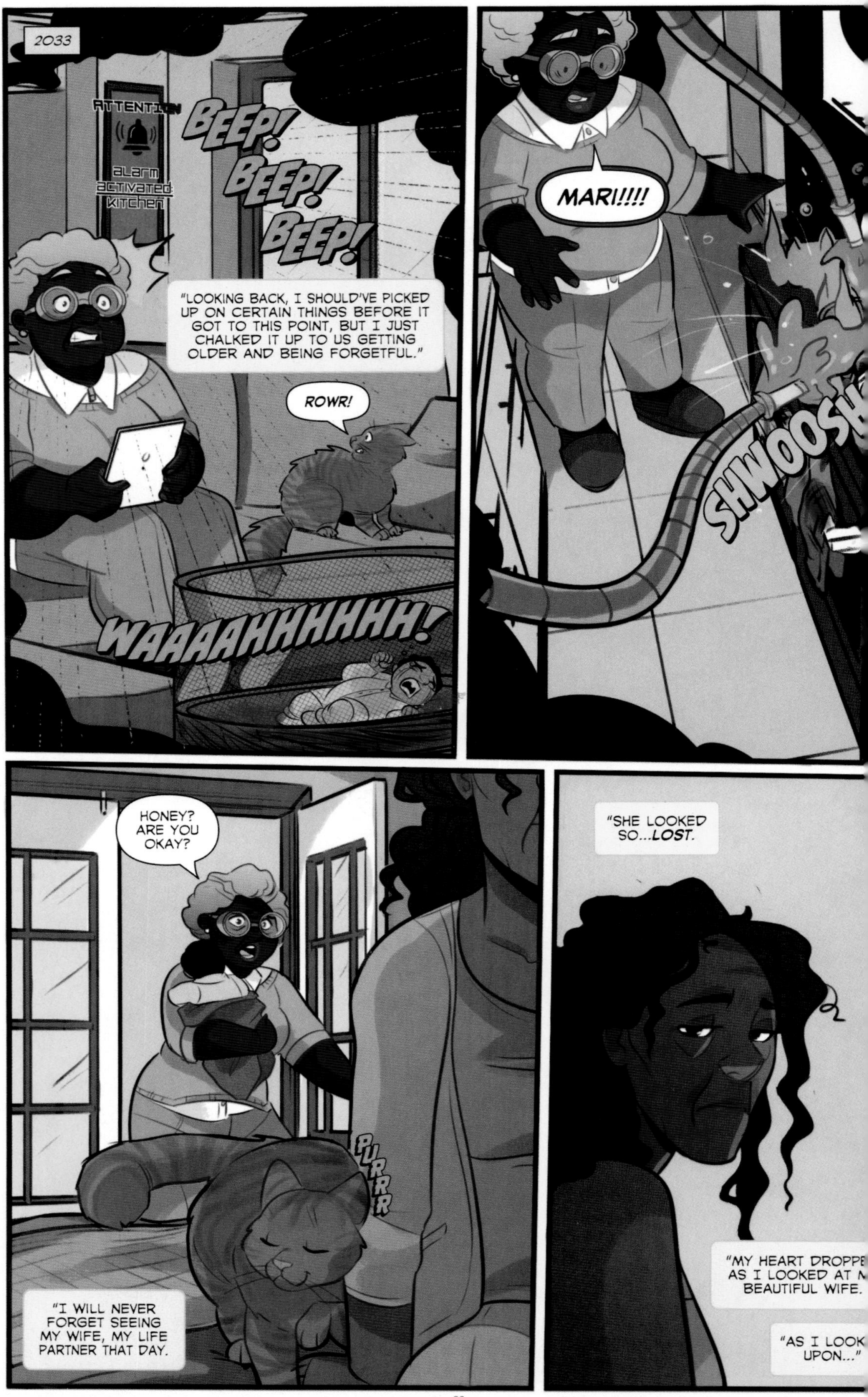
2033
ATTENTION
alarm activated: kitchen
BEEP! BEEP! BEEP!
"LOOKING BACK, I SHOULD'VE PICKED UP ON CERTAIN THINGS BEFORE IT GOT TO THIS POINT, BUT I JUST CHALKED IT UP TO US GETTING OLDER AND BEING FORGETFUL."
ROWR!
WAAAAHHHHHH!
MARI!!!!
HONEY? ARE YOU OKAY?
PURRR
"I WILL NEVER FORGET SEEING MY WIFE, MY LIFE PARTNER THAT DAY.
"SHE LOOKED SO...LOST.
"MY HEART DROPPE
AS I LOOKED AT M
BEAUTIFUL WIFE.
"AS I LOOK
UPON..."

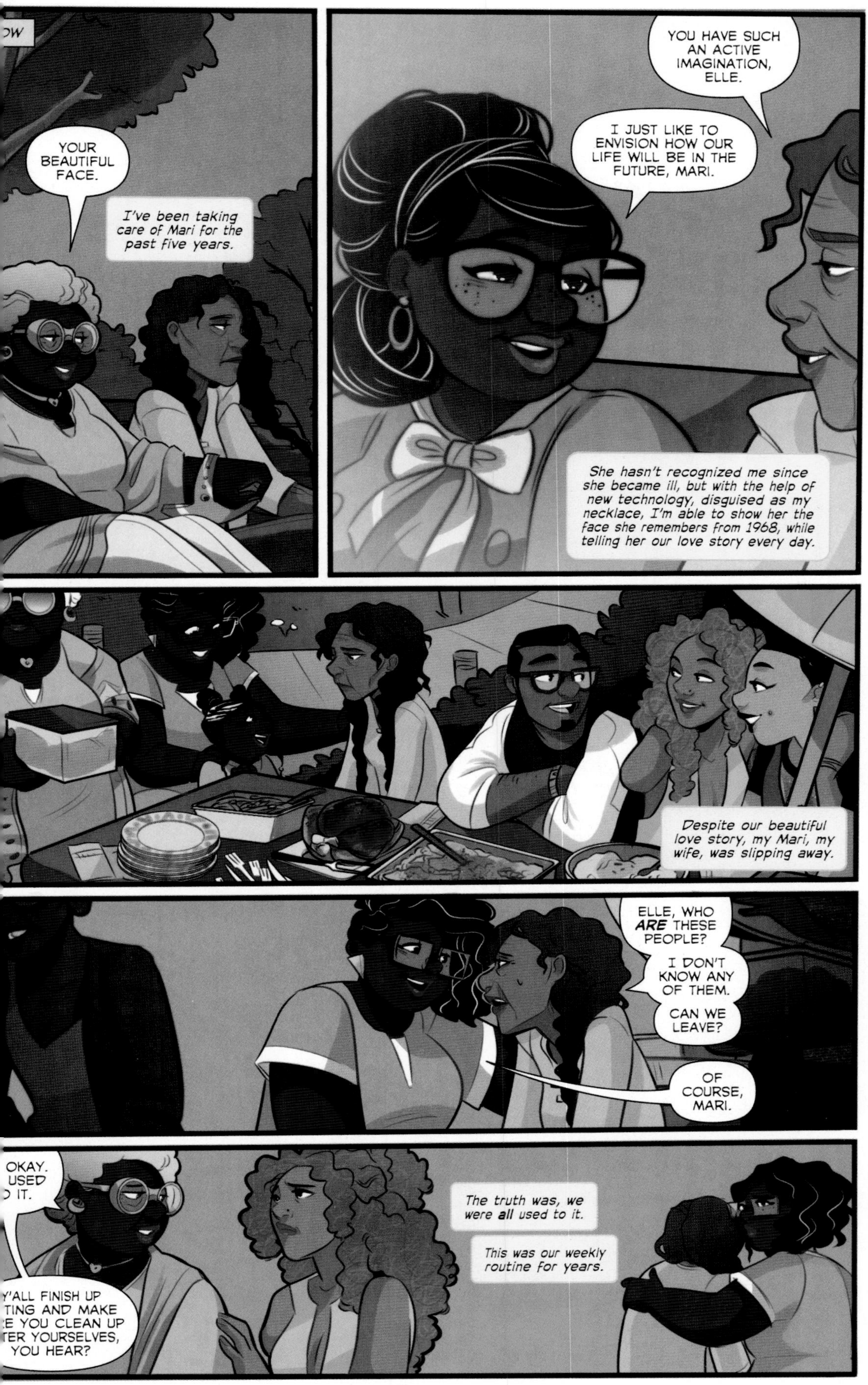
OW
YOUR BEAUTIFUL FACE.
I've been taking care of Mari for the past five years.
YOU HAVE SUCH AN ACTIVE IMAGINATION, ELLE.
I JUST LIKE TO ENVISION HOW OUR LIFE WILL BE IN THE FUTURE, MARI.
She hasn't recognized me since she became ill, but with the help of new technology, disguised as my necklace, I'm able to show her the face she remembers from 1968, while telling her our love story every day.
Despite our beautiful love story, my Mari, my wife, was slipping away.
ELLE, WHO *ARE* THESE PEOPLE?
I DON'T KNOW ANY OF THEM.
CAN WE LEAVE?
OF COURSE, MARI.
OKAY. USED IT.
Y'ALL FINISH UP TING AND MAKE E YOU CLEAN UP TER YOURSELVES, YOU HEAR?
The truth was, we were *all* used to it.
This was our weekly routine for years.

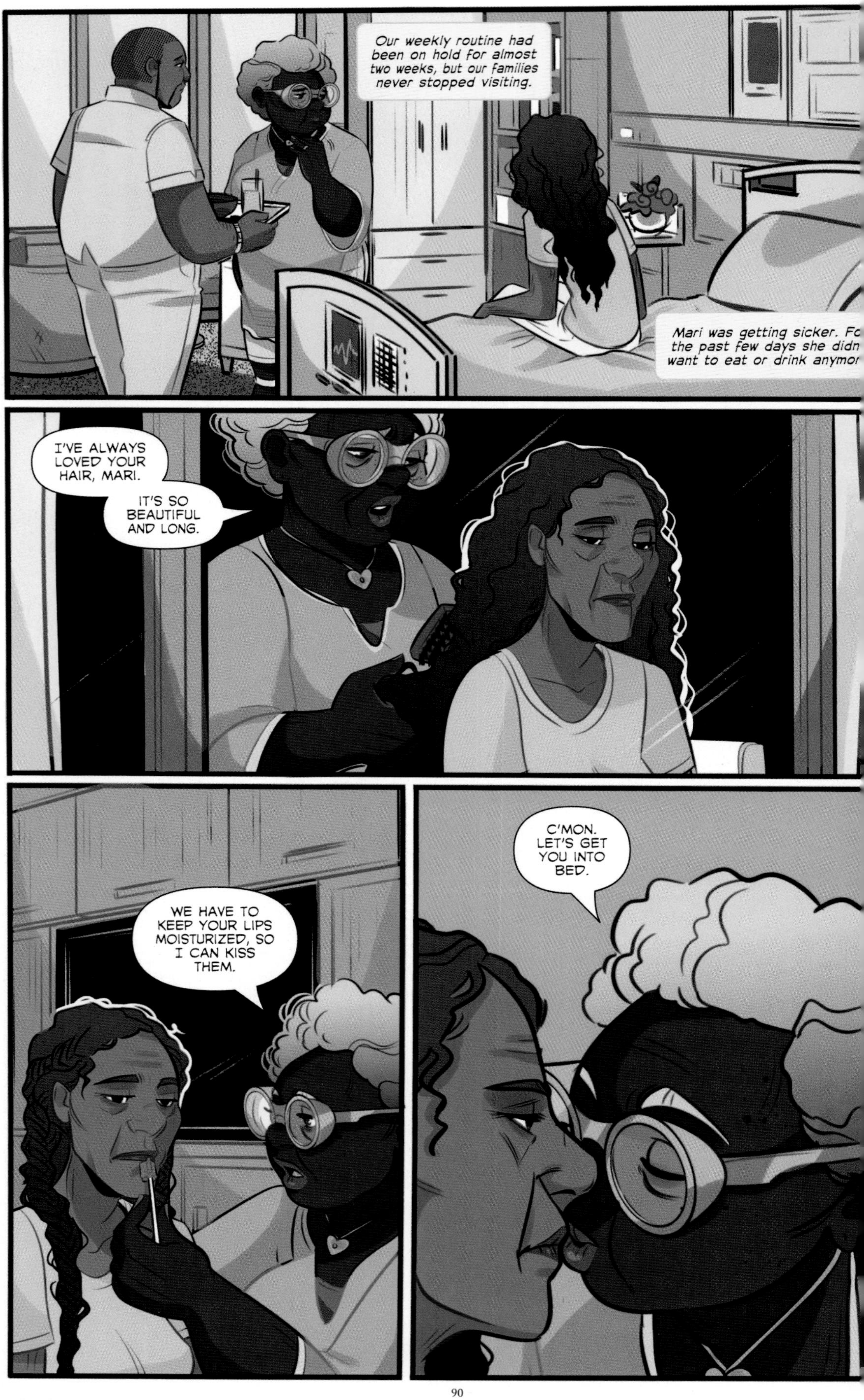
Our weekly routine had been on hold for almost two weeks, but our families never stopped visiting.
Mari was getting sicker. Fo the past few days she didn want to eat or drink anymor
I'VE ALWAYS LOVED YOUR HAIR, MARI.
IT'S SO BEAUTIFUL AND LONG.
WE HAVE TO KEEP YOUR LIPS MOISTURIZED, SO I CAN KISS THEM.
C'MON. LET'S GET YOU INTO BED.

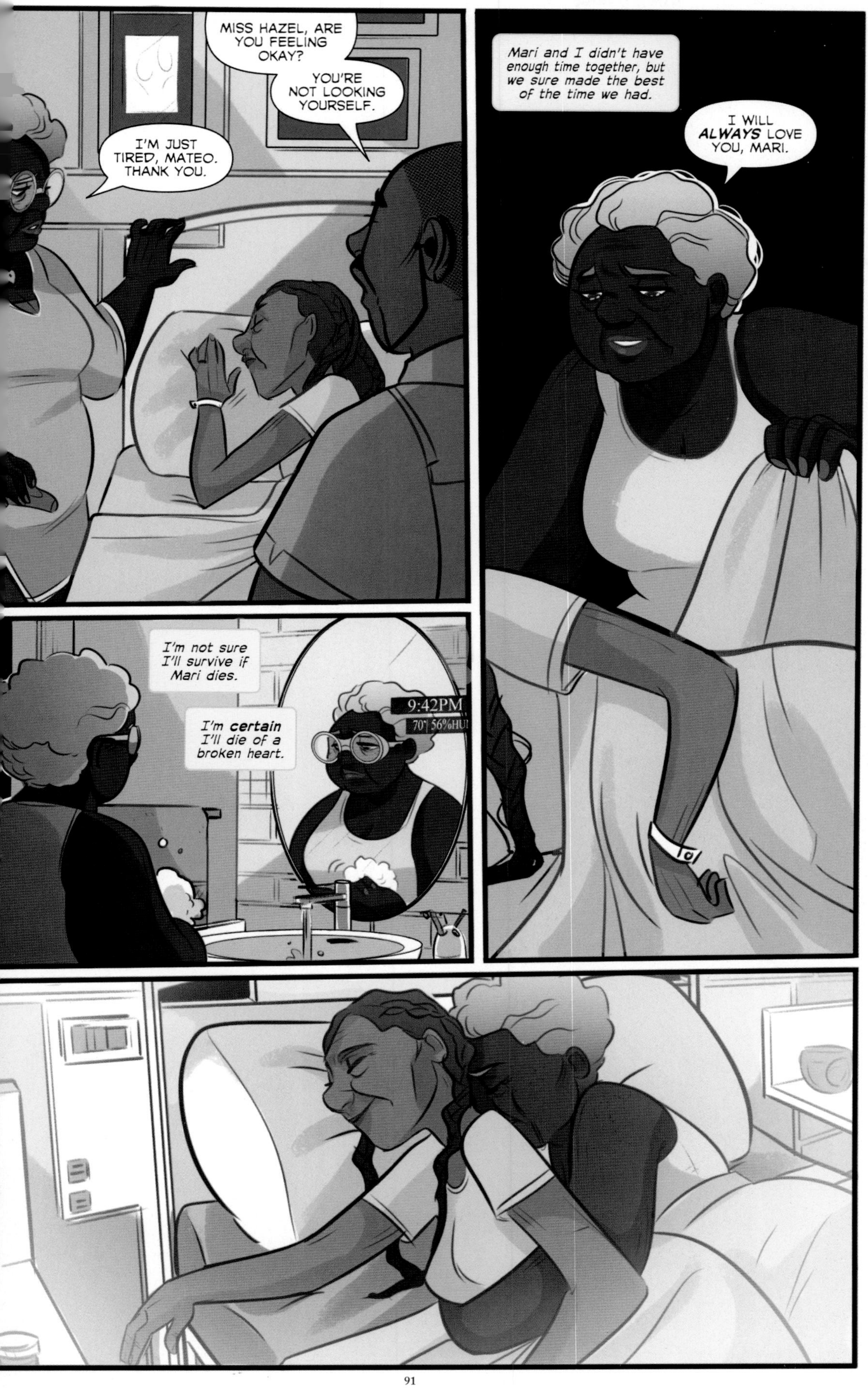
MISS HAZEL, ARE YOU FEELING OKAY?
YOU'RE NOT LOOKING YOURSELF.
I'M JUST TIRED, MATEO. THANK YOU.
I'm not sure I'll survive if Mari dies.
I'm **certain** I'll die of a broken heart.
9:42PM
Mari and I didn't have enough time together, but we sure made the best of the time we had.
I WILL **ALWAYS** LOVE YOU, MARI.

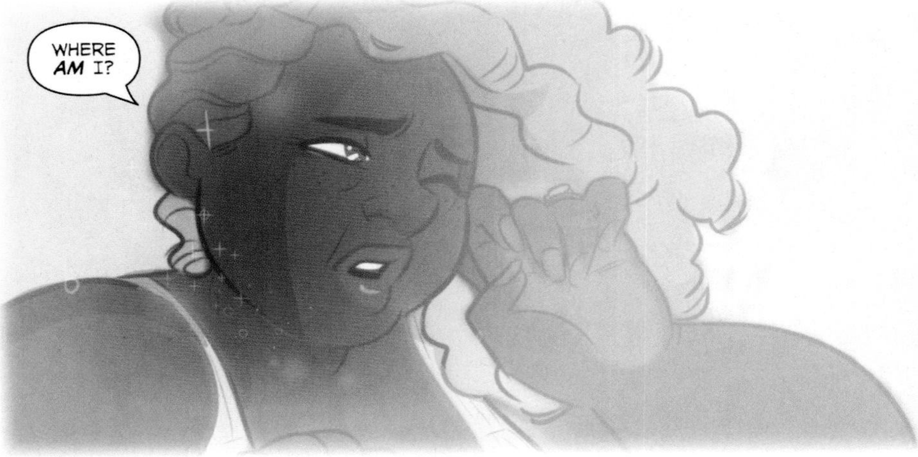
WHERE AM I?

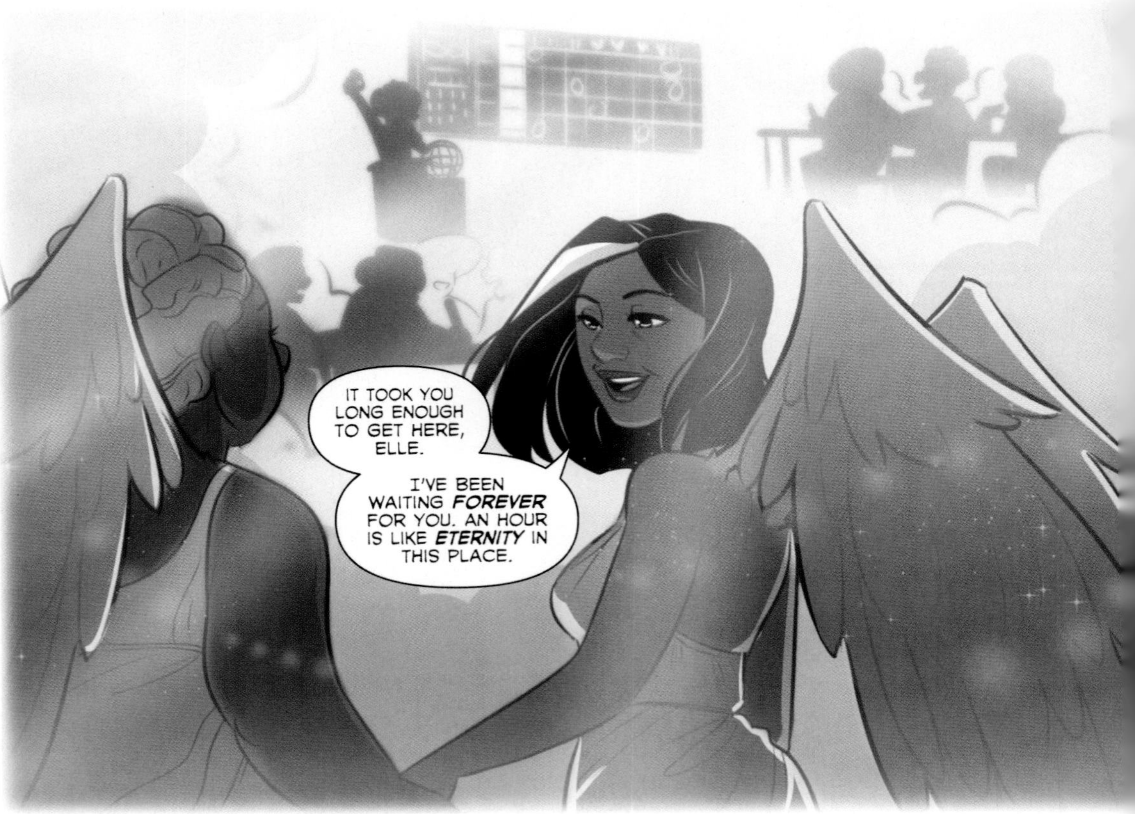
IT TOOK YOU LONG ENOUGH TO GET HERE, ELLE.
I'VE BEEN WAITING FOREVER FOR YOU. AN HOUR IS LIKE ETERNITY IN THIS PLACE.

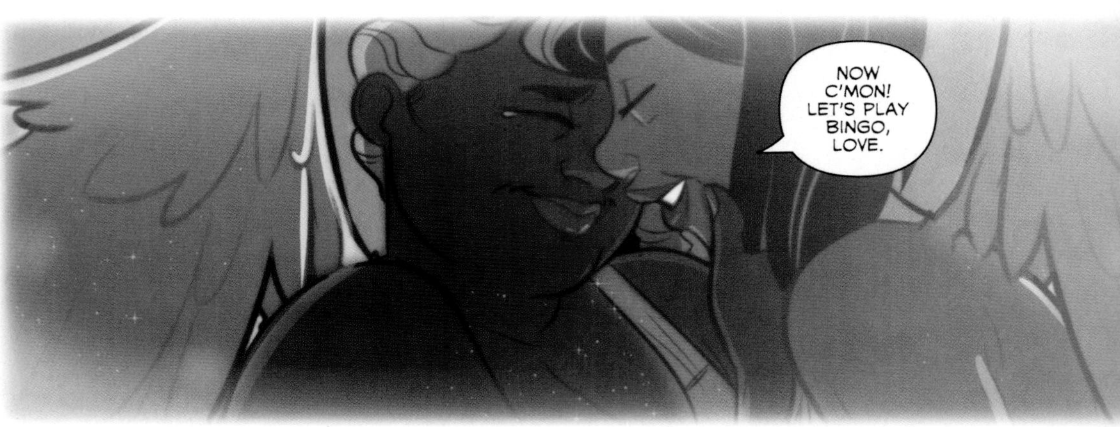
NOW C'MON! LET'S PLAY BINGO, LOVE.

BINGO LOVE

To everyone who supported our story of grandmothers in love, THANK YOU!

YOU made *Bingo Love* the success it is!

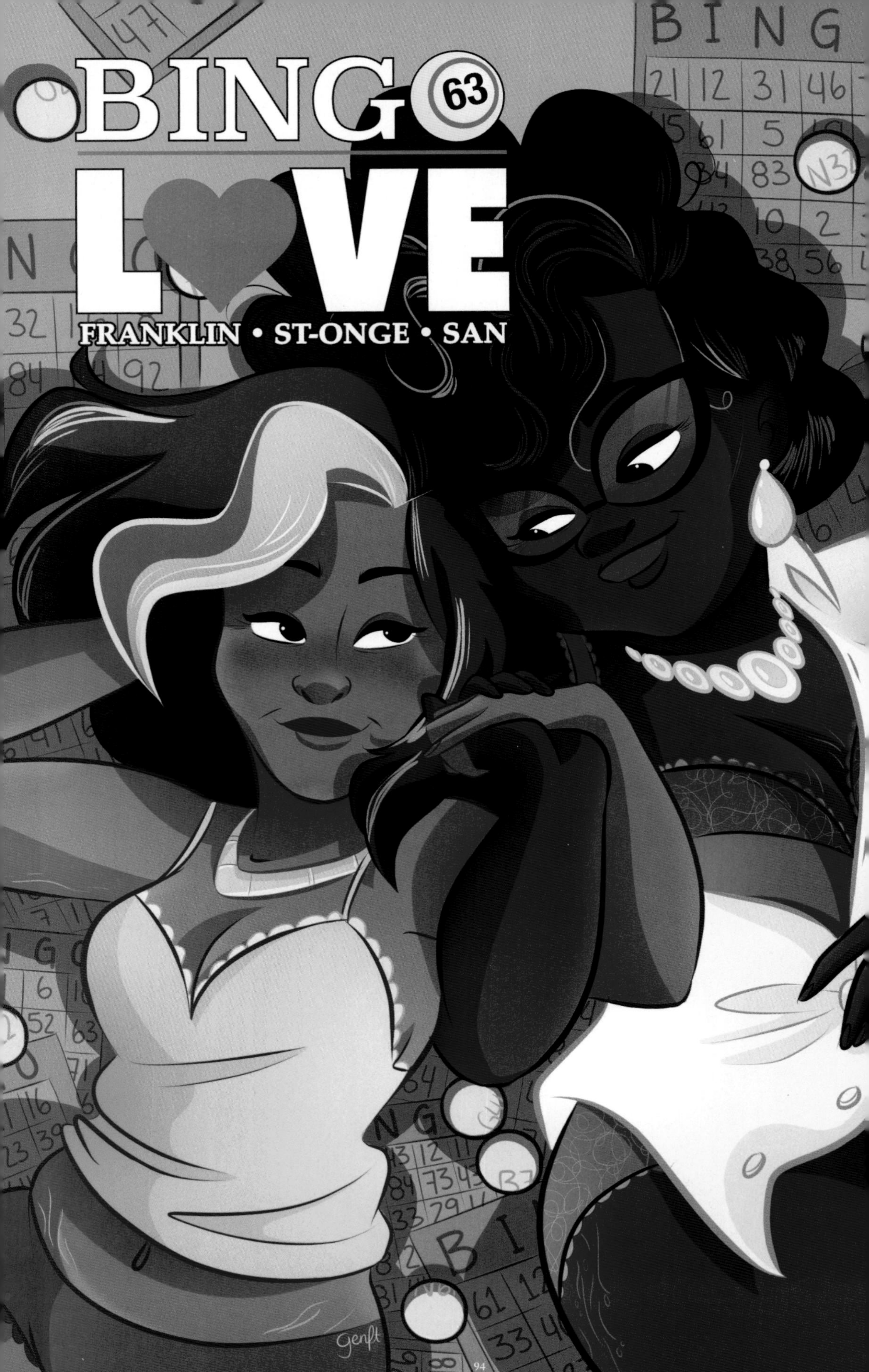
BINGO
63
LOVE
FRANKLIN • ST-ONGE • SAN

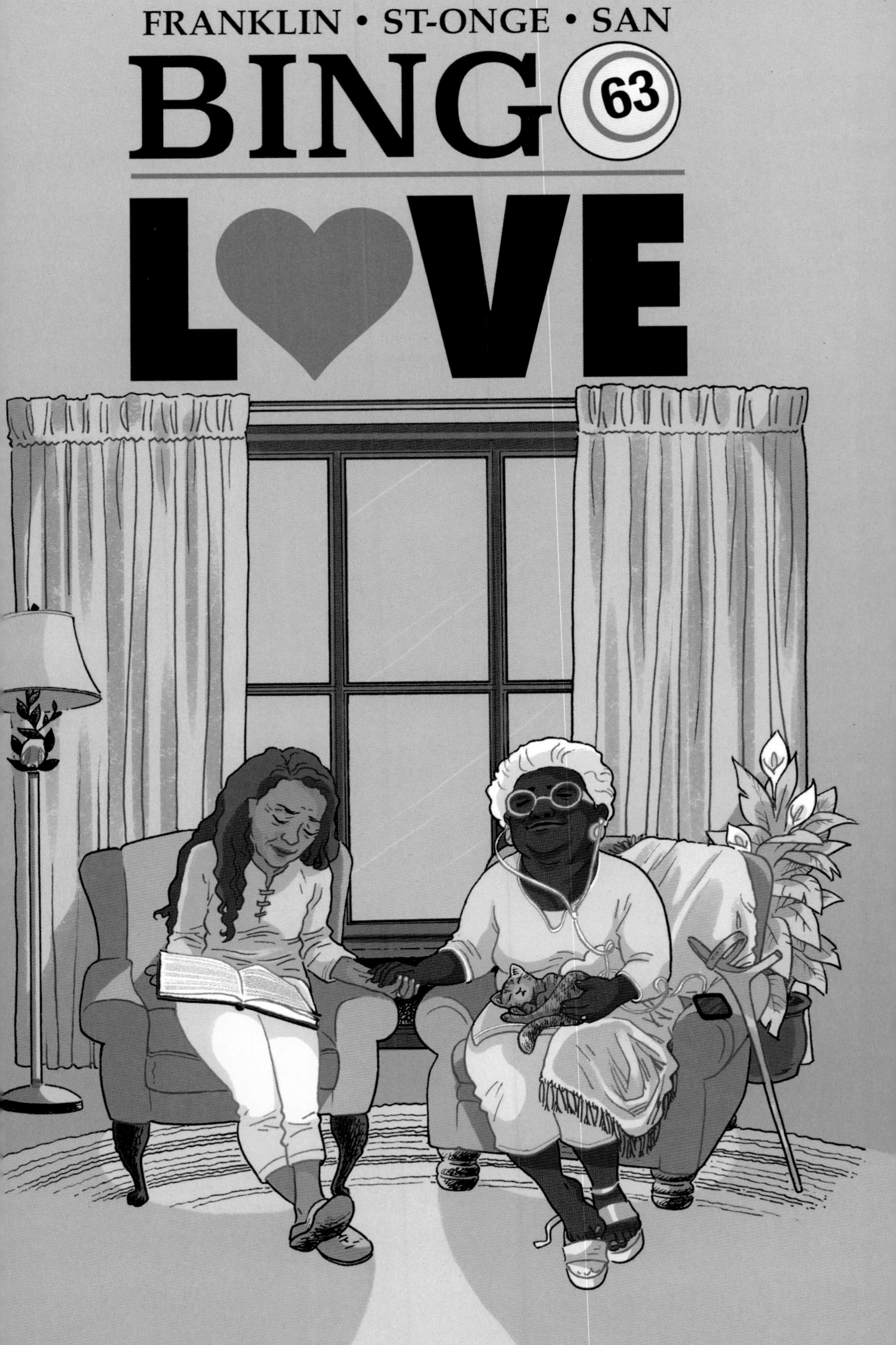
FRANKLIN • ST-ONGE • SAN
BINGO
63
LOVE

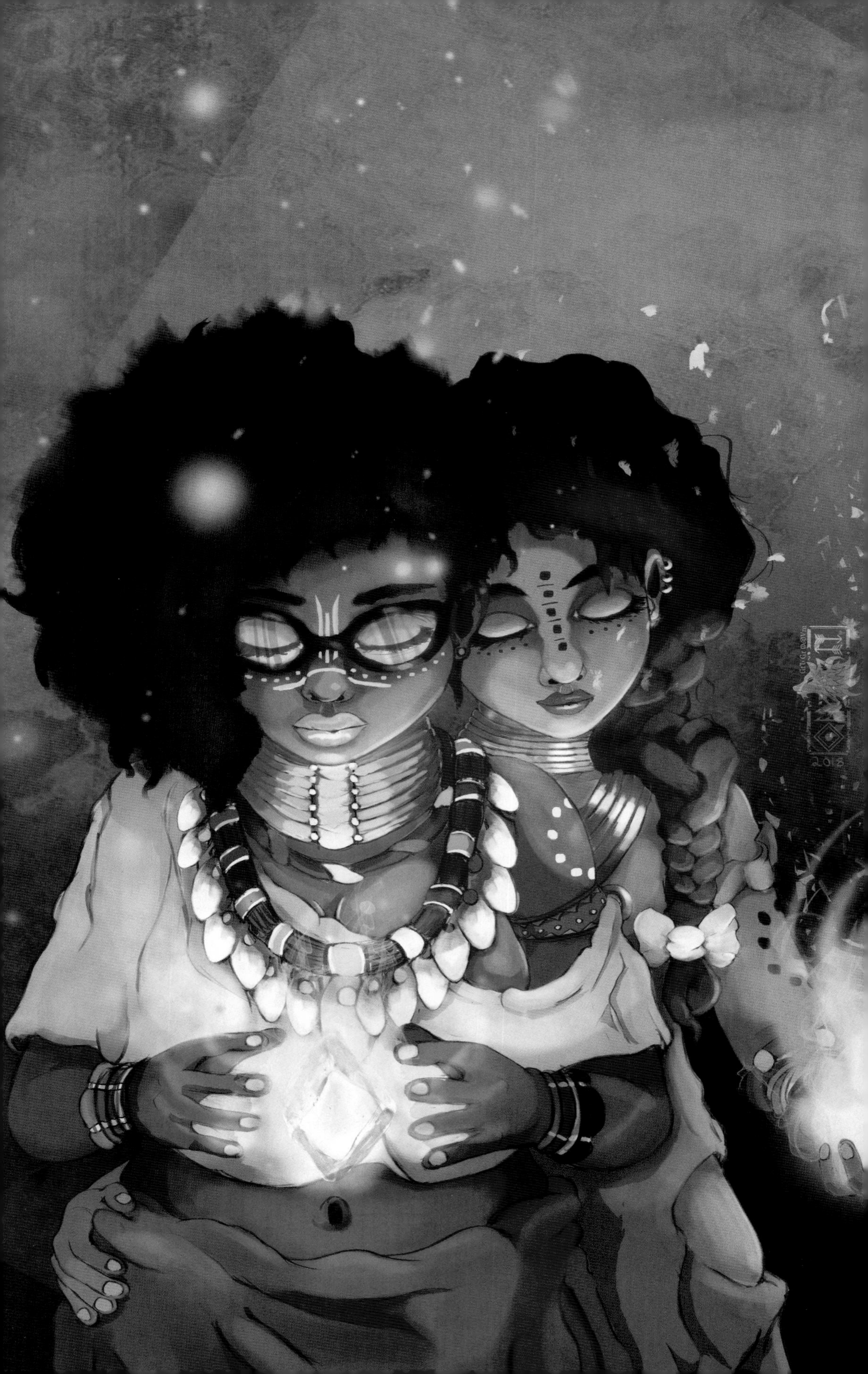

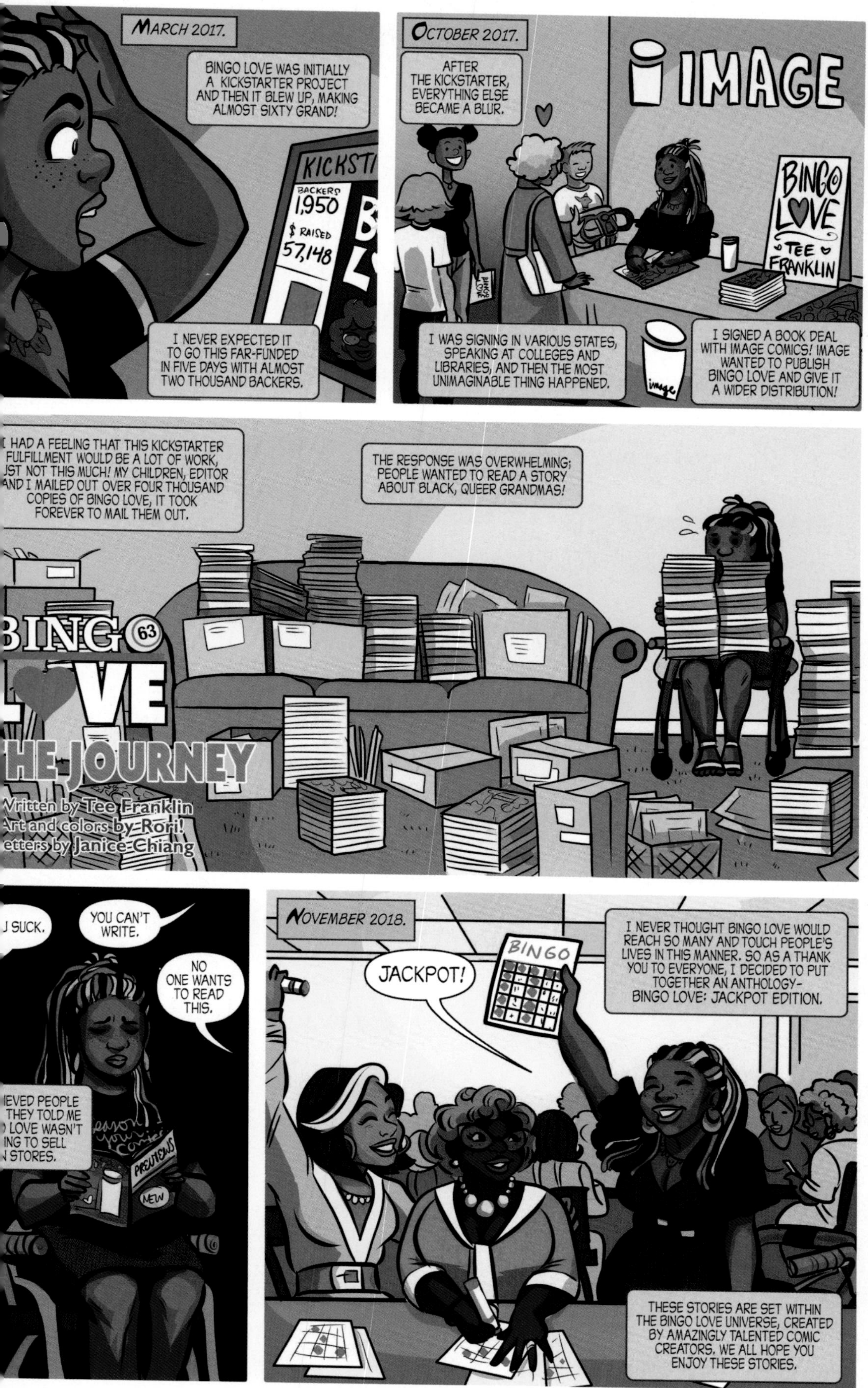
MARCH 2017.
BINGO LOVE WAS INITIALLY A KICKSTARTER PROJECT AND THEN IT BLEW UP, MAKING ALMOST SIXTY GRAND!
KICKST
BACKERS 1,950
$ RAISED 57,148
I NEVER EXPECTED IT TO GO THIS FAR-FUNDED IN FIVE DAYS WITH ALMOST TWO THOUSAND BACKERS.
OCTOBER 2017.
AFTER THE KICKSTARTER, EVERYTHING ELSE BECAME A BLUR.
IMAGE
BINGO LOVE TEE FRANKLIN
I WAS SIGNING IN VARIOUS STATES, SPEAKING AT COLLEGES AND LIBRARIES, AND THEN THE MOST UNIMAGINABLE THING HAPPENED.
image
I SIGNED A BOOK DEAL WITH IMAGE COMICS! IMAGE WANTED TO PUBLISH BINGO LOVE AND GIVE IT A WIDER DISTRIBUTION!
I HAD A FEELING THAT THIS KICKSTARTER FULFILLMENT WOULD BE A LOT OF WORK, JUST NOT THIS MUCH! MY CHILDREN, EDITOR AND I MAILED OUT OVER FOUR THOUSAND COPIES OF BINGO LOVE, IT TOOK FOREVER TO MAIL THEM OUT.
THE RESPONSE WAS OVERWHELMING; PEOPLE WANTED TO READ A STORY ABOUT BLACK, QUEER GRANDMAS!
BINGO 63
LOVE
THE JOURNEY
Written by Tee Franklin
Art and colors by Rori!
Letters by Janice Chiang
U SUCK.
YOU CAN'T WRITE.
NO ONE WANTS TO READ THIS.
IEVED PEOPLE THEY TOLD ME LOVE WASN'T ING TO SELL N STORES.
PREVIEWS
NEW
NOVEMBER 2018.
BINGO
JACKPOT!
I NEVER THOUGHT BINGO LOVE WOULD REACH SO MANY AND TOUCH PEOPLE'S LIVES IN THIS MANNER. SO AS A THANK YOU TO EVERYONE, I DECIDED TO PUT TOGETHER AN ANTHOLOGY- BINGO LOVE: JACKPOT EDITION.
THESE STORIES ARE SET WITHIN THE BINGO LOVE UNIVERSE, CREATED BY AMAZINGLY TALENTED COMIC CREATORS. WE ALL HOPE YOU ENJOY THESE STORIES.

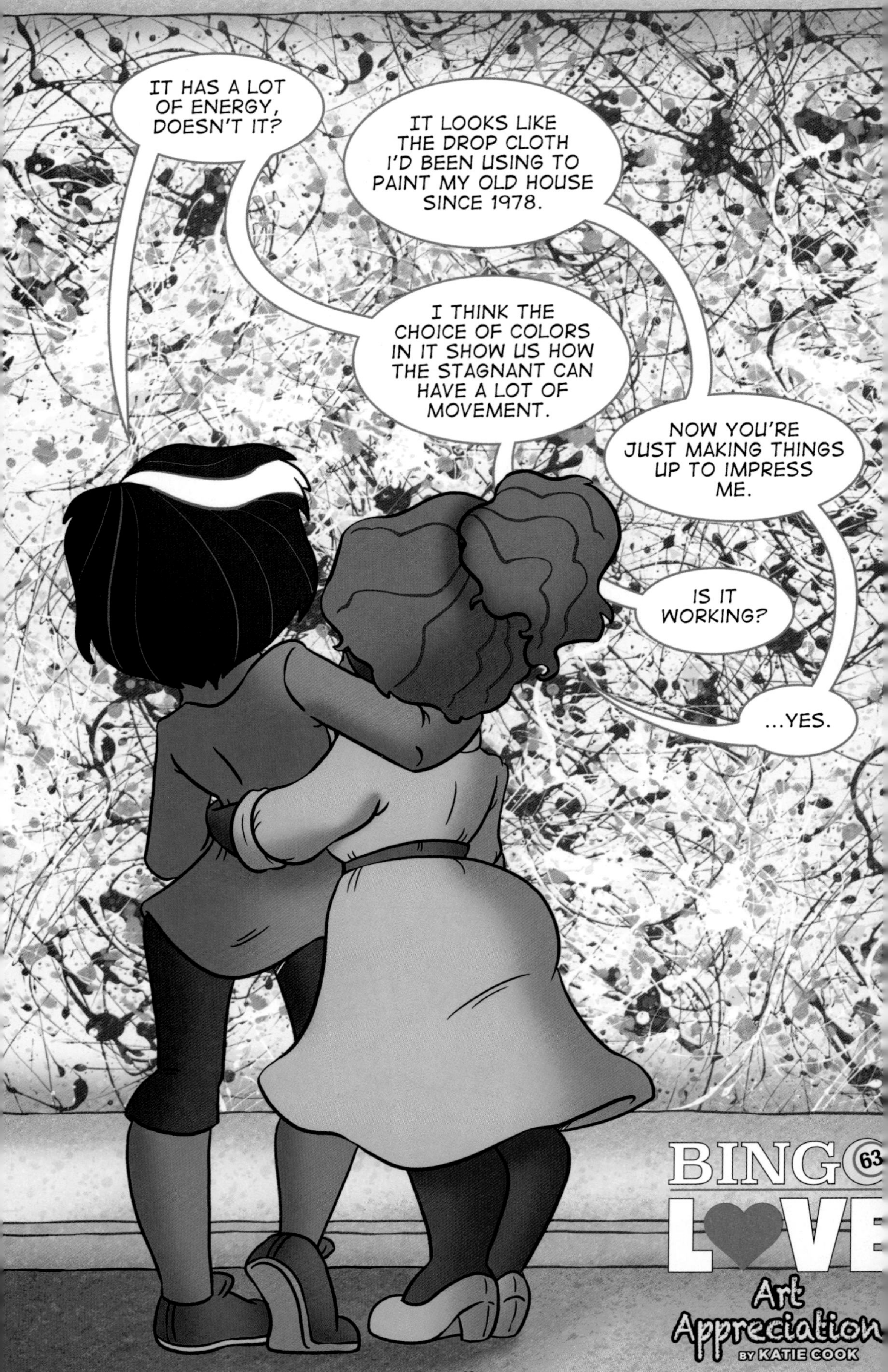
IT HAS A LOT OF ENERGY, DOESN'T IT?
IT LOOKS LIKE THE DROP CLOTH I'D BEEN USING TO PAINT MY OLD HOUSE SINCE 1978.
I THINK THE CHOICE OF COLORS IN IT SHOW US HOW THE STAGNANT CAN HAVE A LOT OF MOVEMENT.
NOW YOU'RE JUST MAKING THINGS UP TO IMPRESS ME.
IS IT WORKING?
...YES.
BINGO 63
LOVE
Art Appreciation
BY KATIE COOK

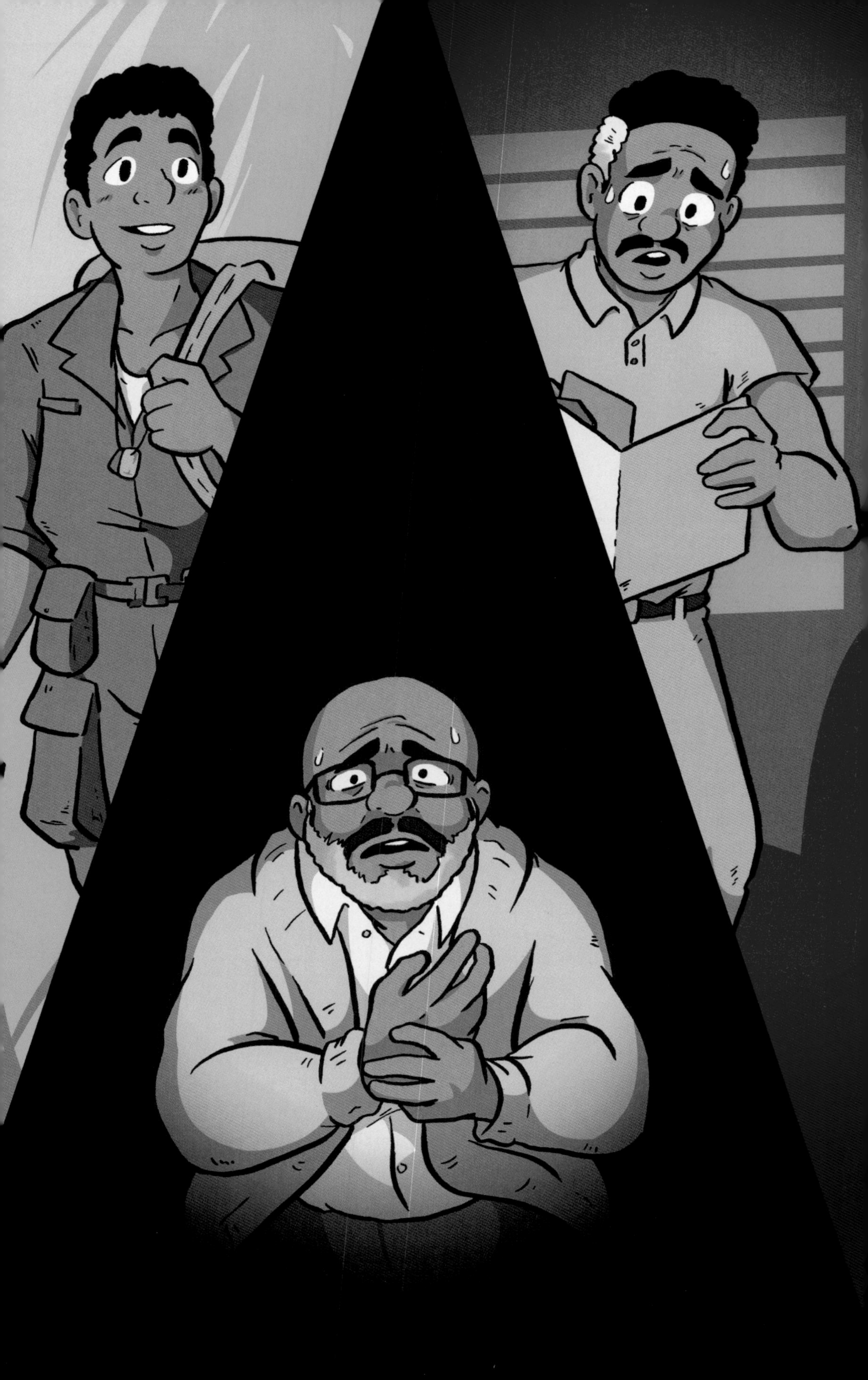

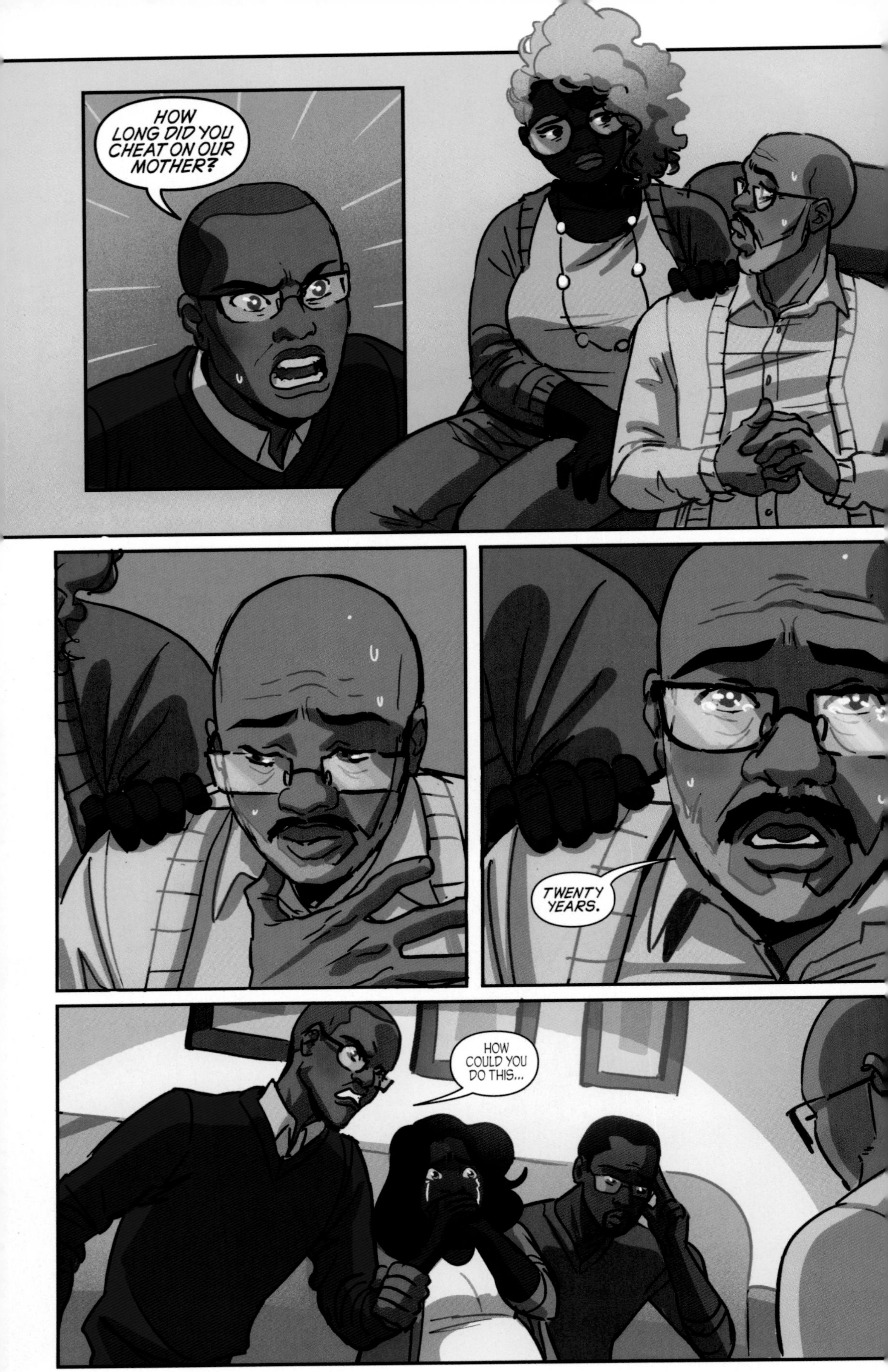
HOW LONG DID YOU CHEAT ON OUR MOTHER?
TWENTY YEARS.
HOW COULD YOU DO THIS...

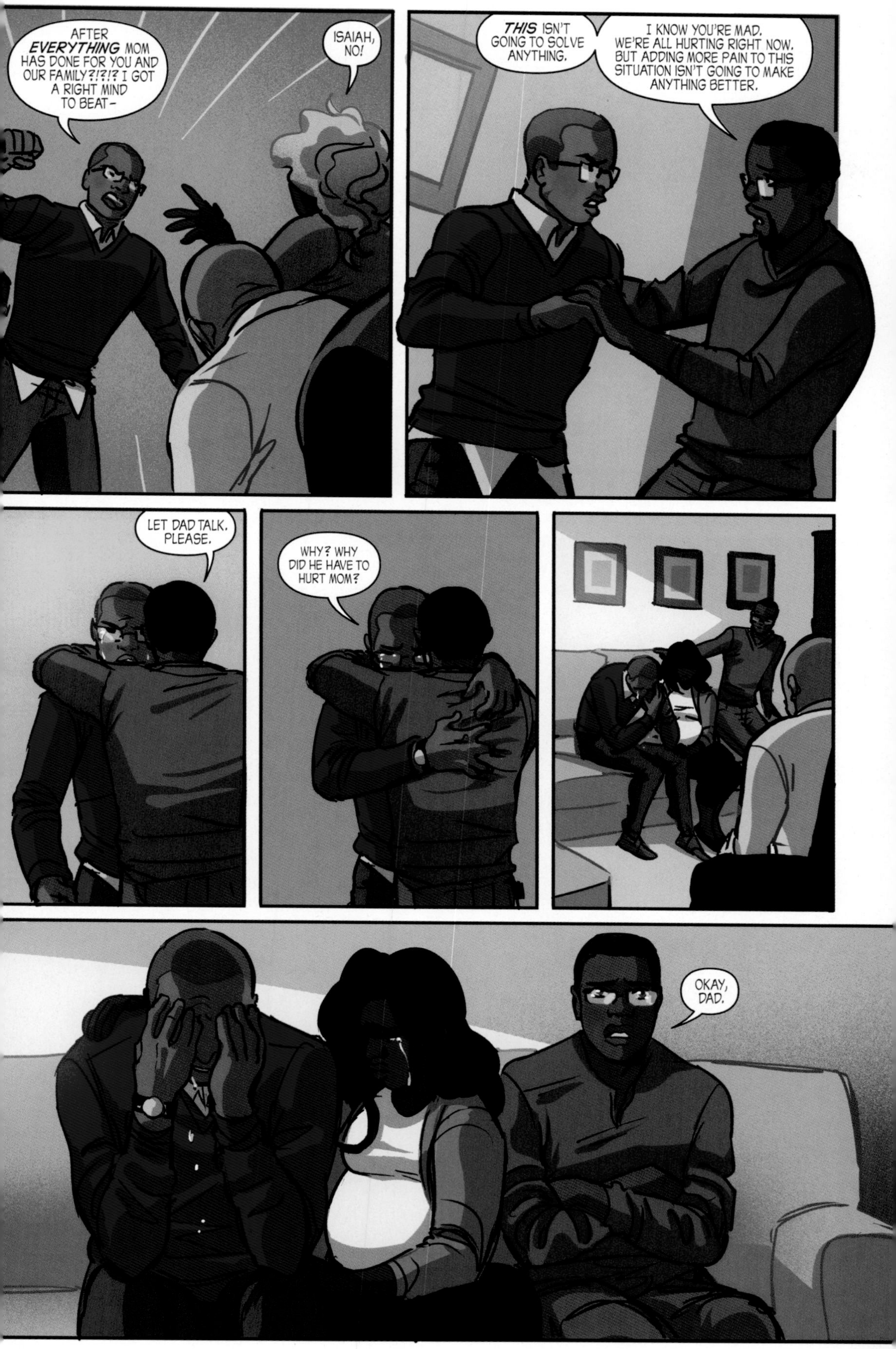
AFTER EVERYTHING MOM HAS DONE FOR YOU AND OUR FAMILY?!?!? I GOT A RIGHT MIND TO BEAT–
ISAIAH, NO!
THIS ISN'T GOING TO SOLVE ANYTHING.
I KNOW YOU'RE MAD. WE'RE ALL HURTING RIGHT NOW. BUT ADDING MORE PAIN TO THIS SITUATION ISN'T GOING TO MAKE ANYTHING BETTER.
LET DAD TALK. PLEASE.
WHY? WHY DID HE HAVE TO HURT MOM?
OKAY, DAD.

SIGH

1968.

"I SERVED IN VIETNAM...

"IT WAS THERE THAT I MET ADAM NGUYEN.

"AFTER A FE WEEKS, WE BEC THE BEST O FRIENDS.

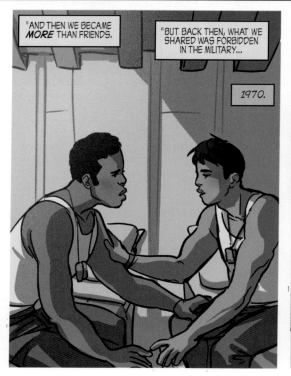

"AND THEN WE BECAME *MORE* THAN FRIENDS.

"BUT BACK THEN, WHAT WE SHARED WAS FORBIDDEN IN THE MILITARY...

1970.

"SO WE DID OUR BEST TO KEEP IT A *SECRET.*"

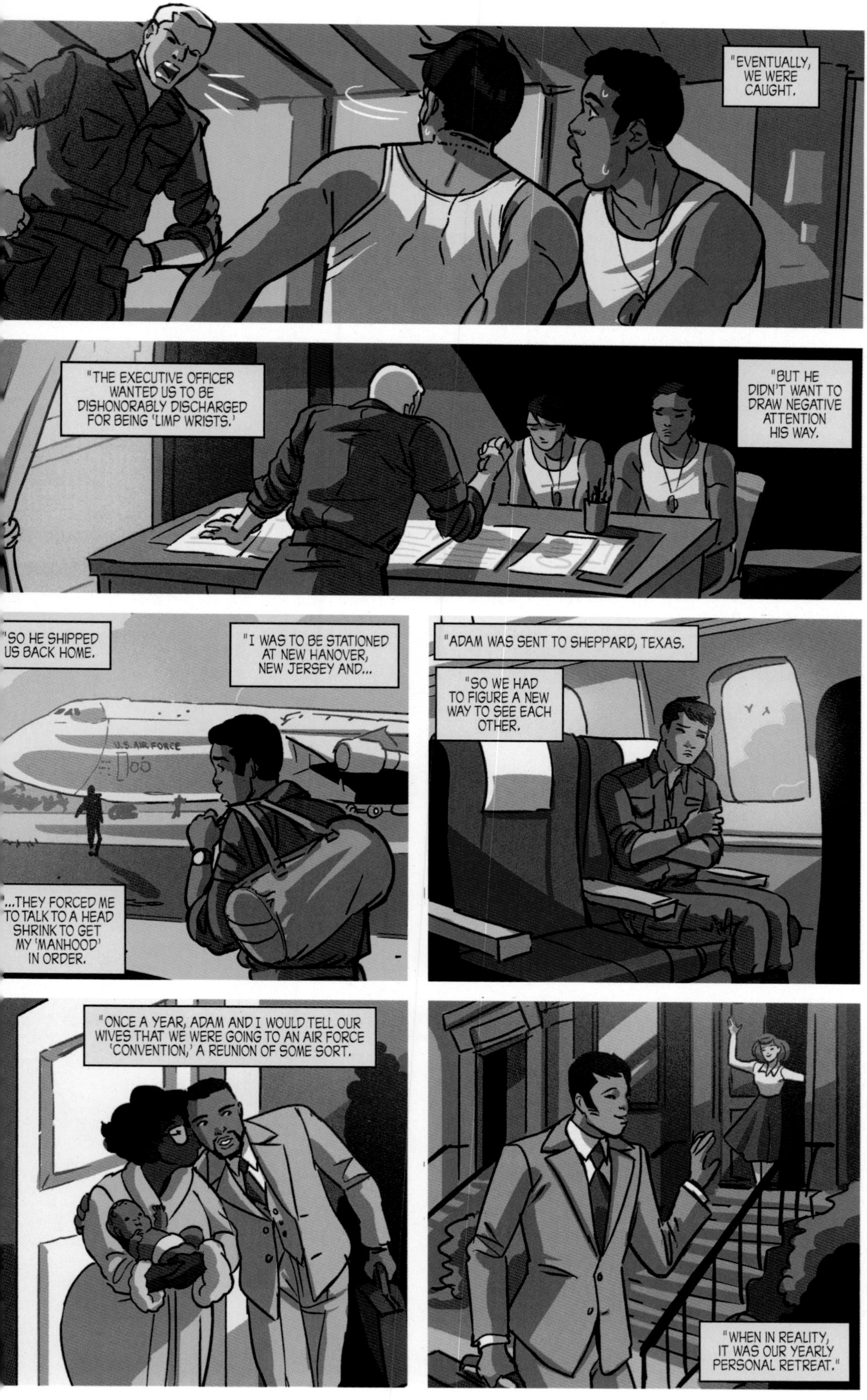
"EVENTUALLY, WE WERE CAUGHT.
"THE EXECUTIVE OFFICER WANTED US TO BE DISHONORABLY DISCHARGED FOR BEING 'LIMP WRISTS.'
"BUT HE DIDN'T WANT TO DRAW NEGATIVE ATTENTION HIS WAY.
"SO HE SHIPPED US BACK HOME.
"I WAS TO BE STATIONED AT NEW HANOVER, NEW JERSEY AND...
...THEY FORCED ME TO TALK TO A HEAD SHRINK TO GET MY 'MANHOOD' IN ORDER.
U.S. AIR FORCE
"ADAM WAS SENT TO SHEPPARD, TEXAS.
"SO WE HAD TO FIGURE A NEW WAY TO SEE EACH OTHER.
"ONCE A YEAR, ADAM AND I WOULD TELL OUR WIVES THAT WE WERE GOING TO AN AIR FORCE 'CONVENTION,' A REUNION OF SOME SORT.
"WHEN IN REALITY, IT WAS OUR YEARLY PERSONAL RETREAT."

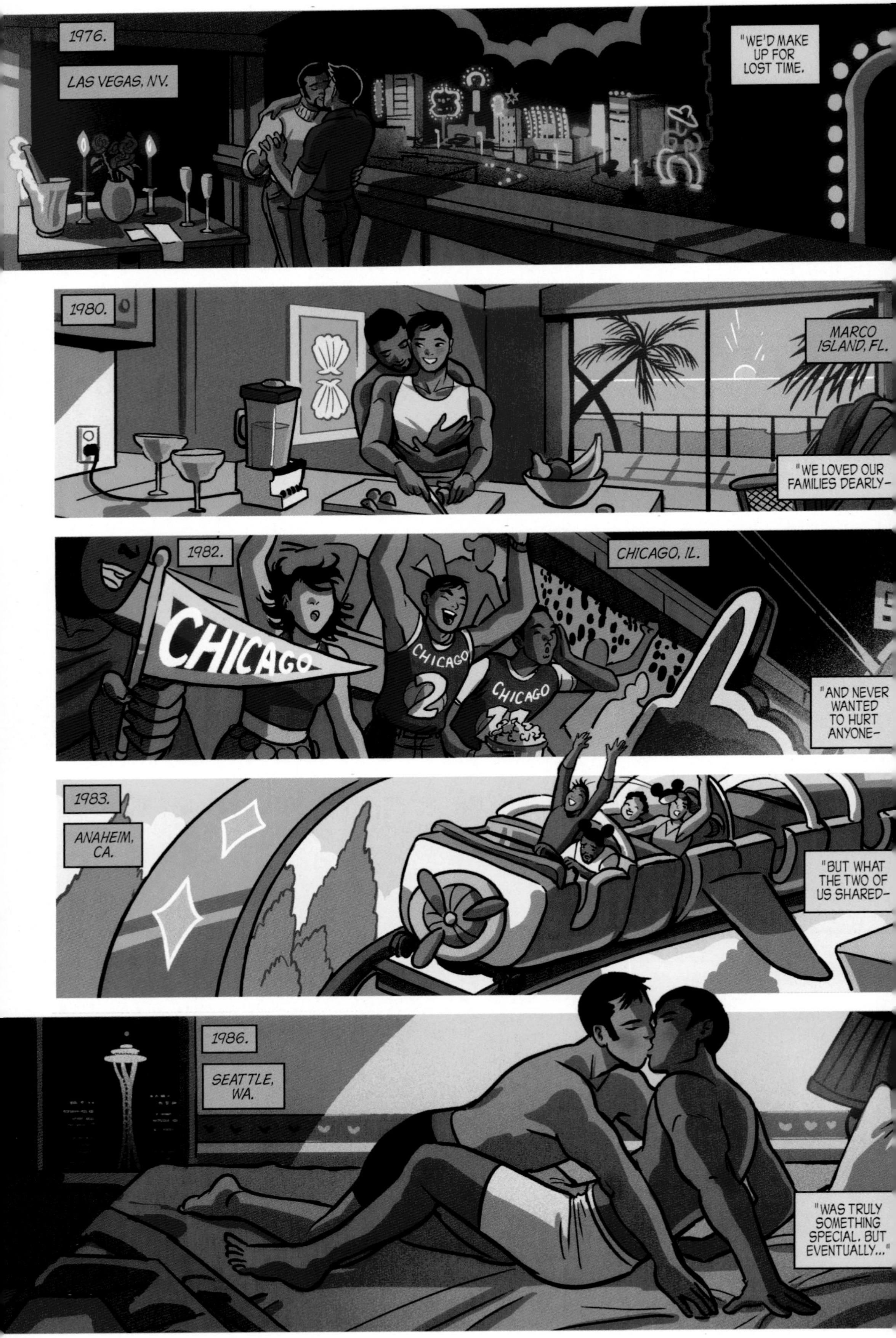
1976.
LAS VEGAS, NV.
"WE'D MAKE UP FOR LOST TIME.
1980.
MARCO ISLAND, FL.
"WE LOVED OUR FAMILIES DEARLY-
1982.
CHICAGO, IL.
CHICAGO
CHICAGO 2
CHICAGO
"AND NEVER WANTED TO HURT ANYONE-
1983.
ANAHEIM, CA.
"BUT WHAT THE TWO OF US SHARED-
1986.
SEATTLE, WA.
"WAS TRULY SOMETHING SPECIAL. BUT EVENTUALLY..."

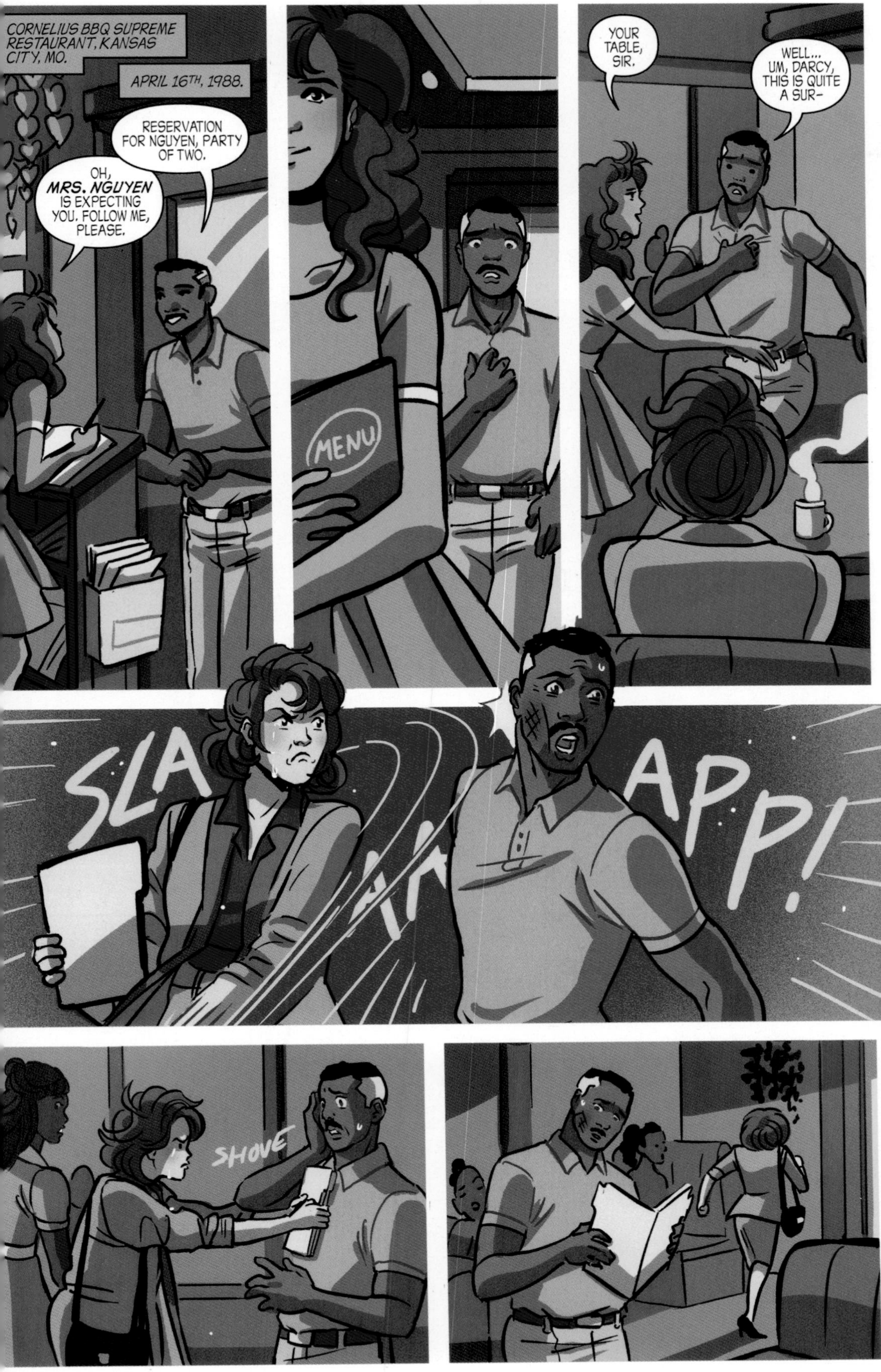
CORNELIUS BBQ SUPREME RESTAURANT, KANSAS CITY, MO.
APRIL 16TH, 1988.
RESERVATION FOR NGUYEN, PARTY OF TWO.
OH, MRS. NGUYEN IS EXPECTING YOU. FOLLOW ME, PLEASE.
MENU
YOUR TABLE, SIR.
WELL... UM, DARCY, THIS IS QUITE A SUR-
SLAAAPP!
SHOVE

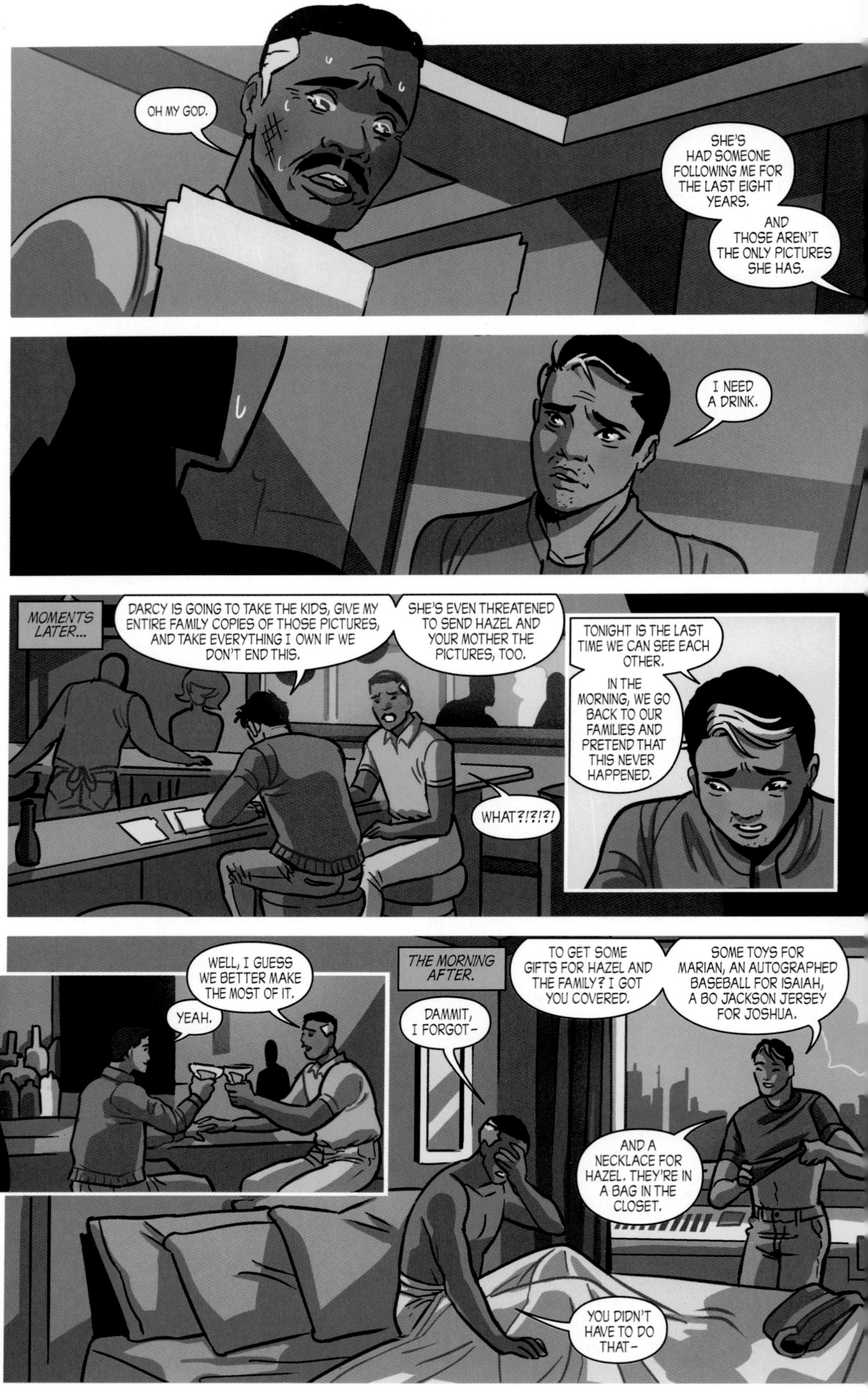
OH MY GOD.
SHE'S HAD SOMEONE FOLLOWING ME FOR THE LAST EIGHT YEARS.
AND THOSE AREN'T THE ONLY PICTURES SHE HAS.
I NEED A DRINK.
MOMENTS LATER...
DARCY IS GOING TO TAKE THE KIDS, GIVE MY ENTIRE FAMILY COPIES OF THOSE PICTURES, AND TAKE EVERYTHING I OWN IF WE DON'T END THIS.
SHE'S EVEN THREATENED TO SEND HAZEL AND YOUR MOTHER THE PICTURES, TOO.
WHAT?!?!?!
TONIGHT IS THE LAST TIME WE CAN SEE EACH OTHER.
IN THE MORNING, WE GO BACK TO OUR FAMILIES AND PRETEND THAT THIS NEVER HAPPENED.
WELL, I GUESS WE BETTER MAKE THE MOST OF IT.
YEAH.
THE MORNING AFTER.
DAMMIT, I FORGOT-
TO GET SOME GIFTS FOR HAZEL AND THE FAMILY? I GOT YOU COVERED.
SOME TOYS FOR MARIAN, AN AUTOGRAPHED BASEBALL FOR ISAIAH, A BO JACKSON JERSEY FOR JOSHUA.
AND A NECKLACE FOR HAZEL. THEY'RE IN A BAG IN THE CLOSET.
YOU DIDN'T HAVE TO DO THAT-

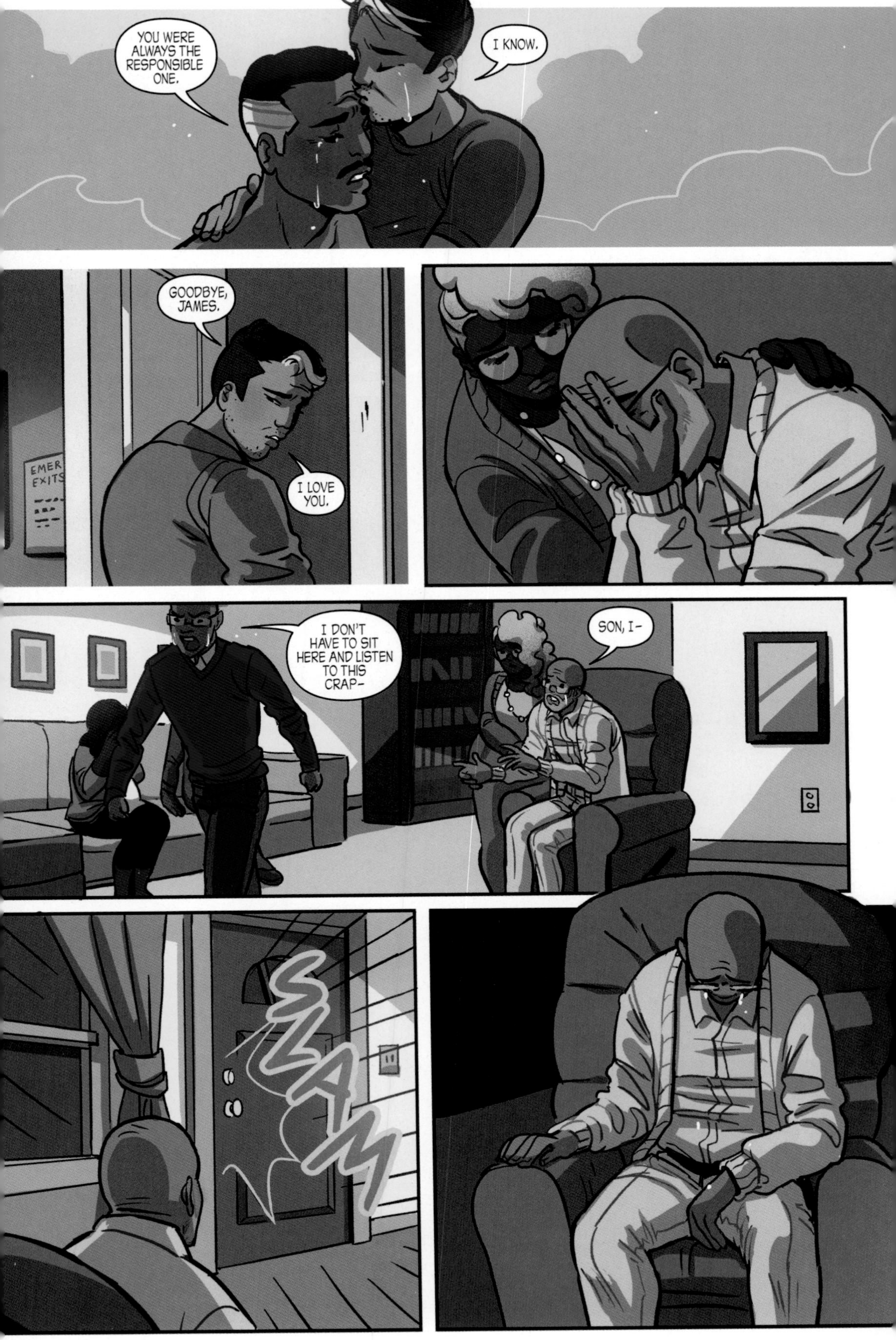

YOU WERE ALWAYS THE RESPONSIBLE ONE.
I KNOW.
GOODBYE, JAMES.
I LOVE YOU.
EMER EXITS
I DON'T HAVE TO SIT HERE AND LISTEN TO THIS CRAP-
SON, I-
SLAM

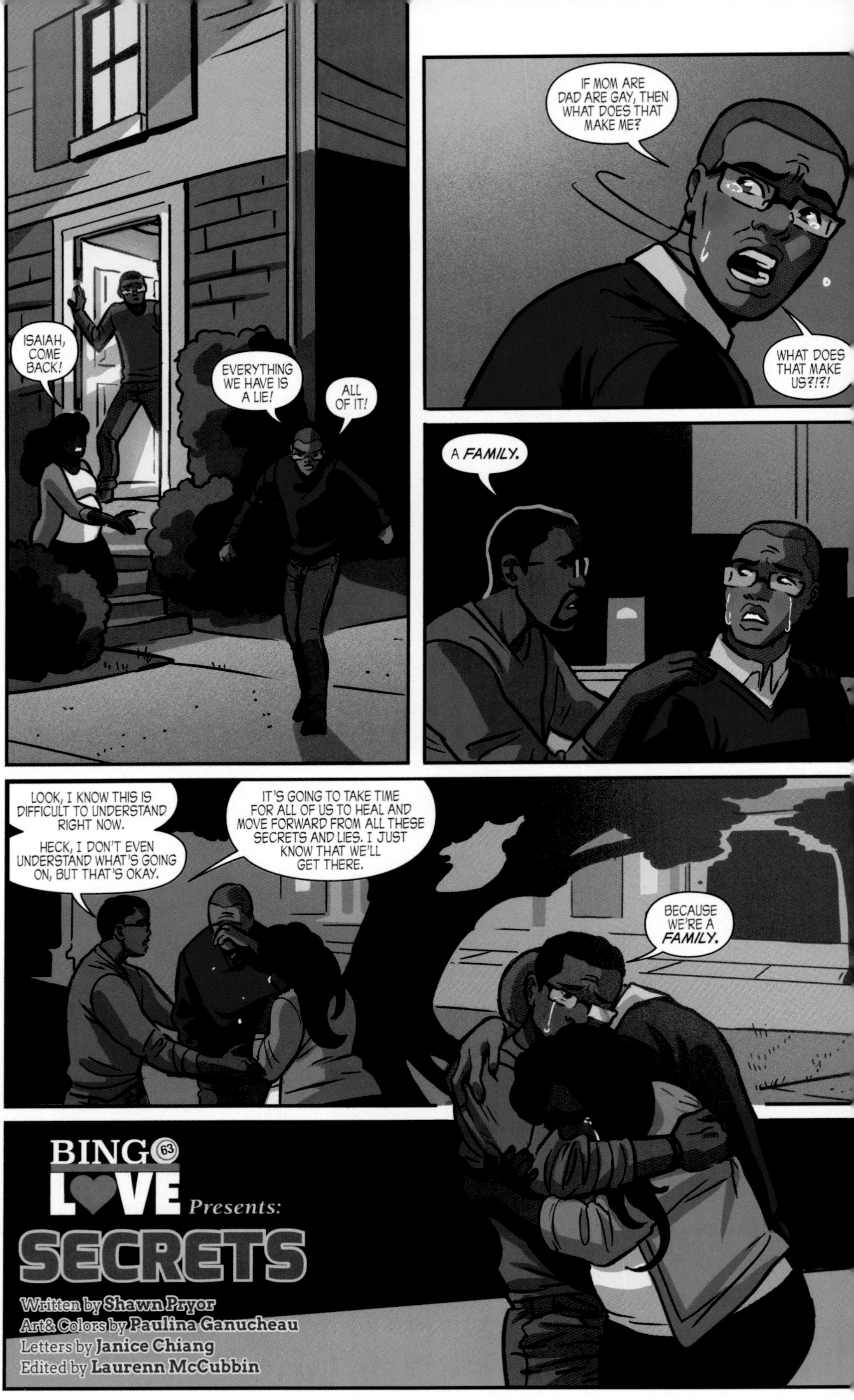

ISAIAH, COME BACK!
EVERYTHING WE HAVE IS A LIE!
ALL OF IT!
IF MOM ARE DAD ARE GAY, THEN WHAT DOES THAT MAKE ME?
WHAT DOES THAT MAKE US?!?!
A FAMILY.
LOOK, I KNOW THIS IS DIFFICULT TO UNDERSTAND RIGHT NOW.
HECK, I DON'T EVEN UNDERSTAND WHAT'S GOING ON, BUT THAT'S OKAY.
IT'S GOING TO TAKE TIME FOR ALL OF US TO HEAL AND MOVE FORWARD FROM ALL THESE SECRETS AND LIES. I JUST KNOW THAT WE'LL GET THERE.
BECAUSE WE'RE A FAMILY.
BINGO 63 LOVE Presents:
SECRETS
Written by Shawn Pryor
Art & Colors by Paulina Ganucheau
Letters by Janice Chiang
Edited by Laurenn McCubbin

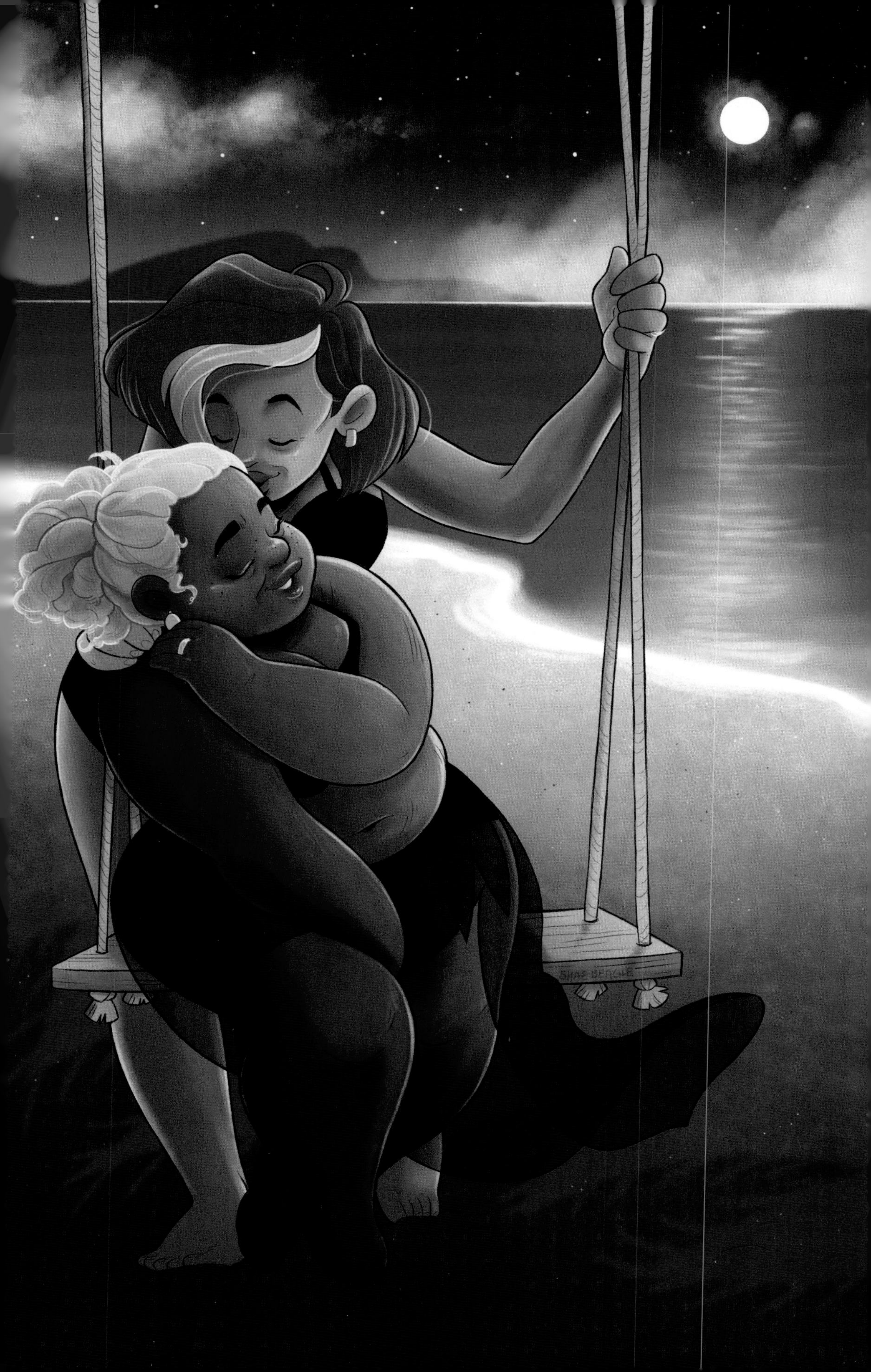
SHAE BEAGLE

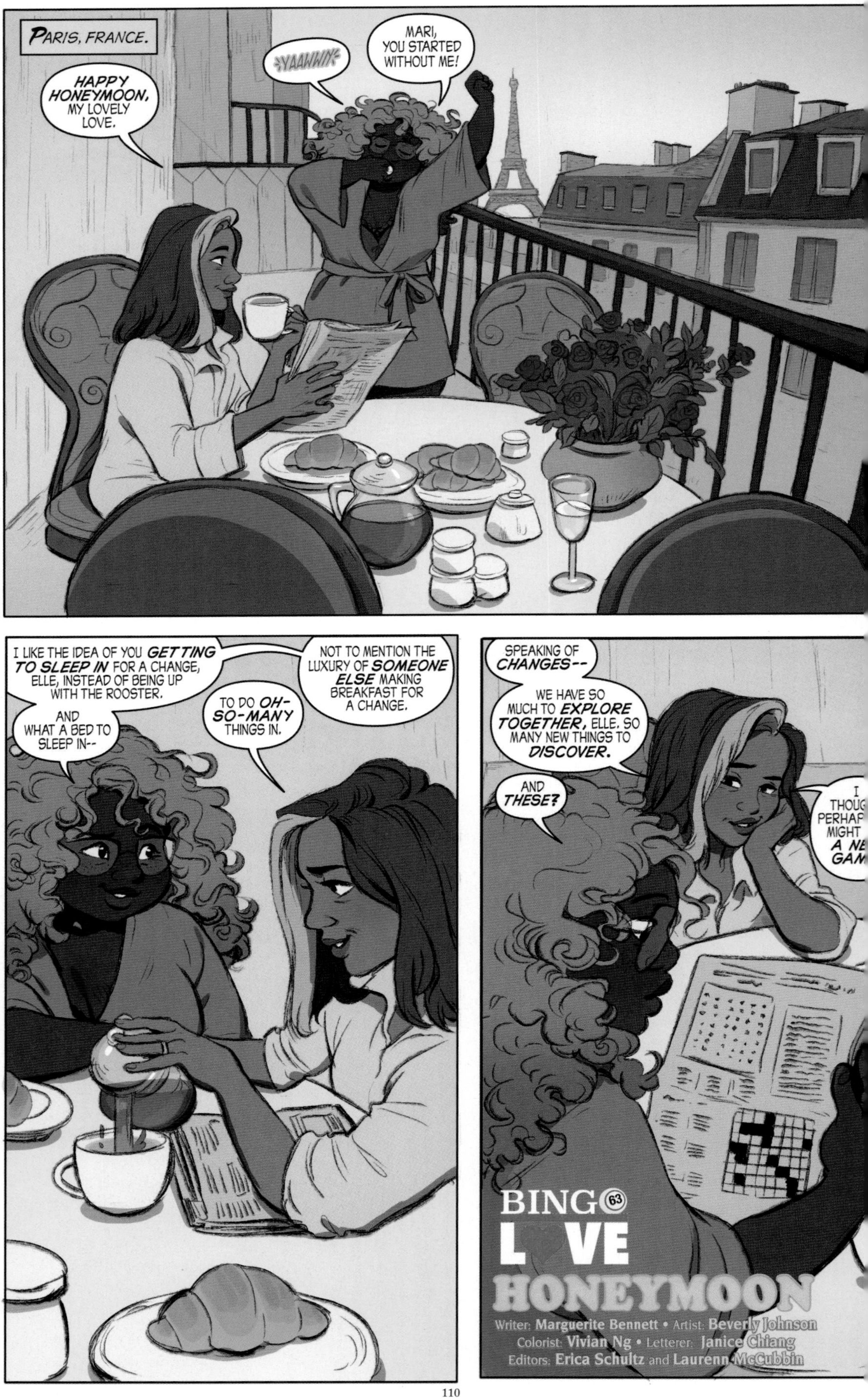
PARIS, FRANCE.
HAPPY HONEYMOON, MY LOVELY LOVE.
YAAWWN
MARI, YOU STARTED WITHOUT ME!
I LIKE THE IDEA OF YOU GETTING TO SLEEP IN FOR A CHANGE, ELLE, INSTEAD OF BEING UP WITH THE ROOSTER.
AND WHAT A BED TO SLEEP IN--
TO DO OH-SO-MANY THINGS IN.
NOT TO MENTION THE LUXURY OF SOMEONE ELSE MAKING BREAKFAST FOR A CHANGE.
SPEAKING OF CHANGES--
WE HAVE SO MUCH TO EXPLORE TOGETHER, ELLE. SO MANY NEW THINGS TO DISCOVER.
AND THESE?
BINGO 63
LOVE
HONEYMOON
Writer: Marguerite Bennett • Artist: Beverly Johnson
Colorist: Vivian Ng • Letterer: Janice Chiang
Editors: Erica Schultz and Laurenn McCubbin

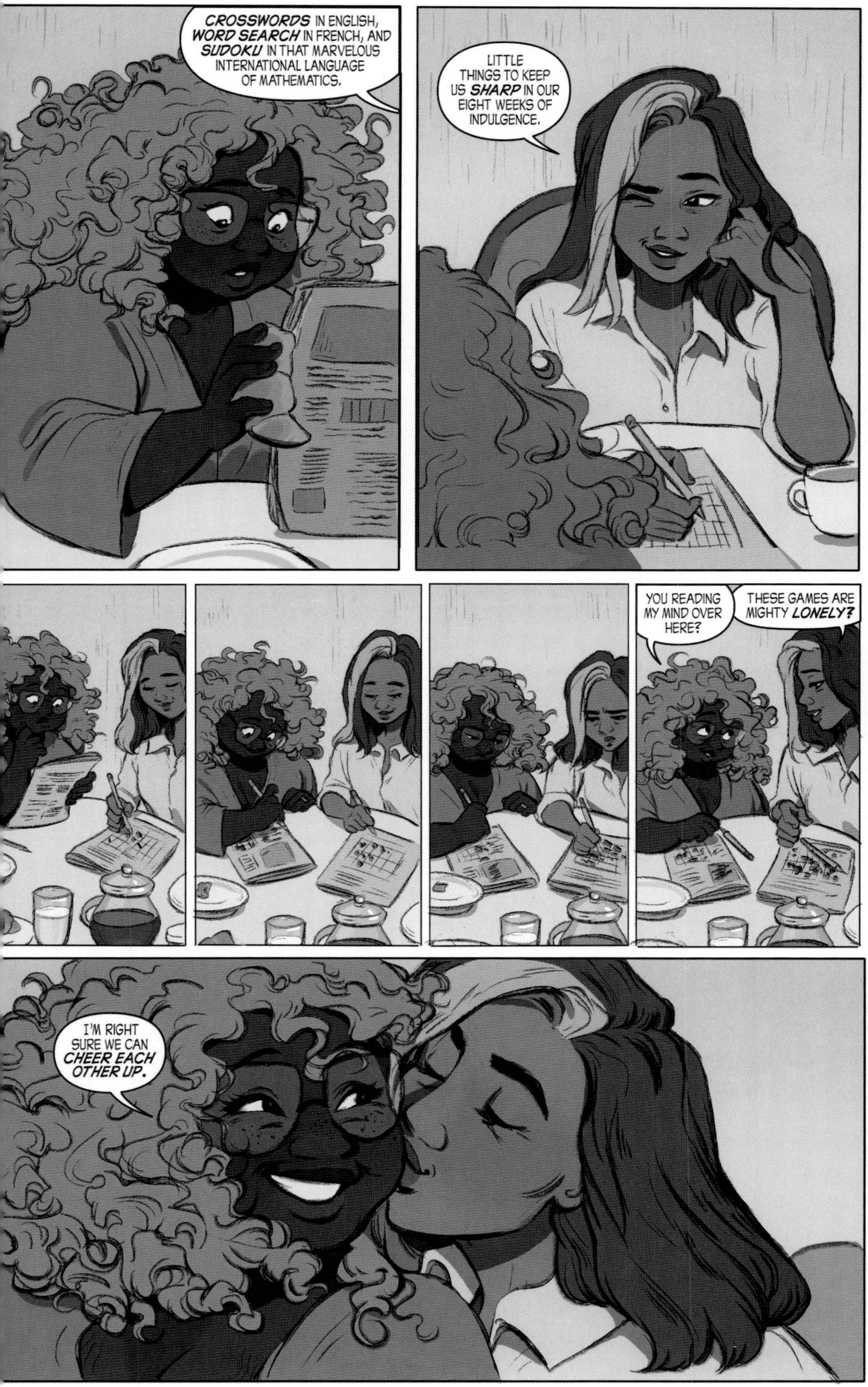
CROSSWORDS IN ENGLISH, WORD SEARCH IN FRENCH, AND SUDOKU IN THAT MARVELOUS INTERNATIONAL LANGUAGE OF MATHEMATICS.
LITTLE THINGS TO KEEP US SHARP IN OUR EIGHT WEEKS OF INDULGENCE.
YOU READING MY MIND OVER HERE?
THESE GAMES ARE MIGHTY LONELY?
I'M RIGHT SURE WE CAN CHEER EACH OTHER UP.

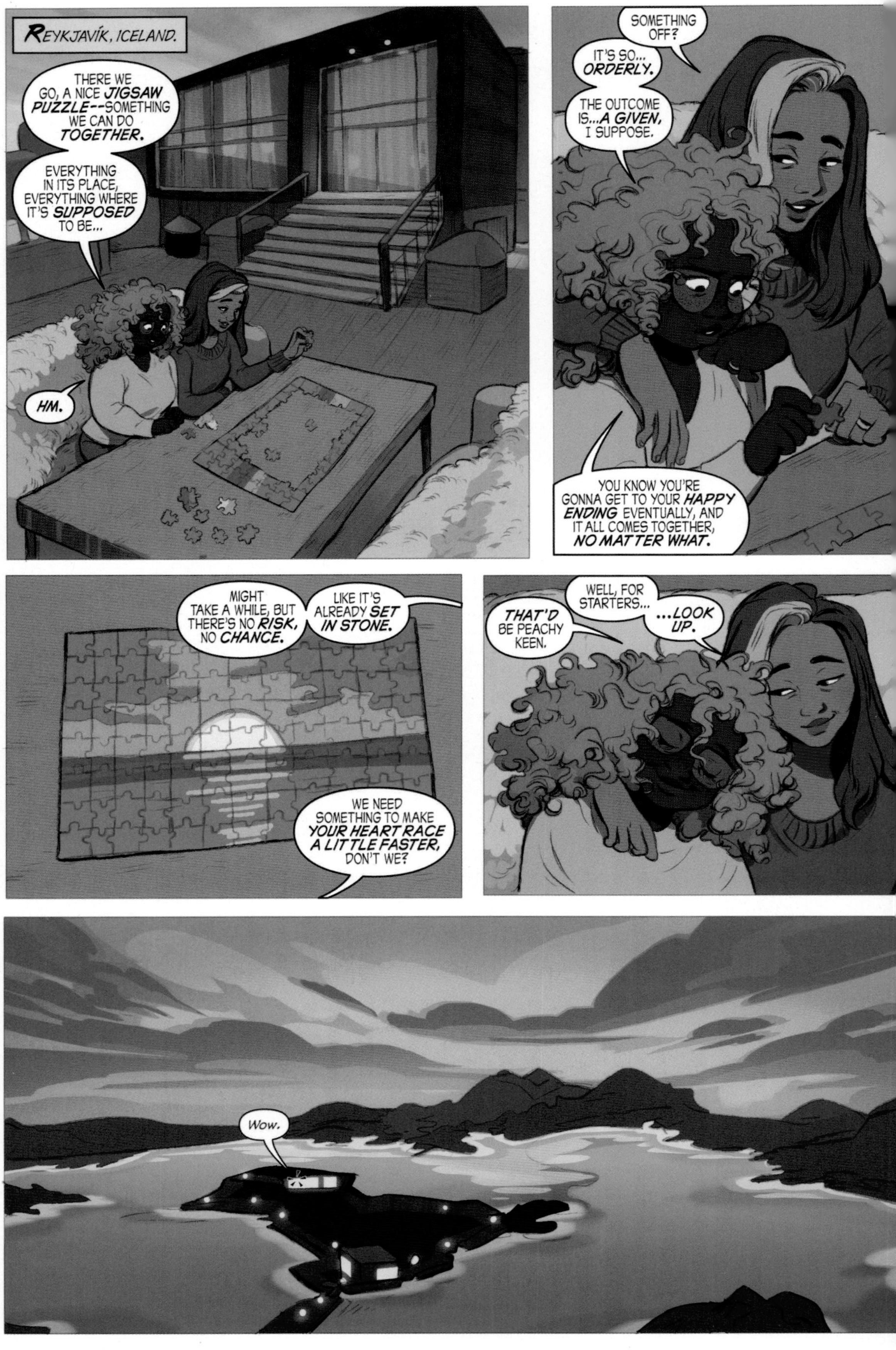
REYKJAVÍK, ICELAND.
THERE WE GO, A NICE JIGSAW PUZZLE--SOMETHING WE CAN DO TOGETHER.
EVERYTHING IN ITS PLACE, EVERYTHING WHERE IT'S SUPPOSED TO BE...
HM.
SOMETHING OFF?
IT'S SO... ORDERLY.
THE OUTCOME IS...A GIVEN, I SUPPOSE.
YOU KNOW YOU'RE GONNA GET TO YOUR HAPPY ENDING EVENTUALLY, AND IT ALL COMES TOGETHER, NO MATTER WHAT.
MIGHT TAKE A WHILE, BUT THERE'S NO RISK, NO CHANCE.
LIKE IT'S ALREADY SET IN STONE.
WE NEED SOMETHING TO MAKE YOUR HEART RACE A LITTLE FASTER, DON'T WE?
THAT'D BE PEACHY KEEN.
WELL, FOR STARTERS...
...LOOK UP.
Wow.

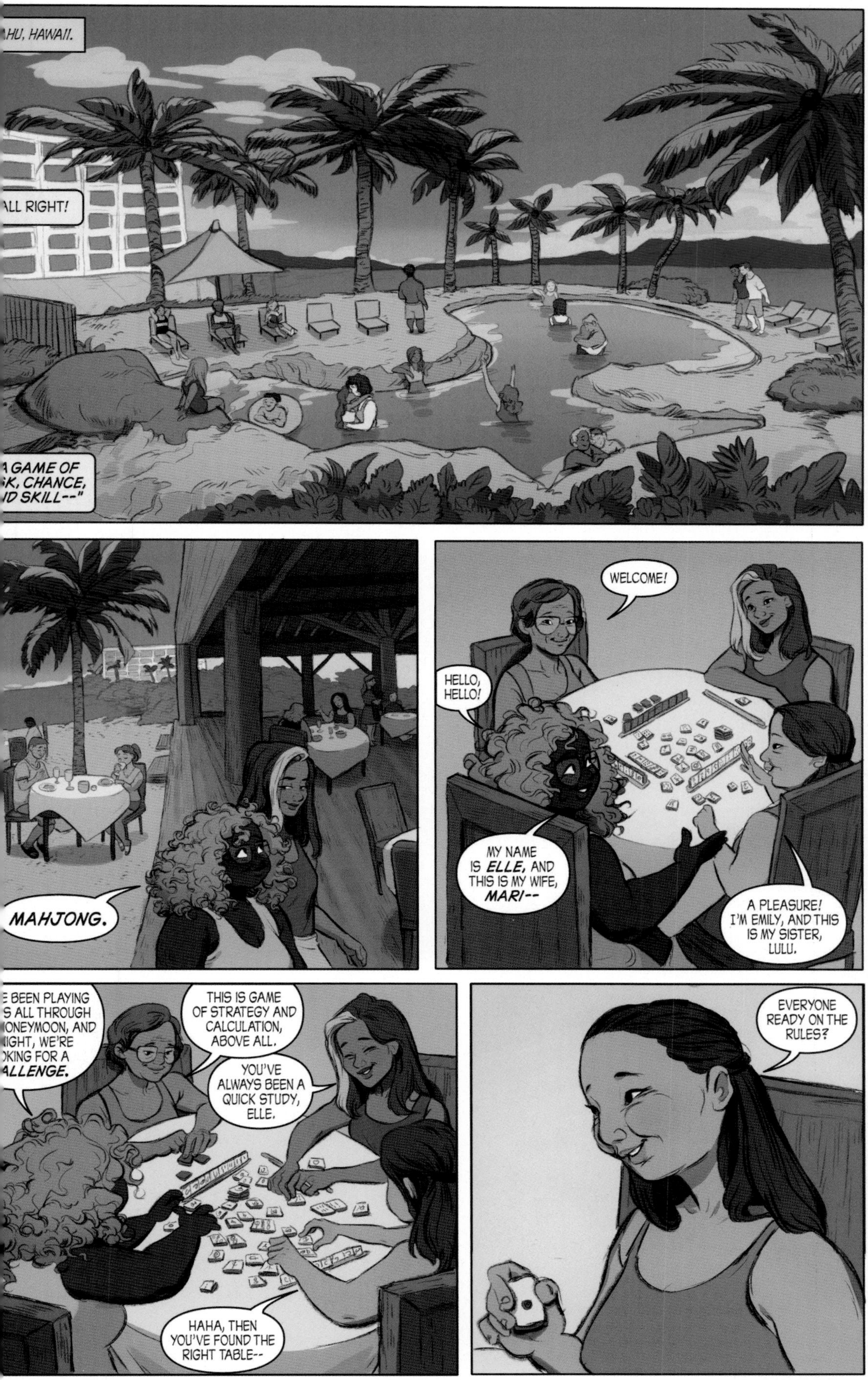

HU, HAWAII.
ALL RIGHT!
A GAME OF
SK, CHANCE,
ID SKILL--"
MAHJONG.
WELCOME!
HELLO, HELLO!
MY NAME IS ELLE, AND THIS IS MY WIFE, MARI--
A PLEASURE! I'M EMILY, AND THIS IS MY SISTER, LULU.
E BEEN PLAYING S ALL THROUGH ONEYMOON, AND NIGHT, WE'RE OKING FOR A ALLENGE.
THIS IS GAME OF STRATEGY AND CALCULATION, ABOVE ALL.
YOU'VE ALWAYS BEEN A QUICK STUDY, ELLE.
HAHA, THEN YOU'VE FOUND THE RIGHT TABLE--
EVERYONE READY ON THE RULES?

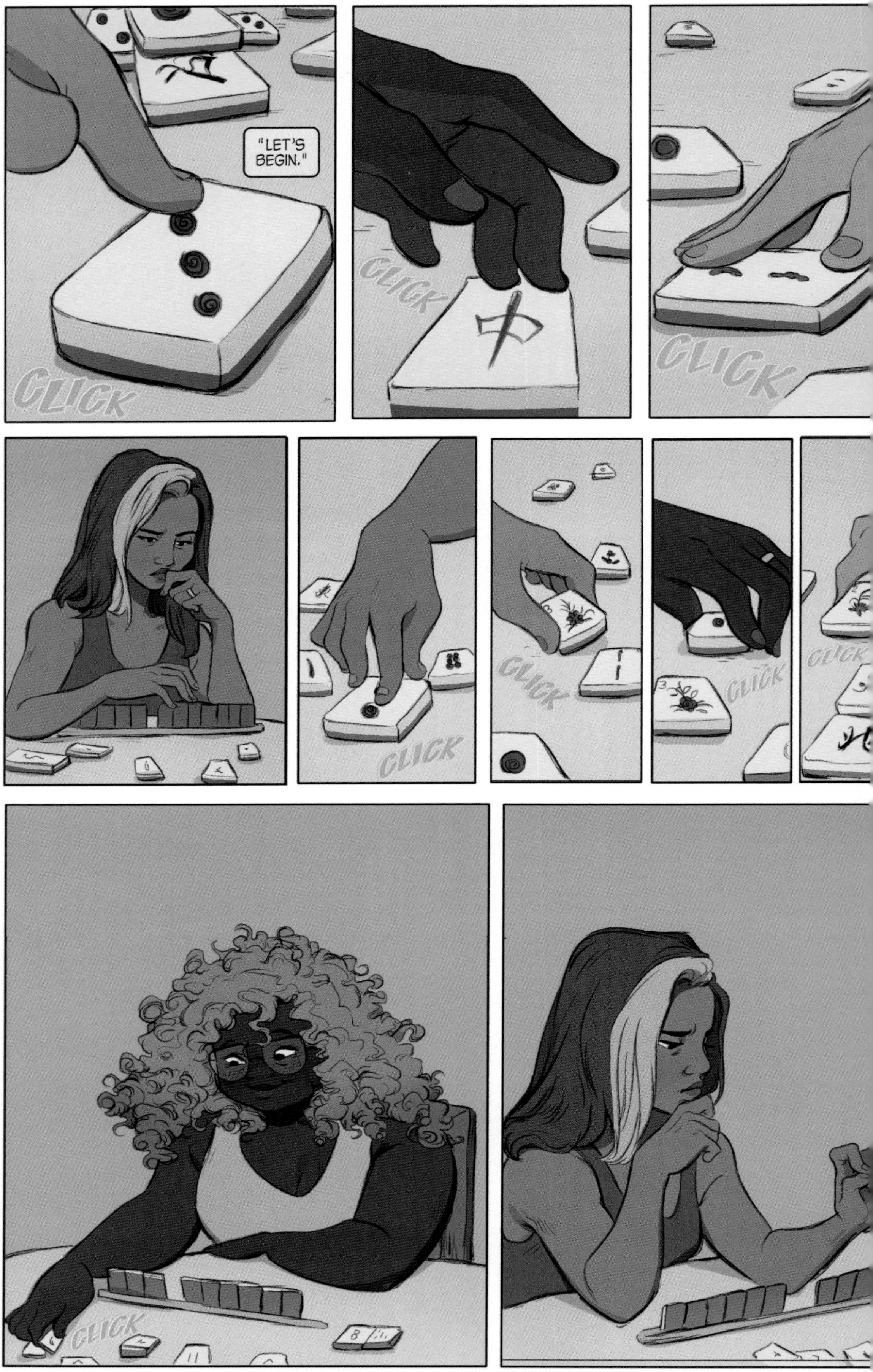
"LET'S BEGIN."
CLICK
CLICK
CLICK
CLICK
CLICK
CLICK
CLICK
CLICK

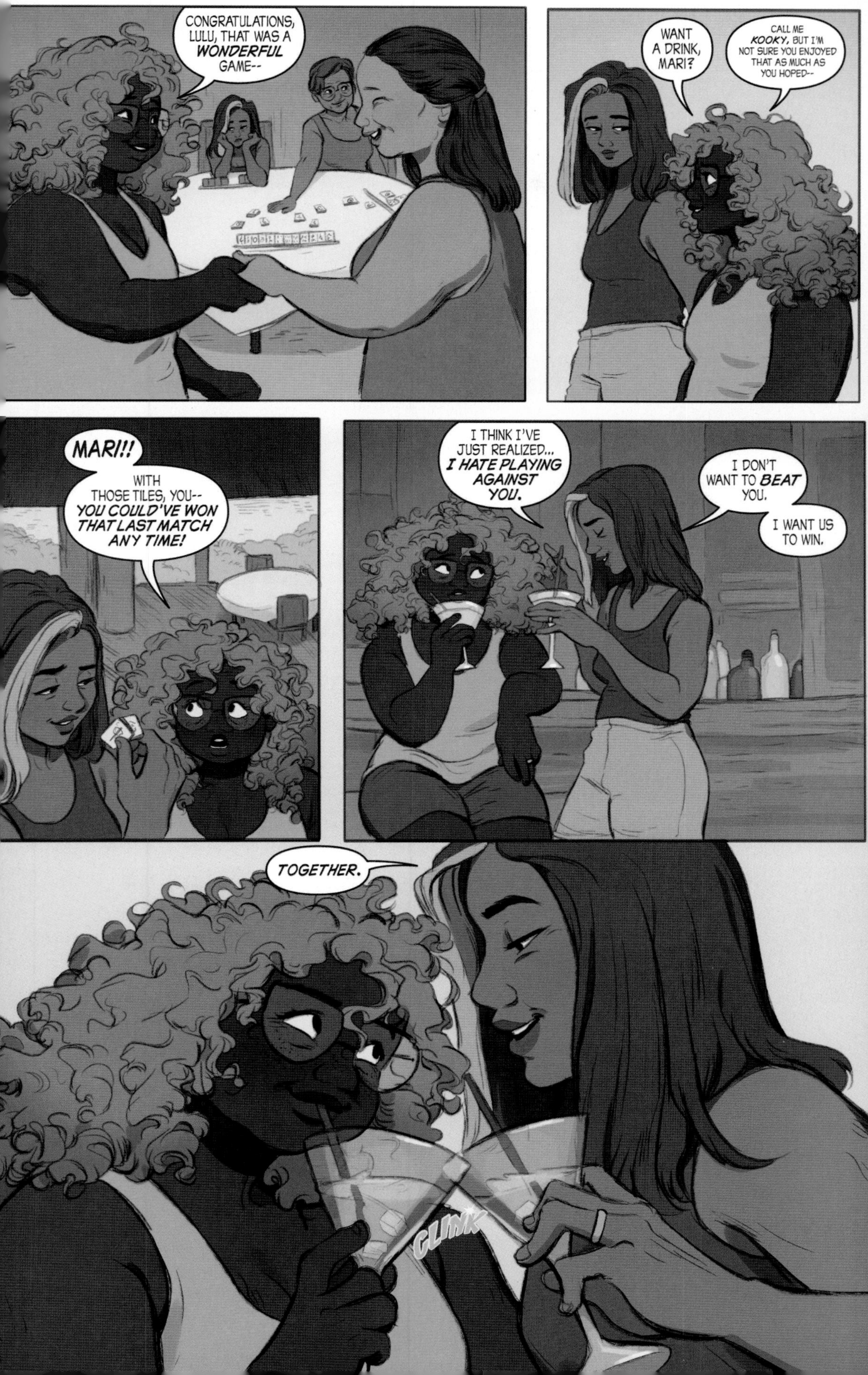
CONGRATULATIONS, LULU, THAT WAS A WONDERFUL GAME--
WANT A DRINK, MARI?
CALL ME KOOKY, BUT I'M NOT SURE YOU ENJOYED THAT AS MUCH AS YOU HOPED--
MARI!!
WITH THOSE TILES, YOU-- YOU COULD'VE WON THAT LAST MATCH ANY TIME!
I THINK I'VE JUST REALIZED... I HATE PLAYING AGAINST YOU.
I DON'T WANT TO BEAT YOU.
I WANT US TO WIN.
TOGETHER.
CLINK

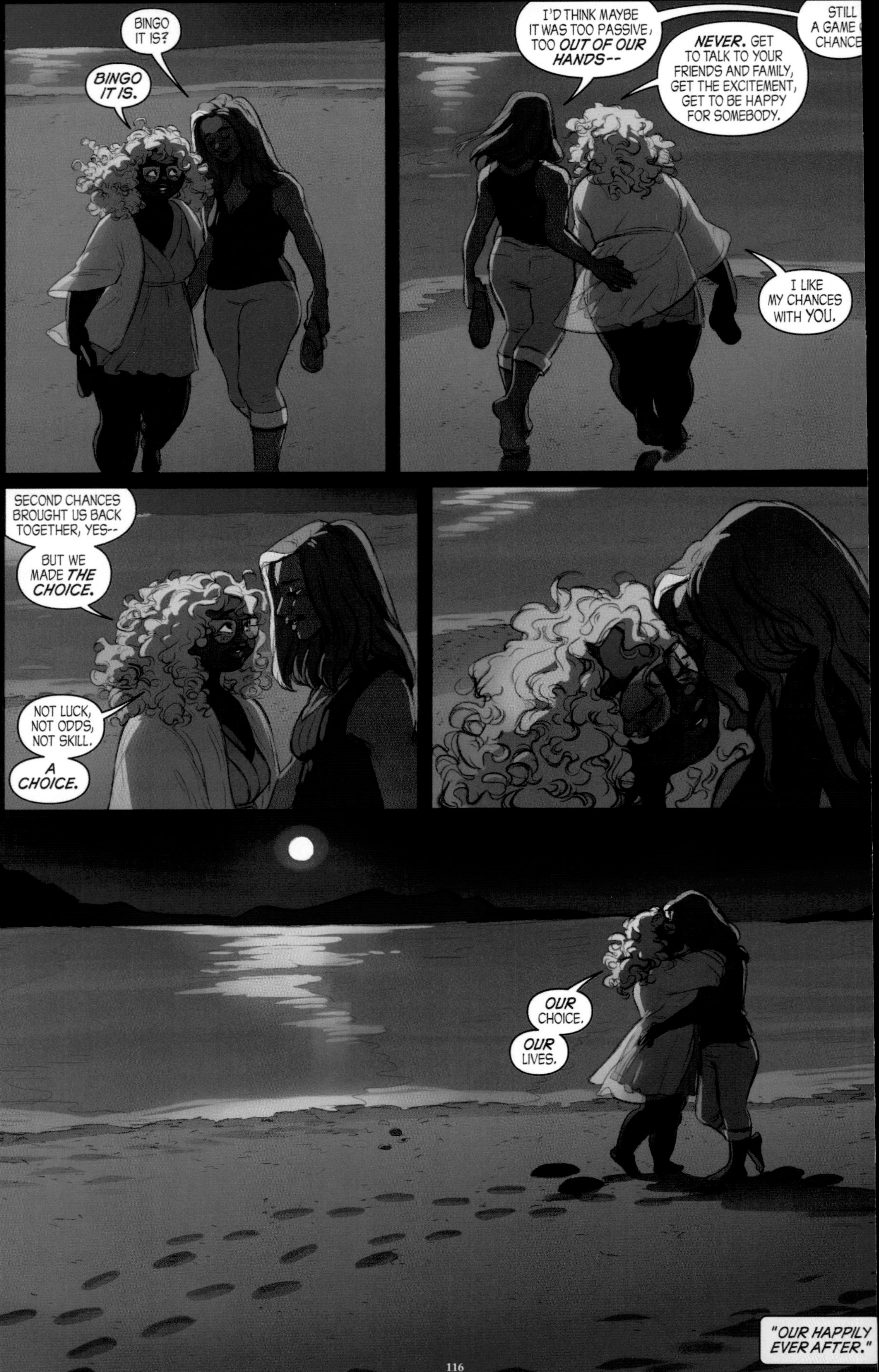
BINGO IT IS?
BINGO IT IS.
I'D THINK MAYBE IT WAS TOO PASSIVE, TOO OUT OF OUR HANDS--
STILL A GAME OF CHANCE
NEVER. GET TO TALK TO YOUR FRIENDS AND FAMILY, GET THE EXCITEMENT, GET TO BE HAPPY FOR SOMEBODY.
I LIKE MY CHANCES WITH YOU.
SECOND CHANCES BROUGHT US BACK TOGETHER, YES--
BUT WE MADE THE CHOICE.
NOT LUCK, NOT ODDS, NOT SKILL.
A CHOICE.
OUR CHOICE.
OUR LIVES.
"OUR HAPPILY EVER AFTER."

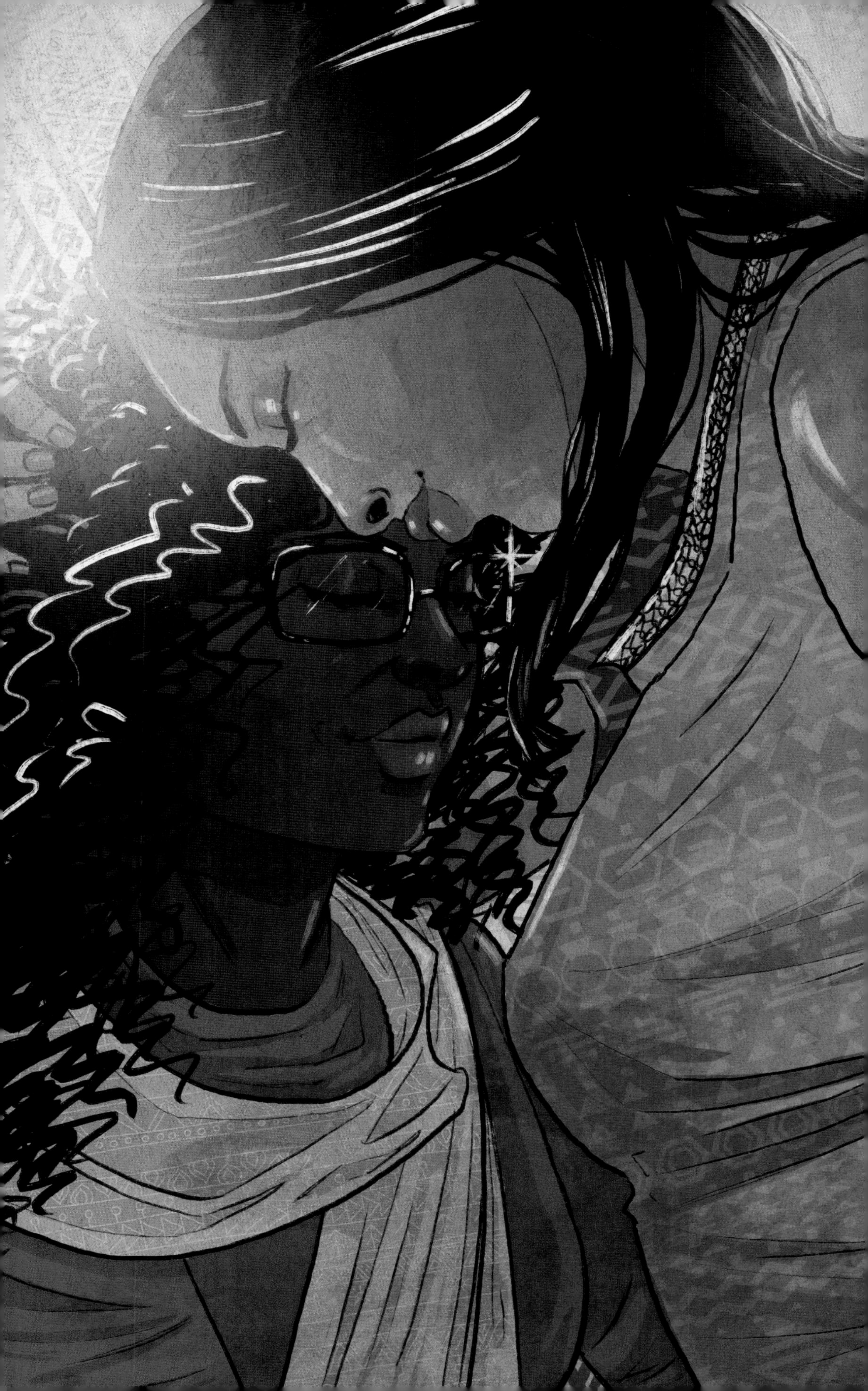

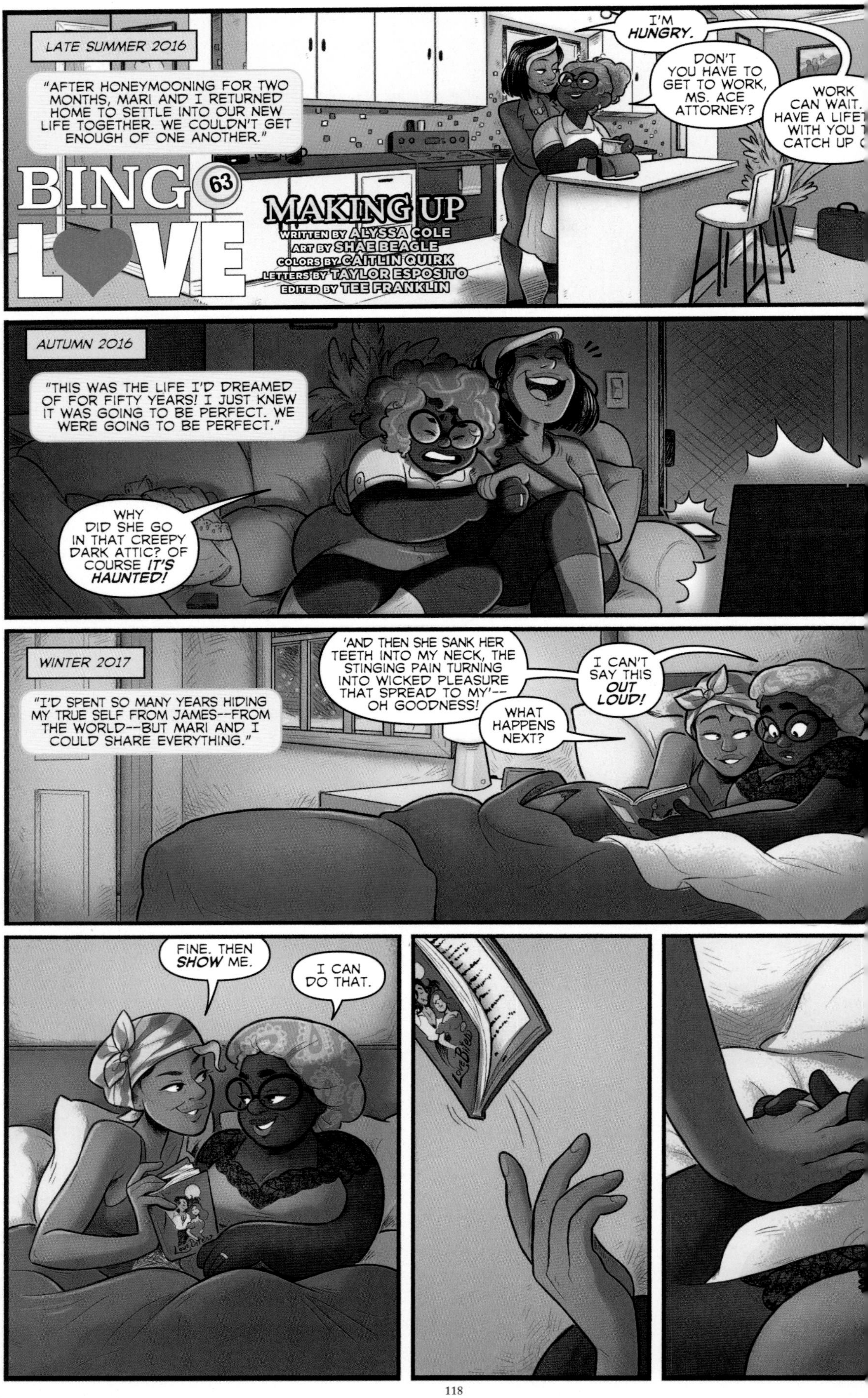

LATE SUMMER 2016
"AFTER HONEYMOONING FOR TWO MONTHS, MARI AND I RETURNED HOME TO SETTLE INTO OUR NEW LIFE TOGETHER. WE COULDN'T GET ENOUGH OF ONE ANOTHER."
BINGO 63 LOVE
MAKING UP
WRITTEN BY ALYSSA COLE
ART BY SHAE BEAGLE
COLORS BY CAITLIN QUIRK
LETTERS BY TAYLOR ESPOSITO
EDITED BY TEE FRANKLIN
I'M HUNGRY.
DON'T YOU HAVE TO GET TO WORK, MS. ACE ATTORNEY?
WORK CAN WAIT. HAVE A LIFET WITH YOU T CATCH UP
AUTUMN 2016
"THIS WAS THE LIFE I'D DREAMED OF FOR FIFTY YEARS! I JUST KNEW IT WAS GOING TO BE PERFECT. WE WERE GOING TO BE PERFECT."
WHY DID SHE GO IN THAT CREEPY DARK ATTIC? OF COURSE IT'S HAUNTED!
WINTER 2017
"I'D SPENT SO MANY YEARS HIDING MY TRUE SELF FROM JAMES--FROM THE WORLD--BUT MARI AND I COULD SHARE EVERYTHING."
'AND THEN SHE SANK HER TEETH INTO MY NECK, THE STINGING PAIN TURNING INTO WICKED PLEASURE THAT SPREAD TO MY'-- OH GOODNESS!
I CAN'T SAY THIS OUT LOUD!
WHAT HAPPENS NEXT?
FINE. THEN SHOW ME.
I CAN DO THAT.

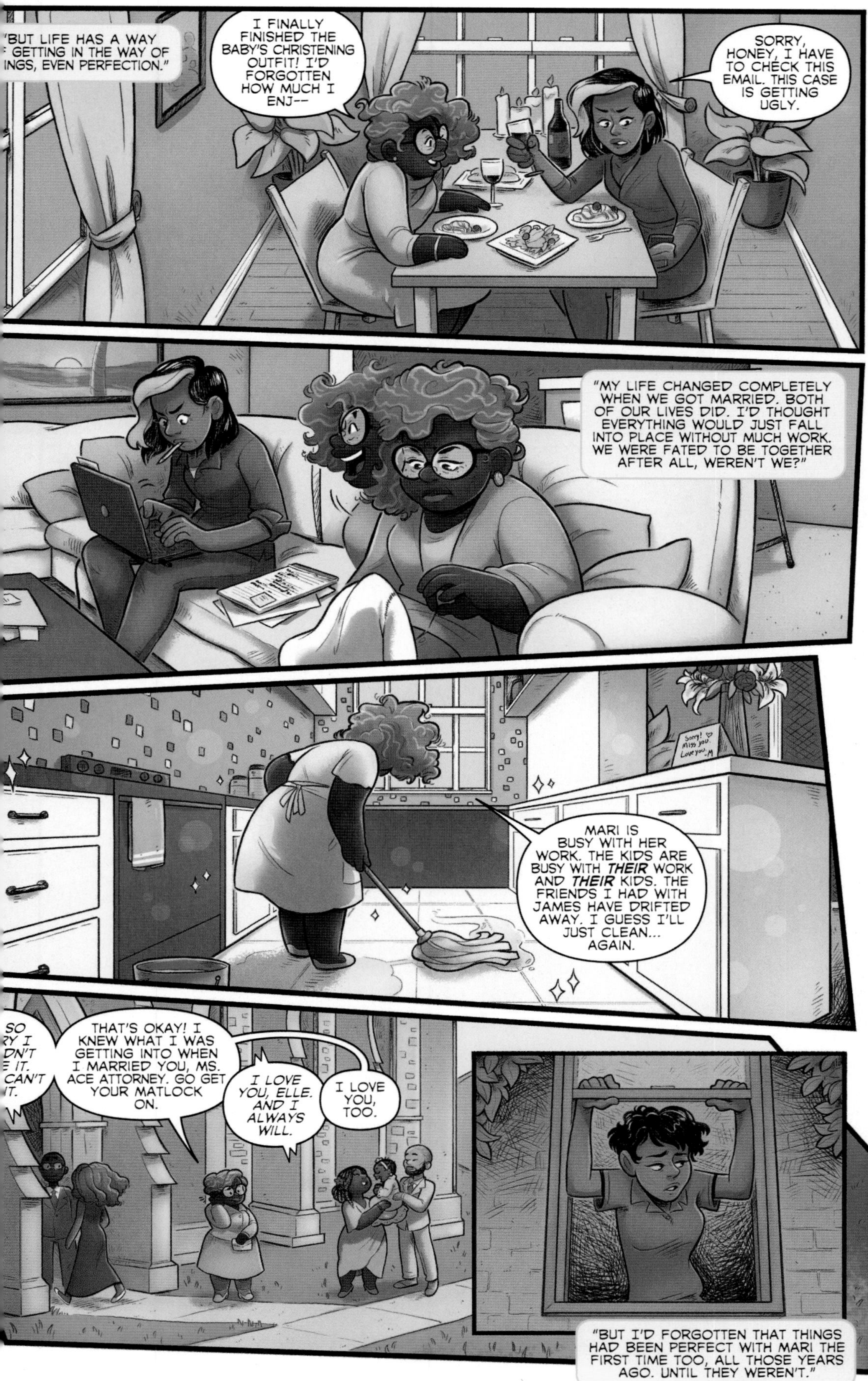

'BUT LIFE HAS A WAY F GETTING IN THE WAY OF INGS, EVEN PERFECTION."
I FINALLY FINISHED THE BABY'S CHRISTENING OUTFIT! I'D FORGOTTEN HOW MUCH I ENJ--
SORRY, HONEY, I HAVE TO CHECK THIS EMAIL. THIS CASE IS GETTING UGLY.
"MY LIFE CHANGED COMPLETELY WHEN WE GOT MARRIED. BOTH OF OUR LIVES DID. I'D THOUGHT EVERYTHING WOULD JUST FALL INTO PLACE WITHOUT MUCH WORK. WE WERE FATED TO BE TOGETHER AFTER ALL, WEREN'T WE?"
Sorry! Miss you. Love you. -M
MARI IS BUSY WITH HER WORK. THE KIDS ARE BUSY WITH ***THEIR*** WORK AND ***THEIR*** KIDS. THE FRIENDS I HAD WITH JAMES HAVE DRIFTED AWAY. I GUESS I'LL JUST CLEAN... AGAIN.
THAT'S OKAY! I KNEW WHAT I WAS GETTING INTO WHEN I MARRIED YOU, MS. ACE ATTORNEY. GO GET YOUR MATLOCK ON.
I LOVE YOU, ELLE. AND I ALWAYS WILL.
I LOVE YOU, TOO.
"BUT I'D FORGOTTEN THAT THINGS HAD BEEN PERFECT WITH MARI THE FIRST TIME TOO, ALL THOSE YEARS AGO. UNTIL THEY WEREN'T."

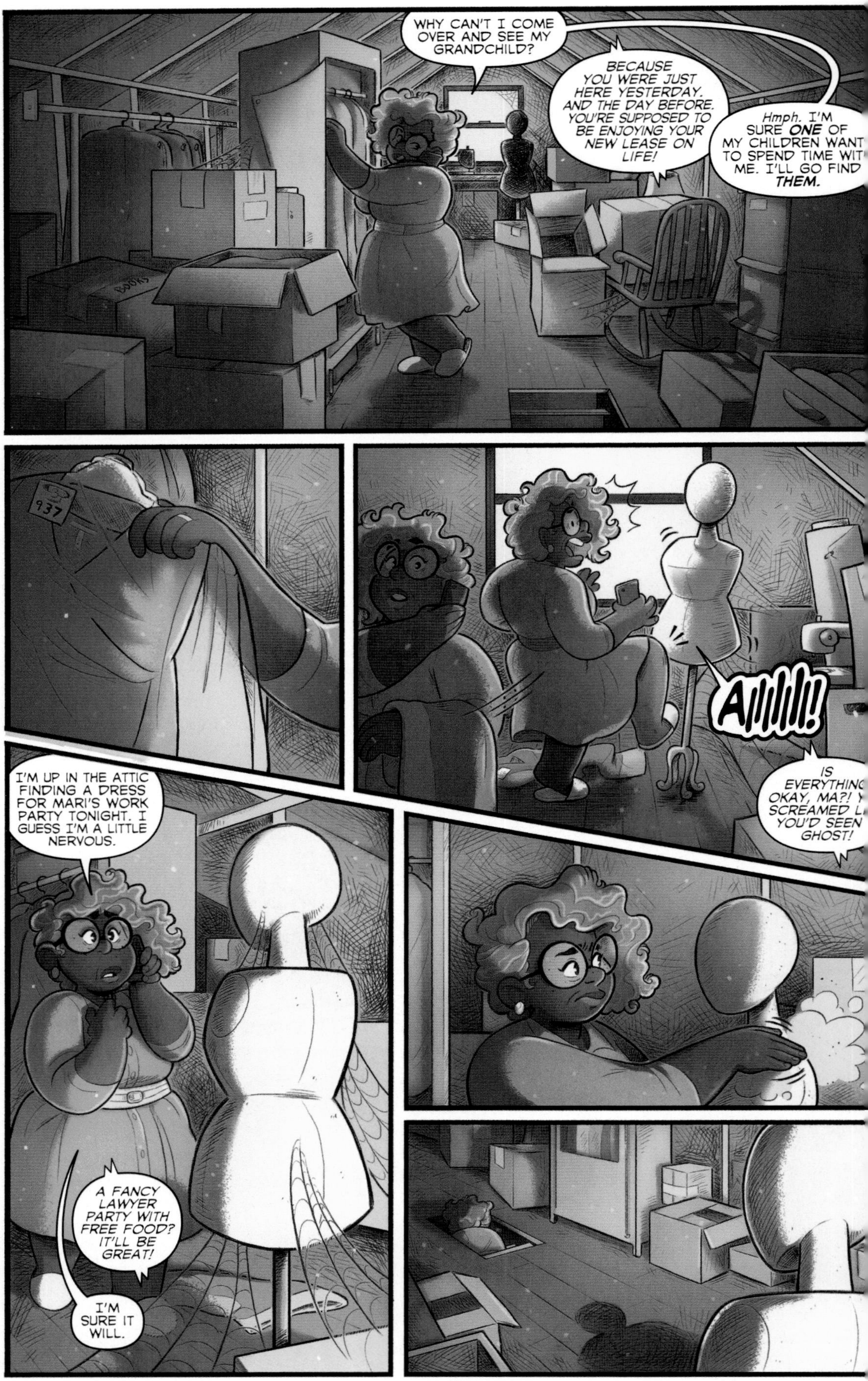
WHY CAN'T I COME OVER AND SEE MY GRANDCHILD?
BECAUSE YOU WERE JUST HERE YESTERDAY. AND THE DAY BEFORE. YOU'RE SUPPOSED TO BE ENJOYING YOUR NEW LEASE ON LIFE!
Hmph. I'M SURE ONE OF MY CHILDREN WANT TO SPEND TIME WIT ME. I'LL GO FIND THEM.
BOOKS
937
AIIIII!
IS EVERYTHING OKAY, MA?! Y SCREAMED L YOU'D SEEN GHOST!
I'M UP IN THE ATTIC FINDING A DRESS FOR MARI'S WORK PARTY TONIGHT. I GUESS I'M A LITTLE NERVOUS.
A FANCY LAWYER PARTY WITH FREE FOOD? IT'LL BE GREAT!
I'M SURE IT WILL.

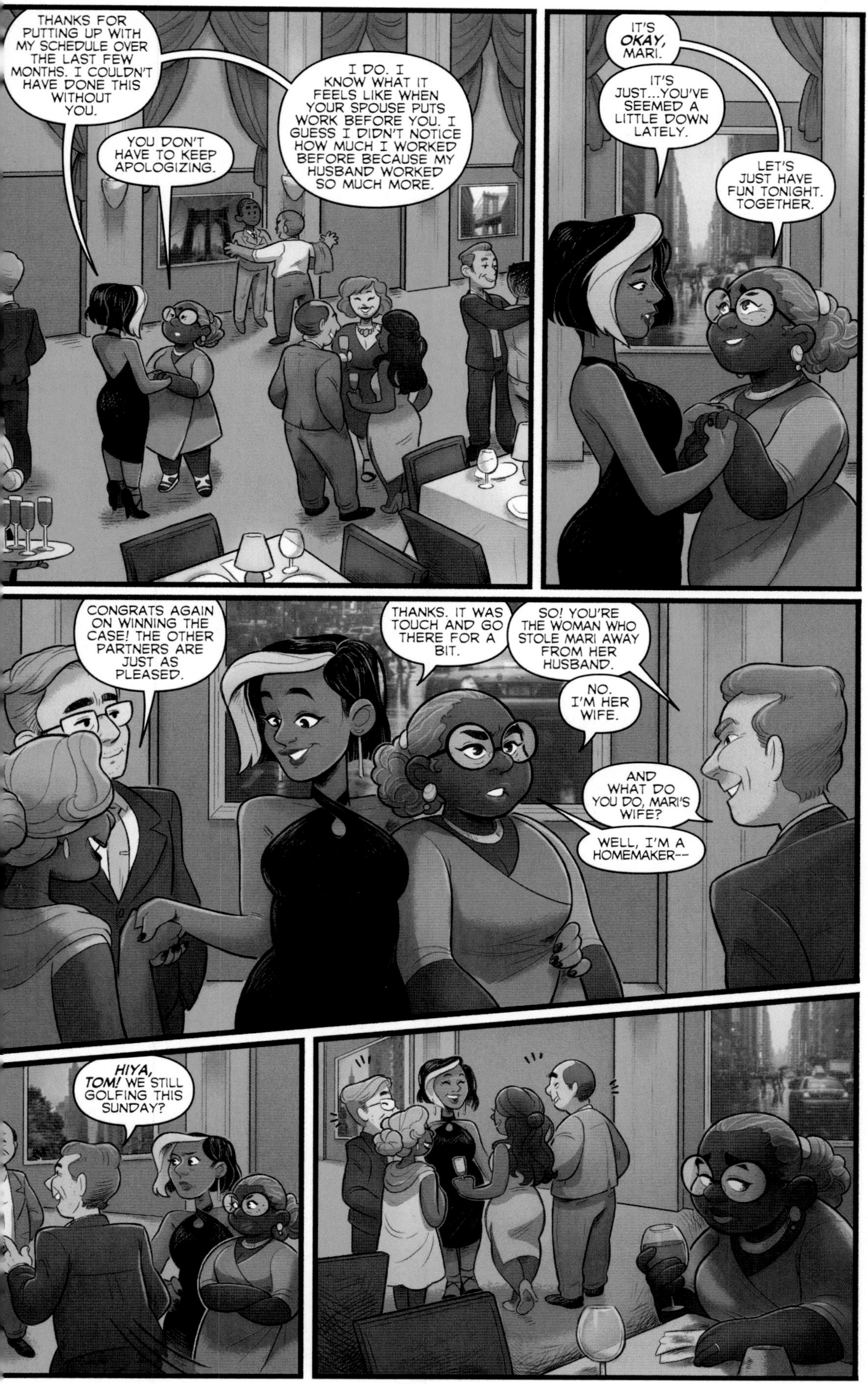
THANKS FOR PUTTING UP WITH MY SCHEDULE OVER THE LAST FEW MONTHS. I COULDN'T HAVE DONE THIS WITHOUT YOU.
YOU DON'T HAVE TO KEEP APOLOGIZING.
I DO. I KNOW WHAT IT FEELS LIKE WHEN YOUR SPOUSE PUTS WORK BEFORE YOU. I GUESS I DIDN'T NOTICE HOW MUCH I WORKED BEFORE BECAUSE MY HUSBAND WORKED SO MUCH MORE.
IT'S *OKAY,* MARI.
IT'S JUST...YOU'VE SEEMED A LITTLE DOWN LATELY.
LET'S JUST HAVE FUN TONIGHT. TOGETHER.
CONGRATS AGAIN ON WINNING THE CASE! THE OTHER PARTNERS ARE JUST AS PLEASED.
THANKS. IT WAS TOUCH AND GO THERE FOR A BIT.
SO! YOU'RE THE WOMAN WHO STOLE MARI AWAY FROM HER HUSBAND.
NO. I'M HER WIFE.
AND WHAT DO YOU DO, MARI'S WIFE?
WELL, I'M A HOMEMAKER--
HIYA, TOM! WE STILL GOLFING THIS SUNDAY?

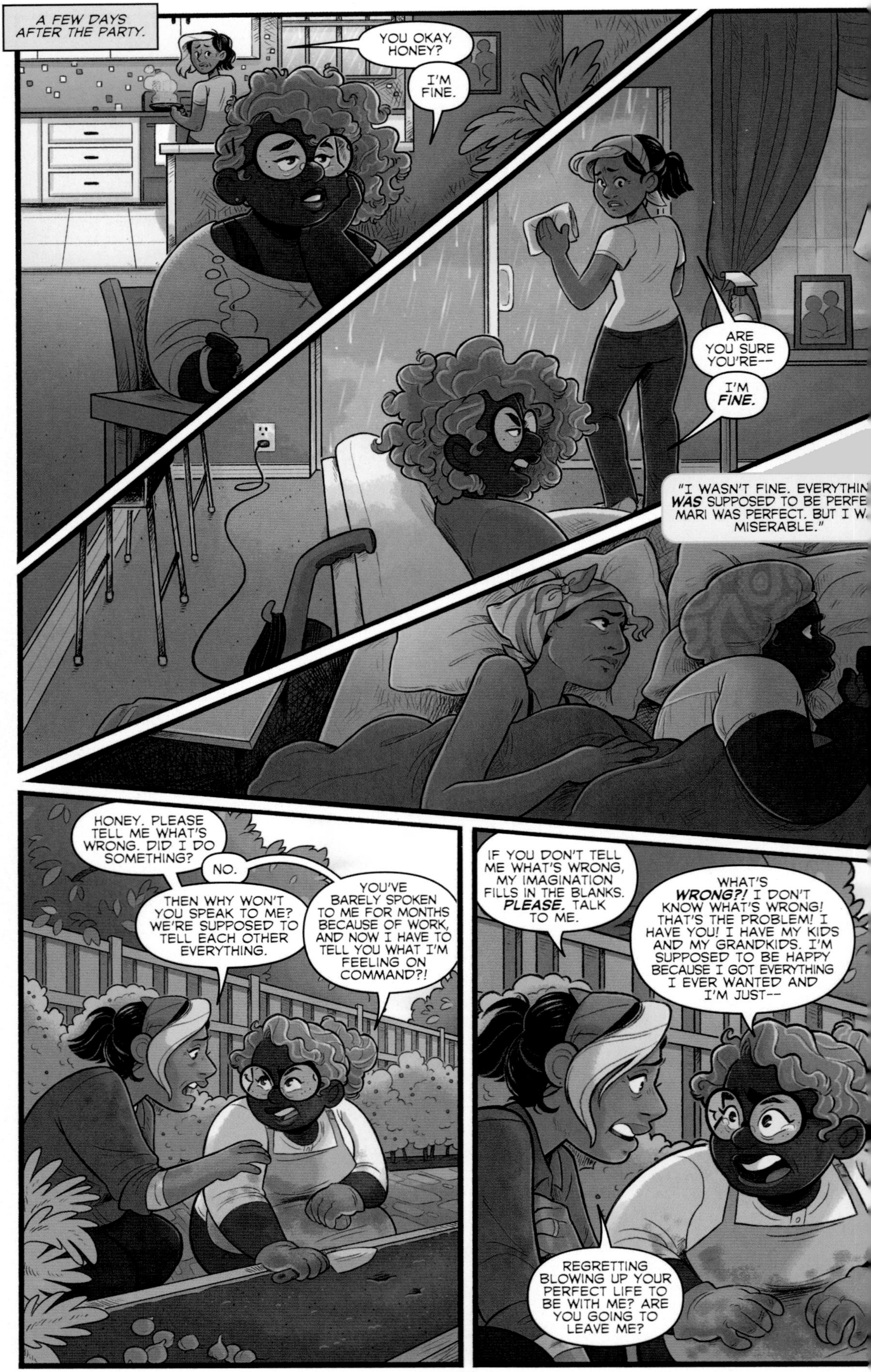
A FEW DAYS AFTER THE PARTY.
YOU OKAY, HONEY?
I'M FINE.
ARE YOU SURE YOU'RE--
I'M *FINE.*
"I WASN'T FINE. EVERYTHIN *WAS* SUPPOSED TO BE PERFE MARI WAS PERFECT. BUT I W MISERABLE."
HONEY. PLEASE TELL ME WHAT'S WRONG. DID I DO SOMETHING?
NO.
THEN WHY WON'T YOU SPEAK TO ME? WE'RE SUPPOSED TO TELL EACH OTHER EVERYTHING.
YOU'VE BARELY SPOKEN TO ME FOR MONTHS BECAUSE OF WORK, AND NOW I HAVE TO TELL YOU WHAT I'M FEELING ON COMMAND?!
IF YOU DON'T TELL ME WHAT'S WRONG, MY IMAGINATION FILLS IN THE BLANKS. *PLEASE.* TALK TO ME.
WHAT'S *WRONG?!* I DON'T KNOW WHAT'S WRONG! THAT'S THE PROBLEM! I HAVE YOU! I HAVE MY KIDS AND MY GRANDKIDS. I'M SUPPOSED TO BE HAPPY BECAUSE I GOT EVERYTHING I EVER WANTED AND I'M JUST--
REGRETTING BLOWING UP YOUR PERFECT LIFE TO BE WITH ME? ARE YOU GOING TO LEAVE ME?

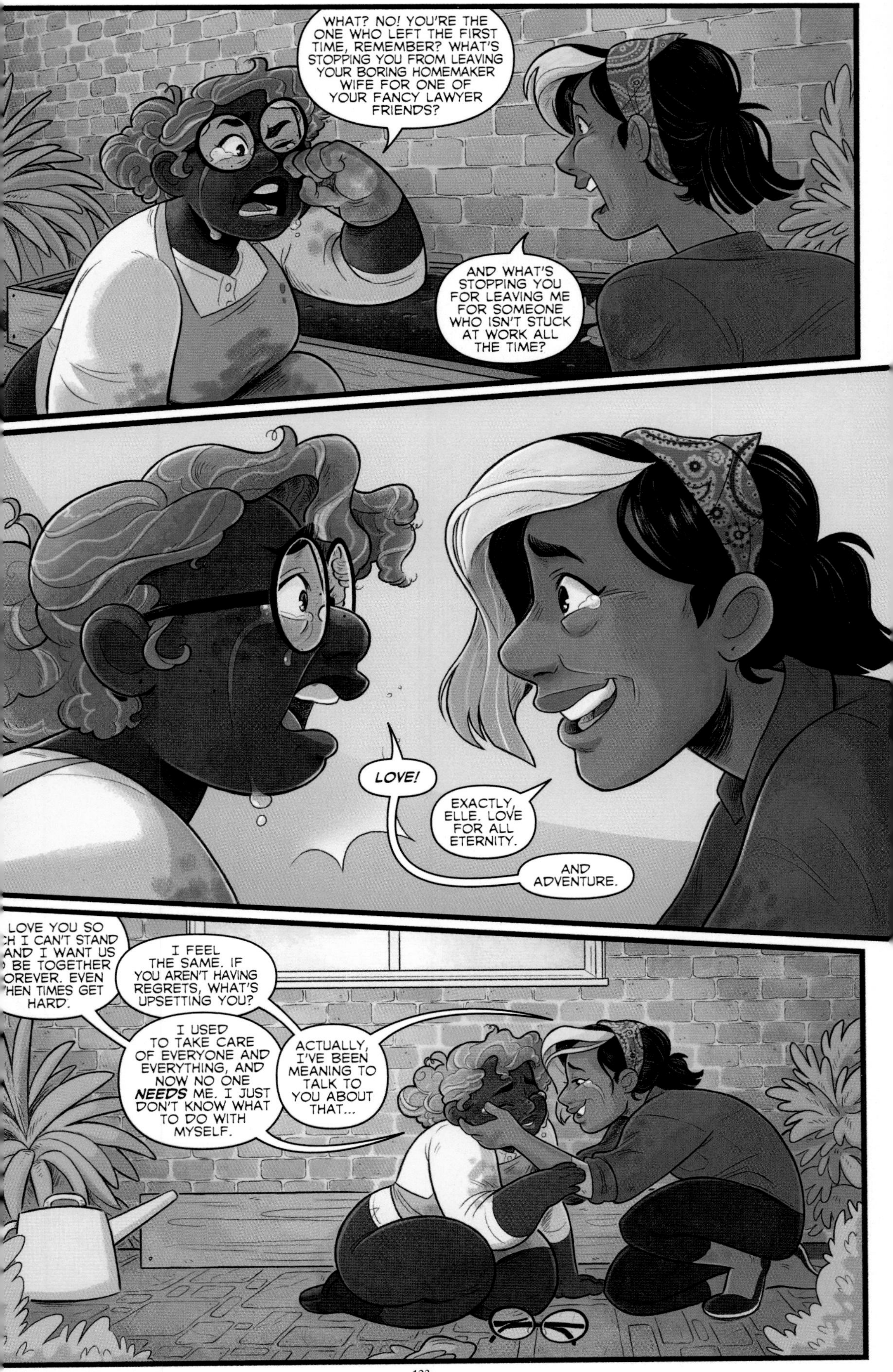
WHAT? NO! YOU'RE THE ONE WHO LEFT THE FIRST TIME, REMEMBER? WHAT'S STOPPING YOU FROM LEAVING YOUR BORING HOMEMAKER WIFE FOR ONE OF YOUR FANCY LAWYER FRIENDS?
AND WHAT'S STOPPING YOU FOR LEAVING ME FOR SOMEONE WHO ISN'T STUCK AT WORK ALL THE TIME?
LOVE!
EXACTLY, ELLE. LOVE FOR ALL ETERNITY.
AND ADVENTURE.
LOVE YOU SO CH I CAN'T STAND AND I WANT US BE TOGETHER OREVER. EVEN HEN TIMES GET HARD.
I FEEL THE SAME. IF YOU AREN'T HAVING REGRETS, WHAT'S UPSETTING YOU?
I USED TO TAKE CARE OF EVERYONE AND EVERYTHING, AND NOW NO ONE NEEDS ME. I JUST DON'T KNOW WHAT TO DO WITH MYSELF.
ACTUALLY, I'VE BEEN MEANING TO TALK TO YOU ABOUT THAT...

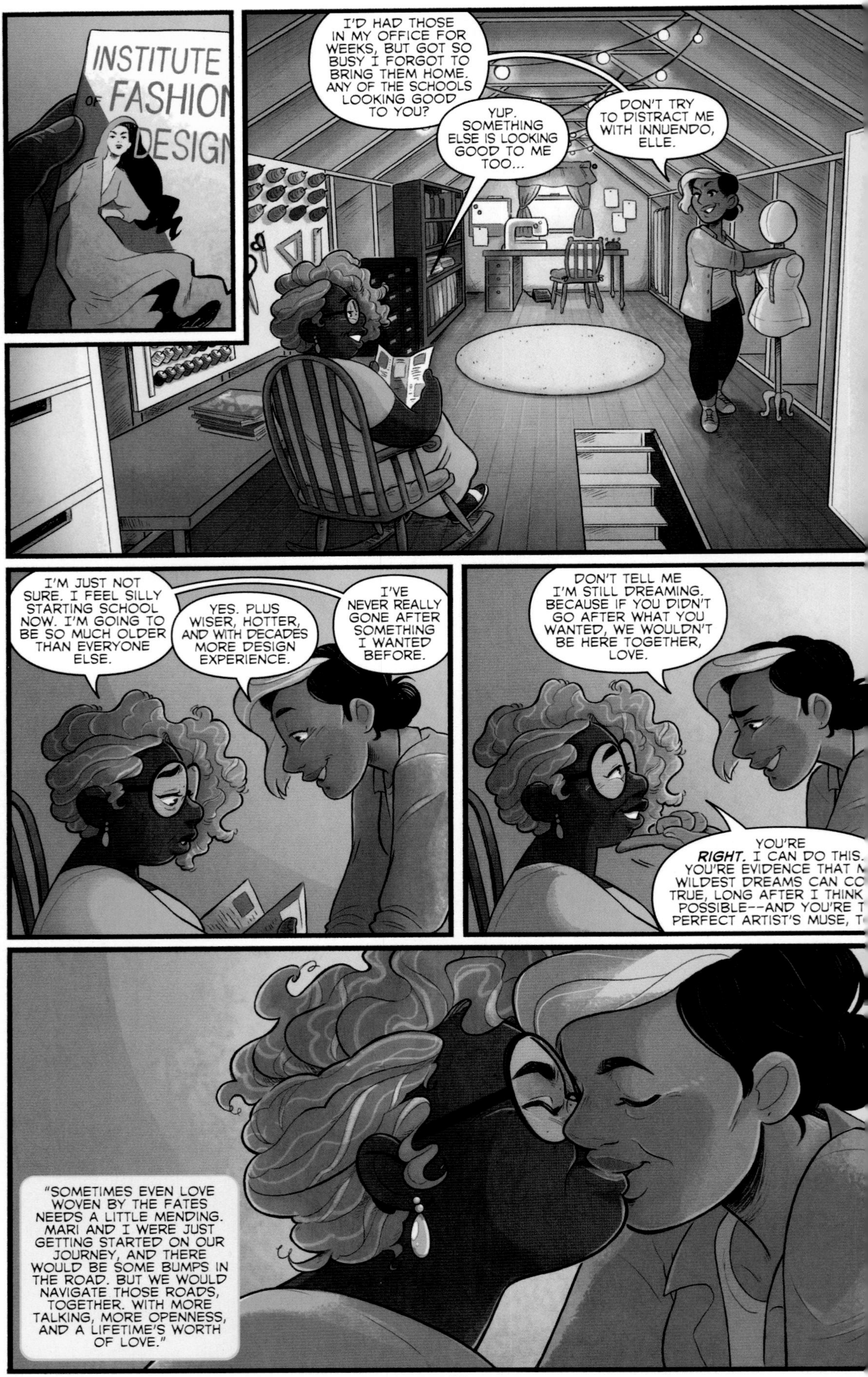
INSTITUTE OF FASHION DESIGN
I'D HAD THOSE IN MY OFFICE FOR WEEKS, BUT GOT SO BUSY I FORGOT TO BRING THEM HOME. ANY OF THE SCHOOLS LOOKING GOOD TO YOU?
YUP. SOMETHING ELSE IS LOOKING GOOD TO ME TOO...
DON'T TRY TO DISTRACT ME WITH INNUENDO, ELLE.
I'M JUST NOT SURE. I FEEL SILLY STARTING SCHOOL NOW. I'M GOING TO BE SO MUCH OLDER THAN EVERYONE ELSE.
YES. PLUS WISER, HOTTER, AND WITH DECADES MORE DESIGN EXPERIENCE.
I'VE NEVER REALLY GONE AFTER SOMETHING I WANTED BEFORE.
DON'T TELL ME I'M STILL DREAMING. BECAUSE IF YOU DIDN'T GO AFTER WHAT YOU WANTED, WE WOULDN'T BE HERE TOGETHER, LOVE.
YOU'RE RIGHT. I CAN DO THIS. YOU'RE EVIDENCE THAT M WILDEST DREAMS CAN CO TRUE, LONG AFTER I THINK POSSIBLE--AND YOU'RE T PERFECT ARTIST'S MUSE, T
"SOMETIMES EVEN LOVE WOVEN BY THE FATES NEEDS A LITTLE MENDING. MARI AND I WERE JUST GETTING STARTED ON OUR JOURNEY, AND THERE WOULD BE SOME BUMPS IN THE ROAD. BUT WE WOULD NAVIGATE THOSE ROADS, TOGETHER. WITH MORE TALKING, MORE OPENNESS, AND A LIFETIME'S WORTH OF LOVE."

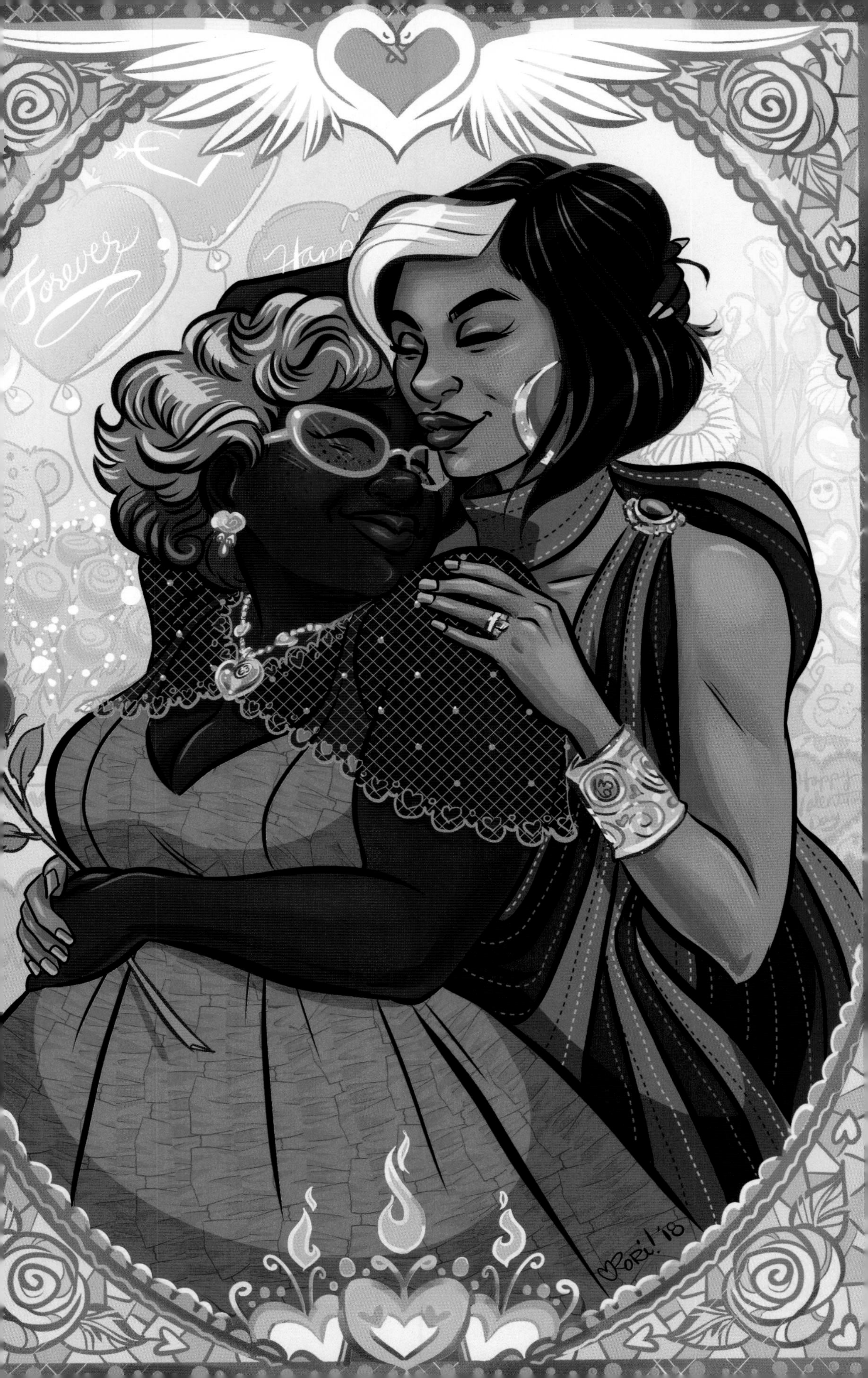
Forever

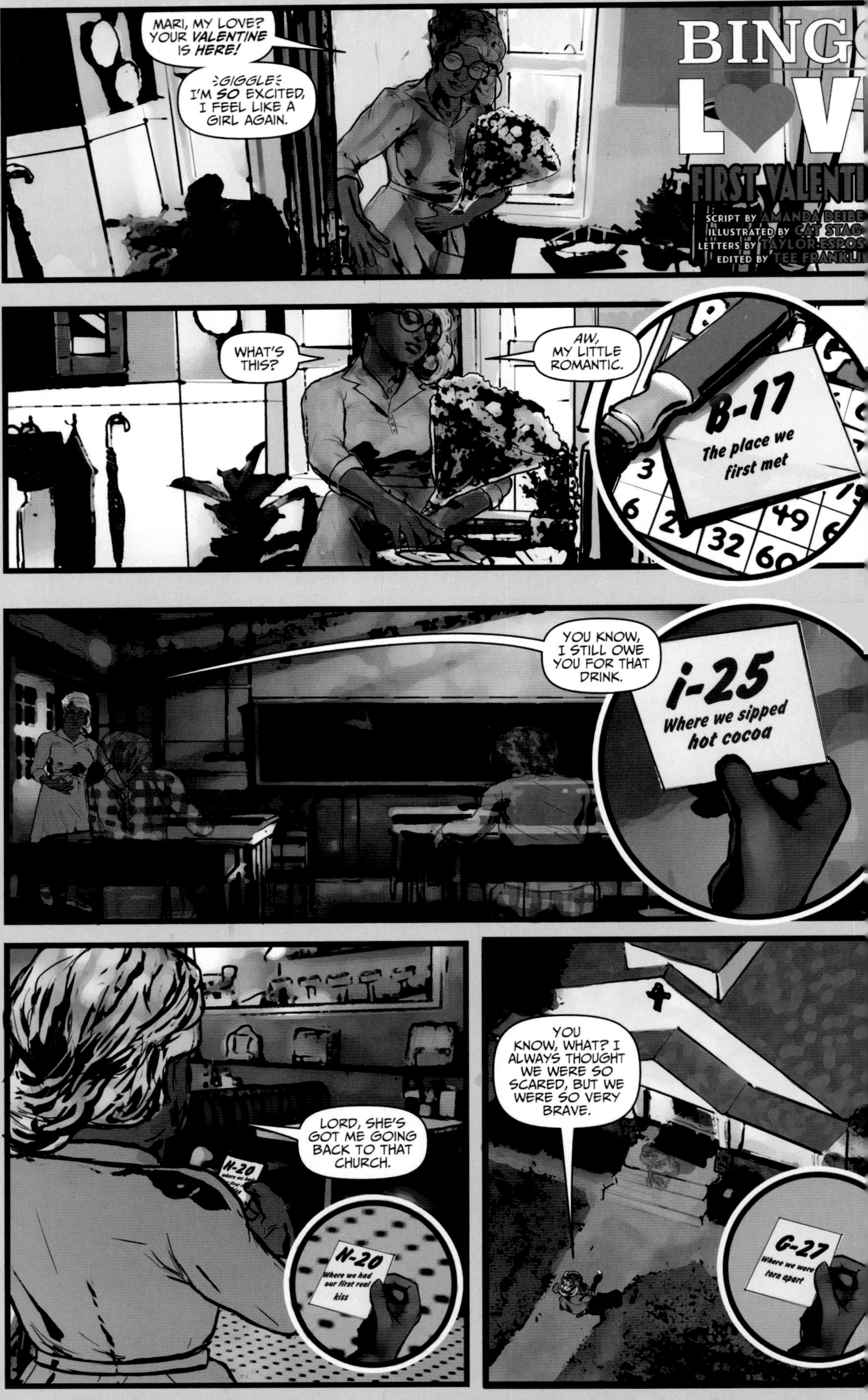
BINGO
LOVE
FIRST VALENTI
SCRIPT BY AMANDA DEIBE
ILLUSTRATED BY CAT STAG
LETTERS BY TAYLOR ESPOS
EDITED BY TEE FRANKLI
MARI, MY LOVE? YOUR VALENTINE IS HERE!
GIGGLE I'M SO EXCITED, I FEEL LIKE A GIRL AGAIN.
WHAT'S THIS?
AW, MY LITTLE ROMANTIC.
B-17 The place we first met
YOU KNOW, I STILL OWE YOU FOR THAT DRINK.
i-25 Where we sipped hot cocoa
LORD, SHE'S GOT ME GOING BACK TO THAT CHURCH.
N-20 Where we had our first real kiss
YOU KNOW, WHAT? I ALWAYS THOUGHT WE WERE SO SCARED, BUT WE WERE SO VERY BRAVE.
G-27 Where we were torn apart

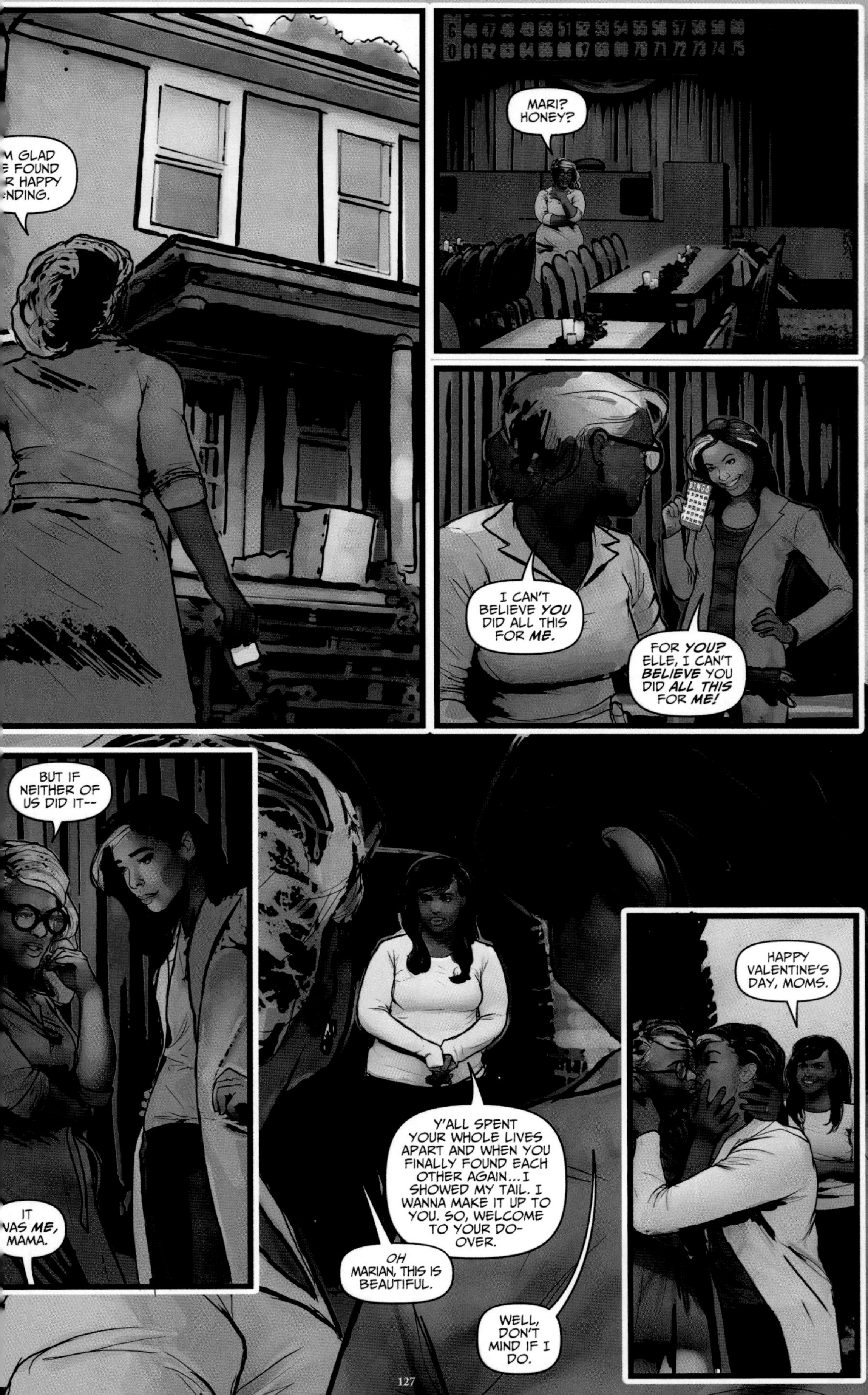
M GLAD E FOUND R HAPPY NDING.
MARI? HONEY?
I CAN'T BELIEVE YOU DID ALL THIS FOR ME.
FOR YOU? ELLE, I CAN'T BELIEVE YOU DID ALL THIS FOR ME!
BUT IF NEITHER OF US DID IT--
IT VAS ME, MAMA.
Y'ALL SPENT YOUR WHOLE LIVES APART AND WHEN YOU FINALLY FOUND EACH OTHER AGAIN... I SHOWED MY TAIL. I WANNA MAKE IT UP TO YOU. SO, WELCOME TO YOUR DO-OVER.
OH MARIAN, THIS IS BEAUTIFUL.
WELL, DON'T MIND IF I DO.
HAPPY VALENTINE'S DAY, MOMS.

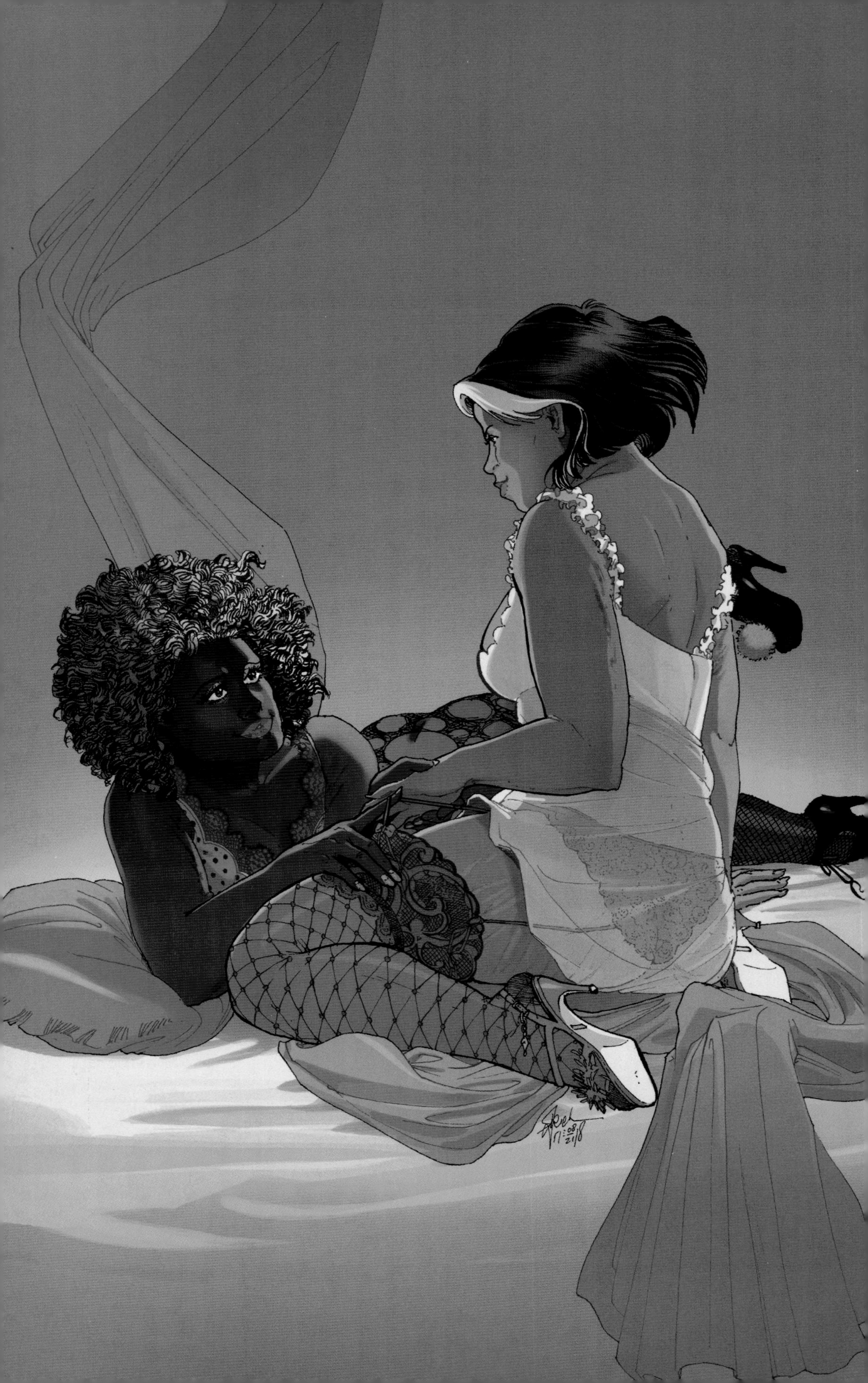

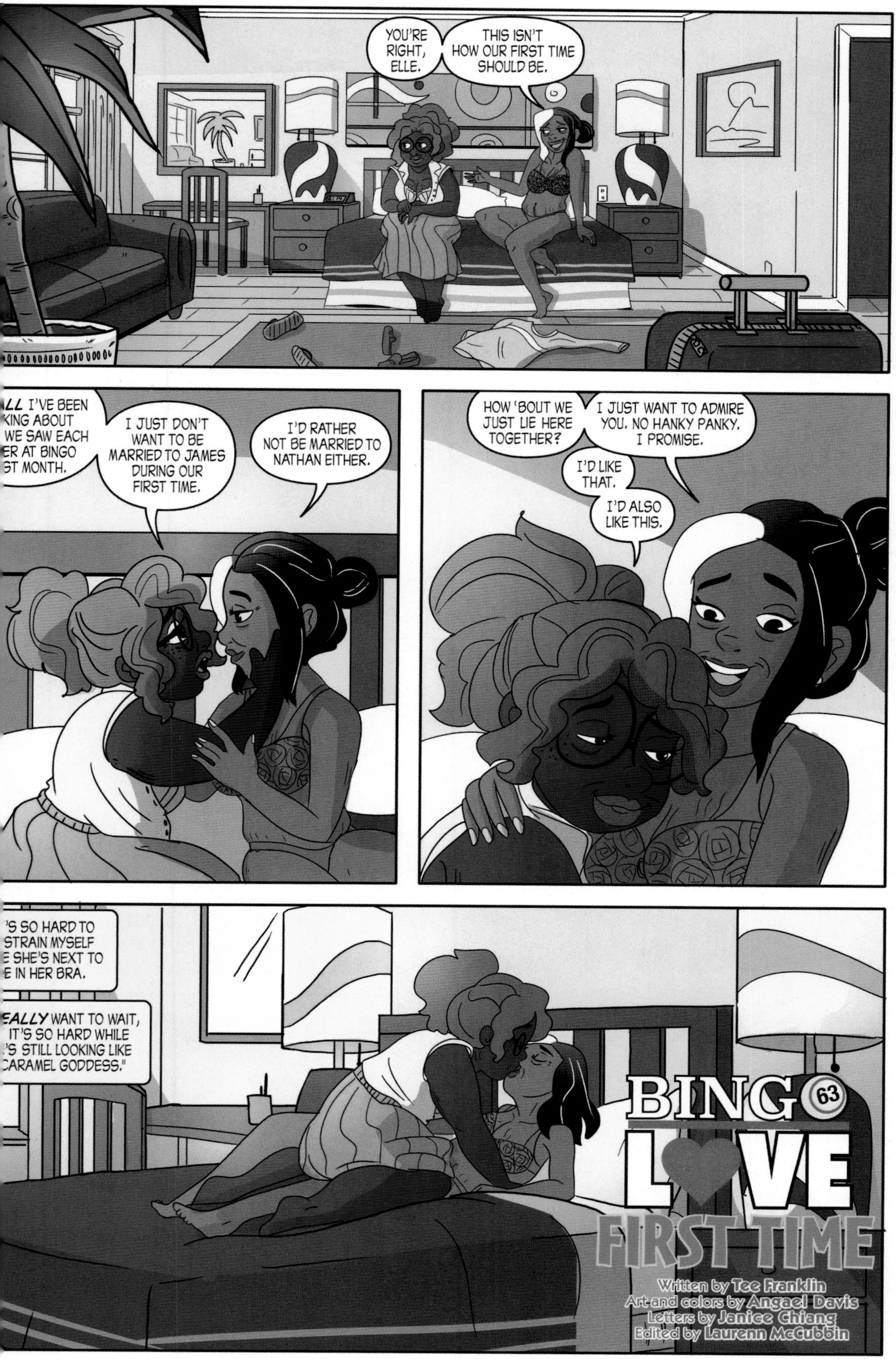
YOU'RE RIGHT, ELLE.
THIS ISN'T HOW OUR FIRST TIME SHOULD BE.
LL I'VE BEEN KING ABOUT WE SAW EACH ER AT BINGO ST MONTH.
I JUST DON'T WANT TO BE MARRIED TO JAMES DURING OUR FIRST TIME.
I'D RATHER NOT BE MARRIED TO NATHAN EITHER.
HOW 'BOUT WE JUST LIE HERE TOGETHER?
I JUST WANT TO ADMIRE YOU. NO HANKY PANKY. I PROMISE.
I'D LIKE THAT.
I'D ALSO LIKE THIS.
'S SO HARD TO STRAIN MYSELF E SHE'S NEXT TO E IN HER BRA.
EALLY WANT TO WAIT, IT'S SO HARD WHILE 'S STILL LOOKING LIKE CARAMEL GODDESS."
BINGO 63
LOVE
FIRST TIME
Written by Tee Franklin
Art and colors by Angael Davis
Letters by Janice Chiang
Edited by Laurenn McCubbin

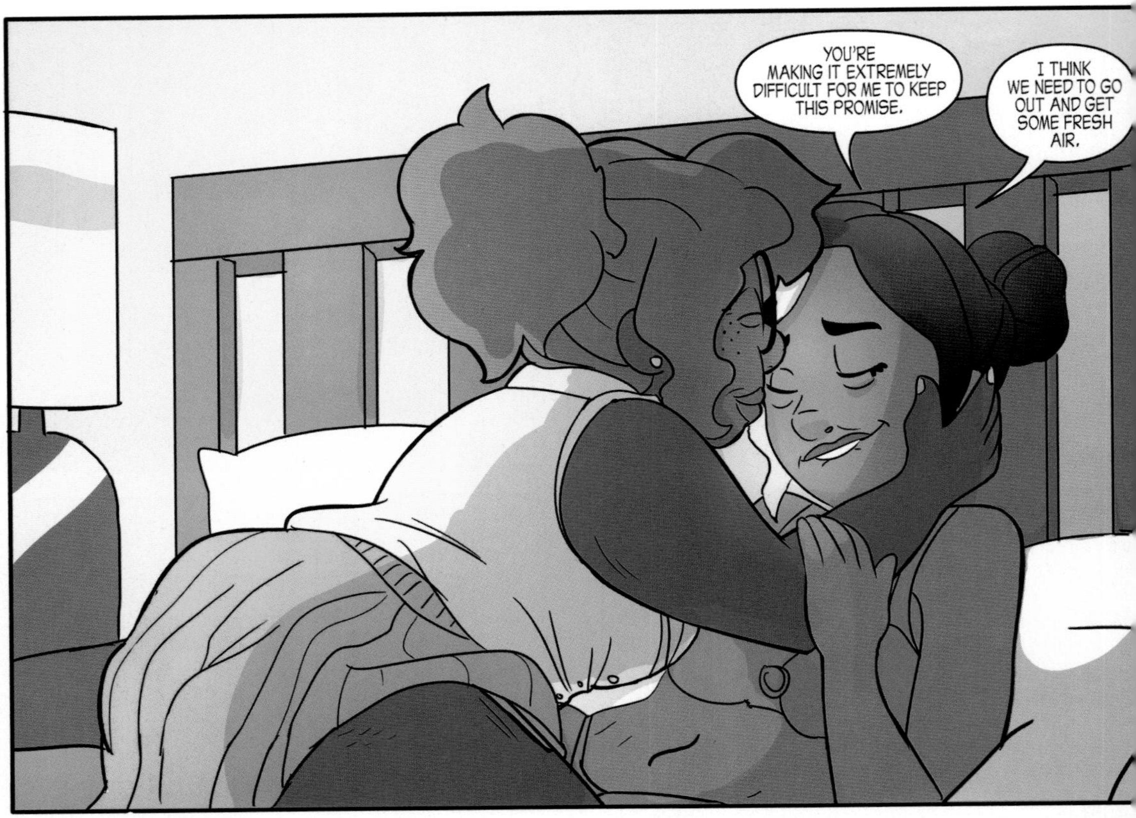
YOU'RE MAKING IT EXTREMELY DIFFICULT FOR ME TO KEEP THIS PROMISE.
I THINK WE NEED TO GO OUT AND GET SOME FRESH AIR.

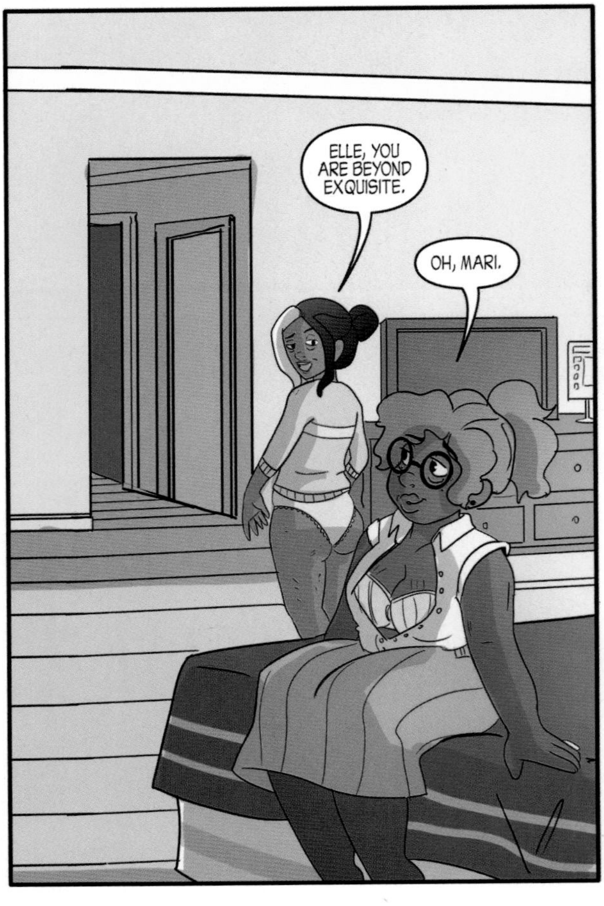
ELLE, YOU ARE BEYOND EXQUISITE.
OH, MARI.

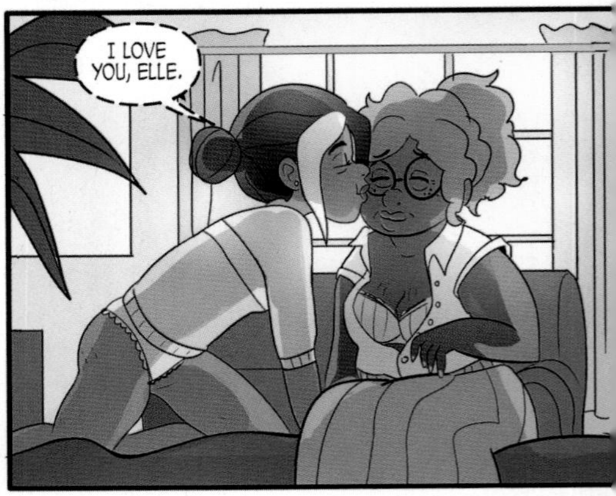
I LOVE YOU, ELLE.

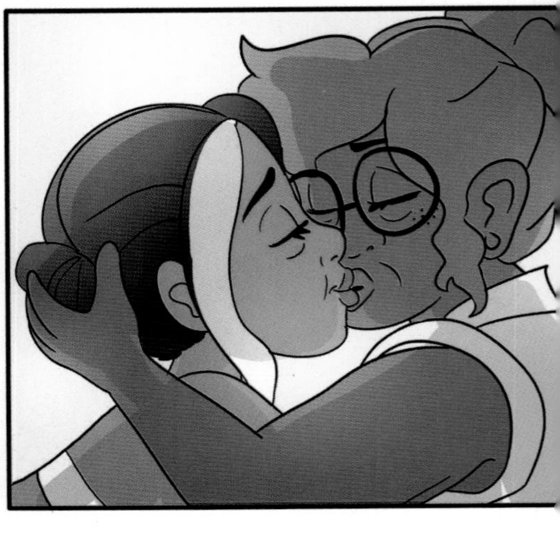

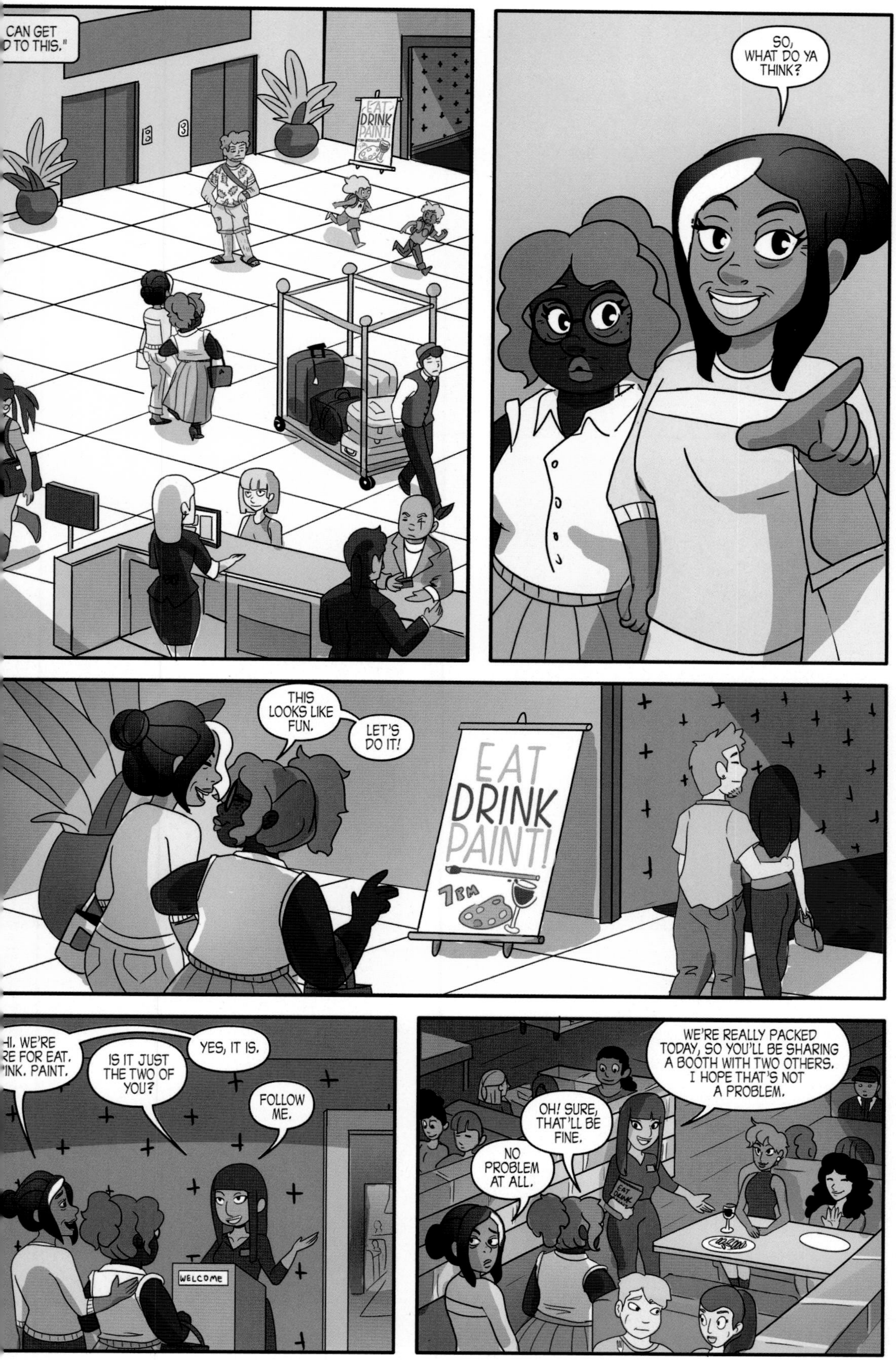
CAN GET
D TO THIS."
EAT DRINK PAINT!
SO, WHAT DO YA THINK?
THIS LOOKS LIKE FUN.
LET'S DO IT!
EAT DRINK PAINT!
7PM
HI. WE'RE
RE FOR EAT.
INK. PAINT.
IS IT JUST THE TWO OF YOU?
YES, IT IS.
FOLLOW ME.
WELCOME
WE'RE REALLY PACKED TODAY, SO YOU'LL BE SHARING A BOOTH WITH TWO OTHERS. I HOPE THAT'S NOT A PROBLEM.
OH! SURE, THAT'LL BE FINE.
NO PROBLEM AT ALL.

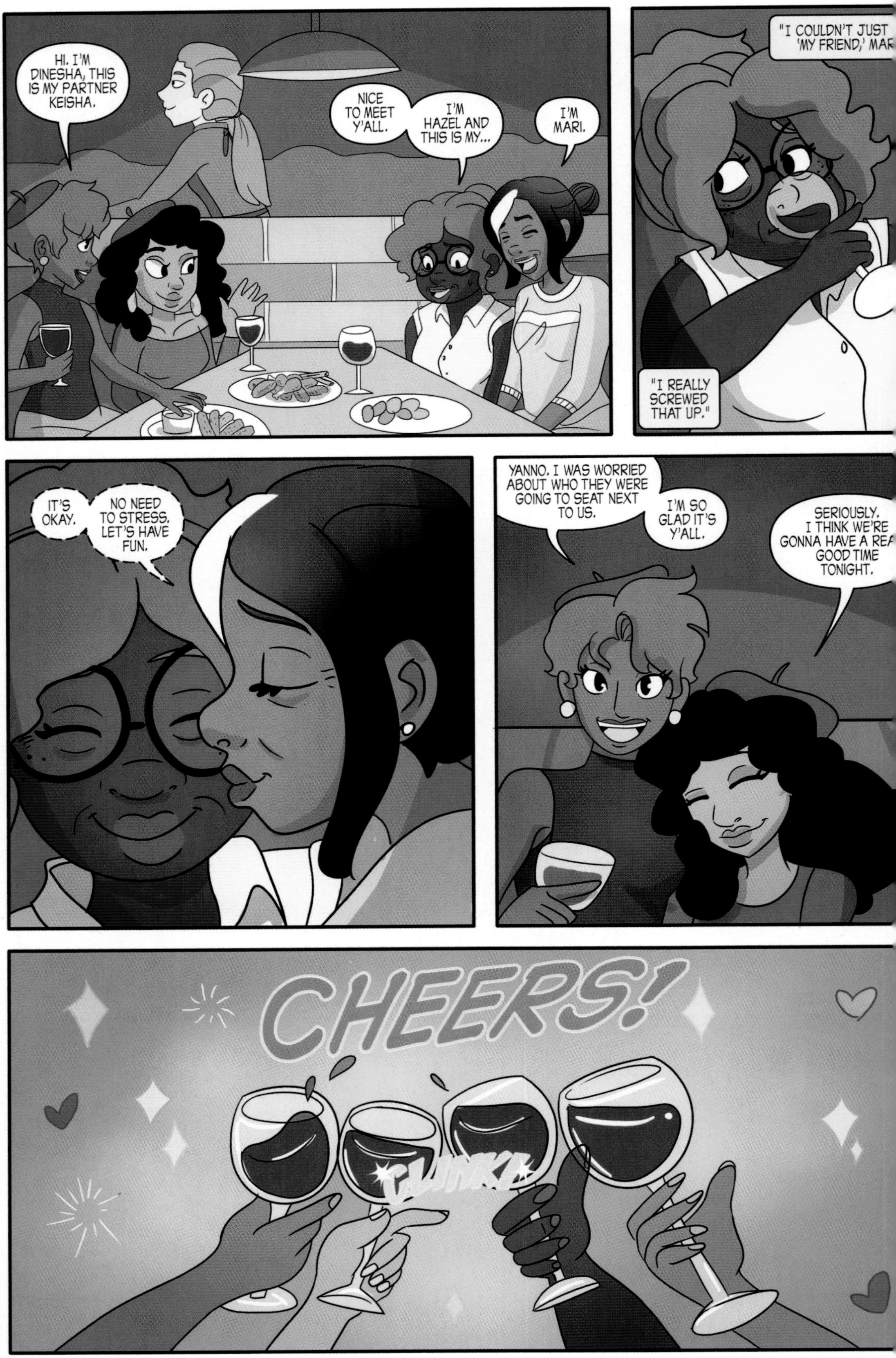
HI. I'M DINESHA, THIS IS MY PARTNER KEISHA.
NICE TO MEET Y'ALL.
I'M HAZEL AND THIS IS MY...
I'M MARI.
"I COULDN'T JUST 'MY FRIEND,' MAR
"I REALLY SCREWED THAT UP."
IT'S OKAY.
NO NEED TO STRESS. LET'S HAVE FUN.
YANNO, I WAS WORRIED ABOUT WHO THEY WERE GOING TO SEAT NEXT TO US.
I'M SO GLAD IT'S Y'ALL.
SERIOUSLY. I THINK WE'RE GONNA HAVE A REA GOOD TIME TONIGHT.
CHEERS!

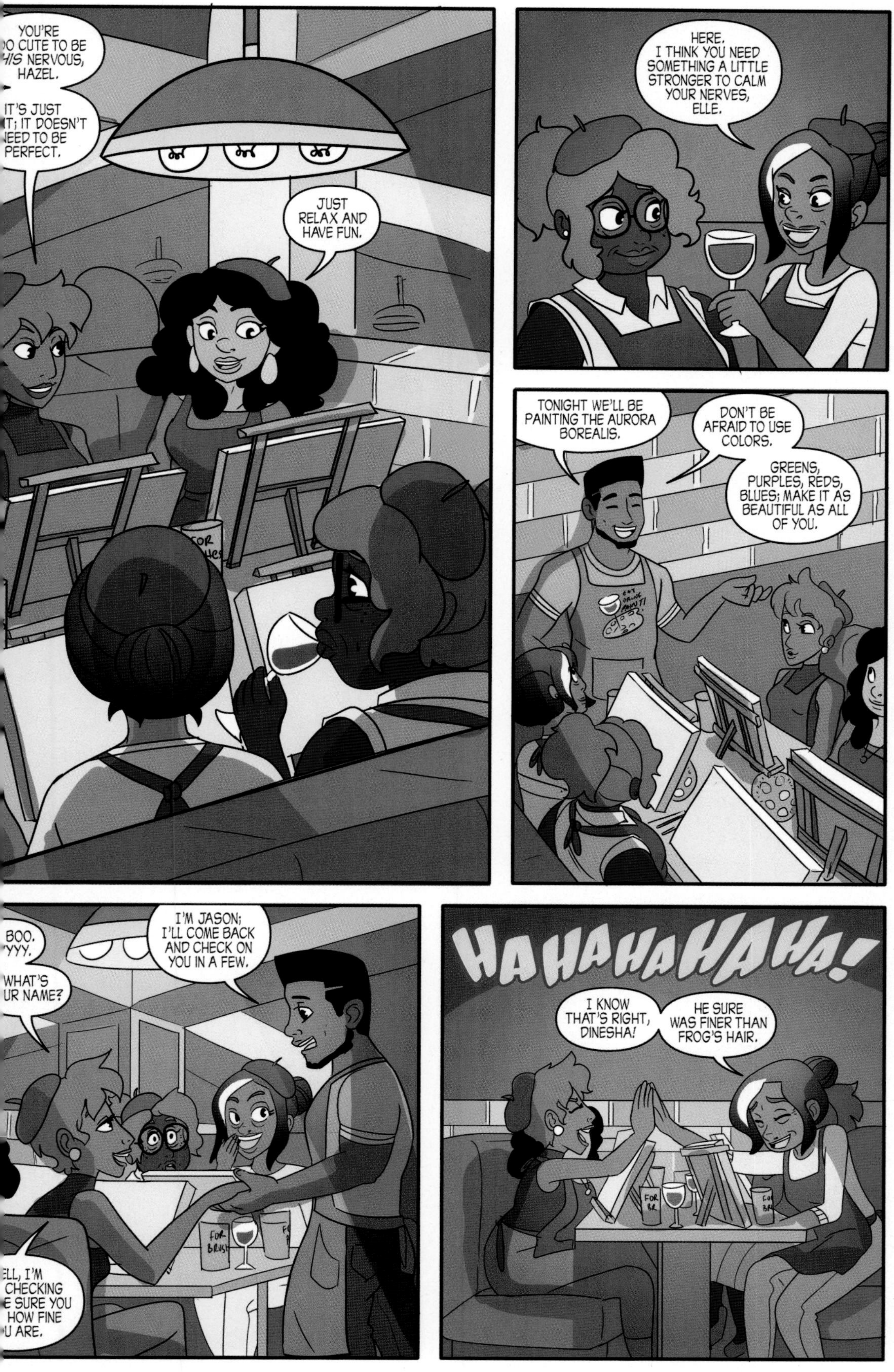
YOU'RE
O CUTE TO BE
HIS NERVOUS,
HAZEL.
IT'S JUST
T; IT DOESN'T
EED TO BE
PERFECT.
JUST RELAX AND HAVE FUN.
HERE. I THINK YOU NEED SOMETHING A LITTLE STRONGER TO CALM YOUR NERVES, ELLE.
TONIGHT WE'LL BE PAINTING THE AURORA BOREALIS.
DON'T BE AFRAID TO USE COLORS.
GREENS, PURPLES, REDS, BLUES; MAKE IT AS BEAUTIFUL AS ALL OF YOU.
BOO.
YYY.
WHAT'S
UR NAME?
I'M JASON; I'LL COME BACK AND CHECK ON YOU IN A FEW.
ELL, I'M
CHECKING
E SURE YOU
HOW FINE
U ARE.
HAHAHAHAHAHA!
I KNOW THAT'S RIGHT, DINESHA!
HE SURE WAS FINER THAN FROG'S HAIR.

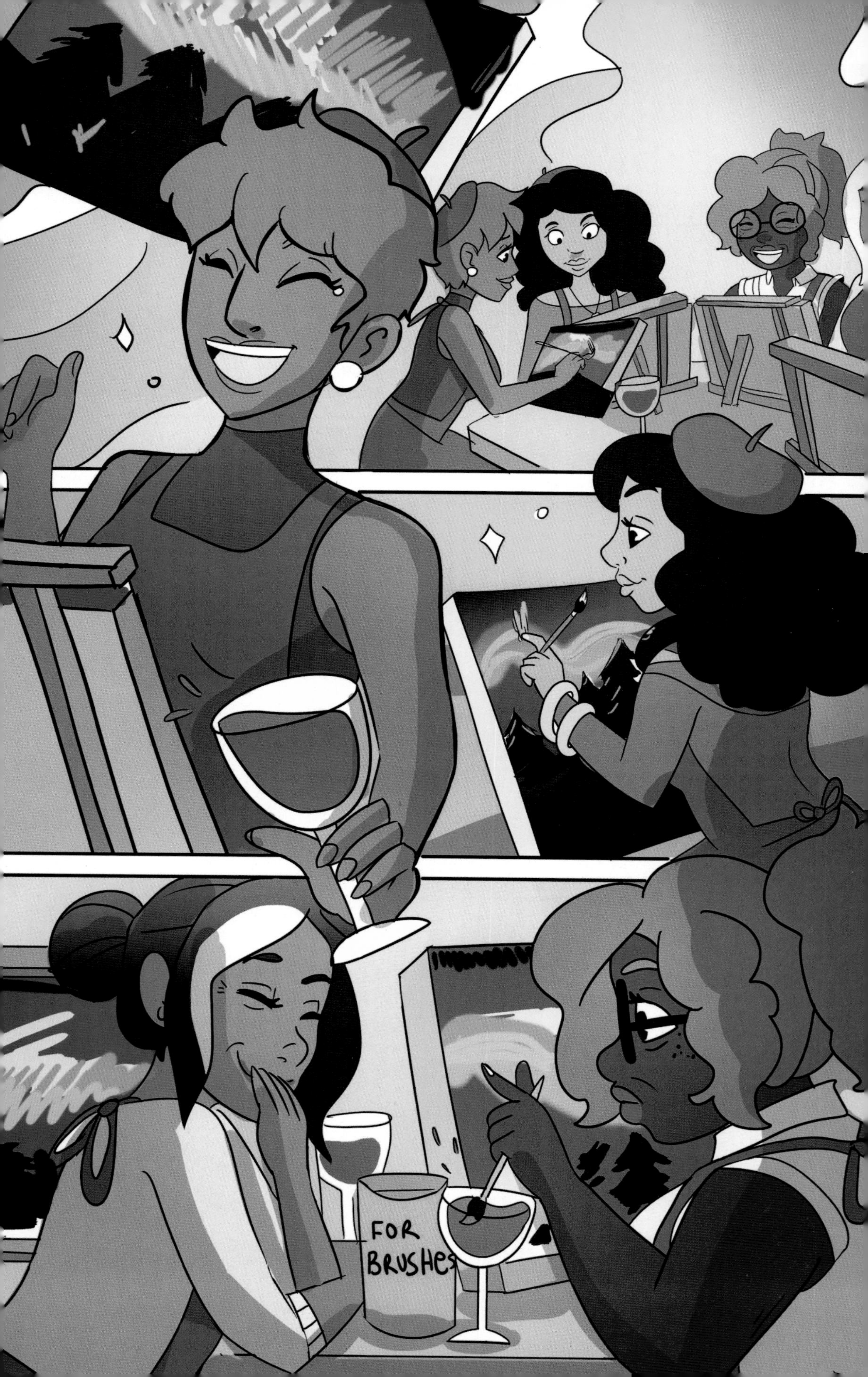
FOR BRUSHES

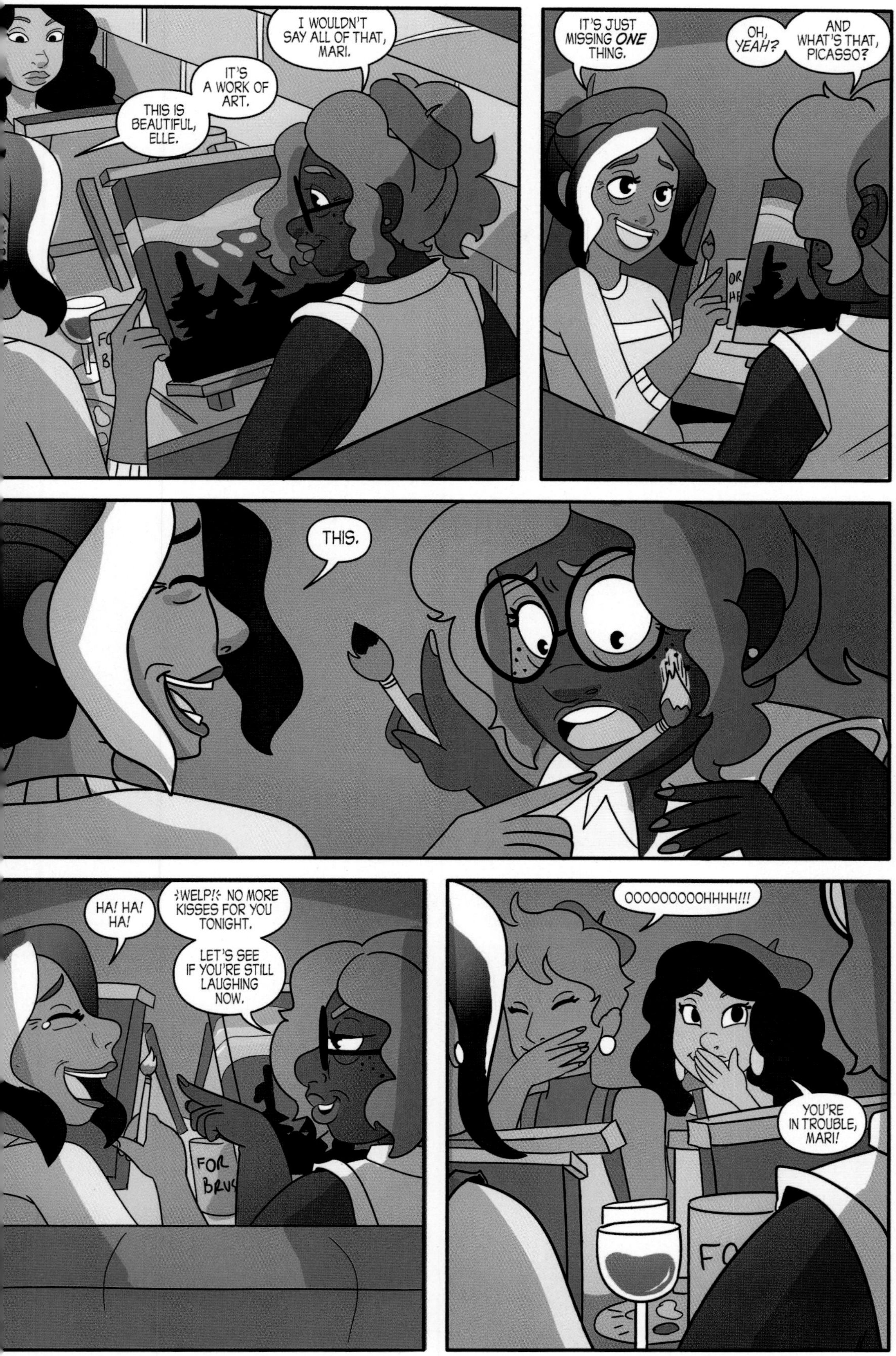
THIS IS BEAUTIFUL, ELLE.
IT'S A WORK OF ART.
I WOULDN'T SAY ALL OF THAT, MARI.
FOR B
IT'S JUST MISSING ONE THING.
OH, YEAH?
AND WHAT'S THAT, PICASSO?
THIS.
HA! HA! HA!
WELP! NO MORE KISSES FOR YOU TONIGHT.
LET'S SEE IF YOU'RE STILL LAUGHING NOW.
FOR BRUS
OOOOOOOOOHHHH!!!
YOU'RE IN TROUBLE, MARI!

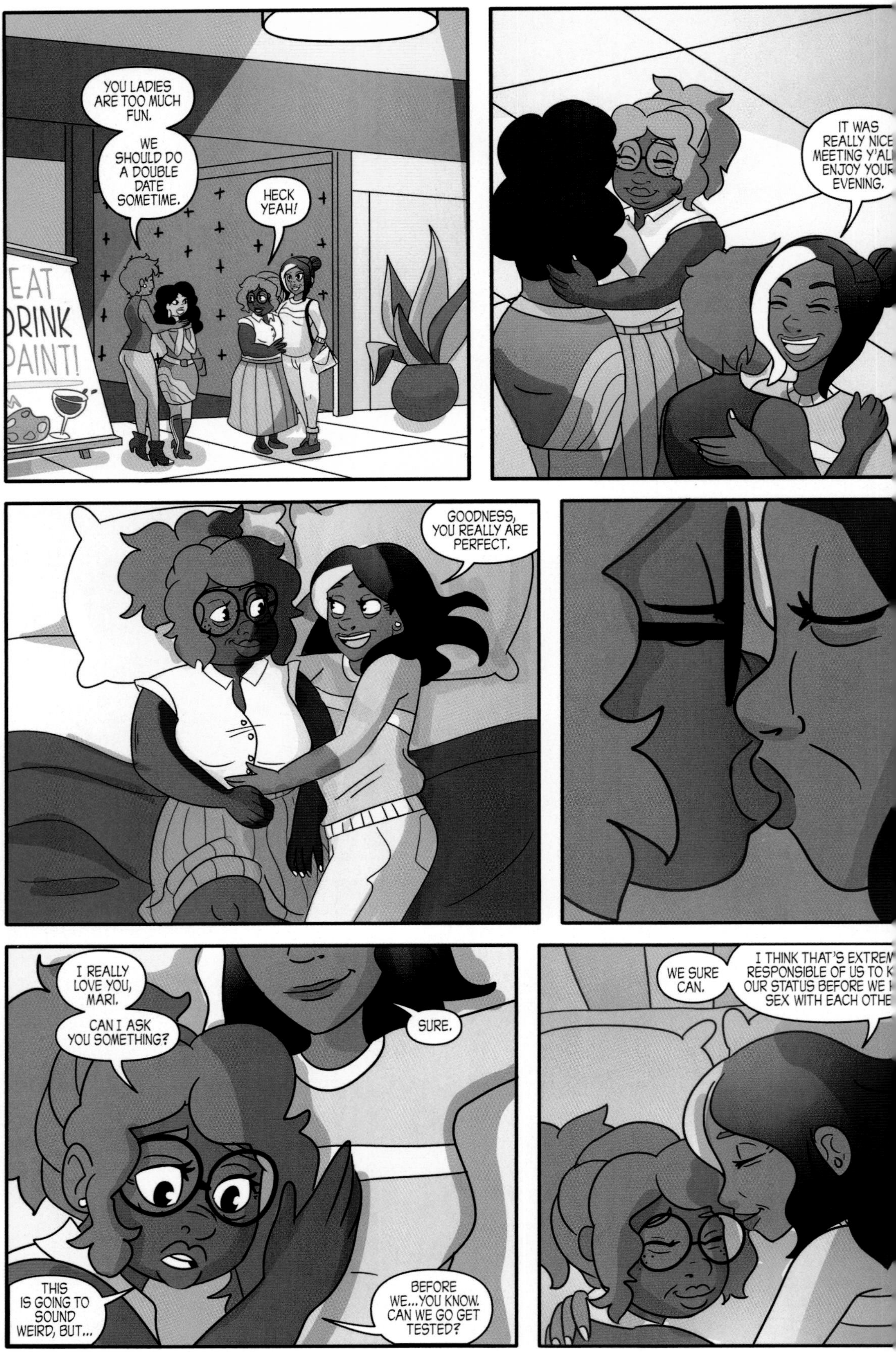

EAT
DRINK
PAINT!
YOU LADIES ARE TOO MUCH FUN.
WE SHOULD DO A DOUBLE DATE SOMETIME.
HECK YEAH!
IT WAS REALLY NICE MEETING Y'AL ENJOY YOUR EVENING.
GOODNESS, YOU REALLY ARE PERFECT.
I REALLY LOVE YOU, MARI.
CAN I ASK YOU SOMETHING?
SURE.
THIS IS GOING TO SOUND WEIRD, BUT...
BEFORE WE...YOU KNOW. CAN WE GO GET TESTED?
WE SURE CAN.
I THINK THAT'S EXTREM RESPONSIBLE OF US TO K OUR STATUS BEFORE WE SEX WITH EACH OTHE

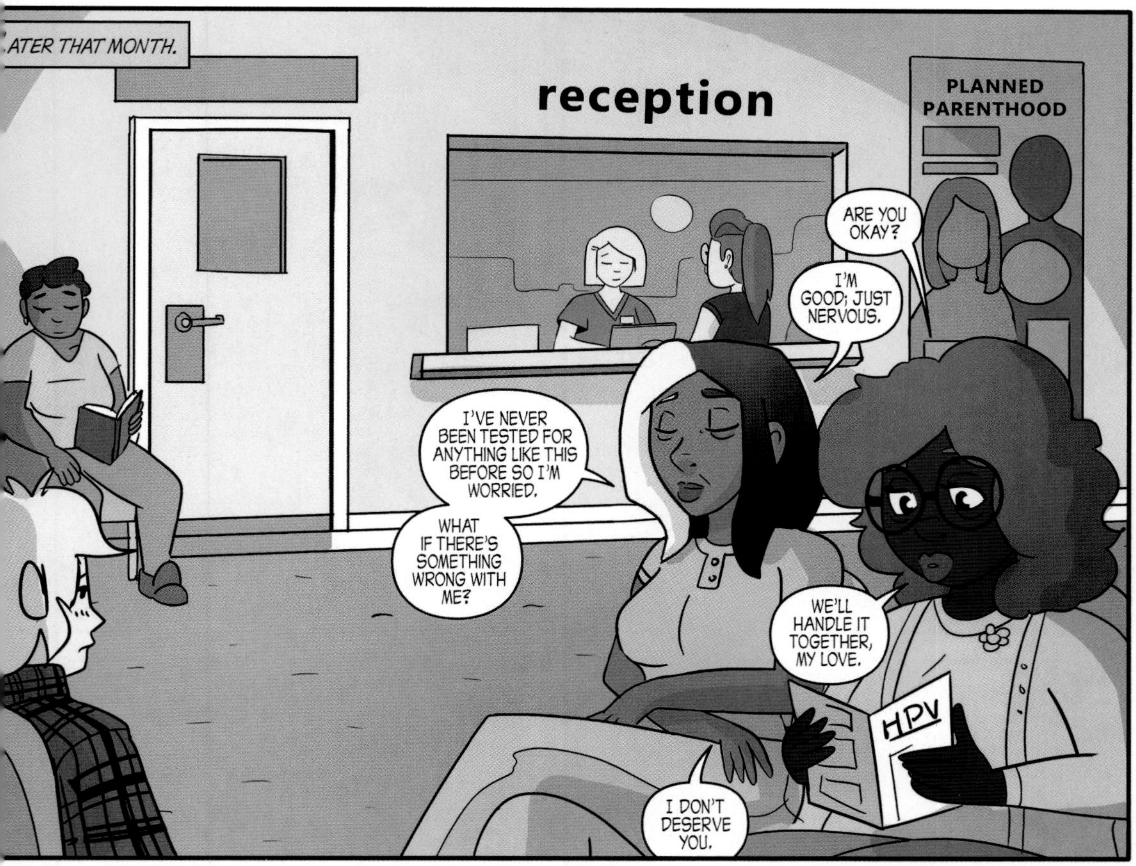
ATER THAT MONTH.
reception
PLANNED PARENTHOOD
ARE YOU OKAY?
I'M GOOD; JUST NERVOUS.
I'VE NEVER BEEN TESTED FOR ANYTHING LIKE THIS BEFORE SO I'M WORRIED.
WHAT IF THERE'S SOMETHING WRONG WITH ME?
WE'LL HANDLE IT TOGETHER, MY LOVE.
HPV
I DON'T DESERVE YOU.

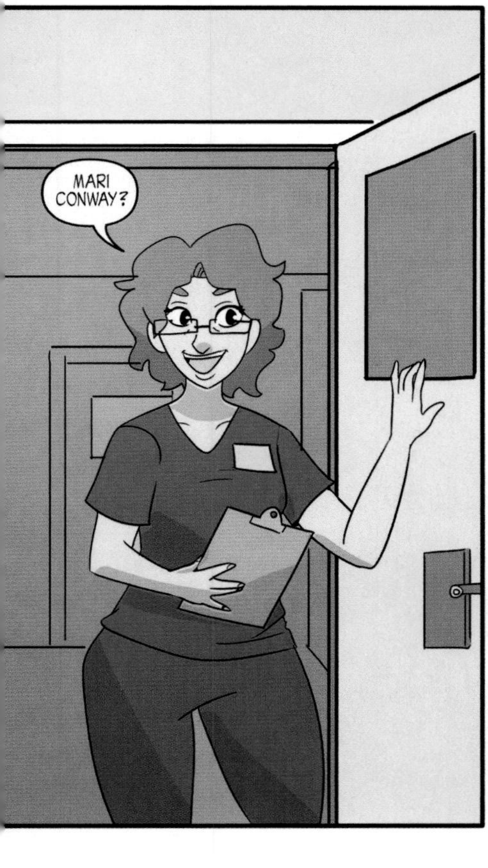
MARI CONWAY?

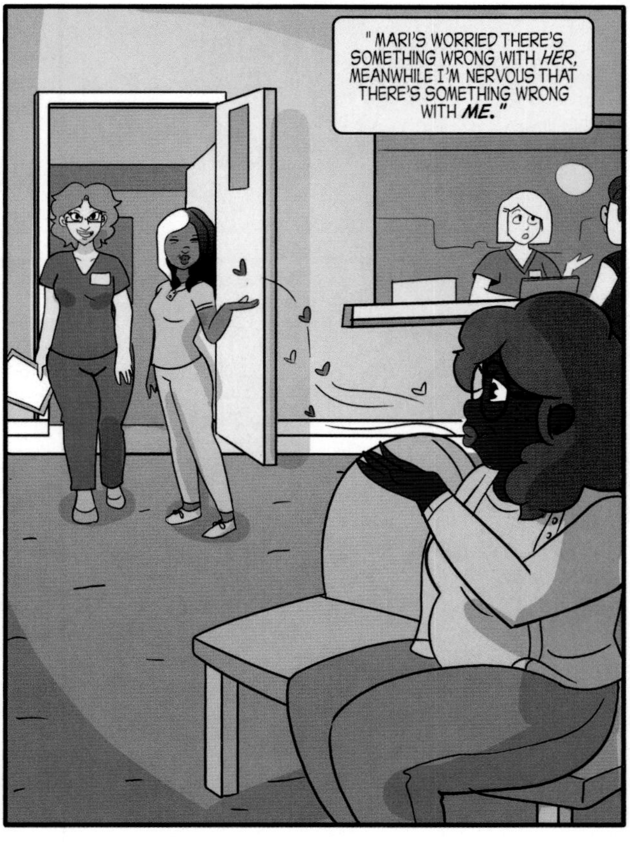
"MARI'S WORRIED THERE'S SOMETHING WRONG WITH *HER*, MEANWHILE I'M NERVOUS THAT THERE'S SOMETHING WRONG WITH ***ME.***"

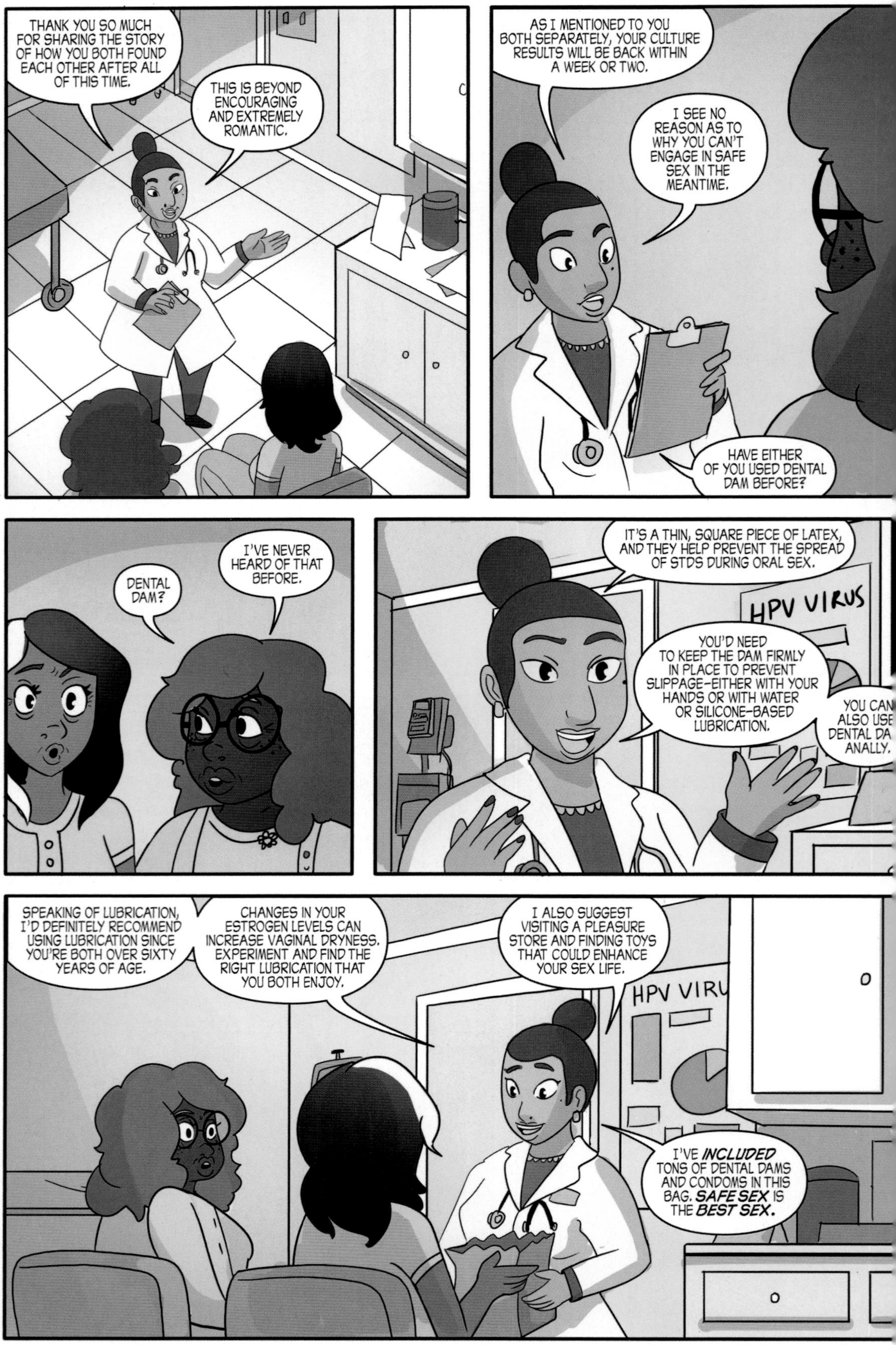
THANK YOU SO MUCH FOR SHARING THE STORY OF HOW YOU BOTH FOUND EACH OTHER AFTER ALL OF THIS TIME.
THIS IS BEYOND ENCOURAGING AND EXTREMELY ROMANTIC.
AS I MENTIONED TO YOU BOTH SEPARATELY, YOUR CULTURE RESULTS WILL BE BACK WITHIN A WEEK OR TWO.
I SEE NO REASON AS TO WHY YOU CAN'T ENGAGE IN SAFE SEX IN THE MEANTIME.
HAVE EITHER OF YOU USED DENTAL DAM BEFORE?
DENTAL DAM?
I'VE NEVER HEARD OF THAT BEFORE.
IT'S A THIN, SQUARE PIECE OF LATEX, AND THEY HELP PREVENT THE SPREAD OF STDS DURING ORAL SEX.
HPV VIRUS
YOU'D NEED TO KEEP THE DAM FIRMLY IN PLACE TO PREVENT SLIPPAGE—EITHER WITH YOUR HANDS OR WITH WATER OR SILICONE-BASED LUBRICATION.
YOU CAN ALSO USE DENTAL DA ANALLY.
SPEAKING OF LUBRICATION, I'D DEFINITELY RECOMMEND USING LUBRICATION SINCE YOU'RE BOTH OVER SIXTY YEARS OF AGE.
CHANGES IN YOUR ESTROGEN LEVELS CAN INCREASE VAGINAL DRYNESS. EXPERIMENT AND FIND THE RIGHT LUBRICATION THAT YOU BOTH ENJOY.
I ALSO SUGGEST VISITING A PLEASURE STORE AND FINDING TOYS THAT COULD ENHANCE YOUR SEX LIFE.
HPV VIRU
I'VE *INCLUDED* TONS OF DENTAL DAMS AND CONDOMS IN THIS BAG. ***SAFE SEX*** IS THE ***BEST SEX***.

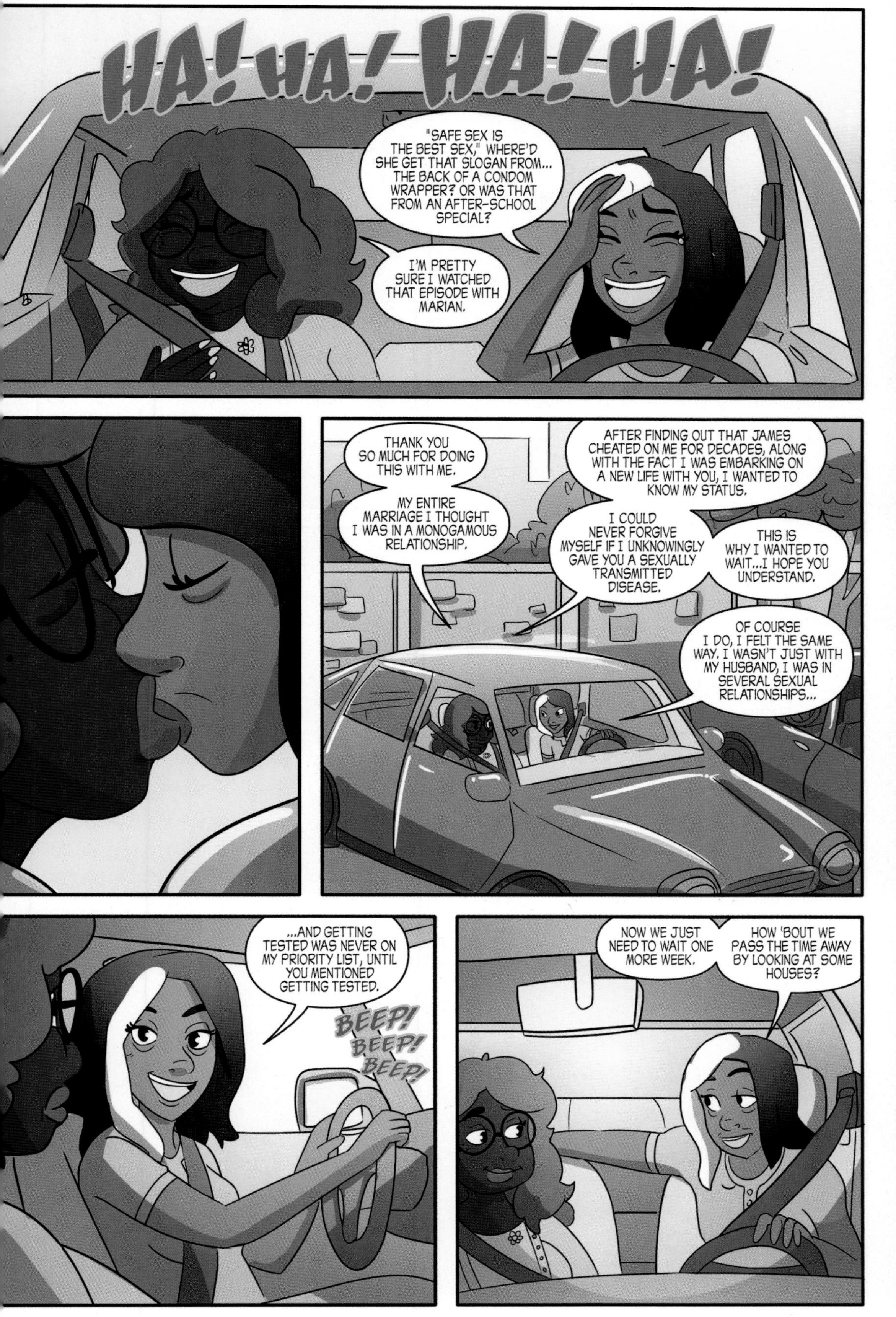
HA! HA! HA! HA!
"SAFE SEX IS THE BEST SEX," WHERE'D SHE GET THAT SLOGAN FROM... THE BACK OF A CONDOM WRAPPER? OR WAS THAT FROM AN AFTER-SCHOOL SPECIAL?
I'M PRETTY SURE I WATCHED THAT EPISODE WITH MARIAN.
THANK YOU SO MUCH FOR DOING THIS WITH ME.
MY ENTIRE MARRIAGE I THOUGHT I WAS IN A MONOGAMOUS RELATIONSHIP.
AFTER FINDING OUT THAT JAMES CHEATED ON ME FOR DECADES, ALONG WITH THE FACT I WAS EMBARKING ON A NEW LIFE WITH YOU, I WANTED TO KNOW MY STATUS.
I COULD NEVER FORGIVE MYSELF IF I UNKNOWINGLY GAVE YOU A SEXUALLY TRANSMITTED DISEASE.
THIS IS WHY I WANTED TO WAIT...I HOPE YOU UNDERSTAND.
OF COURSE I DO, I FELT THE SAME WAY. I WASN'T JUST WITH MY HUSBAND, I WAS IN SEVERAL SEXUAL RELATIONSHIPS...
...AND GETTING TESTED WAS NEVER ON MY PRIORITY LIST, UNTIL YOU MENTIONED GETTING TESTED.
BEEP! BEEP! BEEP!
NOW WE JUST NEED TO WAIT ONE MORE WEEK.
HOW 'BOUT WE PASS THE TIME AWAY BY LOOKING AT SOME HOUSES?

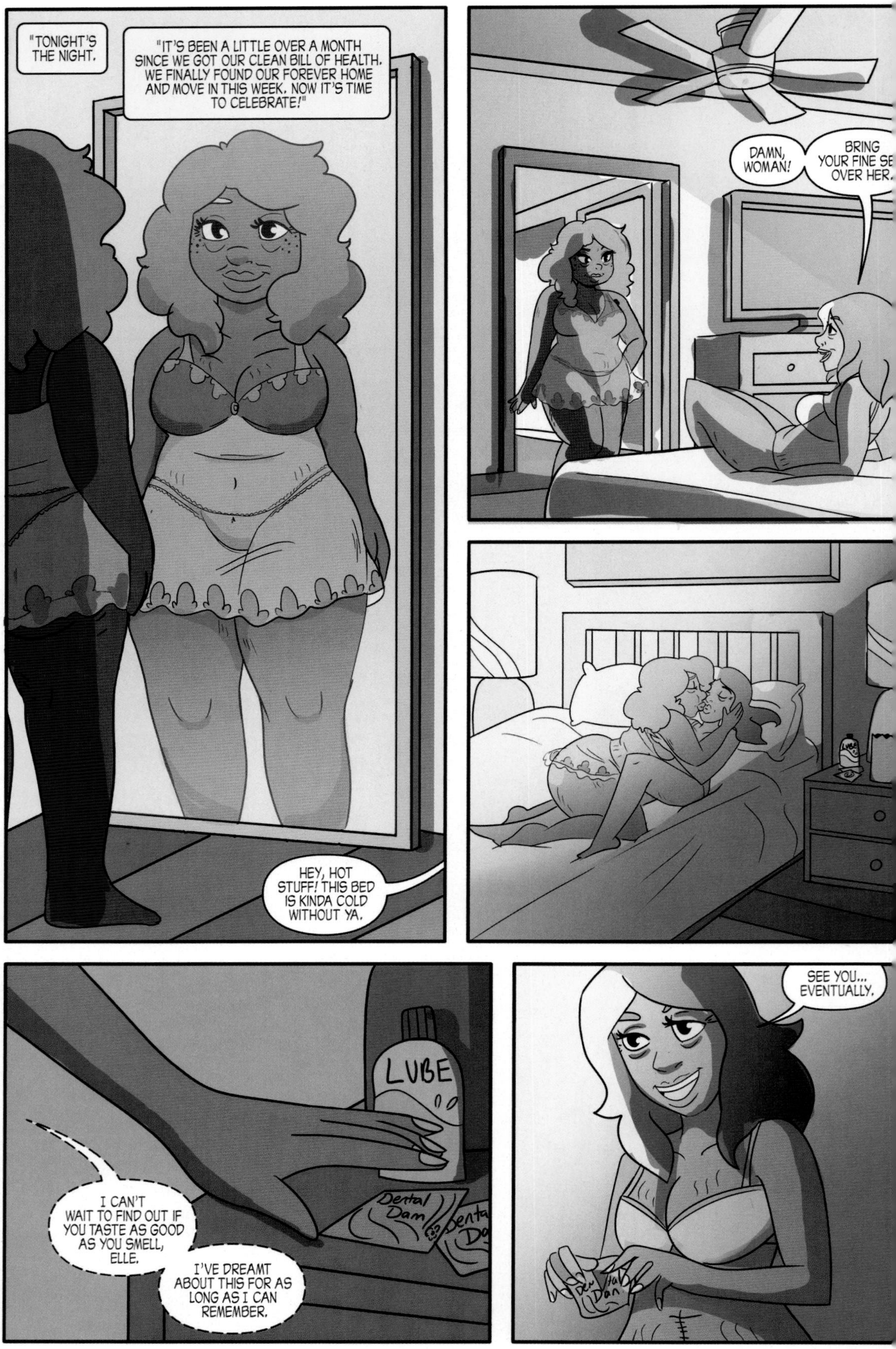
"TONIGHT'S THE NIGHT.
"IT'S BEEN A LITTLE OVER A MONTH SINCE WE GOT OUR CLEAN BILL OF HEALTH. WE FINALLY FOUND OUR FOREVER HOME AND MOVE IN THIS WEEK. NOW IT'S TIME TO CELEBRATE!"
HEY, HOT STUFF! THIS BED IS KINDA COLD WITHOUT YA.
DAMN, WOMAN!
BRING YOUR FINE SE OVER HER
LUBE
I CAN'T WAIT TO FIND OUT IF YOU TASTE AS GOOD AS YOU SMELL, ELLE.
I'VE DREAMT ABOUT THIS FOR AS LONG AS I CAN REMEMBER.
Dental Dam
SEE YOU... EVENTUALLY.

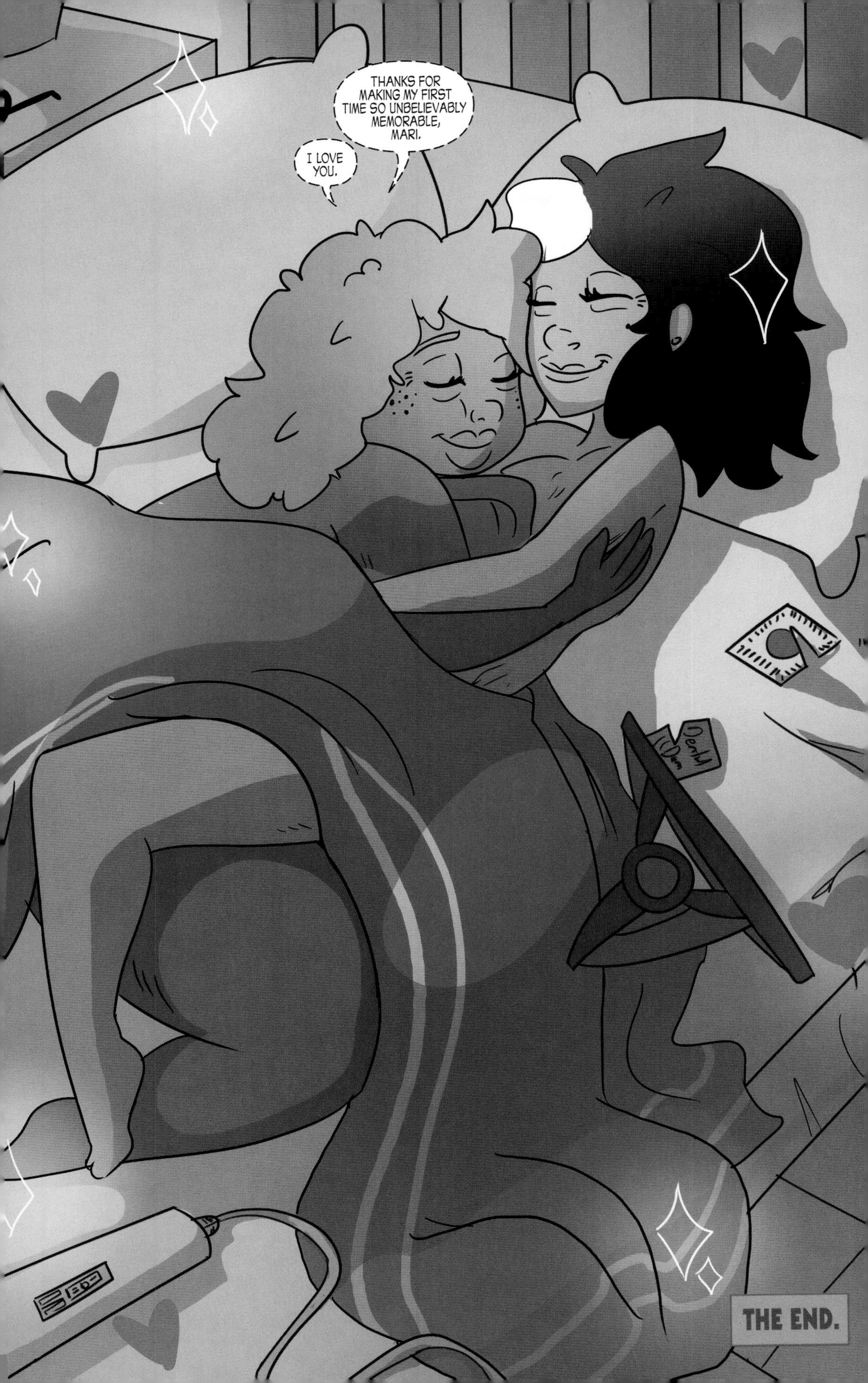
THANKS FOR MAKING MY FIRST TIME SO UNBELIEVABLY MEMORABLE, MARI.
I LOVE YOU.
THE END.

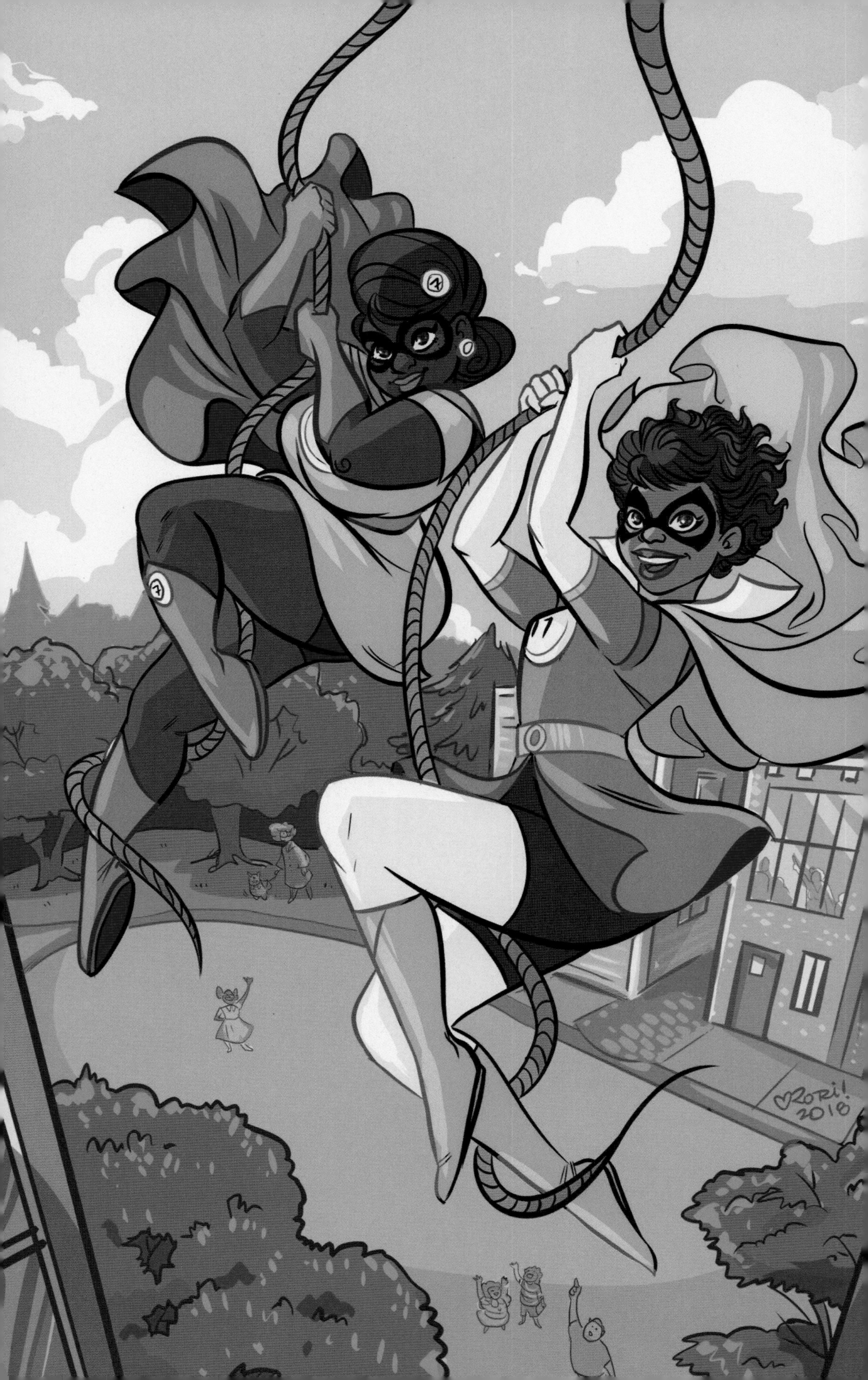
RORI!
2018

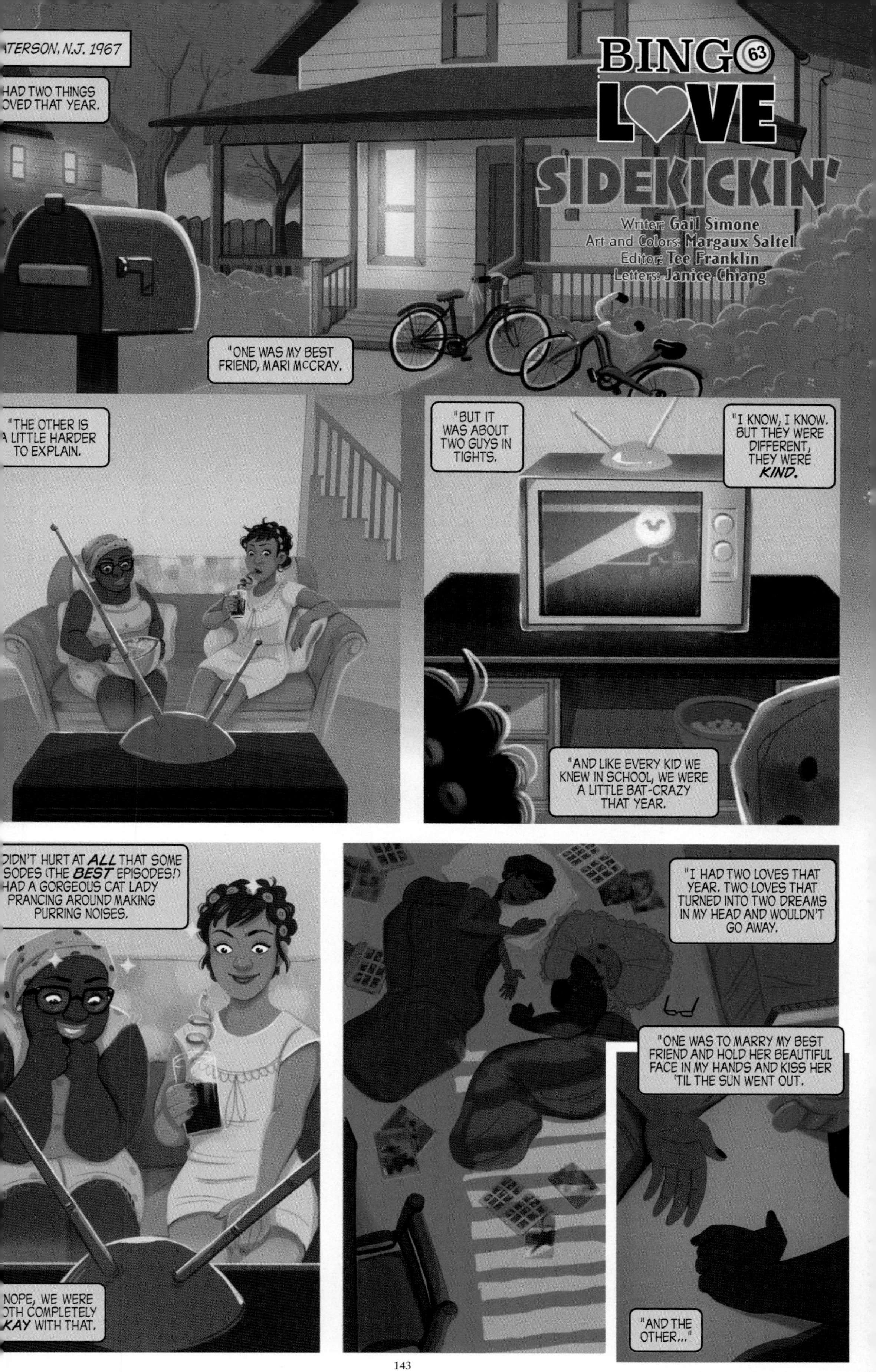
ATERSON, N.J. 1967
HAD TWO THINGS OVED THAT YEAR.
BINGO 63 LOVE
SIDEKICKIN'
Writer: Gail Simone
Art and Colors: Margaux Saltel
Editor: Tee Franklin
Letters: Janice Chiang
"ONE WAS MY BEST FRIEND, MARI McCRAY.
"THE OTHER IS A LITTLE HARDER TO EXPLAIN.
"BUT IT WAS ABOUT TWO GUYS IN TIGHTS.
"I KNOW, I KNOW. BUT THEY WERE DIFFERENT, THEY WERE KIND.
"AND LIKE EVERY KID WE KNEW IN SCHOOL, WE WERE A LITTLE BAT-CRAZY THAT YEAR.
DIDN'T HURT AT ALL THAT SOME SODES (THE BEST EPISODES!) HAD A GORGEOUS CAT LADY PRANCING AROUND MAKING PURRING NOISES.
NOPE, WE WERE OTH COMPLETELY KAY WITH THAT.
"I HAD TWO LOVES THAT YEAR. TWO LOVES THAT TURNED INTO TWO DREAMS IN MY HEAD AND WOULDN'T GO AWAY.
"ONE WAS TO MARRY MY BEST FRIEND AND HOLD HER BEAUTIFUL FACE IN MY HANDS AND KISS HER 'TIL THE SUN WENT OUT.
"AND THE OTHER..."

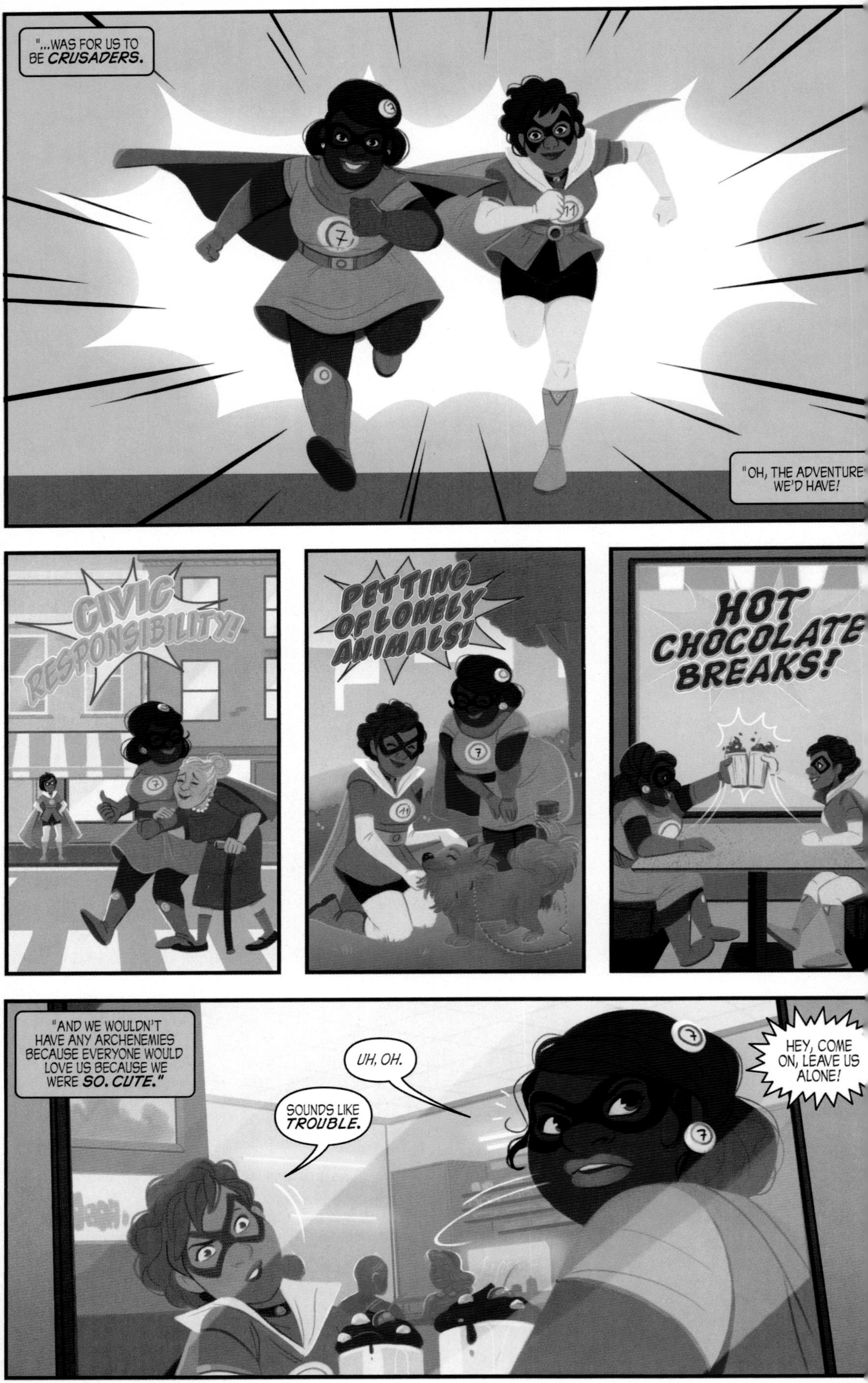
"...WAS FOR US TO BE CRUSADERS.
"OH, THE ADVENTURE WE'D HAVE!
CIVIC RESPONSIBILITY!
PETTING OF LONELY ANIMALS!
HOT CHOCOLATE BREAKS!
"AND WE WOULDN'T HAVE ANY ARCHENEMIES BECAUSE EVERYONE WOULD LOVE US BECAUSE WE WERE SO. CUTE."
UH, OH.
SOUNDS LIKE TROUBLE.
HEY, COME ON, LEAVE US ALONE!

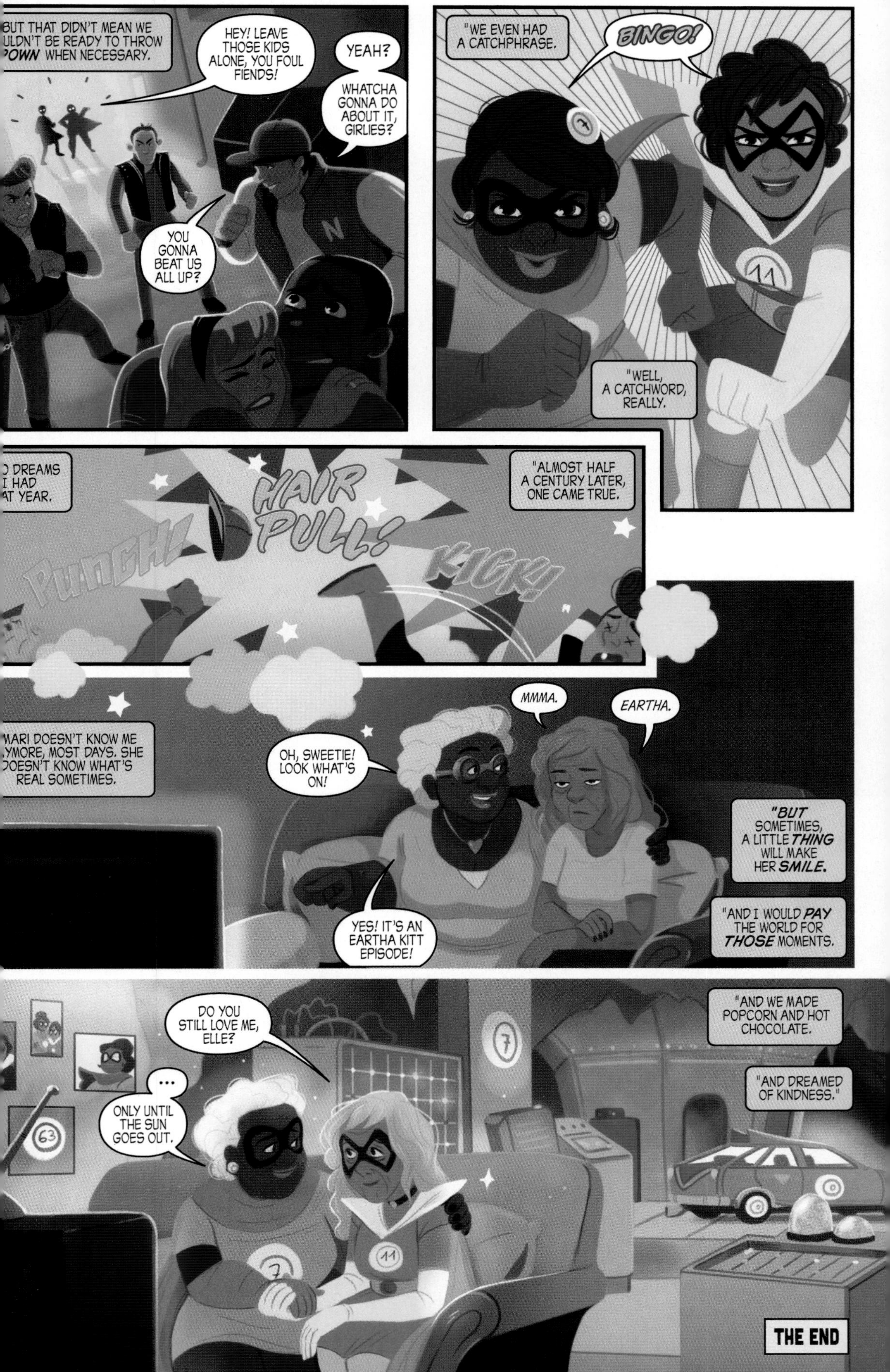
BUT THAT DIDN'T MEAN WE ULDN'T BE READY TO THROW DOWN WHEN NECESSARY.
HEY! LEAVE THOSE KIDS ALONE, YOU FOUL FIENDS!
YEAH?
WHATCHA GONNA DO ABOUT IT, GIRLIES?
YOU GONNA BEAT US ALL UP?
"WE EVEN HAD A CATCHPHRASE.
BINGO!
"WELL, A CATCHWORD, REALLY.
D DREAMS I HAD AT YEAR.
HAIR PULL!
PUNCH!
KICK!
"ALMOST HALF A CENTURY LATER, ONE CAME TRUE.
MARI DOESN'T KNOW ME YMORE, MOST DAYS. SHE DOESN'T KNOW WHAT'S REAL SOMETIMES.
OH, SWEETIE! LOOK WHAT'S ON!
MMMA.
EARTHA.
YES! IT'S AN EARTHA KITT EPISODE!
"BUT SOMETIMES, A LITTLE THING WILL MAKE HER SMILE.
"AND I WOULD PAY THE WORLD FOR THOSE MOMENTS.
DO YOU STILL LOVE ME, ELLE?
...
ONLY UNTIL THE SUN GOES OUT.
"AND WE MADE POPCORN AND HOT CHOCOLATE.
"AND DREAMED OF KINDNESS."
THE END

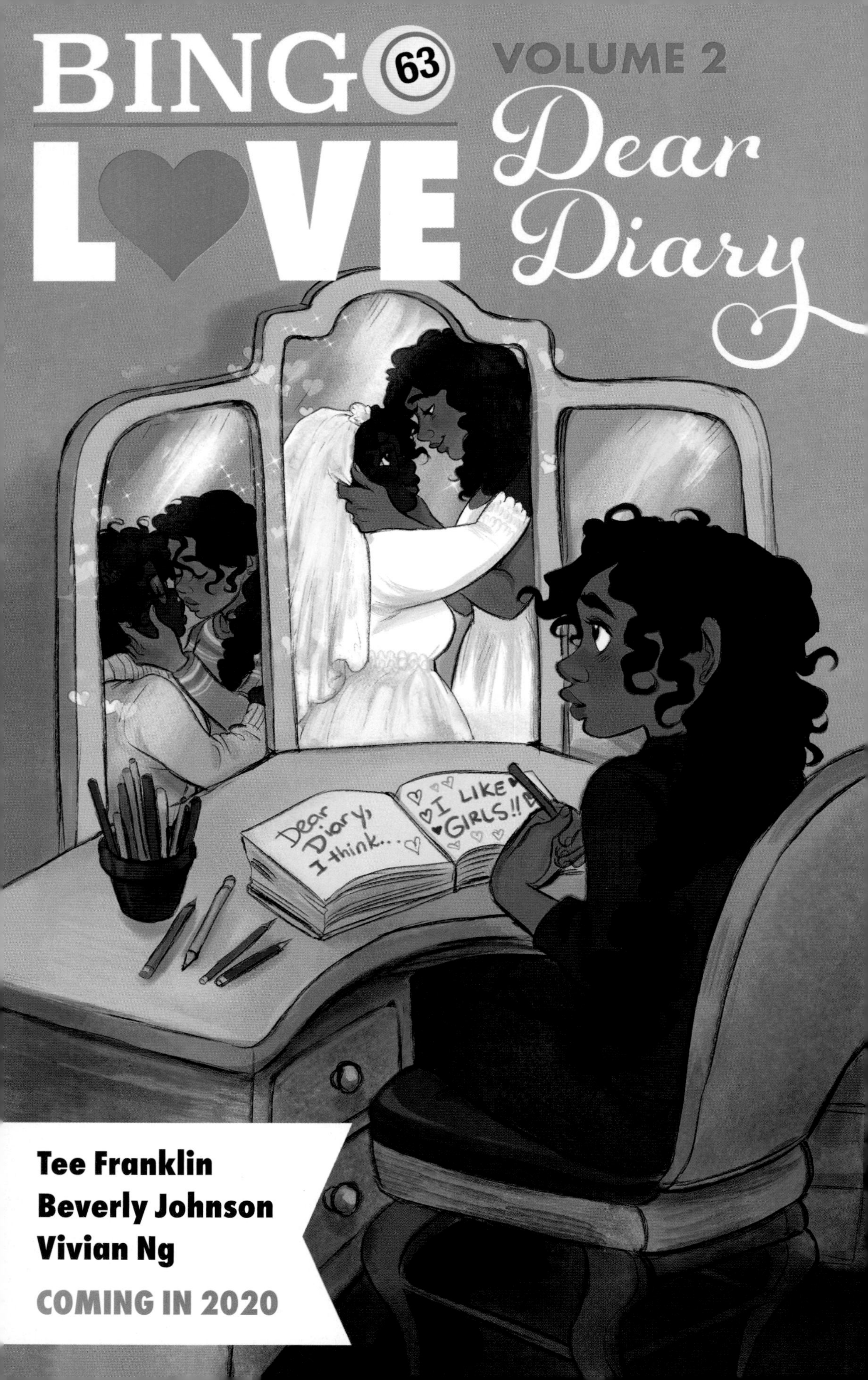
BINGO 63
LOVE
VOLUME 2
Dear Diary
Dear Diary, I think...
I LIKE GIRLS!!
Tee Franklin
Beverly Johnson
Vivian Ng
COMING IN 2020

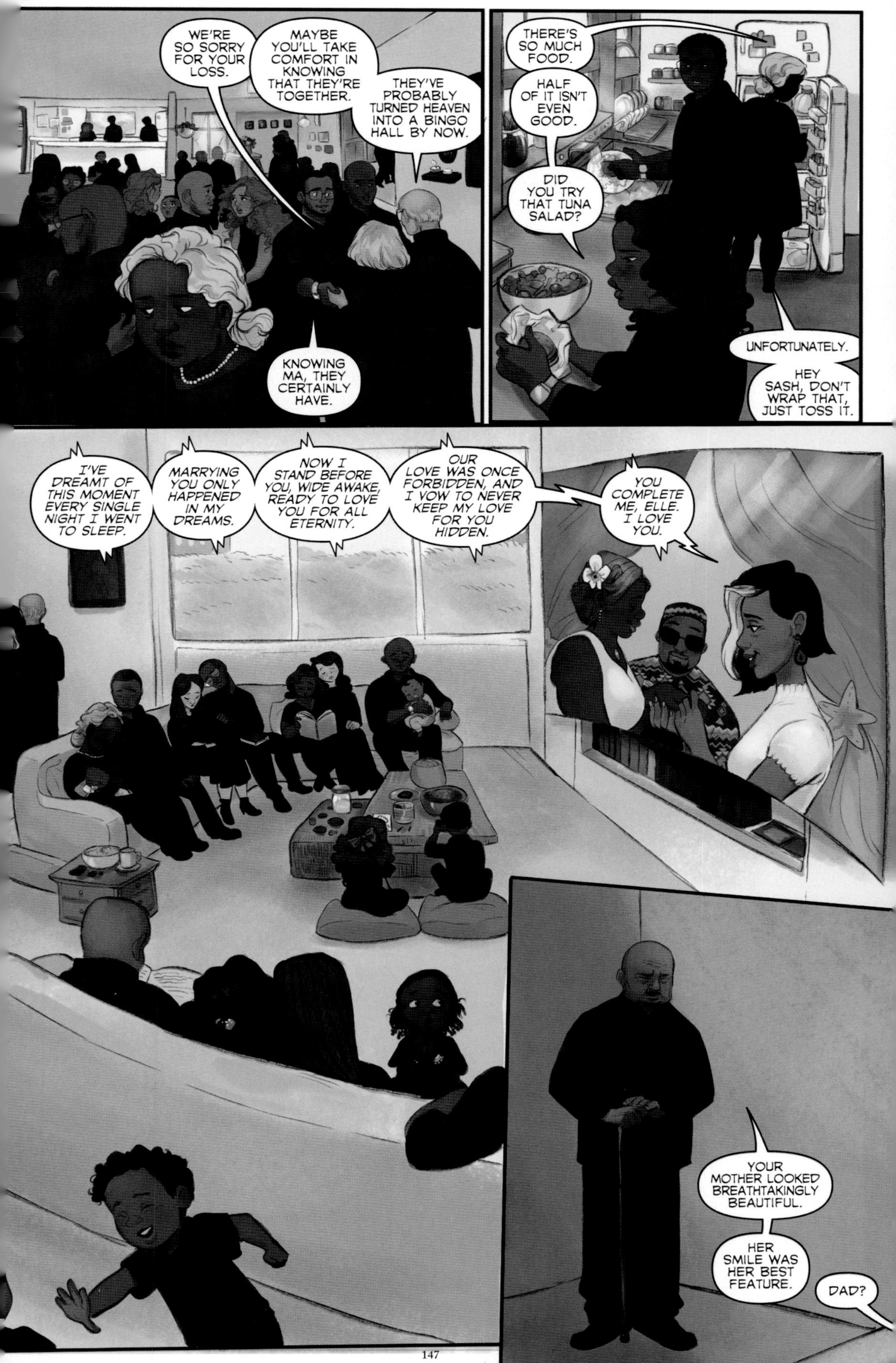
WE'RE SO SORRY FOR YOUR LOSS.
MAYBE YOU'LL TAKE COMFORT IN KNOWING THAT THEY'RE TOGETHER.
THEY'VE PROBABLY TURNED HEAVEN INTO A BINGO HALL BY NOW.
KNOWING MA, THEY CERTAINLY HAVE.
THERE'S SO MUCH FOOD.
HALF OF IT ISN'T EVEN GOOD.
DID YOU TRY THAT TUNA SALAD?
UNFORTUNATELY.
HEY SASH, DON'T WRAP THAT, JUST TOSS IT.
I'VE DREAMT OF THIS MOMENT EVERY SINGLE NIGHT I WENT TO SLEEP.
MARRYING YOU ONLY HAPPENED IN MY DREAMS.
NOW I STAND BEFORE YOU, WIDE AWAKE, READY TO LOVE YOU FOR ALL ETERNITY.
OUR LOVE WAS ONCE FORBIDDEN, AND I VOW TO NEVER KEEP MY LOVE FOR YOU HIDDEN.
YOU COMPLETE ME, ELLE. I LOVE YOU.
YOUR MOTHER LOOKED BREATHTAKINGLY BEAUTIFUL.
HER SMILE WAS HER BEST FEATURE.
DAD?

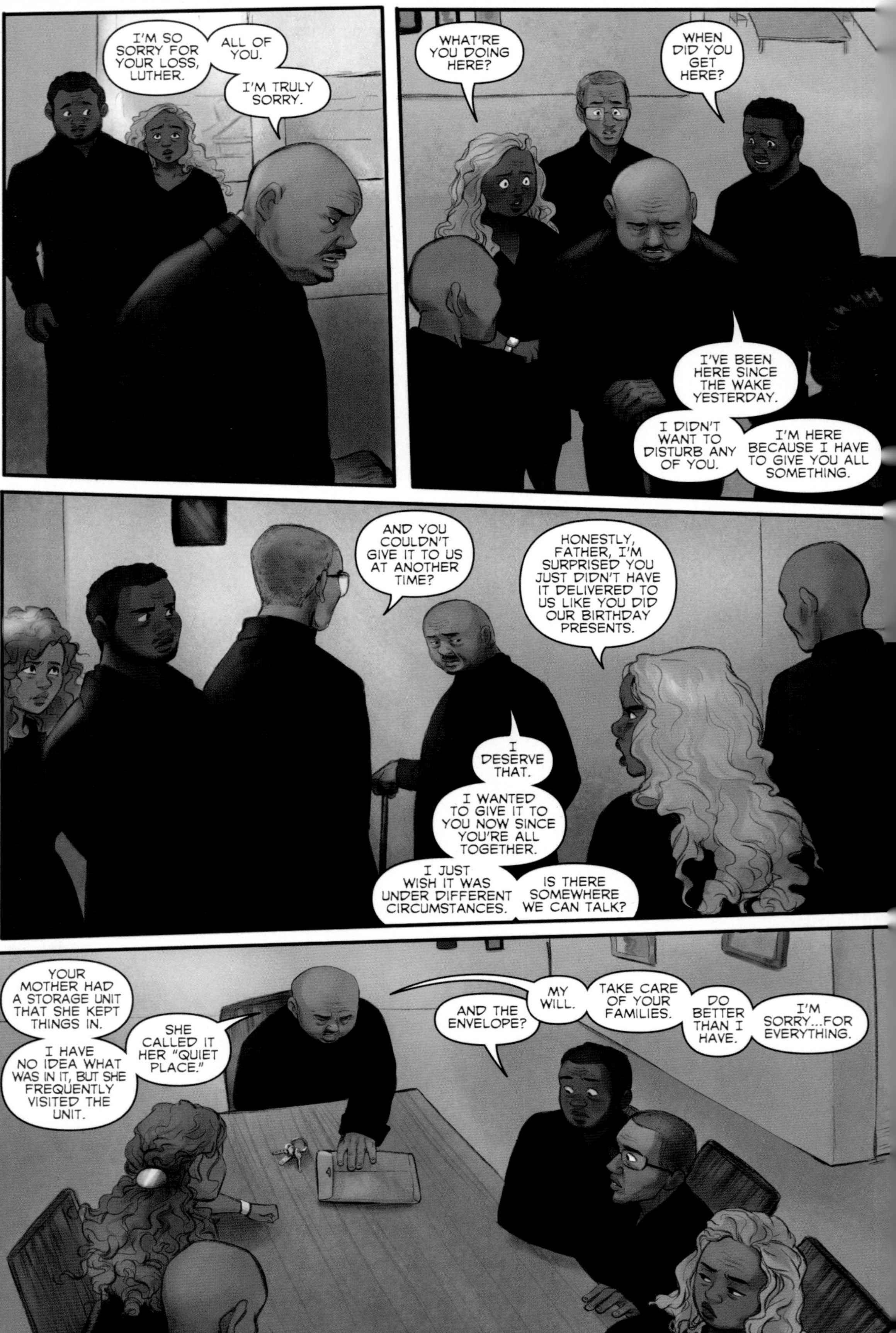
I'M SO SORRY FOR YOUR LOSS, LUTHER.
ALL OF YOU.
I'M TRULY SORRY.
WHAT'RE YOU DOING HERE?
WHEN DID YOU GET HERE?
I'VE BEEN HERE SINCE THE WAKE YESTERDAY.
I DIDN'T WANT TO DISTURB ANY OF YOU.
I'M HERE BECAUSE I HAVE TO GIVE YOU ALL SOMETHING.
AND YOU COULDN'T GIVE IT TO US AT ANOTHER TIME?
HONESTLY, FATHER, I'M SURPRISED YOU JUST DIDN'T HAVE IT DELIVERED TO US LIKE YOU DID OUR BIRTHDAY PRESENTS.
I DESERVE THAT.
I WANTED TO GIVE IT TO YOU NOW SINCE YOU'RE ALL TOGETHER.
I JUST WISH IT WAS UNDER DIFFERENT CIRCUMSTANCES.
IS THERE SOMEWHERE WE CAN TALK?
YOUR MOTHER HAD A STORAGE UNIT THAT SHE KEPT THINGS IN.
I HAVE NO IDEA WHAT WAS IN IT, BUT SHE FREQUENTLY VISITED THE UNIT.
SHE CALLED IT HER "QUIET PLACE."
AND THE ENVELOPE?
MY WILL.
TAKE CARE OF YOUR FAMILIES.
DO BETTER THAN I HAVE.
I'M SORRY...FOR EVERYTHING.

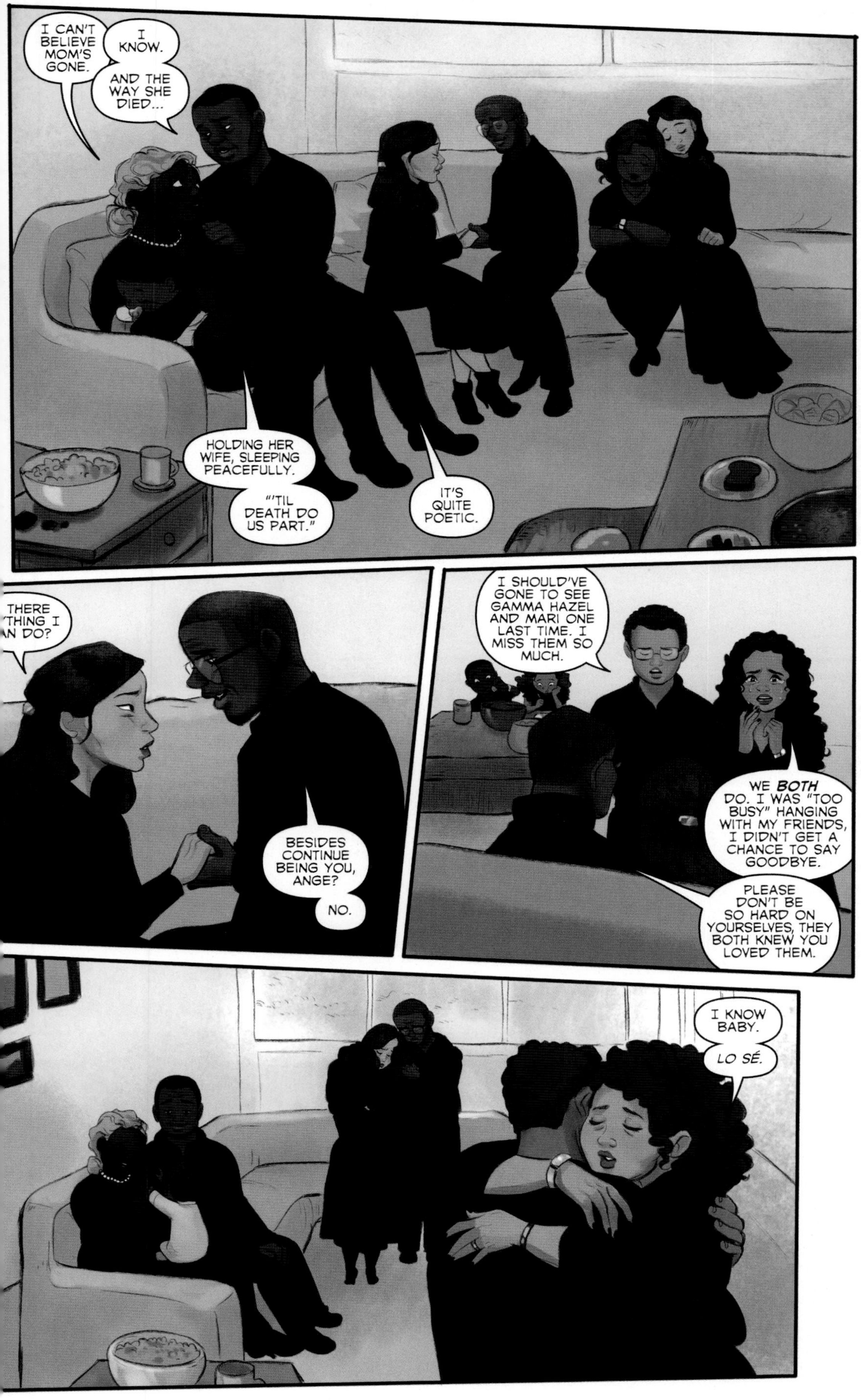
I CAN'T BELIEVE MOM'S GONE.
I KNOW.
AND THE WAY SHE DIED...
HOLDING HER WIFE, SLEEPING PEACEFULLY.
"'TIL DEATH DO US PART."
IT'S QUITE POETIC.
THERE ...THING I ...N DO?
BESIDES CONTINUE BEING YOU, ANGE?
NO.
I SHOULD'VE GONE TO SEE GAMMA HAZEL AND MARI ONE LAST TIME. I MISS THEM SO MUCH.
WE BOTH DO. I WAS "TOO BUSY" HANGING WITH MY FRIENDS, I DIDN'T GET A CHANCE TO SAY GOODBYE.
PLEASE DON'T BE SO HARD ON YOURSELVES, THEY BOTH KNEW YOU LOVED THEM.
I KNOW BABY.
LO SÉ.

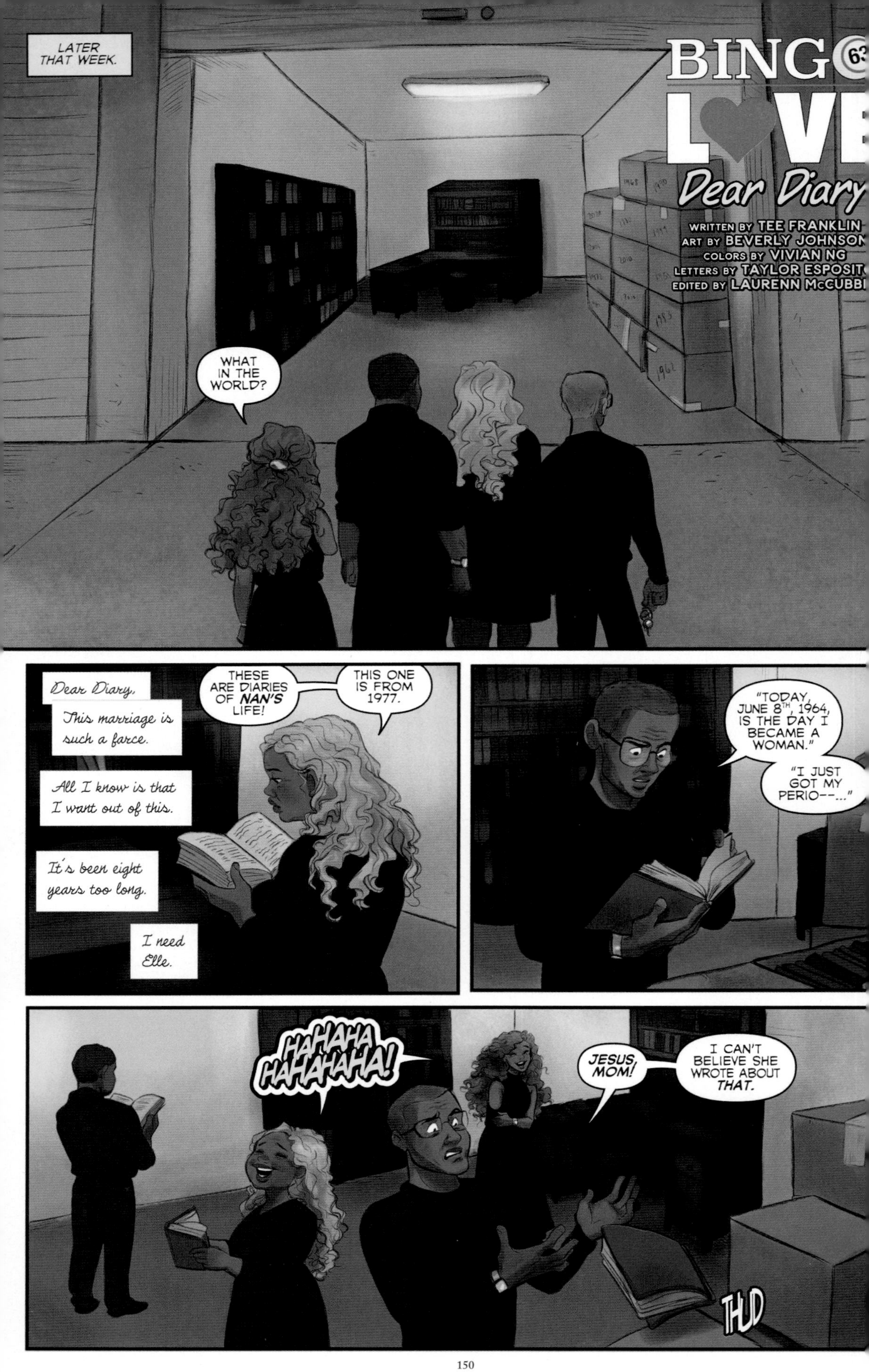

LATER THAT WEEK.
BINGO 63 LOVE
Dear Diary
WRITTEN BY TEE FRANKLIN
ART BY BEVERLY JOHNSON
COLORS BY VIVIAN NG
LETTERS BY TAYLOR ESPOSITO
EDITED BY LAURENN McCUBBIN
WHAT IN THE WORLD?
Dear Diary,
This marriage is such a farce.
All I know is that I want out of this.
It's been eight years too long.
I need Elle.
THESE ARE DIARIES OF NAN'S LIFE!
THIS ONE IS FROM 1977.
"TODAY, JUNE 8TH, 1964, IS THE DAY I BECAME A WOMAN."
"I JUST GOT MY PERIO--..."
HAHAHA HAHAHAHA!
JESUS, MOM!
I CAN'T BELIEVE SHE WROTE ABOUT THAT.
THUD

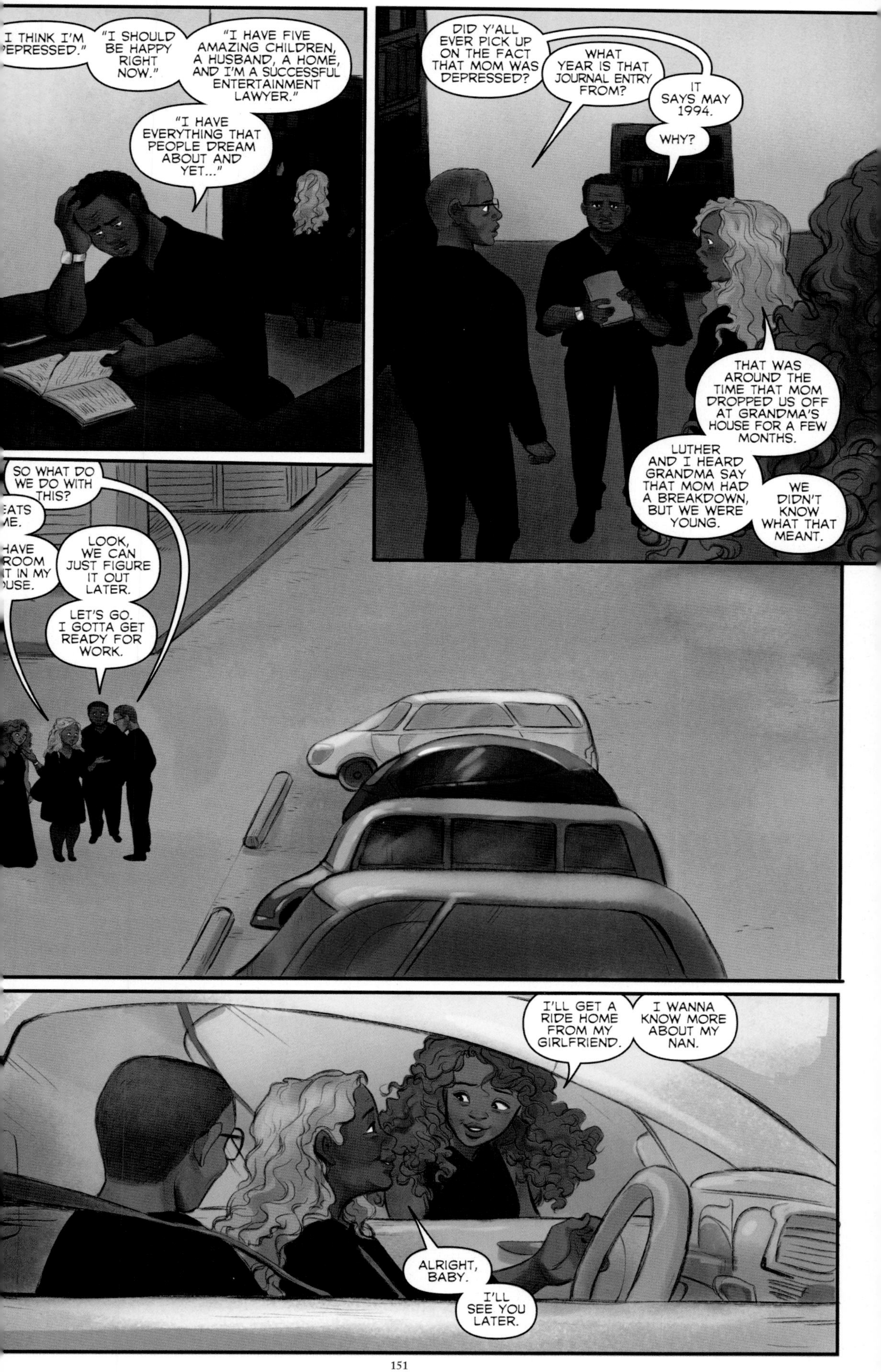
I THINK I'M DEPRESSED."
"I SHOULD BE HAPPY RIGHT NOW."
"I HAVE FIVE AMAZING CHILDREN, A HUSBAND, A HOME, AND I'M A SUCCESSFUL ENTERTAINMENT LAWYER."
"I HAVE EVERYTHING THAT PEOPLE DREAM ABOUT AND YET..."
DID Y'ALL EVER PICK UP ON THE FACT THAT MOM WAS DEPRESSED?
WHAT YEAR IS THAT JOURNAL ENTRY FROM?
IT SAYS MAY 1994.
WHY?
THAT WAS AROUND THE TIME THAT MOM DROPPED US OFF AT GRANDMA'S HOUSE FOR A FEW MONTHS.
LUTHER AND I HEARD GRANDMA SAY THAT MOM HAD A BREAKDOWN, BUT WE WERE YOUNG.
WE DIDN'T KNOW WHAT THAT MEANT.
SO WHAT DO WE DO WITH THIS?
EATS ME.
HAVE ROOM T IN MY OUSE.
LOOK, WE CAN JUST FIGURE IT OUT LATER.
LET'S GO. I GOTTA GET READY FOR WORK.
I'LL GET A RIDE HOME FROM MY GIRLFRIEND.
I WANNA KNOW MORE ABOUT MY NAN.
ALRIGHT, BABY.
I'LL SEE YOU LATER.

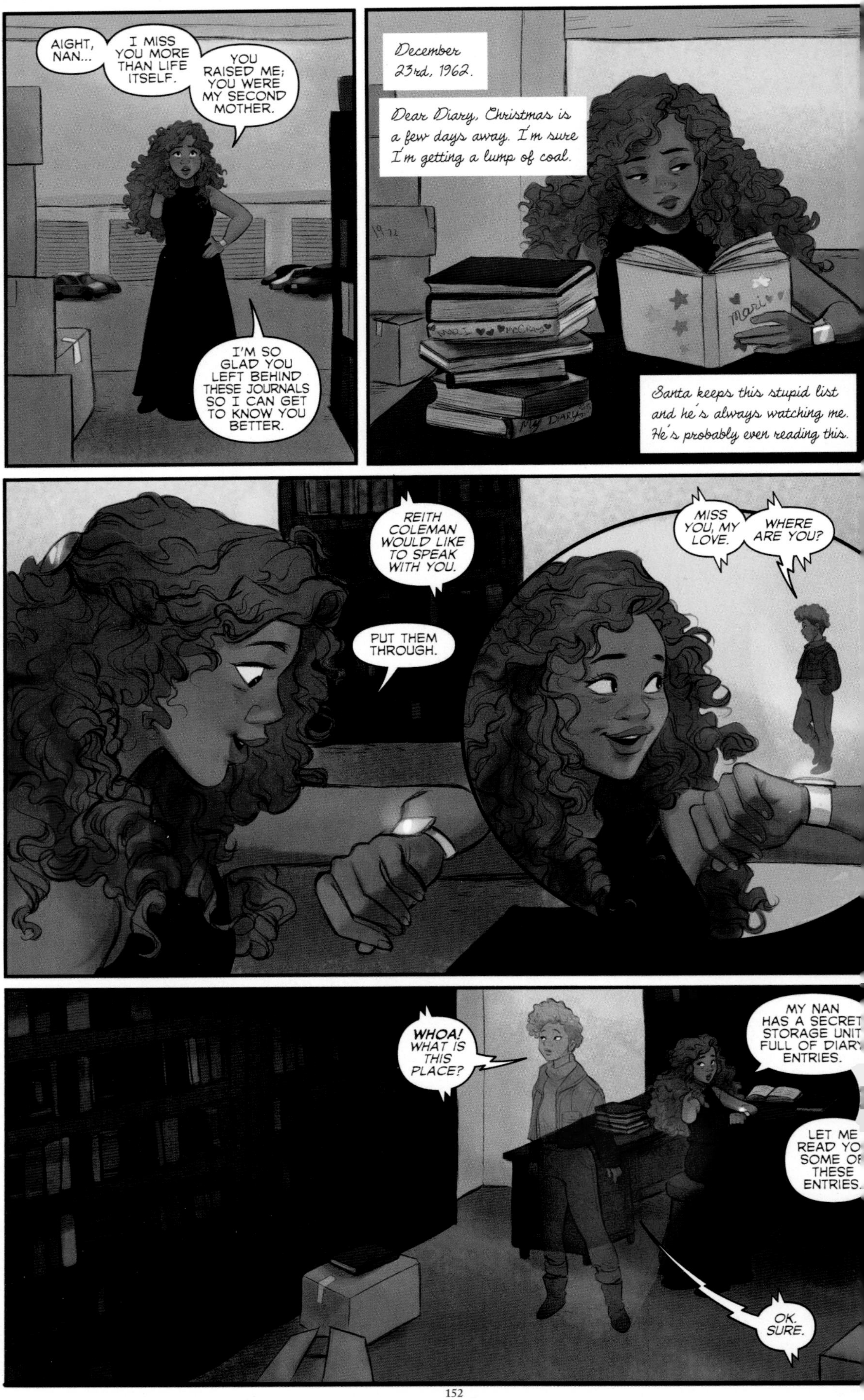
AIGHT, NAN...
I MISS YOU MORE THAN LIFE ITSELF.
YOU RAISED ME; YOU WERE MY SECOND MOTHER.
I'M SO GLAD YOU LEFT BEHIND THESE JOURNALS SO I CAN GET TO KNOW YOU BETTER.
December 23rd, 1962.
Dear Diary, Christmas is a few days away. I'm sure I'm getting a lump of coal.
Mari
Santa keeps this stupid list and he's always watching me. He's probably even reading this.
REITH COLEMAN WOULD LIKE TO SPEAK WITH YOU.
PUT THEM THROUGH.
MISS YOU, MY LOVE.
WHERE ARE YOU?
WHOA! WHAT IS THIS PLACE?
MY NAN HAS A SECRET STORAGE UNIT FULL OF DIARY ENTRIES.
LET ME READ YOU SOME OF THESE ENTRIES.
OK. SURE.

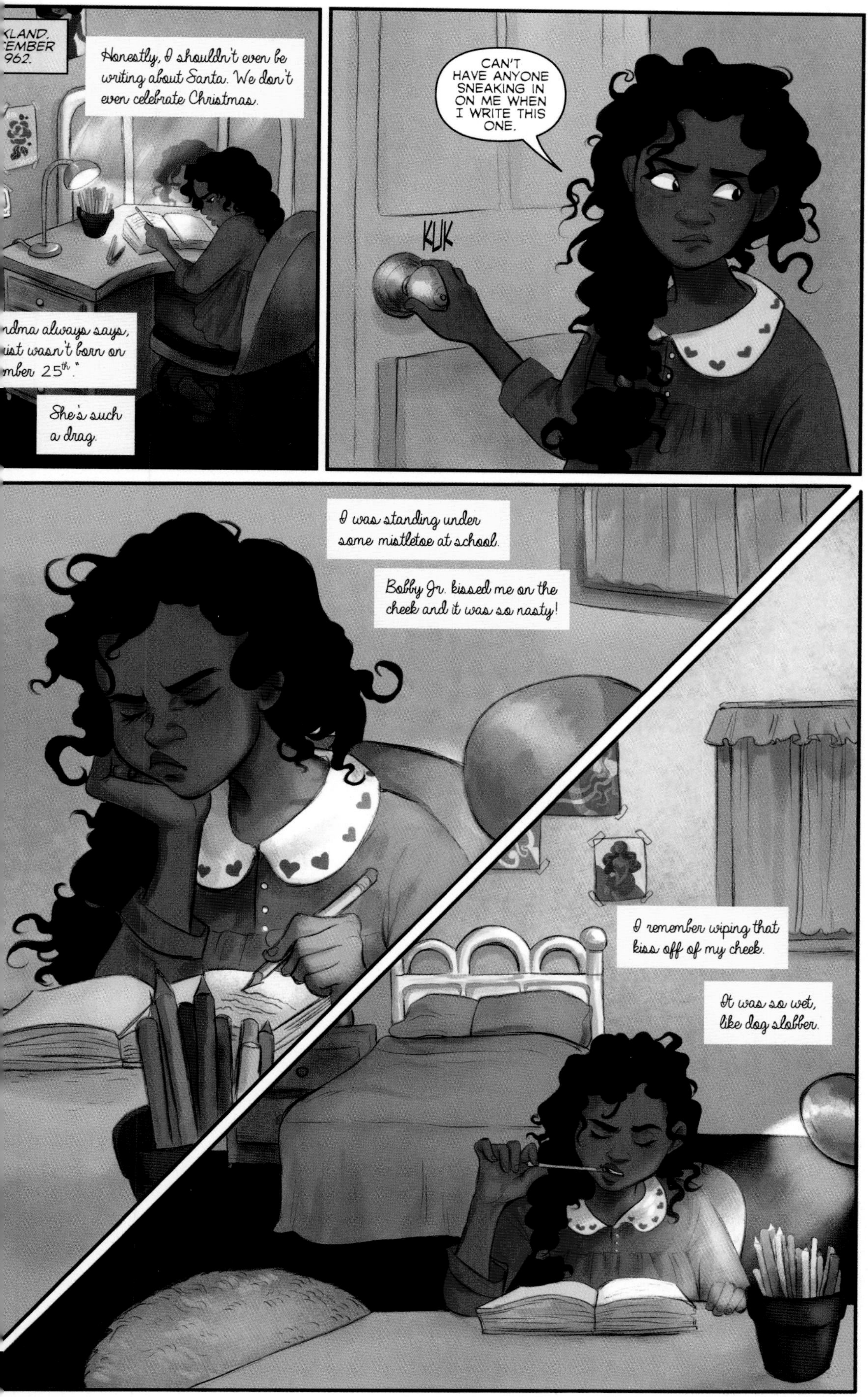
KLAND.
CEMBER
962.
Honestly, I shouldn't even be writing about Santa. We don't even celebrate Christmas.
ndma always says,
rist wasn't born on
mber 25th."
She's such a drag.
CAN'T HAVE ANYONE SNEAKING IN ON ME WHEN I WRITE THIS ONE.
KLIK
I was standing under some mistletoe at school.
Bobby Jr. kissed me on the cheek and it was so nasty!
I remember wiping that kiss off of my cheek.
It was so wet, like dog slobber.

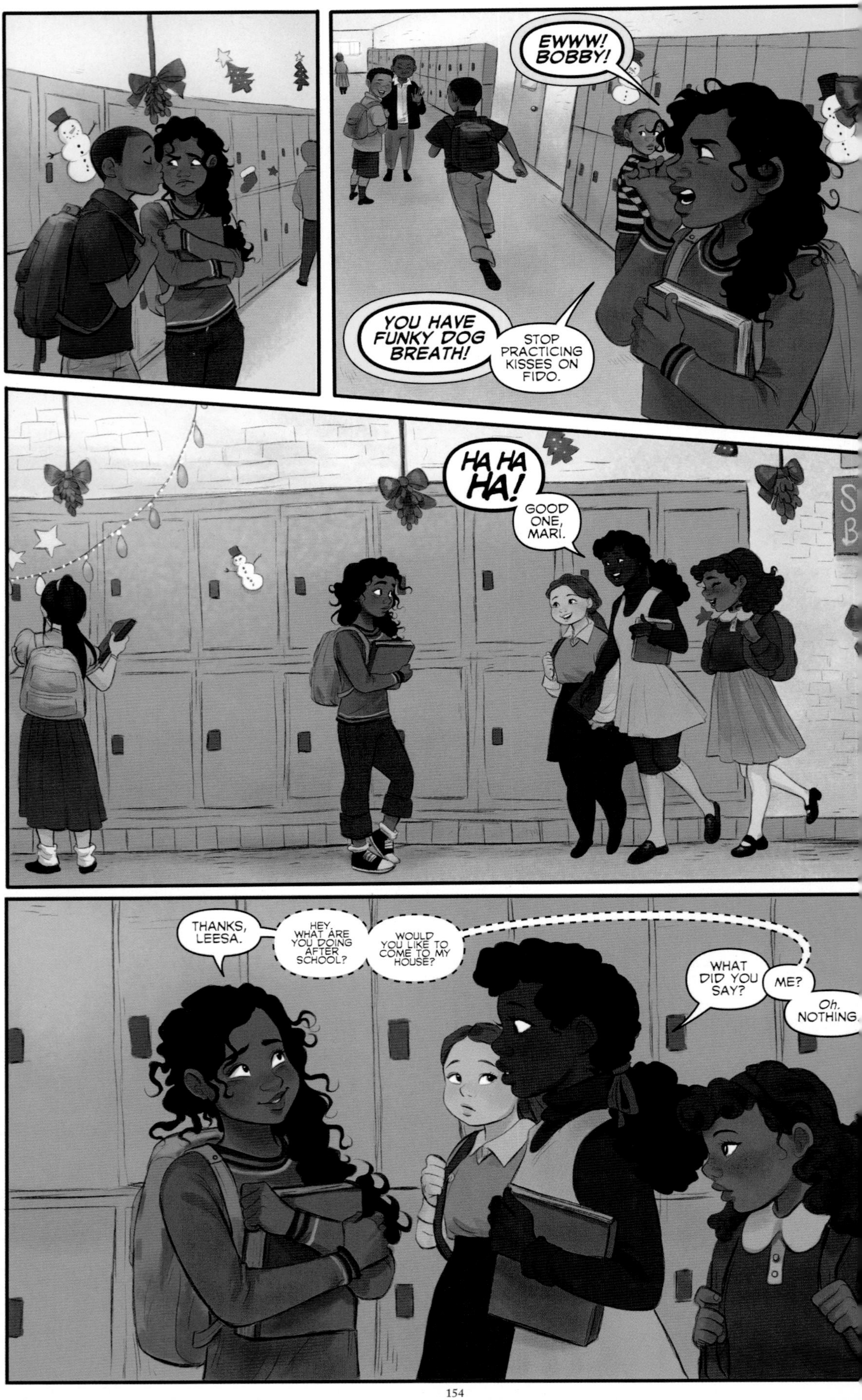
EWWW! BOBBY!
YOU HAVE FUNKY DOG BREATH!
STOP PRACTICING KISSES ON FIDO.
HA HA HA!
GOOD ONE, MARI.
THANKS, LEESA.
HEY. WHAT ARE YOU DOING AFTER SCHOOL?
WOULD YOU LIKE TO COME TO MY HOUSE?
WHAT DID YOU SAY?
ME?
Oh. NOTHING.

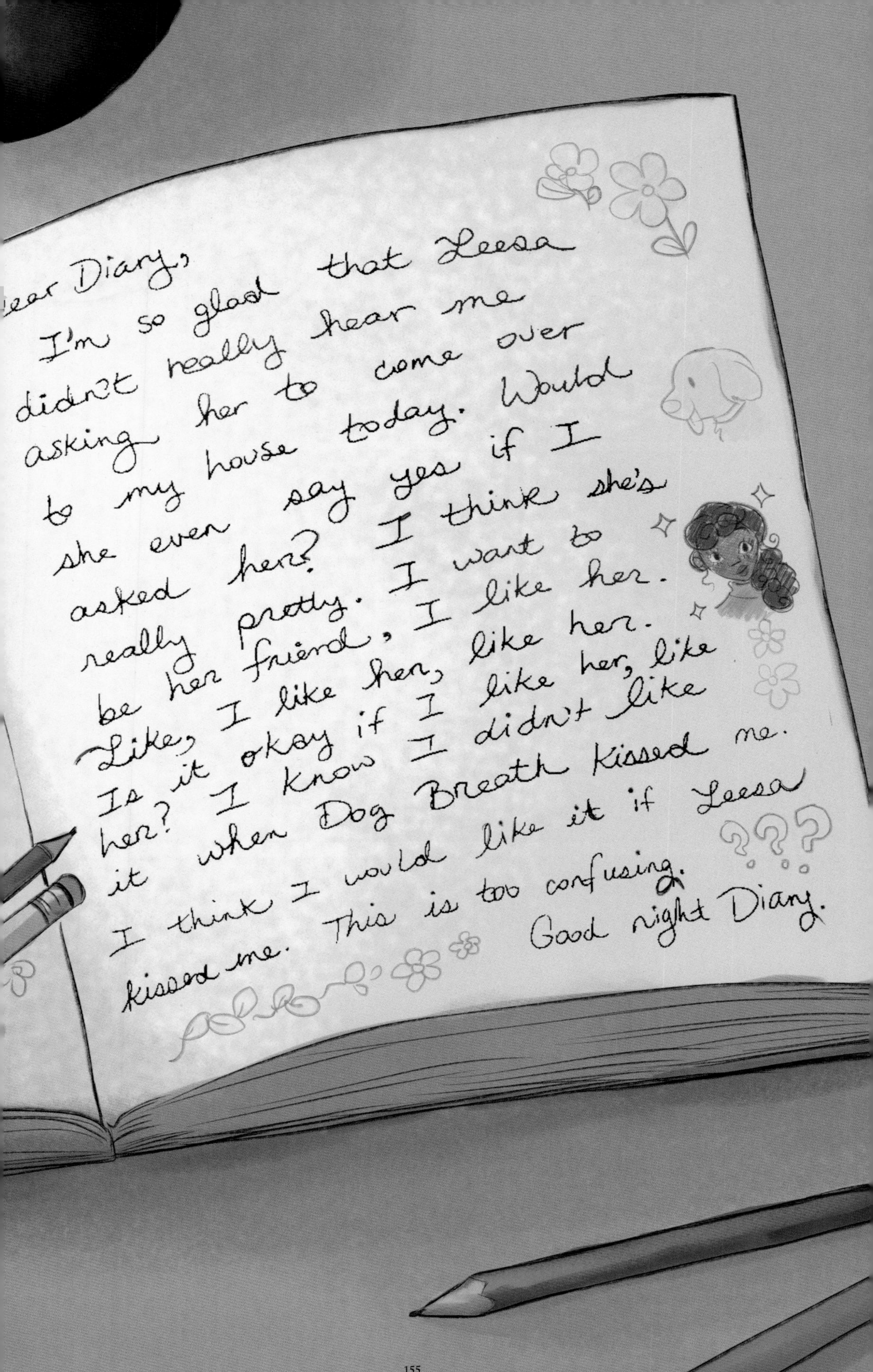
ear Diary,
I'm so glad that Leesa
didn't really hear me
asking her to come over
to my house today. Would
she even say yes if I
asked her? I think she's
really pretty. I want to
be her friend, I like her.
Like, I like her, like her.
Is it okay if I like her, like
her? I know I didn't like
it when Dog Breath kissed me.
I think I would like it if Leesa
kissed me. This is too confusing.
Good night Diary.

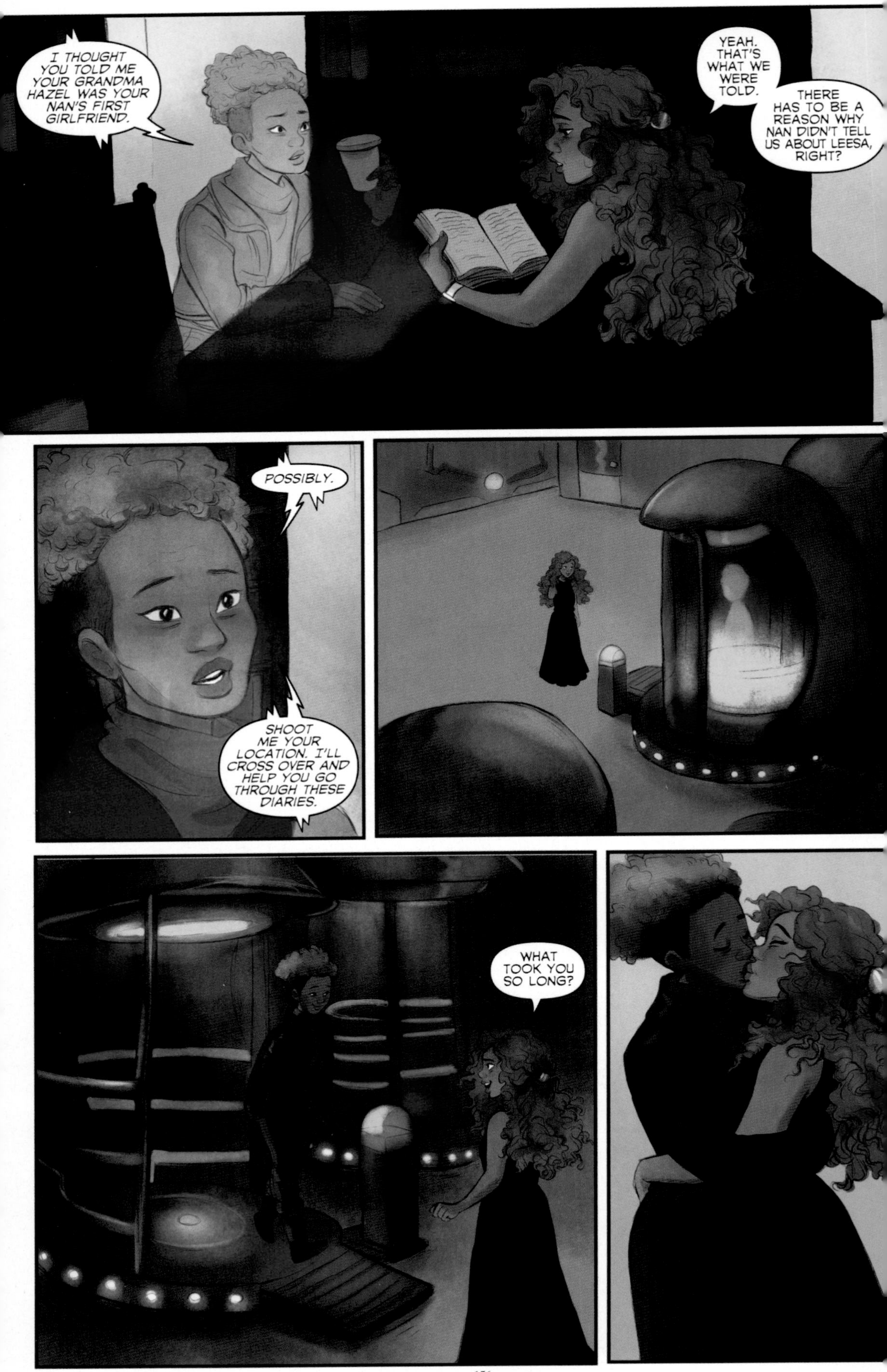
I THOUGHT YOU TOLD ME YOUR GRANDMA HAZEL WAS YOUR NAN'S FIRST GIRLFRIEND.
YEAH. THAT'S WHAT WE WERE TOLD.
THERE HAS TO BE A REASON WHY NAN DIDN'T TELL US ABOUT LEESA, RIGHT?
POSSIBLY.
SHOOT ME YOUR LOCATION. I'LL CROSS OVER AND HELP YOU GO THROUGH THESE DIARIES.
WHAT TOOK YOU SO LONG?

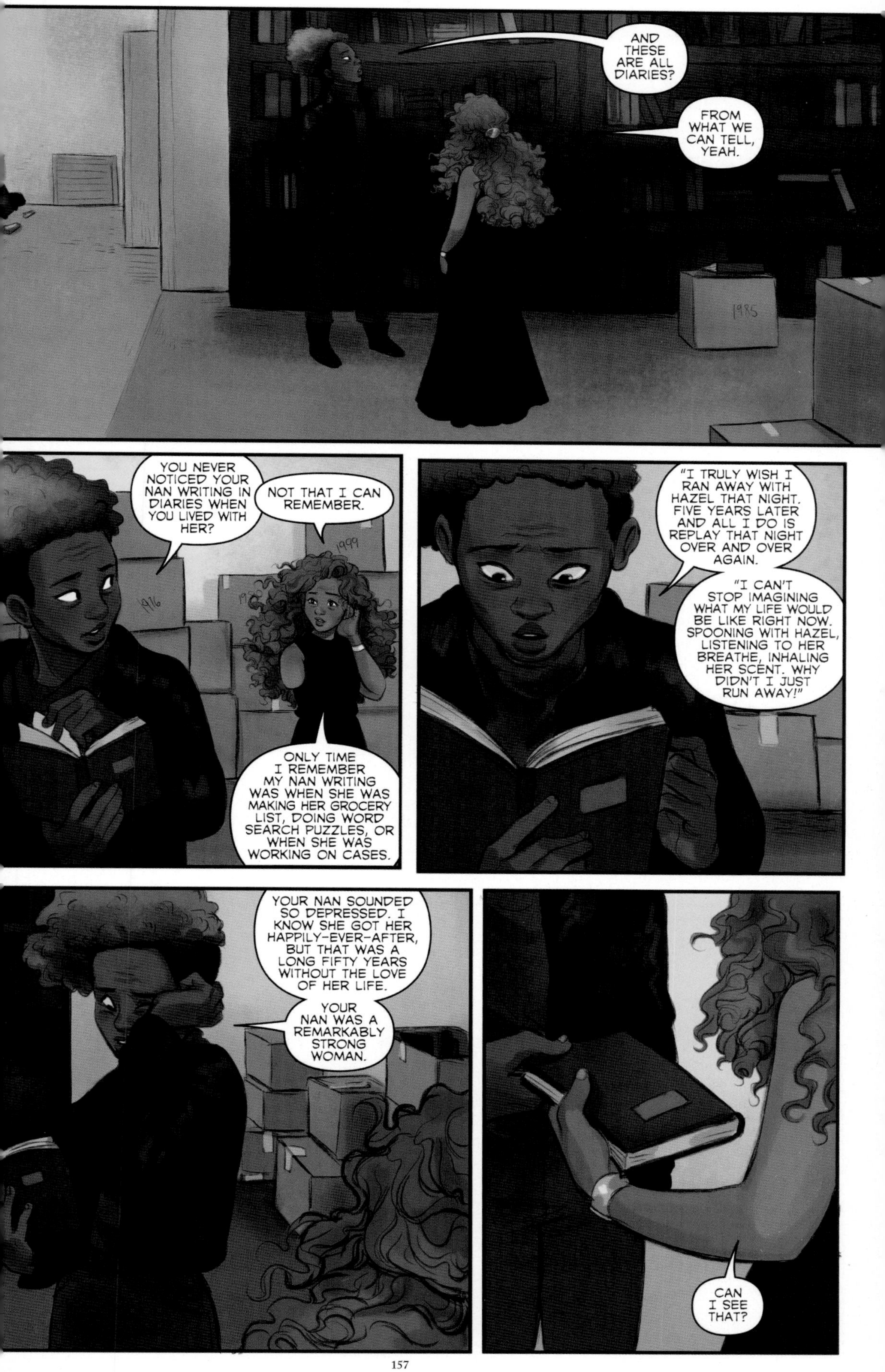
AND THESE ARE ALL DIARIES?
FROM WHAT WE CAN TELL, YEAH.
1985
YOU NEVER NOTICED YOUR NAN WRITING IN DIARIES WHEN YOU LIVED WITH HER?
NOT THAT I CAN REMEMBER.
ONLY TIME I REMEMBER MY NAN WRITING WAS WHEN SHE WAS MAKING HER GROCERY LIST, DOING WORD SEARCH PUZZLES, OR WHEN SHE WAS WORKING ON CASES.
"I TRULY WISH I RAN AWAY WITH HAZEL THAT NIGHT. FIVE YEARS LATER AND ALL I DO IS REPLAY THAT NIGHT OVER AND OVER AGAIN.
"I CAN'T STOP IMAGINING WHAT MY LIFE WOULD BE LIKE RIGHT NOW. SPOONING WITH HAZEL, LISTENING TO HER BREATHE, INHALING HER SCENT. WHY DIDN'T I JUST RUN AWAY!"
YOUR NAN SOUNDED SO DEPRESSED. I KNOW SHE GOT HER HAPPILY-EVER-AFTER, BUT THAT WAS A LONG FIFTY YEARS WITHOUT THE LOVE OF HER LIFE.
YOUR NAN WAS A REMARKABLY STRONG WOMAN.
CAN I SEE THAT?

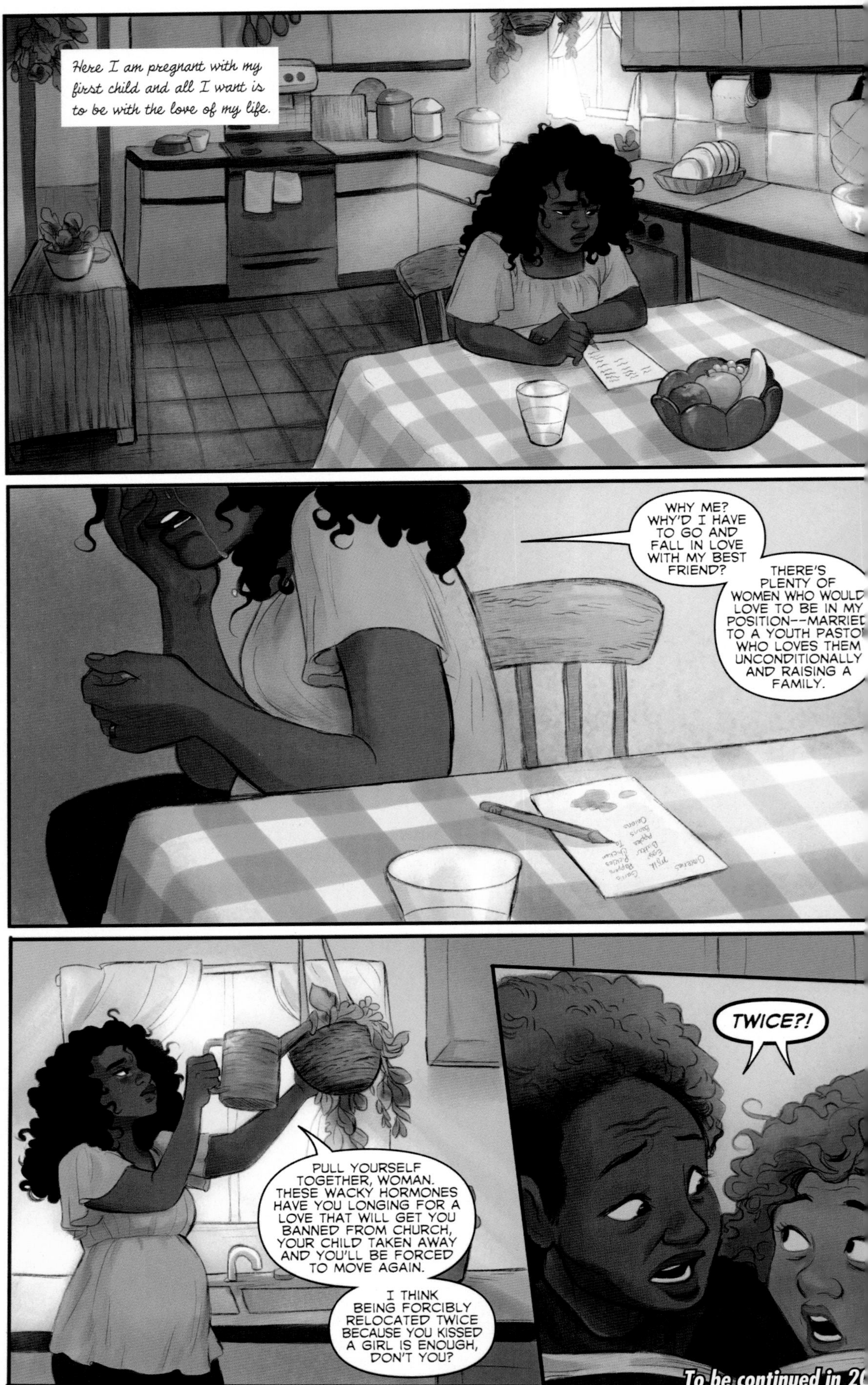

Here I am pregnant with my first child and all I want is to be with the love of my life.
WHY ME? WHY'D I HAVE TO GO AND FALL IN LOVE WITH MY BEST FRIEND?
THERE'S PLENTY OF WOMEN WHO WOULD LOVE TO BE IN MY POSITION--MARRIED TO A YOUTH PASTOR WHO LOVES THEM UNCONDITIONALLY AND RAISING A FAMILY.
PULL YOURSELF TOGETHER, WOMAN. THESE WACKY HORMONES HAVE YOU LONGING FOR A LOVE THAT WILL GET YOU BANNED FROM CHURCH, YOUR CHILD TAKEN AWAY AND YOU'LL BE FORCED TO MOVE AGAIN.
I THINK BEING FORCIBLY RELOCATED TWICE BECAUSE YOU KISSED A GIRL IS ENOUGH, DON'T YOU?
TWICE?!
To be continued in

Afterword
by Gabby Rivera

Confession: I light candles for love every day. The glory of Queer Black, Brown and POC love is all I believe in. It encompasses all genders and all energies beyond gender. Our love is revolution. We are the cosmos, the divine infinity of creation.

At the root of all that glory are queer Black women, always and forever manifesting love here and into the future.

And nowhere is the radical elevation of love between Queer Black women more alive than in BINGO LOVE by Tee Franklin.

The story of Hazel and Mari's love is miraculous. It's a gift that spans decades and dimensions. And in BINGO LOVE: JACKPOT EDITION, Franklin brings back that 1960s Paterson, New Jersey, love and raises us love between queer kins living in the afro-futuristic world of our dreams.

It's ok. Go get some tissues. You're gonna need them.

Hazel and Mari's love is radical and yet it's also unbelievably wholesome. Like pure in the way that puppies and babies are pure, like blue skies over open fields. And damn, I need those types of love stories. Don't you?

BINGO LOVE is a vessel for healing. Hazel and Mari's love offers us a pathway to undoing the damage done to us by homophobia in the guise of concern from our churches and families.

The vignettes by guest writers in JACKPOT are also part of the glorious reimagining of all the places QTPOC have been and all the love we've protected at all points in history.

In "Secrets," written by Shawn Pryor with art by Paulina Ganucheau, we get the All-American QPOC love and war romance of our dreams. (And if you're not forever daydreaming about epic QTPOC period pieces, I cannot in good faith fwu.) James and Adam are young men of color who meet and fall in love during their time as soldiers in the U.S. Army.

159

And try as they might to hide and protect their love, James and Adam can't keep it locked away. The universe rips open their closet door at every turn.

Queer love is the rebirth and reimagining of connection to self, others, and the Divine.

It's the new church.

Hazel and Mari break the cycles of silence and shame.

Bam, it's a whole new world for all of us and for everyone in the BINGO LOVE world.

Once again, Jenn St-Onge gives us full, lush illustrations that evoke the softness of first love and the full sweeping grace of forever love. Joy San's colors bathe each page in the most delicious palette of deep fuchsias, peachy sherbets, and vibrant shades of black and brown everywhere.

Joy is abundant in every panel. "Sidekickin'" gives us Hazel and Mari as a pair of crime-fighting grandma babes. In "Honeymoon" by Marguerite Bennett and Bev Johnson, they're jet-setting gamers in love, bouncing from Reykjavík to Oahu eating croissants and being absolutely radiant.

The world of BINGO LOVE continues to tear away at the toxic cloaks of shame and secrecy placed over QTPOC bodies and joy. The vignettes dive into navigating pleasure-centered conversations about sex and sexual health. We get to see our favorite grandmas having dope-a** sex. Talk about breathing your future into existence, can we all be fresh and free eighty-year-olds like right now, please?

I just kept thinking about all the real life Hazels and Maris all over the globe reveling in each other's magnificence. And all the Adams and Jameses fighting for the survival of tremendous love, terrified for their lives, living in secret. In the future, all the queer kins of all the Hazels and Maris and Adams and Jameses continue to break the cycles of systemic homophobia, transphobia, racism, ableism, sexism, all of it by honoring and manifesting their deepest desires. And doing it all with the guidance of their ancestors mapped out in the constellations above and in the panels of Tee Franklin's BINGO LOVE JACKPOT EDITION.

BINGO LOVE demands that we live free in our truths and move forward in joy.

Hazel and Mari are going to smooch on the lips and tell each other how beautiful they are over and over again. Their hardships are not up for consumption, nor is their pain. Their joy is the ultimate force for revolution and the dismantling of all the f**ks**t.

I want it all forever and then some, times a thousand other baby queers coming to tell their stories of the future. BINGO LOVE is nourishment. It is the foundation of belief in the healing powers of QTPOC love. It is foremost an ode to the sacredness of love between queer black women.

It is an ode to the formation of the universe.

The magic of love.
The Bingo! of it all.